Super Max
and the Last

Tony Kerr

Cover illustration by Phil Gibson

Published in 2008 by YouWriteOn.com
Copyright © Text Tony Kerr
First Edition
The author asserts the moral right under the
Copyright, Designs and Patents Act 1988 to be
identified as the author of this work.
All Rights reserved. No part of this publication may be
reproduced, stored in a retrieval system, or
transmitted, in any form or by any means without the
prior written consent of the author, nor be otherwise
circulated in any form of binding or cover other than
that in which it is published and without a similar
condition being imposed on the subsequent purchaser.
Published by YouWriteOn.com

Chapter One: the potato clock

It was Friday, Maxwell's least favourite day of the week, and this Friday Maxwell Jones faced doom with conkers all around his feet.

This particularly Friday had started out as most days did for Maxwell, at seven thirty precisely, when his potato clock didn't chime.

The potato clock tried to chime every day at seven-thirty – but it never did. The only reason Maxwell ever managed to get out of bed at the right time was a small, rusty (quite smelly) alarm clock he had rescued from the rubbish bin and hidden under his pillow.

Maxwell's problems with the potato clock had begun three months earlier when his mum had walked into the kitchen carrying something large under a tea towel. Maxwell had been eating cornflakes and trying to remember his nine times table. He had a test that morning and was having terrible trouble with nines. He was fine with eights, and sevens were a doddle – but he might just faint if Dr Silex asked him what nine times nine was (as she no doubt would).

'Ta-dadada-da-da-da-*daaaaad*!' his mother bellowed, slamming something heavy on the kitchen table.

'Eightyone!' cried Maxwell, spilling his cornflakes.

'Look at this! *Look* at *this*!' Maxwell's mother squealed, pointing at the thing hidden on the tea towel. Maxwell, gathering together the soggy cornflakes that had landed on the floor, peaked over the table.

'What is it?' Maxwell asked.

'Present! Present!' his mother squealed. She was so excited she was jumping up and down, and the paper hat she was wearing with '15,762' printed on it was lifting off her head with each excited jump.

Maxwell's mum, Bettie Jones, worked in the potato factory at the end of their street, and Bettie was a champion potato peeler. She was, in fact, the greatest potato peeler in history, and held the world record for peeling 15,762 potatoes in one hour.

On the kitchen table was a large, lumpy shape about two feet tall, covered with a tea towel. The tea towel was Bettie Jones's favourite, and was decorated with images of the potatoes of the world. 'Oh . . .' said Maxwell, eyeing a blood red picture of the Nigerian Ginger ("A succulent potato, zingy on the tongue!" was printed underneath the picture) '. . . thanks.'

'Open it! Open it!' his mother virtually screamed. She looked like she was about to faint with excitement.

Maxwell stood up, cleared his throat, and nervously reached for the tea towel.

Maxwell had some justification for being nervous. The last present Bettie Jones had given him (which had also been hiding under this innocent-looking potatoes of the world tea towel) had been a tub of potato bugs; large black beetles with snapping claws, which his mum wanted him to study and train to find rotten potatoes. All Maxwell had succeeded in training them to do was nip his fingers with their large yellow claws . . . and Maxwell suspected they had been quite good at that even before his training.

Maxwell pulled away the tea towel (stepping sharply back as he did so in case a savage potato rat, or a demented potato tiger should leap at him) and looked at what was sitting in the middle of the checked tablecloth.

'What do you think?' his mother asked, breathlessly.

'I think it's . . . erm . . .' Maxwell didn't quite know what to think.

In the centre of the kitchen table was a whizzing, whirring brightly coloured . . . *thing* roughly the size and shape of a wedding cake. It was a machine - or at least Maxwell *thought* it was a machine - made up of four clicking, clacking layers. Each layer grew smaller as the machine rose up, and each layer was connected to the next by brightly coloured, very busy gear wheels. A long red pipe rose out of the topmost layer, and ended in a globe filled with bright green liquid. Maxwell cautiously leaned closer. Inside the green globe silver numbers tumbled, like socks in a washing machine.

'Do you like it?'

'It's . . .' Maxwell began, 'It's . . . What is it, exactly?'

'It is . . . the World's First Potato Clock!' his mother announced grandly.

'A . . . potato clock?'

'A clock,' his mother said, and she began bouncing excitedly again, 'which is made entirely from potatoes!'

'Oh,' said Maxwell. 'Oh good.' His mother suddenly stopped bouncing, and her wide smile began to slowly droop with disappointment. 'It's absolutely fantastic,' Maxwell said quickly.

He almost wished he hadn't.

Bettie Jones let out a squeal of delight that made the windows quiver, and she bounced so high in the air that her record breaker potato peeler hat flew right off her head and landed in the remains of Maxwell's cornflakes.

The potato clock was indeed made entirely out of potato. The gear wheels were made from very thick crisps, the pendulum out of a baked potato skin, and the little number inside the hollowed-out see through potato at the top had been carefully cut from potato, deep fried for three days, and then dipped in molten silver.

It was a brilliant invention. A staggering leap forward in the science of potatoes. It was a creation of true genius.

Unfortunately it didn't work.

Maxwell discovered just how badly the potato clock didn't work when the potato clock hadn't woken him up for his paper round. Looking blearily into the ball at the top, wondering why it was suddenly so sunny in his room, the potato clock told him it was fifteen past thirty-seven.

After a week of not being woken by the potato clock, Maxwell had searched through their bin and retrieved his rusty old metal alarm clock.

Maxwell's mother often tried to put her own shoes on backwards and almost always thought it was Wednesday, even on Christmas Day and on her own birthday. His mother was "eccentric" according to Mrs Trimm, who ran the village shop, or "a bit of a character", according to Mrs Trimm's husband, Hassan.

Maxwell privately thought his mum was more than a bit barmy. But he liked her that way. There were worse things in the world than being a bit barmy.

Your dad, for instance, could be George Pugg, owner of the Pugg Potato Factory and mayor of Virporta Island. You could have a face like a pig that had just run into a brick wall, and your greatest pleasure in life could be beating up small boys with mad ginger hair who wore large spectacles and had eccentric mothers.

Maxwell was fortunate that he was none of these things. He was very unfortunate, however, that the boy who was all of these things - Bartholemew Pugg - was currently chasing him and fully intended to beat his brains out with a hockey stick.

Maxwell ran helter-skelter through the woods, dodging around trees, bounding over logs and splashing through streams, his own hockey stick rapping him the back of his head as his backpack bounced up and down.

The Black Woods flew past him, the trees and undergrowth growing thicker, the air darkening as he ran deeper and deeper into the heart of the woods. But however fast he ran, however much he dodged and jumped, he still heard the thud of heavy feet behind him, and Bartholemew Pugg snorting like an angry bull as he grew closer and closer.

Maxwell came to a great tangle of thorn bushes and ran into their centre without even pausing. He burst through the other side, and skidded to a halt.

He was standing on the edge of a deep ravine. The ground dropped suddenly thirty feet to a muddy stream below. There was no way across.

Maxwell turned back to the thorn bushes - perhaps if he crawled back through he would be able to dodge Pugg's gang . . .

'He went this way!' came Pugg's voice, very close. A second later he heard the whistle and crack of a dozen hockey sticks beating their way though the thick tangle of thorns.

Maxwell turned back to the ravine. He didn't know what to do. He could pull out his own hockey stick and whack the bushes and perhaps hit Pugg's thick head, or maybe . . .

Then something happened.

A large blackbird - for some reason not frightened by the din of Pugg's gang smashing through the bushes - landed at Maxwell's feet.

The blackbird looked up at him, and began to urgently ruffle its wings, almost as if it were trying to tell Maxwell something.

'Fly?' Maxwell muttered to the bird - and was it his imagination, or had the blackbird just *winked* at him? 'Fly!' he said.

Maxwell took two steps back, glanced again at the huge drop, closed his eyes, and crouched low like a runner on his marks.

'Fly!' he hissed. His eyes snapped open and he ran at the ravine as hard as he could, ready to close his eyes the second he jumped -- and the blackbird looked at him, opened its beak, and said, quite distinctly:

'I wouldn't do that if I were you.'

Maxwell was so startled that he forgot what he was doing – and had Maxwell jumped a second earlier he might have made it across - but his startled feet had carried him one step too far - and as he jumped the crumbling edge of the ravine gave way, and Maxwell stumbled out into thin air.

He realised he was going to smash his brains in on the rocks below, he was going to break his arms and legs - he would miss maths and hockey (hurray!) - and he could do nothing to stop it.

Maxwell hit the far bank with a bone-shaking *thud*. All the breath flew out of his body and his spectacles flew off his face. He tumbled backwards down the bank - blue sky swapped places with muddy soil as he tumbled down the ravine like the silver numbers in his potato clock - and then he splashed into cold, muddy water, and came to a stop.

Maxwell lay still for a second, amazed at his luck. His bungled jump had carried him to the far side of the ravine and he had hit soft soil - but his relief evaporated at the sound of a disgruntled *caw!* followed by a loud *crash!*

Bartholemew Pugg heaved himself out of the thorn bush, and looked angrily around. He looked distinctly the worst for wear, with long rips down his school blazer, thick greenish mud covering the knees of his trousers, and several thorns sticking out of his forehead. He glared down at Maxwell, his hockey stick held in both hands like a club.

Maxwell scrambled to his feet. He saw his own hockey stick was lying on the muddy streambed, snapped cleanly in half. He was done for; his only chance was to make a run for it - but to where? His usual confidence that he could always find his way out of the Black Woods had suddenly disappeared.

Pugg stared at Maxwell, his hockey stick still held level . . . then he frowned, looked right then left, and then turned back to Maxwell.

'Where did he go?' Pugg asked.

Maxwell was so surprised that all he could manage to say was, 'Wwha-?'

'The boy who ran through this bush not thirty seconds ago, you moron,' hissed Pugg in his calm, quiet, dangerous voice. 'Where did he go?'

Maxwell goggled at Pugg in amazement. Was he blind? Couldn't he see he was standing right in front of him? Was this some sort of trick--?

'Where did he *go*!' Pugg demanded. He took a step towards the edge of the ravine, shaking his hockey stick furiously.

There was a sudden howl, and Pugg glanced around as a fat boy, also with torn clothes, muddy trousers and thorns stick out of him at several points, fell out of the bushes. The fat boy was Tom Chop - Pugg's main henchman, who had a face like a permanently alarmed gorilla - and he too looked down at Maxwell.

'Did you get him?' asked Chop, his voice wavering and reedy.

'Obviously not, idiot,' Pugg replied without looking round. His eyes were fixed firmly on Maxwell. 'Where did he go?'

Pugg took another step forward, now perilously close to the crumbling edge of the ravine. He frowned, and squinted his piggy eyes at Maxwell - another step and Pugg might recognise him. Another two steps and the edge of the ravine would give way and Pugg and Chop would crash down on top of Maxwell - and there was no doubt they would recognise him then.

'He went that way,' Maxwell said quickly, pointing back over Pugg's shoulder. 'He crawled back into the bushes.'

Pugg's head whipped round. He pushed Chop back towards the thorn bushes, then stopped, and turned back to Maxwell.

The confused frown wrinkled Pugg's face again. 'You've broken your hockey stick,' he snapped. 'Make sure it's fixed the next time I see you, or I'll report you to Dr Silex.'

Pugg marched away from the edge, and poked his hockey stick into Chop's backside just as Chop was preparing to climb carefully back through the bushes. Chop fell headfirst into the thorn bushes with a terrific *yelp* and Pugg stamped through after him.

Maxwell stood staring at the top of the ravine for several minutes, listening as the din from Pugg and his gang slowly died away, hardly believing his luck.

He reached up absently to adjust his spectacles - and found they weren't on his face.

Maxwell spotted his spectacles sticking out of the soil halfway up the side of the ravine, winking in the dim sunlight.

Was it the spectacles? Had his spectacles somehow . . . ?

'Oh!' cried Maxwell, and his eyes shot back up to where Pugg had been standing. But the blackbird had long gone.

Had that blackbird *spoken* to him?

Chapter Two: Mr Vim

Friday was Maxwell's least favourite day for two reasons - Dr Flavia Silex and Potato Hockey.

Of these two (though it was a close competition) he probably detested Dr Silex's lessons the most. Friday morning dawned every week with the prospect of double maths at 9am on the dot. As far as Maxwell was concerned it was two hours of absolute hell, with the added bonus of enough homework to scare Albert Einstein at the end of it.

He had actually arrived at school on time at two minutes to nine. If it had been any other lesson but maths he would have *been* on time. But Dr Silex's lessons began at nine. On the dot. When the school bell rang at five to nine on any other day Maxwell and his fellow classmates would wander in, and start the (sometimes epic) journey to their first class. However, when the bell rang at five to nine on a Friday, if you were wise, you would be seated at your desk in Dr Silex's class.

It nine o'clock precisely when Maxwell eased open the door of the maths class and slipped inside. Dr Silex had her back to the class, her large bottom swaying as she rapidly chalked a mystifying jumble of number on the blackboard. No one turned around as Maxwell crept towards his desk at the far corner of the room. He was sweating heavily as he reached his chair, and slowly eased it out from behind his desk. If his luck would just hold out a little bit longer . . .

'JONES!'

Maxwell gave a squeak of alarm, and jerked his chair back - the chair leg caught the desk, and before Maxwell could do anything, the desk tumbled, and hit the floor with a terrific *CRASH!* spilling the entire contents of his desk - several pens, a pile of paper and half a dozen conkers - all over the classroom floor.

There was a deathly silence. Everyone in the room goggled at him, and then turned wide-eyed to stare at Dr Silex. They all seemed to be holding their breaths.

Dr Silex looked like a volcano on the verge of eruption - if volcanoes ever wore half moon spectacles and mortarboards on their heads.

'I have NEVER,' hissed Dr Silex, 'In all my CAREER,' the class flinched with every word, as though Dr Silex were cracking a whip over their heads, 'Had the MISFORTUNE,' Dr Silex's face, usually the colour of ash, was now the shape and colour of a beetroot, 'To TEACH such a LAZY, IGNORANT, WORTHLESS CREATURE AS YOU MAXWELL JONES!'

Dr Silex was shaking with fury, reminding Maxwell again of an erupting volcano, and the whole class trembled.

'I . . . I . . . I . . .' gurgled Maxwell, his tongue seemed to have grown to twice its normal size.

'I? I? *I!*' roared Dr Silex, and Maxwell felt his whole body go numb with terror. 'SEVEN minutes late! FILTHY from head to toe! Your entire desk scattered over MY CLASSROOM! SEVEN MINUTES LATE!' This was the worst crime by far, Maxwell knew. He was sure he had actually arrived on time, but Maxwell knew from experience that it was pointless, if not downright suicidal, arguing with Dr Flavia Silex.

'Pick up this mess!' Maxwell crouched to pick up his papers. 'Sit down!' Maxwell tried to get to his chair while still crouching. 'Explain yourself!' Maxwell opened his numb mouth, but his seemingly huge tongue didn't even have time to wobble. 'Clean yourself up!' Maxwell was a bit stuck on this one - he looked hopelessly round the mathematics classroom for a sink. 'EXPLAIN YOURSELF JONES!' Dr Silex screeched.

'I . . .' Maxwell looked around the room, and his eyes met Pugg's. Pugg grinned slyly. Maxwell could tell Dr Silex the truth. He could tell the whole classroom that he had run away from that fat idiot and his band of morons. Maxwell said, 'I fell over.' And watched Pugg's grin evaporate with a small twinge of satisfaction.

'You fell . . . ?' Dr Silex blinked her small, mean walnut eyes. 'THAT is your excuse. THAT is your EX-PLAN-AT-ION? "I fell over"?' She turned to the class, and said in a childish voice. 'Poor ickle Jones fell over.'

Several people in the class giggled nervously, and Pugg gave a single loud 'Hah!' Maxwell felt sudden anger burn in his stomach.

'It was an accident!' Maxwell exclaimed.

'"It was an accident"', Dr Silex imitated him in a silly voice. There was more laughter - this time louder, Maxwell felt himself flush with anger and embarrassment.

'I was *trying* to get to school--'

'Trying? *TRYING!* You live ten yards from the gate, you stupid boy!'

'I tripped--'

'If only your brains were half the size of your feet!'

'I didn't--'

'Didn't what, Jones? Didn't think? Didn't move your sluggish body beyond a crawl?' yelled Dr Silex. There was now loud laughter in the classroom, Mickey Prickle's red face looked as if it was about to explode. 'SILENCE!' Dr Silex suddenly roared, and the laughter died instantly. 'Get on with your work! This is not a playground!' Everyone spun round to face the blackboard. Dr Silex advanced on Maxwell - and Maxwell realised something terrible. Dr Silex didn't just dislike him, she didn't just think he was thick, or useless, Dr Silex *hated* Maxwell.

'Stupid, foolish boy! Dr Silex hissed. 'Walking around with your head in the clouds! Just like your mother!'

'Don't you talk about my mother!' Maxwell yelled.

'Don't dare raise your voice to ME boy!' Dr Silex virtually screamed. Everyone had turned to look at them again, their work forgotten. 'Your mother was my pupil! She was as foolish and disorganised as you! I told her the day she left school she would never come to anything, and I was right! I only have to look at you, you worthless, lazy brat, to know how right I was!'

'You can't talk to him like that!' came a voice. Dr Silex spun on her heels, but no one looked up at her. Maxwell thought for a second that he saw Daisy Electra hunch further over her desk.

'My mum is the best person in the world,' said Maxwell.

Dr Silex spun back to Maxwell. 'Your *mum* is an idiot, and you are an idiot,' she hissed so that only Maxwell could hear her. 'You will never come to anything, Jones.' She looked down at her feet, bent forward, and stood up with something held in her hand. 'Look at the trash you bring into my classroom! How DARE you!' She brandished it front of Maxwell's face. 'Professor Magister will hear about this! You have gone too far this time, boy! Too--'

'Put that down,' Maxwell said.

'W...What?' gasped Dr Silex. Her jaws tightened, and her big face, already a bright red, began to turn purple with rage. 'WHAT DID YOU SAY TO ME!'

Maxwell stared into Dr Silex's beady little eyes, and then looked down at what she held in her hand.

A comic book was crushed in her doughy fingers. On the cover, just above Dr Silex's white fist, was the square jawed face of a man with red rays shooting from his eyes.

'I said put that down,' Maxwell replied. He turned his eyes back to meet Dr Silex's. It was the hardest thing he had ever done in his life. He was absolutely, totally petrified - but he was also absolutely, totally furious. The anger bubbled and burnt in him, and it was *him*, after all, that was like a volcano, not Dr Silex at all. 'That was my dad's,' Maxwell said, his voice shaking with fury, his eyes glaring into her piggy little walnut eyes, 'and you'd better put it down right now.'

Dr Silex gaped at him. She took a step back, and her hand fell open. The comic book fluttered to the floor. 'Your . . . ?' murmured Dr Silex - and for a second, for one very odd moment indeed, it was like the whole of the world had turned upside down.

'Tidy this mess up, Jones,' said Dr Silex quietly, and she turned and marched back to the front of the class. Maxwell gaped at her, then, remembering where he was and how much trouble he was in, quickly began gathering the contents off his desk off the floor.

Dr Silex smoothed her black gown over her round body, and glared at the class. 'Haven't you seen a comic book before, you DOLTS!' she barked. 'Face the front of the class! We have had quite enough interruptions for one day!'

Dr Silex returned to the blackboard and continued chalking a sum the length of a bus on it. Maxwell picked his desk up, dumped all his stuff inside, and sat.

He glanced at Dr Silex's busy back, her fat bottom wobbling as she scribbled frantically on the blackboard.

What exactly had just happened?

Maxwell opened his exercise book and started copying down the monster sum, and soon his brain was as pickled as an onion trying to work its way out of a jar.

Though Dr Silex classes always started at five to nine, she was not quite so punctual about finishing them on time. When the class finally staggered out of double maths at ten past eleven, you could almost see the number that had been stuffed into the children's heads over the last two hours dribbling out of their ears.

The second lesson on Friday mornings - and the second reason why Maxwell hated Fridays so much - was hockey with Miss Hummingbird. Maxwell sprinted down halls, across glass corridors, shot down dizzying spiral staircases towards the sports tower, a stark white building which stood alone at the spiky edge of the Watchmen Academy.

The Watchmen Academy was made up of dozens and dozens of towers, of all different colours and all different sizes. By far the largest was the Hall Tower which sat right in the centre of the Watchmen. The Hall Tower was bright orange, and rose over five hundred feet to Professor Magister's office right at its top. Magister's office was bright green, and shaped like a knobbly coconut. All of the other towers circulated from the Hall Tower, and all were connected together by very flimsy looking glass corridors. Some of these corridors were hundreds of feet in the air, and some were actually half buried in the ground. Some of the towers were as wide as motorways, and some so slim that only the smallest of small boys or petite girls could squeeze up their steps with difficulty.

Four boys - Maxwell, Pugg, Chop and Jamie Blip - and four girls - Daisy Electra, Bella Jugg (who had muscles like inflated balloons all over her body), Stephanie Snipe and Tamara Kane - ran into the white sports tower, scattered into separate changing rooms, and frantically dragged on their hockey kit.

Maxwell was sure that Pugg and Chop would see as an ideal opportunity to finish what they had started at the Black Woods, but the prospect of turning up late for Miss Hummingbird's sports lesson was obviously weighing heavily on their minds too, and they left Maxwell alone.

By the time the eight sweaty nervous children ran onto the sports field - Maxwell carrying an ancient school hockey stick to replace his broken one - Miss Hummingbird was running around the large field, standing on her hands, moving as fast doing a handstand as most normal people could run.

'Here you are!' Miss Hummingbird cried, backflipping and landing neatly on her feet right in front of them. 'Only 35 minutes to lunch! This *is* going to be exciting!' Miss Hummingbird grabbed a potato from a pile at the edge of the field, spun a hockey stick in her nimble little hands, threw the potato into the air, and whacked it with a piercing *crack*. The hockey stick snapped clean in half, the potato rocketed into the air with the speed of a missile, and Miss Hummingbird cackled in delight as it vanished over the treetops.

'Four on four! Standard rules!' bawled Miss Hummingbird, discarding the broken hockey stick over her shoulder. 'Maximum aggression! Fast! Fast! Fast! Fun! Fun! Fun!'

Miss Hummingbird cartwheeled away to the edge of the field.

The children trundled onto the hockey pitch, muttering darkly and picking up potatoes as they went. Jamie, Maxwell, Daisy and Bella positioned themselves evenly around the circular pitch facing Chop, Pugg, Stephanie and Tamara. The children waited, potatoes positioned on the ground in front of their hockey sticks.

Potato Hockey had one very simple rule, and it was this: try your very best not to get hospitalised or killed.

The game, according to Miss Hummingbird, was an ancient and noble sport, first devised by the Aztecs. Maxwell knew from Professor Magister's blood curdling history classes that the Aztecs had an ancient and noble tradition of maiming and murdering one another in organised sport.

Miss Hummingbird was a very nice person. Maxwell was almost certain of this. But she did tend to get over enthusiastic. She also had the habit of regarding a broken limb or a gushing fountain of blood a 'little scratch'. Absolutely the best way to ensure that you ended up with a 'little scratch' was to turn up late for Miss Hummingbird's lesson. Coming late to Potato Hockey was a lot like getting into a cage with a starving tiger and telling it you'd run out of raw meat - but would he like a nice scone?

Miss Hummingbird, just over five feet tall and so thin from her constant fleeing around she looked like a breeze would blow her away, now regarded them with her hungry tiger eyes, licked her lips, and blew her whistle.

'That's it Bartholemew! Punt! Punt!' cried Miss Hummingbird as Pugg fired a potato the size and consistency of a rock at Maxwell's stomach. 'Oh! Good block, Maxwell!' she sounded disappointed. 'Bella! Bella! Mark you man! Go left Thomas!

Support Tamara! Support! Jamie! Daisy! Clear goal! Go! Go-go-go-go-go!'

Jamie Blip slipped easily under the hockey stick Chop had aimed squarely at Jamie's head and flipped the potato to Daisy Electra. Daisy drove it into one of the four nets that circled the pitch. Miss Hummingbird cheered ecstatically and leapt twenty feet into the air.

The eight children took up their position round the pitch again, again each one with a rock hard potato on the ground in front of them.

The whistle blew and Daisy blasted her potato across the pitch. It went straight through Pugg's legs and landed squarely in the centre of goal. Miss Hummingbird squealed with delight.

'You'll play for England one day Daisy Electra!' she roared. Daisy's face went bright pink, as Pugg's turned pale with rage. The whistle blew, Bella clumsily passed her potato to Daisy, and Daisy blasted forward again.

The odd thing about Potato Hockey, Maxwell thought, was that it seemed to go on for so long. Other lessons - art, history, biology, even *maths* - seemed to whiz by in comparison to Potato Hockey. The round hockey pitch seemed to exist in a world where seconds turned into minutes and every one of those long seconds was spent trying to avoid exchanging your nose for a large potato, or having your grin permanently widened by a flying hockey stick.

They were down to the last rock hard baked potato now of the original nine they had begun with, with four goals each. Pugg, the other team's 'Hacker' (a worrying accurate name, Maxwell thought) teed up for his strike at goal. Maxwell felt Daisy tense beside him, and beyond her Bella was quivering with terror, the hockey stick the only thing stopping her from falling into a dead faint on the ground.

Maxwell crouched low over his own hockey stick. He could see Jamie at his other side, bent forward, weaving from side to side. Maxwell concentrated on Pugg, ignoring Miss Hummingbird's encouraging tips ('Kill him! Decapitate him!').

Pugg pulled back his enormous muscular arms, his shoulders rising like huge waves - and he looked right into Maxwell's eyes.

'This one's for you, Bumwell,' Pugg hissed, a mean grin flickering across his lips, 'you Mamble's boy.' He fired the potato straight at Maxwell's face.

Maxwell let out a cry of surprise and staggered backwards, trying to bring his stick up in time to stop the potato - but knowing it was too late. He saw Daisy jump towards him, her hockey stick outstretched - but she was not quick enough. It was going to hit him, it was--

The curved blade of Daisy's hockey stick stretched towards the flying potato - and the potato stopped. It spun in mid-air less than an inch from Maxwell's nose. Blue sparks crackled across its skin.

Daisy hit the ground with a painful *thud* - and the potato, completely untouched by Daisy's stick, flew backwards, breezed past Pugg's stunned face, did a fancy little loop, and hit the other team's goal square in the centre.

'WOOOOOHOOOOOOHOOOOOOOO!' howled Miss Hummingbird. She shot across the pitch and skidded to a halt in front of Daisy. Daisy, who had been shakily trying to get to her feet, fell back again with a cry as thick globs of mud covered her from head to toe. 'Magical! ' Yelled Miss Hummingbird. 'Terrific! Stupendous! Remarkable!' she shrieked, waving her arms like windmill sails, then screamed again. 'Magical!' She danced a jig on the

spot, splattering Daisy with even more mud. 'That was simply the most *brilliant*, the most *daring* the most-
-'

'She cheated!' shouted Pugg.

'Don't be ridiculous, Bartholemew.' Bella helped Daisy up onto unsteady legs. 'Genius!' Miss Hummingbird grabbed the wobbly Daisy in a bone crushing embrace.

'She cheated! That goal should be disallowed!' barked Pugg. It was the first time Maxwell had ever heard Pugg raise his voice. His face was twisted in rage, and his hockey stick was dangerously close to Daisy.

'She did not cheat, Bartholemew,' Miss Hummingbird said calmly. She and Pugg were now face to face, and Pugg towered over the little woman. 'It was a perfectly good goal.'

'But she used her--'

Miss Hummingbird raised a tiny finger in front of Pugg's huge red face. 'It was a perfectly good goal, Mr Pugg,' Miss Hummingbird repeated slowly.

'I . . .' Pugg's face writhed. For a second it looked like he was going to bite Miss Hummingbird's finger right off. Then he lowered his head. 'It's not fair.'

'All's fair in love and Potato Hockey!' Miss Hummingbird cried, as she patted Pugg on his beefy shoulder. 'The spirit of competition! Love it! Adore it!' She blew her whistle. 'Game over! Now, hurry off to dinner! A double mash menu today!'

Pugg spun on his heels and loped off, closely followed by his disgruntled team mates. Miss Hummingbird lifted Daisy off her feet with another spine crackling hug, and then sprinted off.

Maxwell turned to Daisy, but she was already half way to the changing rooms, an anxious Bella Jugg pacing beside her.

'Wow!' Jamie Blip appeared beside Maxwell, seeming to jump suddenly from thin air. 'Did you see that shot, Maxy? Wasn't that amazing? Absolutely amazing. Don't you think that was amazing?'

'Amazing,' Maxwell agreed. They began to trudge back to the changing rooms together.

'If she hadn't stopped that ball it would have smashed your face right in!' said Jamie, making it sound like having your face smashed in by a flying potato was the most exciting and desirable thing that could happen to anyone. 'But to score a goal! The winning goal! Absolutely amazingly unbelievable!'

Maxwell had to agree. It was unbelievable. Especially as Daisy hadn't even touched the ball. It was absolutely amazingly unbelievable.

Lunch was always held in the Hall Tower - a hall as big as a cathedral, under a roof five hundred feet high.

Maxwell sat at a small table at the farthest reaches of the Hall Tower. Jamie Blip and Bella Jugg were seated with him - Jamie enthusiastically shovelling mashed potato into his mouth, Bella delicately picking over her small lunch, the fork almost invisible in her massive fist.

Maxwell looked at his own lunch in disgust. It was indeed a double mash menu, the plate was filled almost entirely with potato. Mashed, boiled and roasted potatoes of various sizes shapes and colours were stacked on his plate. At the very edge of the plate, peeking apologetically from beneath a potato whittled into the shape of the school crest, were two very thin, pallid sausages in a drizzle of gravy.

Maxwell pushed his plate away. 'Where's Daisy?' he asked Jamie.

'Bloke ma bib,' Jamie grunted between shovelling more mash into his already bloated cheeks.

'She did what?' he asked Bella.

'Daisy broke a rib,' Bella replied, her voice quavering. 'Oh, it was *terrible*! I helped her back to the changing room and she was wheezing and coughing . . . Poor Daisy!' Bella swallowed, her eyes filling with tears. 'I *told* Miss Hummingbird, but *she* said it was just a *bruise*, and Daisy should run some water on it.' Bella shot a fierce glance at the teacher's table, where Miss Hummingbird was talking animatedly to a very irritated Dr Silex. 'Luckily, Lance was passing or goodness knows *what* might have happened.' Bella's angry face melted into a dreamy expression. 'Lance is *so* useful.'

'I bet you'd make use of him, wouldn't you, Bella?' said Jamie, looking up from his empty plate.

'I don't know what you mean.' Bella looked down at her own plate, her dreamy expression falling away.

'You'd give him a nice big useful kiss,' Jamie smacked his lips together. '"Oh Lance, you're so lovely! Kiss me, you handsome devil, you! Take me in your arms and embrace me like you embrace your mop!"'

Maxwell snorted, and covered his mouth with his hand.

Lance, the Watchmen's janitor, grounds keeper, and occasional nurse, was a tall, muscular teenager with wavy blond hair and piercing blue eyes. All of the girls turned to jelly whenever he passed within a hundred yards of them.

Bella looked furious, her ears turning a deep crimson as she bent her fork double in her hand with a single squeeze. Bella Jugg was huge. She wasn't fat, but she was twice as muscular as a heavyweight boxer.

'Is Daisy going to be all right?' Maxwell asked, changing the subject before Bella decided to to bend Jamie into the same shape as her fork.

'Lance said--' Jamie made a loud, sloppy noise with his lips, Bella tutted, and turned an even deeper shade of red '--Lance said she'd be back at school by Monday.'

'Brilliant shot, though,' said Jamie. 'I'd gladly break all my ribs and both my legs to make a shot like that!'

'Don't be stupid!' Bella said. 'I mean it!' Jamie replied, and they began arguing about whether it was worth breaking various bones ('Well what about your little toe bone?' 'Don't be ridiculous!' 'It's not me who's being ridiculous!' 'Yes it is') to score a winning goal.

Maxwell wished Daisy was here. He thought about asking Jamie and Bella whether they had seen the potato pause in mid-air or that strange blue electricity that had surrounded it - but they obviously had not. If Jamie had seen anything like that he would have talked endlessly about it, and would have already have come up with a dozen outlandish theories to explain it. Bella would have been quaking in terror and telling everyone that the hockey potatoes were haunted. Perhaps he had imagined it? Perhaps he had imagined Pugg and Chop not being able to recognise him with his spectacles off? Perhaps he had imagined the talking crow?

That seemed like an awful lot of perhapes and imaginings.

'Are you eating that?' asked Jamie, poking his fork in Maxwell's lunch. 'Can I have it then? I'm starving.'

Maxwell passed him the plate, and Jamie started to dig happily into another mound of potato, oblivious to Bella's scowls.

Maxwell's eye wandered around the Hall Tower. There were several small tables here and there, and in the centre of the room a large table which

seated Pugg and the hangers on he considered cool
enough to eat with him. The teacher's table was on a
raised platform that doubled as a stage for school
assemblies and Miss Hummingbird's occasional, and
always disastrous, school plays. Only Miss
Hummingbird and Dr Silex were seated at the table.
Maxwell wondered where Professor Magister was. He
could not remember the headmaster ever missing
lunch before.

As usual Pugg's table was rowdy, with most of
the noise coming from people laughing at Pugg's
unfunny remarks. Maxwell didn't even bother to
listen. All Pugg ever talked about were his hockey
skills and people he had beaten up.

'Bella?' said Maxwell. 'When Pugg fired that
potato at me - did you hear what he called me?'

Bella shook her head.

'A twit?' suggested Jamie helpfully.

'No, he--'

'A specky twit?'

'No--'

'A short specky twit?' Jamie suggested.

'No!' Maxwell liked Jamie, but trying to get
him to shut up for even two seconds was like trying to
get Dr Silex to tell a joke during a maths test. 'Bella?
He called me . . .' Maxwell searched his memory for
Pugg's exact words. 'I think he called me a Mamble's
Boy. Do you know what that means?'

Bella shook her head, and continued pushing
food around her plate.

'He probably meant Mummy's Boy,' said
Jamie. 'What with you living with your mum.'

'He said "Mamble's Boy",' Maxwell said. Bella
didn't look up from her plate.

'No, you didn't hear him right,' said Jamie. 'He
said "Mummy's Boy".'

'I don't think he--'

'Because you are a bit, aren't you?'

'What's that supposed to mean!'

'Well, you do live with your mum, don't you?'

'So do you!'

'So do I,' interrupted Bella. 'My dad's dead, like Maxwell's. So what does that make me, Jamie?'

'I don't know,' Jamie stuffed more potato into his mouth. 'A mummy's girl? A girly girl? A womany girly?'

'Honesty, you're just so . . . so stupid sometimes!' said Bella. 'You're as bad as Pugg.'

'Am I?' Jamie chuckled, delighted. 'Are you eating that dinner?'

'Yes I am, you greedy pig!' yelled Bella. 'What about Daisy? Daisy lives with her dad--'

'Weirdo!' Jamie said promptly.

'He is not a weirdo! He's a very nice man, isn't he, Maxwell?'

'He is a weirdo!' Jamie said before Maxwell could reply. 'He's as loopy as a piece of string! He's as fruity as a nut cake!'

Maxwell did think that Daisy's dad, Tesla Electra, *was* a very nice man - but he was also a very, very weird man. He had several strange hobbies, including collecting light bulbs and flying his aluminium kite during lightning storms. Maxwell had actually seen Mr Electra do this - cackling manically with his hair sticking up like a porcupine's quills while lighting bolts blasted his frantically bobbing kite.

Bella liked Mr Electra a lot, and was very sensitive about her own dad, perhaps because her own dad had been a circus strongman who had been eaten by a rampaging herd of hippopotamus. Despite this Maxwell had often thought that Bella was quite lucky - he had never known his own dad, who had died in a plane crash in Buenos Aires in Brazil when Maxwell was only a month old.

'Well about Pugg, then? His mum's dead, so what would you call him?' demanded Bella.

'I would call him a prat,' Jamie replied. 'Pugg!' he shouted. Pugg and his gang turned as one at the sound of Jamie's voice, all wearing match scowls. 'You're a prat, Pugg!' Jamie shouted.

Pugg's face twisted in fury, and for a second it looked like he was going to run across the room at Jamie when a bell chimed once, and everyone in the room turned to the teacher's table and fell silent. Professor Ludo Magister stood at the table looking self conscious, the school bell held in his hand. 'Good day, ladies and gentlemen,' his murmuring voice said into the sudden silence. 'I am sorry to interrupt your meal, but I have a few short announcements.'

Professor Magister placed the school bell back on the table, and coughed nervously. At the end of the table Dr Silex was glaring pointedly at Jamie. She had obviously heard Jamie call her favourite pupil a prat. Beside her Miss Hummingbird was unusually still. She was staring across the table as if hypnotised, and Maxwell followed her gaze to the seat beside Professor Magister.

A tall thin man sat at the teacher's table, his long fingers steepled under his chin.

'Who's that? Maxwell whispered to Jamie.

'Ludo Magister,' Jamie whispered back. 'The headmaster.'

'Not him, stupid, the man sitting beside him!'

'Jangle Mumbles,' hissed Bella. Maxwell looked at Bella. She was wearing a similar awestruck expression to Miss Hummingbird's.

'Who's--' Maxwell began.

'First of all, I would like to congratulate Miss Hummingbird on her recent production of Oliver Twist on ice.' Maxwell turned his attention back to Professor Magister, who was smiling dubiously at Miss

Hummingbird. 'A highly imaginative interpretation, Miss Hummingbird, and I'm informed by the hospital that Bill Sykes will be on the mend any day now.

'Also, Lance would like me to tell you that corridors 596 through 603 are no longer under water. He assures me that the problem with the plumbing has been resolved, which I'm sure we are all very relieved to hear.'

Maxwell had no idea where corridors 596 through 603 were, didn't know there had been a flood, and wasn't listening to Magister anyway. Maxwell's eyes were glued to the man sitting at Professor Magister's side.

He looked a very odd person to be sitting at the teacher's table.

The man was dressed in an electric blue suit which was crumpled and frayed, and didn't seem to fit him very well. Maxwell could clearly see at least four inches of pale wrist above his sleeves. The man's long, thin chin ended in a long, thin silvery grey goatee beard, and he was totally bald. It was quite dark in the windowless Hall Tower, but what little light there was reflected off the man's sunglasses, which covered his eyes with a metallic band that looked thick as steel plate.

'Who's Janet Munsie?' hissed Jamie.

'Jangle Mumbles!' Bella replied in a whisper. 'He's a--'

'As you may have noticed we have a visitor,' said Professor Magister. He turned and smiled at the man in the metallic sunglasses. The man did not look round, or even indicate he had heard Magister, but continued to stare ahead. 'This is Mr Vim,' Magister announced, 'the school inspector.'

Miss Hummingbird began to applaud excitedly, and Professor Magister frowned at her. Dr

Silex gave a single limp clap, and then continued to glare at Jamie.

'You're mad,' Jamie whispered. 'He's a school inspector. Who ever heard of a school inspector called Jangle Mumbles?'

'It is Jangle Mumbles!' Bella insisted. 'He was a friend of my dad's! He--'

'Mr Vim will be conducting a test of all student beginning Monday morning,' Magister continued. 'This test will comprise . . .' he looked at Mr Vim questioningly. 'It is a three part test, Mr Vim?'

'Yes,' Vim replied. His voice was as deep and strangely hollow, and cracked as though he hadn't spoken for years, but it carried across the large hall with ease. 'Standard aptitude, physiological attributes and cognitive ability.'

There was a worried murmur among the students. 'What's cog ability?' Jamie asked. Maxwell shrugged.

'You will be pleased to note that you will not have to revise for these tests,' said Magister. 'Additionally, any homework you have been set is officially cancelled - along with all of this afternoon's classes.'

A much louder, much more approving murmur of voices filled the hall. If Dr Silex hadn't been scanning the hall like a fat hawk looking for her dinner, Maxwell would have cheered. 'No maths! No physics! No biology!' chuckled Jamie. 'Bless you, Mr Vim!'

Professor Magister held up his hands and the happy rumble of voice died down. 'Also, you may see a few new faces in school on Monday. We have asked the parents of children born on Virporta to return for the forthcoming test. Many of these children will not have been on our island since they were born, so I would ask that you make them feel welcome during their visit.'

Maxwell and Jamie exchanged an astonished look, and from the expressions on the faces of most of the children in the hall Maxwell saw they were equally surprised by this news. Maxwell hadn't thought that anyone had ever moved away from Virporta. When he considered it, of course, it made perfect sense - after all, why would everyone living on the little island continue to live here indefinitely? Still . . . Maxwell didn't even know anyone who had moved away, or who had even visited the mainland - wherever that was.

Maxwell wasn't actually sure where Virporta Island was. He was pretty sure it was somewhere between England and Ireland - but whether it was nearer Lands End, John O' Groats, Liverpool or Belfast, Maxwell didn't have a clue.

'Well, I hope you all have a very enjoyable weekend,' Magister was saying over the excited hubbub. 'And try not to break any bones or crack open your heads, as you will need both limb and brain come Monday morning.' He turned to Mr Vim, who throughout his entire speech and the excitement which met it, had sat as still as a statue, not moving a single inch. 'Is there anything you would like to add, Mr Vim?' the Professor asked.

For a second it looked as if Mr Vim wasn't going to answer. Then, quite slowly, he pushed back his chair, and rose to his feet.

For the first time Maxwell could see that, far from being thin, Mr Vim was powerfully built. His shoulders looked huge, and his shrunken blue suit was pulled tight against his wide chest. He looked more like a boxer than a school inspector. He stood almost seven feet tall.

His head moved slowly to take in all the faces goggling up at him, his sunglasses glinting dully, his pale face as expressionless as stone, and the room fell silent instantly.

'Children,' he growled, and as he spoke Maxwell could have sworn he was looking straight at him. 'Stay out of the woods.'

Mr Vim slowly sat again, the room filled with uneasy silence. Magister was blinking at the school inspector with a perplexed expression.

'Yes . . . Well . . .' said Professor Magister. 'Wise words.' He cleared his throat. 'Thank you, Mr Vim.' He paused, and then smiled at them all. 'You are all dismissed!'

Even Dr Silex's grim expression couldn't stifle the loud cheer that followed these words; dozens of chairs scraped across the floor and everyone began to rush to the doors.

'Come on, Bella!' Jamie yelled. He was jiggling on the spot, obviously itching to join the people streaming past.

But Bella did not move. She was still staring at the teacher's table. Professor Magister, Dr Silex and Miss Hummingbird were huddled together at one end of the table, talking quickly, almost arguing, Maxwell thought. At the other end of the table Mr Vim sat unmoved.

'That is Jangle Mumbles,' Bella said.

'It's Mr Vim!' Jamie cried, exasperated.

'It is Jangle Mumbles,' Bella insisted. 'He was a friend of my dad's. I'd know him anywhere.'

'You are totally mad,' Jamie replied flatly. He turned to Maxwell. 'Come on, Maxwell. Let's go and get an ice cream or something?'

The Hall Tower was now empty apart from the three friends, the teachers and Mr Vim. Maxwell looked out of the open doors at the enticing April sunshine, and then he looked back at Bella, who was ringing her hands together as she stared at Mr Vim, her lunch still untouched on the table. 'I'll catch you up,' Maxwell said.

'Catch me up! But we've got to . . .' Jamie looked like he was about to explode on the spot. 'Don't be long!' he barked, he ran out of the hall without looking back.

'It is him, Maxwell,' Bella said. 'I'm *sure* it's him.'

'Well, let's go and asked him,' Maxwell said.

They walked over to the teacher's table, their footsteps sounding very loud in the empty hall. As they drew closer to the stage Maxwell saw for the first time that despite his powerful build Mr Vim was obviously a very old man. His immobile face was deeply lined, and the backs of his hands were covered in little brown spots. He did not move as they approached, and he seemed more than ever like a marble statue.

'Ex . . . Excuse me, sir?' stammered Bella, 'but are you . . . that is . . . did you ever--?'

'JONES! JUGG!' barked Dr Silex. 'You have been DISMISSED! What are you still doing here?'

'I . . . I wanted to speak to Mr Vim--' Bella began.

'Get out! You have no business here! You are dismissed!'

Maxwell turned hurriedly to leave. He had walked two steps before he realised Bella was not following him. Maxwell turned back, and saw that Bella was staring at Mr Vim and completely ignoring Dr Silex.

'It is you, isn't it?' Bella said.

'Are you DEAF girl?' Dr Silex howled. 'I TOLD you--'

'Silence, Flavia,' said Mr. Vim.

Mr Vim had stood up. Dr Silex stared at him with opened mouthed amazement. Mr Vim turned and looked at her, and Dr Silex took an involuntary step back. Mr Vim walked around to the front of the stage, and stepped down beside Bella. 'Come with me, Bella,' he said, and they both walked to the back of the Hall Tower, the door slamming closed behind them.

'JONES!' roared Dr Silex, and even Professor Magister jumped. 'School is CLOSED!'

'But I wanted to wait--'

'OUT!' screamed Dr Silex.

Maxwell glanced at Dr Silex's murderous face, and ran out of the Hall Tower.

Jamie wasn't waiting outside the school gates. This didn't really surprise Maxwell, as there was more chance of Dr Silex naming him pupil of the year than there was of Jamie Blip waiting for anyone or anything. He was relieved to see no sign of Pugg. He wasn't worried about Jamie - one of the reasons that Miss Hummingbird was so keen to have Jamie play potato hockey was that Jamie did not appear to have any bones in his body, or, at least, the bones he had were made of rubber. You couldn't catch Jamie Blip in a fishing net.

Maxwell often fantasised about giving Pugg just one good hard punch - pow! - a right hook right in the middle of his dumb face. But Maxwell knew that even if by some miracle that punch landed Pugg flat on his back in the middle of the school yard, his problems would only get worse, not better.

Still, Maxwell thought dreamily as he sat on the wall opposite the school, just imagine that one great punch. Ka-POW! Pugg flat on his back with Maxwell looming over him. The look of amazement on Chop and Prickle's faces. Wonderful.

Maxwell sighed, closed his eyes, and felt the warm sun on his face. Two and a half days with no school and no homework. He would go home, grab a pile of comics . . .

'March, damn you! Keep your legs up at the front there! Left-left-left! Right-right-right!'

Maxwell's eyes flew open. The schoolyard was deserted. Yet he could have sworn--

'987326! Keep up the pace you shower! Yes, I'm talking to you, laddie!' came a distant voice.

Maxwell looked up and down Spudmore Avenue but there was no one in sight.

'Left-left-left! Right-r-- 987326! Lift your feet! Cretin!' Came the voice again. 'You are a disgrace to this army!'

Because there was no where else left to look, Maxwell looked down, and saw a line of ants walking across the pavement in front of his feet. Maxwell leant forward, and saw the small ant at the back of the line raise its head, and say: 'Stay in line you slovenly shower!'

'Er . . hello?' said Maxwell.

The small ant at the back of the line looked around. 'Who's talking in rank! 987326, I'll have your feelers, laddie!'

'It wasn't me, sergeant,' came the timid reply from a large ant at the front of the group.

'SILENCE!' screeched the drill sergeant, reminding Maxwell distinctly of Dr Silex. 'RABBLE! I have never in my six months at the front line of this ant's army encountered such insolence--'

'Excuse me?' said Maxwell. He knelt down beside the line of ants. 'It wasn't that . . . it wasn't 987326 speaking, sergeant, it was me.'

The ant raised its tiny head. 'You?' it spluttered. You? Speaking?'

'Yes. Don't be frightened. I'm--'

'You? A foot speaking? Did you hear that, lads? A talking foot!'

The line of ants all began to laugh. Maxwell opened his mouth to reply, but was suddenly struck by the absurdity of what he was doing. Not only was he talking to a group of ants, they were all laughing at him. One, indeed, was lying on its back in fits of giggles, waving six legs in the air. 'Which one of you set this up, eh? The sergeant was saying. 'Was it you 987326? 423861 - it was you, wasn't it! It was, wasn't it?' It occurred to Maxwell that if anyone knew what he was doing they would think he'd gone totally bonkers. Maxwell was beginning to wonder if they would be right to think exactly that.

'Maybe he's a spy, sergeant!' rose a fearful voice, and all the ants stopped laughing instantly.

'A . . . *spy*. . .?' said the drill sergeant, and he raised his tiny face to Maxwell's. 'A spy! Well, you'll not get anything out of us, foot boy!'

'I'm not--' Maxwell began.

'Collaborator!' cried the drill sergeant. 'Not an ant in my troop will break, you spying scum!'

'I'm not a spy, I just want--'

'You can stamp on us! You can burn us! You can drown us! You can feed us to your foul masters! We shall not bend! We shall not break!' The ants cheered. 'Onwards, lads! Stand proud 987326! All stand proud! He may flatten our bodies, but he shall never break our spirits!'

'I don't want to flatten you!' said Maxwell, but the troop was already marching away. 'I just want to know how you can understand me?'

'Beetle loving scum!' cried 987326 shrilly.

'Wait! Please! Listen to me, I just--'

'Maxwell?'

'Please, if you just wait--'

'Maxwell? What are you doing?'

Maxwell looked up. Bella was standing looking down at him, a worried expression on her face. 'What was that funny clicking sound you were making?' she asked.

'It was - I was just . . .' Maxwell got quickly to his feet. 'Nothing. I . . . I lost a marble.' Bella didn't look convinced; in fact she looked more worried than ever at the thought of Maxwell misplacing his marbles. 'What did Mr Vim say?' He said quickly.

Bella's concerned expression transformed into a beaming grin. 'It was him, Maxwell! I knew it was him!'

'Joe Mangle?'

'*Jangle Mumbles*,' Bella corrected him. 'He says he isn't involved in the entertainment industry any more. Oh - he was a busker, didn't I tell you that?'

'A busker?' Remembering Mr Vim's stony face Maxwell couldn't think of anyone he'd feel less inclined to give fifty pence to.

'Well, more of a one-man band. Anyway, he doesn't do that anymore, he told me . . .' Bella looked up and down the street, just as Maxwell had done when he'd first heard the ant sergeant major.

'What is it?' Maxwell asked.

'He said I shouldn't tell anybody . . .'

'You can tell me, I can keep a secret.'

'He told me . . .' she glanced up and down Spudmore Avenue again, and then said in a whisper: 'He told me my dad is *still alive*.'

'But Bella . . .' Maxwell stopped. He was about to say something like - don't be stupid Bella, don't you know a hippo ate your dad? But he couldn't say that. 'That's brilliant, Bella,' he said. 'That's absolutely wonderful.'

Bella squealed and threw her thick arms around him. As Maxwell felt his spine crack, he began to wonder just who Mr Vim really was.

Chapter Three: Billy Barker

Maxwell spent the rest of what he had begun to think of as the strangest day of life in his bedroom.

Bella had run home almost as soon as telling Maxwell about Mr Vim's revelation, leaving him standing alone at the end of Spudmore Avenue, feeling confused and shaky. He had gone home to his room, and had remained there for the rest of the day while the April sun shone outside and the distant sound of laughing children drifted through his window. The prospect of sitting in the garden with his dad's old comics didn't seem particularly attractive any more. The comics, which all his life had seemed so wonderful, suddenly seemed dull, useless things.

Maxwell's dad, Andy, had been a reporter. Before Maxwell was born his mum and dad had travelled the world 'Top to toe and side to side,' as his mum said, adding, typically: 'And what a variety of potatoes!' Andy had died in a plane crash in Brazil. Maxwell had been one month old.

What Andronicus Titus Jones liked more than anything else was superhero comics. He had collected thousands and thousand, and Maxwell's mum had kept them all after his death. There were comics crammed into every spare corner of the tiny two bedroomed house on Spudmore Avenue. Bettie Jones had not kept any photographs of Maxwell's dad - 'He didn't like getting his picture done' - and she hadn't kept any of his newspaper report - 'He hated showing off' - but she had kept the things he had most loved. And Maxwell, with only the comics to remind him of Andy Jones, loved them too.

When Maxwell opened the comics it was like his dad had come back to life. All the colourful pictured and wild stories of flying men and terrible villains were a little doorway into his dad's head. The comics were the little piece of Andy's heart that Maxwell could still feel inside his own heart.

And if Bella's dad was still alive . . . Well, that was wonderful! . . . Wasn't it?

But as he lay in bed all through that day and long into the night looking at the rows of yellowing comic books that lined his bedroom wall, Maxwell couldn't help but wish that Mr Vim had told him that it was Andy Jones who was still alive, not Cyril Jugg.

The next morning his rusty alarm clock woke him and Maxwell dressed quickly and ran out of the house in the chilly air. It was a cold, cloudless morning and as Maxwell trudged down Spudmore Avenue and turned into Front Street he decided one thing - if he did nothing else today he would solve at least one of the previous day's mysteries.

Front Street looked out across a mile-long stretch of sand dunes that reached to the unseen sea. Though Virporta Island had only two streets most of the two or three hundred people who lived on the island fitted comfortably into Spudmore Avenue. Mrs Trimm's general store was halfway down Front Street, and a good half-hour walk from Maxwell's gate, past literally hundreds of empty houses.

No matter how much he thought about it there was no way he could just dismiss what had happened. If it had just been Pugg not recognising him with his glasses off, or if it had just been the talking blackbird, then Maxwell could have said it was an hallucination, or coincidence, or a bonk on the head. But those ants had definitely spoken to him. Or rather, those ants had shouted at him, laughed at him, and had accused him of "collaborating" (he had looked this word up in the dictionary and had discovered a "collaborator" was a sort of spy). It was stupid trying to fool himself that hadn't happened - *it had.*

How had Daisy made that potato stop in mid-air?

If Mr Vim was telling the truth about Bella's dad being alive, where was Mr Jugg now?

Maxwell didn't know the answers to any of these question, but he was determined he was going to find those answers.

There was a loud crash, and a bicycle wheel appeared in the doorway of Mrs Trimm's general store, followed by a high, excited voice shouting: 'I *know*! It's so *thrilling* isn't it?'

Without another thought Maxwell snatched off his spectacles and dropped them into his newspaper satchel.

Miss Hummingbird came out of the shop pushing her bright red bicycle. As well as being a teacher Miss Hummingbird was also the island's postman. A large stack of mail sat in the trailer at the back of her bike, and she was wearing a dazzling pink t-shirt with the words POST BABE written on the front in vivid golden letters.

As Maxwell approached Miss Hummingbird leapt onto her bicycle. Now or never, thought Maxwell.

'Morning,' he said, in a voice that he hoped sounded natural. Miss Hummingbird looked at him, and blinked.

This was it! The proof he needed! Miss Hummingbird didn't recognise him without his glasses--

'Hello Maxwell, didn't see you there!' Miss Hummingbird cried. 'Must be off! Busy, busy, busy!'

She shot away from the shop like a bullet from a gun, missing running over Maxwell's toes by millimetres.

So much for that theory.

Trimm's general store was the only shop on Virporta Island, and far from being general it catered for everything you could ever possibly need.

Behind the small two-windowed front the store was vast. Trimm's was in fact half a dozen of the small houses of Front Street, their inner walls knocked down to form a space as big as any city supermarket. It was a post office, a newsagents, a greengrocers, an ironmongers, a clothes shop and a food store. If what you wanted wasn't on the shelves then Mr or Mrs Trimm could always spirit it up from the store's legendarily cavernous basement within a minute.

If there was anything you couldn't buy at Trimm's Maxwell had yet to find out what it was.

Mrs Trimm was sitting behind the counter smoking a large cigar, the Blue Danube playing through the open door behind her. Mrs Trimm was a stocky, steely-eyed woman with a lot of grey hair, which she shaped into interesting sculptures on her head. Maxwell's personal favourite had been the Sydney Opera House, but her yearly Santa Claus hair sculpture was a close second.

This morning, however, Mrs Trimm's hair was tied into a business-like plat, which trailed five feet across the shop counter.

'Maxwell,' she said, looking up from the Virporta Morning News. 'On time this morning. Good.'

'Morning, Mrs Trimm.' Mrs Trimm was staring at him. 'Is something wrong?' Maxwell asked.

'You look different . . .' Mrs Trimm looked him up and down suspiciously. She clicked her fingers. 'Got it! Specs!'

Maxwell sighed, retrieved his spectacles from his satchel and slipped them on. His spectacles were just spectacles after all, and Pugg was even dimmer than even Maxwell had suspected.

'Bit of a change today, Maxwell,' Mrs Trimm slammed a stack of newspapers down on the counter... 'We have a new paperboy.'

'What . . . ? You mean - I'm sacked?' Maxwell said in amazement.

'Of course not,' said Mrs Trimm, impatiently. 'I mean we have an *extra* paperboy.' She turned to the open door behind the counter, and bellowed: 'BILLY!'

A boy slouched through the door, and blinked blearily at Mrs Trimm. He was almost a foot taller than Maxwell, with blond hair that was sticking out at all angles from his head. He wore small, silver spectacles and was dressed in shorts and a t-shirt.

'Maxwell, this is Billy Barker, my nephew.'

Mrs Trimm's lanky nephew held up a hand in greeting, and let out a jaw-cracking yawn. Maxwell smiled back uncertainly, and turned back to Mrs Trimm, who had disappeared under the counter.

'Mrs Trimm?' Maxwell said as a second bundle of Virporta Morning News appeared on the counter. 'I don't think I really need any help, Mrs Trimm?'

'I *told* you, Aunty Magnolia,' said Billy. He dropped onto the stool behind the counter and slumped against the wall. He looked like he was going to drop off to sleep any second.

Another bundle of newspapers appeared on the counter. 'Mrs Trimm?' Maxwell didn't want to split his pay with anyone. He had to replace his broken hockey stick. 'Mrs Trimm, I've never needed any help before. I don't really think . . .' Maxwell stared as Mrs Trimm continued adding to the pile of newspapers.

'Are you getting changed, Billy?' Mrs Trimm demanded. 'It's a cold morning.'

Billy jumped - he had fallen asleep. 'You must be joking, mate, I'm *boiling*,' he replied.

Mrs Trimm ushered Billy off the stool, handed him a satchel, and gave Maxwell a very long list of houses. Maxwell goggled at the pages and pages of numbers - who were all these papers for?

'Well, don't dilly-dally!' Mrs Trimm commanded. 'People need their newspapers!'

Maxwell didn't bother to argue, looking at the amazing stack of newspapers he obviously had a busy morning ahead. He began shoving bundles of the Virporta Morning News in his satchel and (after a warning bark from Mrs Trimm woke him) Billy joined him.

'I am absolutely knackered,' said Billy, collapsing into a beanbag. 'How do you *do* that every morning, Max?'

'I don't,' Maxwell replied, slumping onto his bed.

It had taken both Billy and Maxwell over an hour to deliver all the copies of the Virporta Morning News. Maxwell's round usually took him only half an hour by himself - less if he ran, or had his skateboard. This morning, however, his usual pile of fifty or sixty papers had grown to two or three hundred.

They had delivered to almost every house in Front Street and Spudmore Avenue, and the two streets seemed a lot longer than usual. As the paper round wore on Maxwell spotted several children he had never seen before playing in the sand dunes or heading for the Watchmen's playing fields.

When they went to pick up the last two bundles of newspapers Mrs Trimm told Maxwell that she wasn't splitting his wages with Billy as he'd feared - she was actually doubling his money to twenty pounds a week.

Dragging the heavy bag around didn't seem so bad after that, and Maxwell imagined the fantastic hockey stick he could afford with his sudden riches.

As it turned out Billy Barker did more than his bit. After falling asleep at a couple of letterboxes he had volunteered to deliver to all of Front Street. 'It's cooler,' Billy said. He didn't mean that Front Street was somehow better than Spudmore Avenue, it was just that he preferred to work in the cold sea wind.

'I've been living in Antarctica for the last few months,' Billy explained as they trudged back to Trimm's for the umpteenth time.

'Antarctica? What were you doing there?' Maxwell asked.

'My mum and dad are journalists,' Billy replied.

'My dad was a reporter!' said Maxwell excitedly. 'He's dead now, though,' he added.

Maxwell was ready to tell Billy the story of how his dad had died, but Billy had stopped him with a puzzled expression. 'That's odd,' he said. 'You're the third kid who's told me that since I arrived on this island.'

When they had finally finished the mammoth paper round Maxwell had asked Billy if he'd like to come back to his house for a drink.

Maxwell's mum was out, as she always was on a Saturday morning. She worked every weekend, and though she loved her job and had never been late even once in all the years she'd worked at Pugg's Potato Factory, Maxwell suspected she spent weekends there mostly because she was never entirely sure it wasn't Wednesday. They grabbed a glass of lemonade each (Maxwell advised Billy to keep away from the large jug of Spud O' Cola) and Maxwell, remembering he'd had no breakfast, managed to find a packet of chocolate biscuits that he was fairly sure had no potato in them.

Between stuffing biscuits and guzzling down ice-cold lemonade, Billy had told Billy about his journey to Virporta.

'We came by husky from the base to Johnson's Sound - that's, like, on the coast of Antarctica - then we took a steamer ship to Argentina.' Billy winced. 'Shockingly hot in Argentina. Then we got a plane to Boston - in America, like - then another plane from America to Spain, another from Spain to England. My dad hired a car in London, and we drove to Rhyll - that's in Wales. Then a train to Liverpool, and from there we got a ferry to Virporta.'

Maxwell was impressed. He had never even been in a car, never mind an aeroplane, let alone a steam ship crashing through the ice of Antarctica. 'Where did the ferry land?' he asked. He hadn't even been aware that there was a ferry to Virporta.

'Dunno,' Billy said, taking another biscuit from the almost empty packet. 'I fell asleep on the train. I woke up in bed in Aunty Magnolia's.'

'Funny though, isn't it?' Maxwell said. "All these people coming to Virporta all at the same time?'

'For the test, init?' Billy replied.

'You've come here for the test?' said Maxwell in surprise.

'Yeah. Some sort of thing they make you do when you're eleven, my dad said.' Maxwell was surprised again. Billy was eleven? He was almost as tall as Maxwell's mum, and he looked at least fifteen. 'You have to, like, do an assault course, or something, and answer questions on maths and stuff.'

Maths? Oh no! 'Your dad did the test?' Maxwell asked.

'Everybody does the test, my dad said.'

'And they all have to come back to Virporta Island?' Maxwell imagined a massive flood of people, millions and millions crammed into Spudmore Avenue like the world's biggest conga line.

'Well, the people who were born here, anyway,' Billy replied, deflating Maxwell's vision of every eleven year old from Pakistan to Australia descending on the small island. 'Until a week ago I didn't even know I *was* born here. I'd never even heard of this place.' Billy looked around as if it was Maxwell's room he had been born in. 'Very weird,' Billy took another chocolate biscuit. 'What's this test thing about, then? Dad didn't tell me much about it?'

Maxwell told him about Mr Vim with his strange sunglasses, his scarred and wrinkled skin and his amazing news about Bella's dad.

When he'd finished Billy was lying back on the beanbag again looking thoughtfully at the ceiling, his hands crossed over his stomach. 'Jangle Mumbles,' he murmured. He sat up suddenly 'Your mate? Whatchacaller - Bella?' Maxwell nodded. 'Did she tell you where Mr Vim said her dad was?'

'No,' Maxwell said. Of course, that should have been the first thing he asked Bella, but he couldn't very well tell Billy he had been distracted by talking ants, so he said nothing else.

'There's something well weird going on here, Max,' said Billy. 'Where does this Bella live?'

'Number 302,' Maxwell replied - then realising Billy hadn't lived on Virporta all his life, he added. 'Just down the end of Spudmore Avenue, near the factory.'

'Let's go and see her, then,' Billy stood.

Maxwell looked at the gangling boy in alarm. 'And do what? Ask Bella where her dad has been hiding all these years after abandoning her and her mum?'

'My dad says good reporters report facts, not rumours,' said Billy. 'I think we should find out exactly what this Vim bloke said to your mate Bella.'

'There is definitely something going on,' Billy announced as he marched down Spudmore Avenue, sweat popping from his brow despite the chilly morning breeze. 'All these people coming back to this island, this test thingy, all this stuff with Mr Brim . . .'

'Vim,' Maxwell corrected him, as he jogged along, trying to keep up with Billy's very long legs.

'Whatever,' Billy waved this unimportant fact away. Maxwell noticed that once Billy was fully awake he seemed to do a lot of waving, pointing and flapping his arms. He was like a blond haired windmill. 'Conspicuous disconnections,' Billy said.

'Pardon?' said Maxwell.

'That's what my dad calls it when facts about the same thing don't seem to be connected,' Billy explained. He was now walking as fast as Maxwell could jog, and his arms were waving in every direction. '"Conspicuous disconnections" - like, stuff that seems to have nothing to do with other stuff - it *suspiciously* has nothing to do with other stuff.' Billy stopped walking, and Maxwell almost ran into him. Billy turned to Maxwell, his eyes narrowed behind his spectacles. 'There hasn't been nothing else funny happening, has there?' he asked.

Maxwell considered telling Billy about what had happened the previous day - actually opened his mouth and was about to say something like, 'Well, actually, now you come to mention it I've just discovered I can talk to animals. I'm kind of like Dr Doolittle, although I'm not a doctor, of course. Tell you what - find me a worm and we'll have a quick chat about where to pick up the best turnips.'

He *almost* said something like that - but he changed his mind at the last minute and simply replied: 'No.' Billy still wore a suspicious look. 'Not that I've noticed, anyway,' Maxwell added nervously.

Billy shrugged, spun on his heels, and started marching down the street again.

Maxwell followed. He didn't know why he hadn't told Billy about the strange things that had happened to him. It was just that . . . Billy Barker was an interesting person, Maxwell thought, and he would make an interesting friend . . . and the last thing Maxwell wanted was Billy thinking he was odd.

Bella was out. They rang her doorbell several times, and Billy tried to peek through the window - but the house was deserted.

'I hate it when a lead dries up,' Billy said.. 'You haven't any idea where she could be do you, Max?'

Maxwell shook his head. He supposed she might be with Daisy Electra. Bella had been very concerned about her after the accident.

'I wonder what my dad would do now?' murmured Billy. 'I'll tell you what, Max, you're not a very good lead.'

'What do you mean?' said Maxwell.

'Well, we've got nowhere have we? And you told me this house was near the factory,' Billy pointed at the house, then up the street at the factory. 'It's flipping miles away! It's a good job I wasn't following this story up by myself!'

Maxwell looked up Spudmore Avenue. From where they stood to the gates of Pugg's Potato Factory was at least ten minutes walk. He looked back at the house. 302. It was Daisy's house for sure.

'But it *was* close to the factory,' Maxwell said in amazement.

'Eh?'

'It was! Bella's house is - was - only three or four doors from the factory gates.'

'Are you saying,' Billy said slowly, an expression of deep concentration on his face, 'that this house has moved?'

'No I'm not. I'm telling you that this street is longer than it was yesterday, Billy. It's much longer.' Maxwell looked up and down Spudmore Avenue again. The street, which yesterday morning had perhaps two hundred houses in it, now had twice as many. At *least* twice as many houses. 'But that impossible!' he exclaimed.

'It can't be impossible if it's happened,' Billy replied reasonably. 'Perhaps they built more houses and you didn't notice?'

'How could I not notice? I deliver newspapers up and down this street every morning,' said Maxwell. 'And anyway, it's not just more houses - the street is longer, Billy. How could they make the street longer unless they moved Pugg's or the Watchmen?'

Billy rubbed his chin thoughtfully. He was staring at Maxwell, and Maxwell began to feel uncomfortable. Billy did think he was odd after all. But something *had* happened. The street *was* longer.

'Max?' said Billy, and Maxwell was ready for Billy to say – "Max – you're barmy" or "Max – is everyone on this island as nutty as you?" – but Billy simply said: 'This is because of Mr Vim.'

'Mr Vim? But how—'

'I don't know *how*, not yet, but all this weird stuff started the day Mr Vim came, right?' Maxwell nodded. He did not point out the fact that all this "weird stuff" had also begun as Billy had arrived on Virporta. 'So all this *must* be connected to him, right?' Billy continued. '*That's* the conspicuous disconnection.' Billy nodded his head. 'Did Mr Vim say anything else?' he asked.

'Like what?'

'I dunno! Did he say anything, like, odd or unusual?'

Maxwell thought about Mr Vim with his shrunken suit, his elongated limbs, his bald head and metallic sunglasses – everything about him was odd and unusual. Then Maxwell remembered something. 'Mr Vim told us to stay out of the Black Woods,' he said.

'Brilliant!' Billy cried, and he began marching back up the street.

Maxwell ran after him. 'Where are we going?' he asked.

'Where do you think?' Billy replied with an excited grin. 'We're going to the Black Woods!'

Chapter Four: The Black Monastery

It soon became obvious to Maxwell and Billy that very few people had taken Mr Vim's warning about entering the Black Woods seriously. The woods were teaming with children – children climbing trees, children collection leaves and bugs, even children playing hockey and football at the edges of the thick undergrowth.

Maxwell was stunned by how many children there were. The mammoth paper round hadn't prepared Maxwell for this noisy, jumping, muddy proof that Virporta Island's population had grown enormously.

'There must be thousands of new kids,' Maxwell exclaimed, goggling at the noisy tribes racing all around them and dangling from the trees above them.

'Don't exaggerate,' Billy said. 'Hundreds, maybe.' He ducked as a baked potato whizzed over his head. 'It must be important this test.'

They walked into the woods dodging flying balls, punted potatoes, and children falling out of trees. Maxwell reflected that must be a *very* important test indeed to bring this many new people to the small island in such a short space of time. But how had they transported so many people to Virporta in just one night?

'The ferry?' Billy suggested.

'Until today I didn't even know there was a ferry,' Maxwell replied.

'Well how did you think people got on and off the island?'

'They didn't. Nobody ever leaves Virporta.' Saying that out loud made it sound ominous, like something you'd read in a ghost story – "Nobody leaves Virporta Island alive!" But it wasn't as if they were *trapped* on the island. Nobody ever left, true, but that was because . . . Well, no one had ever wanted to leave.

'Nobody *ever* leaves this place?' asked Billy curiously.

'No . . . Well – Professor Magister,' said Maxwell.

'Who's he?'

'The headmaster. He leaves the island for research trips.'

'Research, eh?' said Billy, mysteriously.

Soon Maxwell and Billy had left the other children behind and it seemed they had heeded Mr Vim's warning after all. There was no one to be seen in the depths of the Black Woods, only the gentle rustle of the trees and bird song accompanied them.

'Crikey,' said Billy. 'How *big* is this island?'

'Oh, not very . . .' Maxwell trailed off as he looked at his watch and saw they had been walking for over an hour without him noticing. He had been listening carefully to the birds – half expecting to hear them chatting about the weather or where to find the best worms – but he was relieved to discover (and perhaps a *little* disappointed) that all he could hear was their twittering song.

'I'll have to have a rest,' said Billy, sitting on a log. 'I am cream crackered, mate.' He was sweating again, despite the fact that barely a glimmer of sun came through the thickening leaves above their heads.

Maxwell was still staring at his watch. 'Billy...?'

'What mate?' Billy produced a large bottle of black liquid from his shorts pocket. 'I like this Spud O' Cola,' he said, and took a swig. 'Want some?'

'No. Billy . . . The island is . . . We've been walking for over an hour, Billy. The island is bigger than it was.'

Billy took another swig of Spud O'Cola – and now, Maxwell thought, surely *now* he will think I'm strange.

But Billy simply said, 'Course it is,' and took another huge gulp from the bottle.

Maxwell sat beside Billy on the log, and looked at him questioningly. Eventually, after he had drunk almost the whole bottle of Bettie Jones's disgusting brew, Billy sat back, burped, and sighed.

'Look, Max, it's common sense, in it? I mean you said that street . . . whatchacallit?'

'Spudmore Avenue,' Maxwell said.

'Right. You said Spudmore Avenue is longer, so when you think about it, it makes perfect sense that the whole of Virporta Island has grown, not just one street.'

'It makes absolutely no sense to me,' Maxwell replied. 'How can Virporta have grown? An island *can't* grow.'

'I dunno how,' said Billy, 'But I'm gonna find out.' He lay back against the fallen tree and fanned his face with his hand. 'Fearful hot on this island, init? Did it get hotter when it got bigger, do you think?'

Maxwell was dressed in jeans, a shirt and a denim jacket, and was still feeling chilly. 'It's not hot. You're just not used to the climate. What were your mum and dad doing in Antarctica anyway?'

For the next half hour Billy told Maxwell about the Barker family's world adventures. In Antarctica they had been reporting on illegal oil drilling, 'Never found no evidence, though,' Billy said. Billy had been more interested in the stories the scientists on the base had told about a mysterious snow beast that attacked expeditions during blizzards. Billy had wanted to investigate the snow beast, but had been confined to the base with a tutor most of the time. He had spent his eleventh birthday in a mud hut in Zambia, and while his parents had been looking into ivory smuggling, Billy had investigated a giant man-eating snake that lived in the jungle. In Tasmania the year before his parents had tracked down crocodile poachers while Billy had looked for a dinosaur which, according to local legend, lived in a remote lake and ate 100 sheep a night.

'Are you sure your mum and dad aren't looking for monsters?' Maxwell said at one point.

Billy just laughed. 'As if!' he replied.

Maxwell was disappointed to discover that Billy had lived in a large, luxurious research base in Antarctica, with satellite TV, a swimming pool, and three restaurants (including a MacDonalds) and not in an igloo, as Maxwell had imagined. Billy was horrified when Maxwell told him that TV didn't work very well on Virporta Island.

'No telly!' gasped Billy, clutching his heart.

'Well, we do have TVs,' said Maxwell. 'It's just that they don't work very well. You can watch TV though - for about three hours a day.'

'Which hours?' Billy asked urgently.

'All different hours. It changes all the time. Most people just don't bother switching them on, but mum keeps ours on with the sound turned down, in case a gardening programme comes on. Mum likes gardening programmes.'

This was not exactly true. Bettie Jones liked to shout at gardening programmes, then write letters of complain to TV companies. On the rare occasion they did see a show, it was invariably about roses or bushes or hanging baskets, and was never about potatoes. Bettie Jones was almost constantly writing angry letters to the BBC and the Discovery Channel about the shocking lack of potato coverage on television.

'No footy!' Billy moaned, slumping back against the log as if someone had shot him.

Maxwell had to admit to Billy that he had never actually seen a football match on television, and then had to break the news that they didn't actually play soccer at the Watchmen Academy.

'Hockey!' exclaimed Billy in disgust. 'Bleeding hockey! That's a girl's game!'

Maxwell said nothing. Five minutes on the pitch would change Billy's mind about Potato Hockey. Assuming he was still conscious after five minutes.

It was now almost mid-day according to Maxwell's watch (under the shade of the trees it didn't look like noon, if anything it had become gloomier) and Maxwell was starving hungry. He was just about to suggest to Billy they head back for lunch - when a small voice behind Maxwell whispered: 'He's coming!'

Maxwell looked at Billy, but Billy was still slumped on the tree, his eyes closed, groaning softly about the Premier League. Maxwell looked around. There was no one else here. Odd. He must have imagined . . .

'Can you see him yet?'

'Yes - Yes! Look! He's just passing that blackberry bush!'

'Are you *sure* it's him?'

'I know the Eye when I see him!'

'All right, all right.'

'Well - *really.*'

Maxwell stood up and looked around him. A few yards away from where he and Billy were a red squirrel stood in the branches of a tree. Perched above the squirrel was a large seagull.

'What's up?'

Billy was looking at him curiously. Maxwell shook his head, held a finger to his lips - *shh* - and turned back to watch the animals. To *listen* to the animals.

'But are you *sure* it's him?' Asked the squirrel, peering into the woods. 'Are you *positive*?'

'Look!' the seagull sounded angry. 'I am twenty-three summers old. I was here during the Big Combination. And I know the Eye when I see him!'

'All right, all right,' mumbled the squirrel. 'Keep your beak on.'

'What's wrong, Max?' Billy sat up and looked over the log.

'Someone's coming,' said Maxwell. 'Quick - duck!'

Billy dived back behind the log, and Maxwell squatted beside him.

They did not move for several minutes. The only sound in the woods was the swoop of the blowing branches high above them. 'Are you *sure* you heard--'

'Shh!' hissed Maxwell. 'Look!'

Through the dirt encrusted roots of the fallen tree the boys saw a blue shape moving quickly through the Black Woods. The blue thing never paused or slowed, and despite the thick coating of branches and leaves covering the ground, it didn't make a single sound. As the figure grew closed Maxwell saw that the blue was the electric blue of a suit jacket, above that a glint of something metallic was revealed, and finally he recognised a face which was the shape of an almond with a little white beard.

Mr Vim stopped below the branches where the seagull was perched. The squirrel had vanished.

'You know who I am?' said Mr Vim in his rumbling, cracked voice. The seagull ducked its head, its body trembling. 'You know why I'm here?' Mr Vim asked.

'M . . . Master Eye,' stuttered the seagull. 'I am just a humble old bird. I would not presume to know the mind of such a great and majestic--'

'Silence, bird,' said Mr Vim. He did not raise his voice, and there was no hint of a threat in his words, but it was just like he had struck the seagull. The bird cowered on the branch, and tried to duck its head under its wing. 'I know your ways, bird. You are vermin, an eater of the dead, you are *his* creature, are you not?' The seagull didn't answer, it seemed paralysed with fear, and was now shaking so hard that Maxwell was sure it would fall off the branch any second. 'You know what I seek, bird,' said Mr Vim, 'and you will take me to it.'

'I . . . I am not sure it is there, master,' squealed the seagull.

'You know,' said Mr Vim. 'Take me to it.'

'I . . . I will have to fly above the big trees . . .'

'I will see you,' said Mr Vim. 'I will see you where ever you go, bird.'

The seagull shuffled on the branch, its feet working up and down as if it was preparing to flee. Then it bowed its head, and said quietly, 'Yes, master Eye.'

The bird took flight with a loud, frightened caw. Mr Vim watched it fly up to the treetops, and when it disappeared above him, Mr Vim *still* watched it.

Mr Vim walked into the Black Woods, and had vanished into the greenery within seconds.

'Blimey!' Billy exclaimed suddenly, making Maxwell jump up and thump his head on the tree. 'What the bleeding Nora was all that about!'

'The seagull's taking Mr. Vim to something,' Maxwell said, rubbing his throbbing head.

Billy looked at him oddly. 'How do you know that?' he asked.

'I heard Mr Vim ask the seagull,' Maxwell replied slowly, suddenly aware that Billy was looking at him the way he might look at a deadly snake. 'Mr Vim said "Take me to it" - didn't you hear him?'

'Max . . . he . . .' Billy bit his lip thoughtfully. 'Mr Vim didn't say nothing. He just made this funny squawking noise. I thought he'd gone barmy, or something. Max . . . you understood what he said?'

Maxwell paused. He had tried his best not to appear odd in front of Billy, but, he supposed, whatever had happened to him couldn't be any stranger than what he had just seen and heard, so he simply replied, 'Yes.'

'You can understand what birds say?'

'Yes . . . But not just birds, any animal.' Maxwell realised this wasn't true as soon as he'd said it. 'Well . . . seagulls, and squirrels, and blackbirds. Oh - and ants.'

'Ants!' Billy said in disbelief. 'How long have you--'

'Does it matter?' Maxwell interrupted. 'You said Mr Vim is the link between everything that's happening.'

'Well ... yeah . . .' Billy replied slowly, but he still looked unsure. 'But this is all, like, just a little bit *too* weird, you know?'

'I'm going after Mr Vim,' Maxwell said. 'By myself, if I have to.'

The uncertainty fell away from Billy's face immediately. 'You're right,' he said, to Maxwell's enormous relief. The thought of following Mr Vim alone was very frightening. 'What am I thinking of!' Billy exclaimed. 'This is the story of a lifetime! Let's go!'

It wasn't just the size of the woods that was different. They saw strange plants: bright purple bushes and strangely twisted trees looped and bent around them, and once they came upon a bright pink flower as tall as a man and as wide as a car, which reeked like rotting meat. Like the plants, the animals also seemed to have changed. They saw a golden bird bigger than a seagull flit momentarily between the trees up ahead. They saw dragonflies the size of tennis balls buzz past. And, as they passed a large bubbling swamp, something huge crossed their path. They heard its snorting breath twenty feet above their heads, and glimpsed a massive, lizard-like hide through the trees.

'Was that . . . ?' Billy murmured, looking at Maxwell in alarm.

'No. No, it couldn't be,' said Maxwell, but his head was filled with names from Professor Magister's history class - *brachiosaurus, euoplocephalus, tyrannosaurus rex*.

The woods were so thick and dark now that they could see no sign of Mr Vim's trail, but Maxwell could still hear the seagull's nervous instructions as it led the school inspector through the woods.

'Are you sure it's the same seagull?' Billy said.

'It sounds like the same one,' Maxwell replied uncertainly.

'Maybe Mr Vim's fooling us,' Billy said. 'Maybe he *knows* you can talk to animals, and he's making that seagull trick us.'

'I don't think so,' Maxwell said, remembering the seagull's very real terror, 'And anyway, how would he know--'

Billy grabbed Maxwell from behind, and dragged him behind a bush. Mr Vim was standing just feet from where they were hidden looking curiously at a large thorn bush. If Billy hadn't grabbed Maxwell they would have both walked right into him. It was the thorn bush Pugg had chased him through yesterday, Maxwell realised. There was a broad path in front of Mr Vim where Pugg's gang had beaten their way through.

'Get down!' Maxwell hissed, and they both fell flat on their bellies behind the bush a second before Mr Vim turned to look in their direction.

Maxwell held his breath, expecting to feel Mr Vim's hand on his shoulder at any second; sure that Mr Vim could hear his thundering heartbeat. He heard Mr Vim's almost soundless feet whispering over the ground, moving away, until there was only silence.

Billy looked cautiously over the bush. 'Come on, he's gone.' He lead Maxwell through the broken thorn bushes to the clearing where the day before Maxwell had jumped head first into this mystery.

'Look,' said Billy, pointing to a flattened bush on the other bank of the deep ravine. 'He must have jumped across.' He peered over the crumbling edge to the rocky stream below. 'Blimey, that's some jump. Do you think we can make it across, Max?'

Maxwell was about to say - no, nope, no way, Billy boy - then he realised something. He didn't just *want* to see what was beyond those bushes on the far bank of the ravine, he *needed* to see. He needed, right down to his bones, to know what Mr Vim was looking for.

'Yes,' Maxwell said. 'I think we can make it across. Together.'

'Cool,' Billy replied. Maxwell felt Billy take his hand, and when he looked round Billy scowled at him. 'Just cos I'm holding your hand it don't mean I'm gonna give you a kiss, okay?' he said.

'Okay.' Maxwell laughed. 'Are you scared?'

'Absolutely blinking terrified,' Billy replied, laughing himself.

'Me too. On three, all right?'

'Right,' Billy squeezed his hand tight. 'One ... Two ...'

'Three!' yelled Maxwell.

They ran at the ravine, and both jumped at the same time. They soared over the gurgling water below, and for a second Maxwell was certain they were going to crash into the bank, no way they could make it across. They were both going to lose their spectacles and bust their heads open on the rocks below.

Then Maxwell felt himself *lift* . . . he had the oddest sensation, like his body was made of nothing more than air, he felt sudden electricity shudder up his spine, and Billy's hand grew hot in his - *boiling* hot, *burning* hot - and they landed on the far bank with a *THUD* that shook every bone in Maxwell's suddenly heavy body, and they crashed into the bushes.

'Ow! Oww!' yelled Maxwell.

'What is it?' said Billy in alarm. 'Have you bust your leg?'

'Let go of my hand!' Maxwell cried. Billy's hand flew open. Maxwell was sure he saw a puff of smoke. The palm of his hand was covered in blisters. 'Did you feel that?' Maxwell said, rubbing his stinging hand on the damp grass. 'Did you feel that, sort of *push* . . .?'

'Max . . .'

'It was kind of like a hand or something pushed me up . . .'

'Max?'

' . . . then your hand got all hot. It was like holding a coal from a fire, or--'

'MAX!' Billy yelled. Maxwell looked up at him. He was standing looking over the broken bushes in front of them. Maxwell stood.

'What is . . .' Maxwell followed Billy's eyes, and he gasped '. . . it?'

Beyond the bushes the Black Woods ended and the land dropped away into a wide rolling meadow filled with thousands upon thousands of blood red poppies. Maxwell could follow a broad line where Mr Vim had walked through the meadow. Beyond the poppies the land rose again to a stark grey hill which was dotted with white gravestones. At the top of this hill, massive, black and crumbling, was a huge ruin.

'How come you never told me about *this*?' Billy exclaimed.

'I never . . .' Maxwell began. 'This wasn't here before, Billy,' he said.

The ruin hung over the crashing ocean, huge and black. It seemed to lean towards Maxwell and Billy. Four towers stood at one end, the other end a blasted, crumbling wreck.

'Vim's gone in there?' said Billy. Maxwell nodded. 'We've got to go in there?'

'We don't *have* to,' Maxwell said - but he knew that Billy hadn't asked him a question.

The white gravestones were corroded so badly by wind and rain that the boys could not make out any names or dates.

Billy was sweating more than ever as they climbed the steep bank towards the black castle, or church, or whatever it was. Maxwell could feel the heat from Billy's body even though his friend stood several feet away from him. Maxwell himself was shivering in the cold wind that swept down the hill from the crashing sea.

'What do you think we'll find here?' Maxwell asked.

'Who knows?' Billy replied. 'Talking giraffes, tap dancing worms? Nothing would surprise me anymore, Max.'

As they reached the last of the gravestones they found themselves looking over a drop. A moat ringed the black ruin, and at the bottom of the dried out moat stood Mr Vim.

Maxwell and Billy ducked behind a gravestone, and peered cautiously round either side.

Mr Vim was crouched at the bottom of the moat beside a small puddle of water. As they watched Mr Vim stretched out a hand and touched the surface of the puddle.

'What's he doing?' whispered Billy.

Maxwell shook his head

Mr Vim stood still as a statue. The heat was pulsing off Billy in waves. Even the ancient gravestone felt warm. Maxwell turned to ask Billy if he felt okay - actually, to ask him if he was just about to burst into flame - when he heard a loud *splash!*

Maxwell looked back down into the moat. Mr Vim had vanished.

'Where did he go?' Maxwell looked behind him, sure for a second that the gaunt figure of Mr Vim would be standing right there.

'He jumped in,' Billy said. Billy turned to look at Maxwell, and Billy's face was slack with shock. 'He jumped into that puddle!'

'Don't be--'

Something hit the ground behind them with a heavy *thump* - and it was they who jumped as a voice said:

'He's gone to void.'

Chapter Five: the bat man

A large seagull stood on the ashen ground of the graveyard. It weaved and bobbed like a nervous boxer, its black eyes darting from Maxwell to Billy and back again. 'I could not stop the Eye!' it cawed. 'I could not stop it! Mercy, I beg you mercy!'

'Oh crikey,' said Billy, pushing himself back against the gravestone, his eyes wide. 'It's gonna attack us!'

'I led it from you! I did! But you came after! I could not prevent!' The seagull fluttered its large wings. Billy let out a shout of alarm as the creature darted suddenly forward . . . then it laid its white head on the ground at Maxwell's feet.

Maxwell and Billy looked at each other wide eyed, and then both looked down at the quivering bird.

'Are you all right?' Maxwell asked.

'Well, I'm a bit shaken up to be honest. And I'm *sweating* like a--'

'Not you, Billy,' Maxwell said. He cautiously reached out a hand and touched the seagull's head. 'Are you all right, bird?'

'I could not help it,' the seagull whimpered, its long yellow beak stirring up the ashen ground. 'I did not mean to lead The Eye to you, great Everyman.'

Great Everyman? What did that mean?

'Can you understand it?' Billy asked, leaning closer to the bird, Maxwell nodded. 'What did it say?'

The seagull spoke again, and though its words were quite clear to Maxwell, Billy looked at him questioningly. 'He says that he had to lead Mr. Vim here because he commands the beasts,' Maxwell paused, 'Like me.'

'You command the beasts?' said Billy. 'Cool.' He leant forward and scratched the seagull's white head. It shivered and closed its eyes. 'Does he know where Vim's gone?'

'He said he's gone into the Void. Bird?' The seagull's eyes opened at the sound of Maxwell's voice. 'Where is the Void?'

'Nowhere,' replied the seagull. 'The nowhere between everywhere.'

'Well that's crystal clear, in it?' said Billy after Maxwell had translated the seagull's words. 'Why's he gone to this nowhere that's everywhere, then?'

'He seeks the Rended,' said the bird. 'He seeks your broken powers, Everyman.'

'Is he trying to be mysterious on purpose or are all seagulls this thick?' Billy said in exasperation. 'Who's Everyman, anyway?'

'Me, apparently,' Maxwell replied. 'Why do you call me that?' he asked the seagull.

'I have not forgotten you, Everyman, though I was just a fledgling when you last commanded us.' The seagull lifted its head and looked at Maxwell, blinking in fear - or maybe it was wonder. 'You are young again, strong again, and we have not forgotten our oath, great and powerful Everyman.'

'This bird's cuckoo,' said Billy.

The seagull rose suddenly to its feet and let out a cry of alarm. 'It returns! I did not betray you, Everyman! I swear!' The seagull shot into the air, its wings flapping frantically. Maxwell watched it disappear over the treetops.

'Max!' whispered Billy. 'Look! He's back!'

Maxwell scrambled round to the gravestone, and looked down into the moat. He was just in time to see Mr Vim drag himself from the puddle and flop onto the wet ground.

Mr Vim turned onto his back and lay, his chest rising and falling rapidly. After a few minutes he climbed unsteadily to his feet, and turned in a circle.

The boys ducked as he turned towards where they were hidden.

'What's he looking for?' whispered Billy.

Maxwell shrugged. 'May be the seag--'

Mr Vim let out a great roar. Maxwell and Billy cowered behind the gravestone. 'I know where you are!' came Mr Vim's harsh, booming voice. 'I know you can hear me! You coward! You worm! I will find you and tear you to pieces! I will hunt you for a thousand years, creature! I will *never* stop!'

Billy and Maxwell exchanged a look of terror.

'What are we going to do?'

Maxwell thought frantically, but there was nothing he could do, there was nowhere they could *go*. Then he remembered. His glasses! If he took of his spectacles maybe Mr Vim, like Pugg, wouldn't be able to recognise him!

Maxwell turned to Billy to tell him his plan, but Billy had his back turned to Maxwell, as he looked around the gravestone. Was he *trying* to get them caught? Maxwell was just about to drag him back into hiding, when Billy turned back to him. Billy's face was as pale as the gravestone.

'Oh blimey, Max,' he whispered. 'Look at him.'

Maxwell turned from Billy's shocked face, fairly sure that he did not want to see whatever it was Billy had seen.

Mr Vim still stood beside the small puddle of water. He had removed his silver sunglasses, and beneath the thin-faced man's scarred brow he had no eyes. Where his eyes should have been were flaming red pits. Out of Mr Vim's back grew enormous black bat wings, and his feet were three toed, wrinkled pink talons.

Maxwell looked in disbelief as Mr Vim rose above the small pool, bobbing up and down with each muscular stroke of his enormous black wings. Mr Vim raised his face to the sky, and let out an inhuman roar. Mr Vim's gaze fell back to the pool, and flames shot from under his brow. The little pool boiled, and suddenly, with a single thrust of his bat wings Mr Vim rocketed into the air in a column of rising steam.

He was a bird-like shape, then a black dot, and then he had vanished into the cloudy sky.

Maxwell realised his mouth was hanging open. He closed it with a loud *clop*, and turned to Billy.

'You know?' Billy said. 'Maybe this island isn't such a boring place after all.'

The puddle into which Mr Vim had dived was about six feet wide and a murky green colour. Steam still rose off its surface where Mr Vim had blasted it with his flaming eyes.

Billy looked at the water for several seconds, murmuring under his breath and rubbing his chin. He turned abruptly from the pool, and returned seconds later with a long stick. He jabbed the stick into the water, but it only sank a few inches into the water before it hit the muddy bottom.

'Is he a monster ?'

'Must be, mate,' Billy threw the stick aside. 'What the bleeding heck else could he be?' He sighed. 'Flipping teachers.'

Maxwell could barely believe what he had seen - but he *had* seen it, he had no doubt about that.

'I have a theory,' Billy announced. He dipped a toe into the pool, stirring its thick green depths.

'What?' Billy took another step into the pool. 'Don't, Billy,' Maxwell said nervously.

Billy's feet sank ankle deep in the green water. 'Don't worry, Max. Mr Vim did something to the pool. Magic or physics, or something. Now he's gone it's normal again.' Billy demonstrated this by walking right to the centre of the pool. He held out his arms, the water up to the top of his socks. 'See?'

'Yes, I see. But I really think you should get out now.' Maxwell held out his hand.

Billy waved him away. 'It was only yesterday that you found out that you could talk to animals, right?'

'Yes, that's right. A blackbird talked to me. Billy, I really don't think you should be--'

'And Mr Vim came yesterday,' Billy interrupted. 'When Mr Vim came into the woods they changed, right? And when he stood in this pool, the pool changed, yeah?'

'Yes, yes, and he grew wings and shot fire from his eyes - okay!' Maxwell said, exasperated. 'Come on, Billy, get out of there, will you?'

'It's perfectly safe,' Billy said, and to demonstrate how safe it was he jumped up and down in the water. 'See? He's gone, so it's just a pool again, dopey.'

'Yes, but Billy, he's gone and that enormous castle thing is still there, isn't it?'

Billy grinned. 'Not for much longer it isn't - look.'

Maxwell looked up. The black ruin was fading. It was no longer black, it was a dingy grey. A cloud sailed through its highest turret. The once solid and fearful black structure looked like a castle built from dirty ice.

'Anyway, it's a monastery, not a castle,' said Billy. 'Don't they teach you nothing at that school?' Billy looked down at the dirty pool. 'Water. That's all. Water.'

'So Mr Vim is making these things happen?' Maxwell looked up at the shape of the gravestone they had hidden behind - and now that's all that it was - a shape. Like a slab of clear glass. He turned back to

Billy. 'But I still don't think you should be standing there.'

'Oh cor blimey O'Riley! All right, all right!' Billy started to walk back to the side. 'Honestly, Max, if you want to be an investigative journalist like me, you've got to learn to take a few little ris--'

But Billy didn't finish. With a look of embarrassed astonishment he vanished into the pool with a soft splash, leaving barely a ripple.

'Billy?' Maxwell took a step towards the pool. The waters were still. 'Billy!' His voice echoed only once off the fading walls of the Black Monastery, then died.

Maxwell quickly grabbed the stick Billy had thrown aside, and thrust it into the water.

This time the stick sank its full length in the depths . . . but Billy didn't grab it.

He looked frantically around. He should get help - but where? Who could help him? If the Black Woods were still expanding it would take him at least an hour to get back to the village, and by then . . .

Maxwell threw the stick aside, pulled off his jacket, and without another thought, he dived head first into the pool.

Chapter Six: the Nurgler

The icy waters gripped Maxwell like a fist. He was instantly freezing cold and it was all that he could do not to shout out in shock and empty all the precious air from his lungs.

He swam vertically downwards, deeper and deeper into the cold, black waters. For the first time in his life he felt grateful to Miss Hummingbird. Her swimming lessons in the Watchman's huge pool were called "the not drowning lessons" by Maxwell and his classmates, as they mostly consisted of sitting at the bottom of the twenty foot deep pool holding your breath for as long as possible.

Maxwell was very good at holding his breath. In fact he was probably the school's not drowning champion; but as he swam deeper into the darkness he felt the cold nip at his lungs as the weight of the pitiless water grew and grew.

And the deeper he swam the darker it became, until he could no longer even see the shape of his spectacles at the end of his nose. There was no sign of Billy.

At last, with his lungs heaving in his chest and his throat working, Maxwell turned and swam back upwards.

As the dim light from above began to turn the dark waters grey Maxwell realised a terrible thing - Billy was gone.

Maxwell kicked his legs and reached up towards the light. What would he tell Billy's mum and dad? Would they blame him? How could he explain--

His fingers hit something, and a second later his face hit a hard, freezing slab of light. Ice. He was trapped under a sheet of ice.

Maxwell let out a shout of horror. The scream made no sound. Little bubbles rose from his mouth

and settled, bobbing, on the ice above. He hit the
sheet with his fists, then spun around and kicked it
with his feet - but all that did was thrust him back
down into the water. He swam back up and began
scrabbling and punching and clawing at the ice, his
lungs screaming hot, and now black points flickered in
front of his eyes and his arms grew heavy.

Maxwell felt himself fall slowly into the
embrace of the black waters, the little slab of cold
sunlight growing hazy and distant . . .

There was a sudden explosion of white light.
Something grabbed Maxwell by the hair and pulled
him upwards. A second later Maxwell burst out of the
ice and was dragged by his hair onto solid ground.

'Cor blimey O'Riley I thought you'd had your
chips there matey and no mistake,' gasped a familiar
voice. 'Chips, salt, vinegar and sauce.' Billy added, his
face appearing in front of Maxwell's. 'Are you alright
Max, mate?' he asked.

'I ... I nearly ... drowned,' Maxwell gasped.

Billy took Maxwell's arm and helped him to his
feet. 'Well, I think you're exaggerating a bit there, like,
mate,' Billy said seriously. Maxwell goggled at him,
and Billy began to laugh. There was something odd
about Billy, for some reason ...

Maxwell's thoughts stopped dead as he noticed
for the first time what was over Billy's shoulder.

'I know!' Billy said, sniggering, 'Bleeding
amazing, init?'

Maxwell was more than amazed; he was
absolutely astounded by what he saw.

They were no longer in the moat beneath the
Black Monastery. They were nowhere Maxwell had
ever seen before. They stood on a frozen river which
stretched to distant purple mountains in each
direction, their summits heavy with snow and cloud.
A vast forest rose up at both banks into thick, busy

darkness. Snow flakes the size of golf balls fell. Not a creature stirred, not a bird, nor a distant car or a barking dog, even the still air was silent.

'Where are we?' said Maxwell breathlessly.

'Not a clue!' said Billy, his voice filled with glee. 'No idea at all! Crackin, init?'

Maxwell closed his eyes tight, sure that when he opened them again he would be in bed at home. He was soaking wet, shaking with cold, and could feel snow pattering on his face - but he had probably left his bedroom window open. Yes, that was it, he'd open his eyes and he'd see the potato clock and the fish bowl beside his bed--

'Max, it isn't a dream so you might as well open your eyes,' said Billy.

Maxwell did open his eyes, and he was still standing on a frozen river, and, strangely . . .

'You're dry,' said Maxwell. 'How are you dry?'

Billy started. 'I'm ... er, I've been here a bit,' he said, unconvincingly.

'How long?'

'I dunno. A bit,' Billy looked away, then said: 'I wonder where here is, though?'

Billy walked to the closest bank and stood looking up at the huge trees. Maxwell stood beside him and he noticed something very odd - there was no snow in Billy's hair, even though thick flakes whirled all around them.

'Siberia, do you think?' Billy asked. 'Or maybe we're still on the island?' As he spoke a snowflake landed on his cheek and simply vanished - it evaporated with a tiny puff of steam and a slight hiss. 'Maybe we've travelled forwards in time? Or maybe backwards in time? That would explain the dinosaur, yeah?'

Maxwell looked around again. That distant mountain range didn't look like anywhere on Virporta, or anywhere else on earth for that matter. 'The main thing is, how do we get back?'

'Through the ice, of course. But what you want to go back for?'

'I'm freezing to death!' Maxwell exclaimed.

'Nah - when you stop shivering, that's when you have to worry.'

'Why's that?'

'Cos when you stop shivering, that's when you die,' Billy clapped his hands together. 'Anyway, before we go back we have to find out where we are, don't we? Common sense, init?' He took a step into the forest, rubbing his hands together eagerly. 'Maybe if we go into these woods for a bit--'

'Don't go into the forest.'

Billy stopped dead, and took a step back. He looked at Maxwell, his eyes wide. 'Did you hear--'

'There are things in the forest,' came the voice again, and both Maxwell and Billy took a step back. The voice - low and cold and somehow *wet*, spoke again: 'You do not belong here.'

Maxwell couldn't agree more. He grabbed Billy by the collar and they both walked quickly backwards across the frozen river, looking in every direction at once as they went. Nothing moved in the dark, thick trees, and there was no sound except the soft patter of snow and the quick sound of the boys' frightened breath.

'Did you see anything?' Billy whispered when they were back in the middle of the river. Maxwell shook his head. 'I think it's gone--' he began.

'I know you,' whispered the soft gargling voice. 'You are Maxwell.'

Maxwell shivered again at the sound of his own name spoken by that alien voice. 'He means you, Max,' hissed Billy.

'I know!' Maxwell hissed back.

'Ask it where we are.'

'You ask it!'

'You're the one who commands the beasts, ain't ya?'

'It's not a beast!' whispered Maxwell furiously.

'I have waited for you,' said the voice, and something moved high up in the trees, a thick shape.

'What . . .' Maxwell began. He stopped and cleared his throat. It was probably a bit rude to ask someone *what* they were, even if that someone probably wasn't human, so he asked: 'Who are you?'

'I am a forgotten thing,' said the voice. 'A part of something else. A forgotten piece of the great whole.'

'Well, that's as clear as mud,' Billy murmured. 'What's your name, mate?' he shouted to the trees.

'I had a name long ago, yes. The beasts who live in this world call me the Nurgler.' The Nurgler chuckled, it was like someone choking on mud. 'In their language it means "Devil".'

'Well that's not a good sign,' whispered Billy. 'Ask it where we are.'

'You ask it!'

'It's your mate.'

'It is not--'

'You have escaped Virporta,' said the Nurgler. 'I had always hoped that you would. But this, perhaps, is not the best place to escape too.'

'We haven't escaped,' said Maxwell. 'We're here by accident.'

'Accident? But you followed Optar here, didn't you?'

'Why does it think we want to escape from the island?' Maxwell whispered to Billy.

'The creature Optar came for me, but he was held back by the beasts,' the Nurgler continued. 'Many have tried to find me over the years, but I have hidden well. I have waited for you, Maxwell.'

Maxwell was beginning to get very confused. Optar must be Mr Vim, he guessed, but for some reason the Nurgler thought they had been chasing Mr Vim, hoping to find the Nurgler.

'Why would we want to escape from Virporta Island?' Billy asked suddenly. 'I mean, I know they've got no telly and they play hockey like girls and that, but . . .'

'Virporta is a prison,' said the Nurgler, and a large shape flitted through the trees again, closer to the boys. But it was still almost impossible to see, partly because of the thick shadows of the forest, but mostly, Maxwell thought with a chill, mostly because the Nurgler didn't seem to have a proper shape.

'A prison?' exclaimed Billy, looking at Maxwell.

'That's just stupid!' said Maxwell. 'How can it be a prison?'

'Your idiot parents are Virporta's guards and it's executioners if need be. You and your friends are its inmates,' gurgled the Nurgler. 'You will never leave Virporta Island alive.'

'I have never heard such rubbish,' said Maxwell hotly. 'It isn't a prison at all. Is it, Billy? Billy?'

But Billy didn't reply. He was staring at the opposite bank of the frozen river, his back to the Nurgler, his eyes wide, his mouth open and closing like a fish's.

'What's wrong with . . .?' Maxwell began to say, turning to look at whatever it was Billy was staring at - and his next words died in his throat.

'Beasts,' whispered Billy.

Chapter Seven: beasts

The beasts were all shapes and sizes. One was a thick green-grey barrel with flat feet and ape-like arms which propelled it forward in leaps and bounds - it had no face at all, the top half of its body a chaos of gnashing teeth. Another was the size of football, and every inch of its black skin was covered in dripping claws like a scorpions' stinger that sent it scuttling over the ice. One looked like a furry blue giraffe - only it stood on its hind legs, and its front legs ended in large red crab-like pincers, its small head twisted in an evil grimace at the end of its long neck.

They came out of the forest on the distant bank of the frozen river, loping, bounding, crawling, flying and scuttling, all moving fast, all glaring insanely at Maxwell and Billy, their open jaws dripping with hunger.

'Billy! Quickly!' shouted Maxwell, and he began battering the ice with his foot.

Billy was staring at the beasts, frozen in terror. Maxwell reached out to shake him, and sprang back with a shout of pain and surprise - Billy's body was as hot as a naked flame. 'Help me, Billy!' Maxwell yelled, holding his blistering hand and battering at the ice with his feet.

Behind them the Nurgler chuckled, a sound like bubbling mud. 'Leave him for them,' it said. 'Run into the forest, Maxwell. Save yourself.'

Maxwell looked up, and felt the strength run out of him. The beasts were seconds away, rocketing towards the boys in a stampeding herd. There were dozens off them, some of them too terrifying to even look at, some you simply *couldn't* look at - their ghastly shapes didn't seem to fit into the world somehow, and looking at them made your eyes water and your mind ache. Yet Billy was looking at them. He was staring at them, his expression as dead as a waxwork's.

Maxwell reached for Billy again, but he couldn't even get near that searing heat. The impossible heat from Billy's body was now so intense that the ice was melting under his feet ...

Melting under his feet!

Maxwell threw himself at Billy, and was enveloped in terrible, choking heat. Billy crashed to the ice with a yell, and Maxwell landed on top of him. Maxwell's shirt burst into flame. He tried to push himself away from the unbearable heat and with a loud *crack* the ice broke beneath them, and they were both plunged into freezing water.

Maxwell struggled back to the surface, coughing and spluttering. A moment later Billy reappeared, steam was rising off his body in great clouds and he looked *furious*.

'What the bleeding Nora do you think you're--' Billy began yelling, but his angry words turned into a scream as the spiky black ball Maxwell had seen scrabbling across the ice landed on Billy's head - and promptly burst into flame.

'DIVE!' Maxwell screamed, and he plunged back into the icy water.

The water grabbed him in its bitter embrace - he felt the unbearable cold tear at his burnt skin and he couldn't stand it - he would have to go back up!

A hand grabbed his, and he felt heat fill his body, and the momentary panic evaporated with the warmth. Billy stared at him, goggle eyed and green faced in the water, and pointed downwards. Maxwell nodded, and they both dived.

They swam down and down until Maxwell only knew for sure that Billy was beside him by the warmth that radiated from him. Everything was black, as it had been when he had first dived into the water.

Maxwell squeezed Billy's hand, and knew his friend had understood when they both turned and began swimming upwards again.

The black waters turned slowly grey, and now Maxwell could see Billy's face again in the light that fell from above. Two more strokes of their legs and they would break the surface, back to the Black Monastery, and then home--

Billy's eyes widened in shock, and bubbles exploded from his mouth as he yelled out in terror.

Maxwell looked up.

Above them was a sheet of ice, only this time it wasn't like looking through a grimy window into daylight - this time the ice was dark with huge lumbering shapes.

The beasts.

Maxwell felt Billy's hand pull at his - but they couldn't swim up or down, they were trapped.

Billy's hand pulled at his again. Maxwell turned just as Billy's hand was wrenched from his. For a second Maxwell saw Billy's hands reaching out desperately, his eyes wide in terror . . . and then he disappeared into the black depths.

Maxwell felt exhausted dizziness wash over him, the waters filling his head with their blank cold, his body losing feeling, giving up the fight. *No*, he though fiercely, *I* won't *give up!* Maxwell turned in the water, saw the chaotic shapes of the beasts loom over him through the ice, and he kicked towards the bottom again. He would find Billy, he would get back to the surface, and, somehow they would fight the beasts--

Something grabbed his throat. He opened his mouth to scream and the last few bubbles of precious oxygen rose out of his mouth. The thing tightened round his throat, and in a second it was dragging him down into darkness. Maxwell grabbed at his throat, and his fingers sank into something thick and slimey and muscular. As he struggled hopelessly it dragged him deeper and deeper into the freezing water. He realised there was no escape now. Even if he could pull free he would never make it back to the surface. Blackness engulfed Maxwell, the distant surface quickly blotted out by blackness between his wavering feet. Cold bit at him angrily, jabbing his skin like broken glass. He was finished . . .

He was breathing.

'It is remarkable,' gurgled a horribly familiar voice, 'that your spectacles haven't fallen off, don't you think?'

'Nurgler?' whispered Maxwell. His voice was quite clear, though there was no air to carry his words.

'I used to wear spectacles myself, and like yours they never fell off,' the Nurgler chuckled. 'I had quite forgotten about my spectacles.'

Maxwell tried to peer into the black waters, but it hopeless. If it wasn't for the cold rush of the waters around him he could have been in a very dark room - if he didn't have a tentacle wrapped around throat. 'You're hurting my throat,' he said.

'That is a shame,' said the Nurgler. 'Perhaps I should let you go and see how well you can breathe water?'

Not very well, Maxwell thought, but he said, 'Did you rescue Billy too?'

'Rescue?'

Maxwell didn't much like the sound of that. 'Where are you taking me?'

'Somewhere safe. Somewhere the beasts won't go,' said the Nurgler. 'A little place I know, a little place called home.' It chuckled its horrible, gurgling laugh.

They plunged deeper and deeper, the Nurgler's tentacle tight around Maxwell's throat. It was icy cold, and the only part of his body Maxwell could feel was his throat where the hot tentacle writhed and pulsed. He began to think about his spectacles again - the Nurgler was right, it was remarkable that they clung to the end of his nose despite the fact that he was upside down and what felt like a hundred miles under water. What was so special about these things that he had thought absolutely useless (and horribly ugly) up until now . . . ?

With a start Maxwell realised he was looking at the world through his spectacles frames. The black water had been pierced by a thick beam of green light. Long thick undulating tentacles rose around him, and Maxwell saw something sway in the rushing water.

'Billy!'

'Poor Billy hit his head on the ice, the silly boy' said the Nurgler. 'But his spectacles stayed on too. How very odd.' The Nurgler chuckled thickly. 'Look, Maxwell, look! Home, sweet home!'

Maxwell looked where all of the tentacle met at the thick of the Nurgler's body and beyond at a circle of sky. 'Are the beasts still there?'

'The beasts, my dear Maxwell, are several billion light years away. That is Virporta, your pretty little prison.' The creature had come to a stop in the waters now, a featureless mass blotting out the sun of Virporta, 'You don't belong there, Maxwell.'

Maxwell was desperate to get free of the Nurgler and back into his world - even if his world was suddenly filled with bat-winged men, talking animals and dinosaurs. 'Why don't you just say what you want to say and let us go?' he pleaded.

The Nurgler chuckled. 'It is your fate to discover what you are, it is not my fate to tell you. But ... you are extraordinary, Maxwell.' The tentacle tightened painfully around Maxwell's throat and he felt himself moving again, rising - or perhaps falling -

towards Virporta. 'You must swim quickly to the surface when I let you go, Maxwell,' said the Nurgler. 'As soon as I release you you won't be able to breathe, and you have no air in your lungs--'

'Wait!' said Maxwell. 'What about Billy? He's unconscious. He can't swim to the surface!'

'Billy isn't important,' snapped the Nurgler. 'Now, when I release you--'

'Billy's my friend!' Maxwell struggled against the Nurgler. But the muscular tentacle wouldn't budge. 'I won't leave him!' Maxwell shouted, thrashing frantically in the water. 'Let me go!'

'I let you go, you die,' replied the Nurgler. 'I let your friend go, he dies. Which part of this don't you understand? I will look after Billy,' it said. 'I have been looking for someone like Billy.'

Maxwell looked at Billy, dangling unconscious in the forest of tentacles. 'What do you mean?' he whispered.

'I am tired of this beast's body,' said the Nurgler, 'And I think your friend would adapt well to the ice and snow. He is perfect, in fact.' The Nurgler's tentacle dragged Billy, and he rose up towards Maxwell, his blond hair waving, his silver spectacles still fixed firmly on the end of his nose. 'Say goodbye to your friend, Maxwell,' said the Nurgler. 'But don't worry, I will not hurt him. At least . . . I will not hurt his body. The rest of him is of no use to me.'

Maxwell tried again to free himself from the grip of the tentacle as the Nurgler pulled Billy back into the water, but it was no use. And as Billy fell into the green depths Maxwell was rising slowly towards the mouth of the pool. The Nurgler was calculating the best place to let him go, and Maxwell knew that as soon as the Nurgler released him he would have to escape into the air or drown. He looked back at Billy, now motionless in the jungle of tentacles . . . and then with a start he realised that Billy wasn't motionless at all.

Billy's fingers spread out stiffly, as if he was stretching after waking from a sleep . . . but then Billy bent his thumb towards the palm of his hand, and then he bent his index finger . . . 10 - 9 ...

'Why are you doing this?' said Maxwell desperately.

'Because I must,' the Nurgler replied.

... 8 - 7 - 6 - and Billy closed his right hand.

'What are you?' said Maxwell as Billy bent the thumb on his left hand.

'I am a forgotten thing,' said the Nurgler. 'A part of something else. A forgotten piece of the great whole.'

... 5 - 4 - 3 ...

Maxwell looked down at the shapeless mass of the creature, and he whispered, 'But who were you?'

The Nurgler chuckled, wet and horrible. 'My name was Titus M--'

'GO MAX!' screamed Billy, drowning out the Nurgler's words. The creature turned on Billy with a roar of rage, and with a quick tug, Maxwell pulled the startled monster's tentacle free.

Maxwell's lungs stopped working. The water he had been breathing so easily just a second before filled his lungs like cement, his heart suddenly pounding. Maxwell looked down and saw that the creature was turning in the water, ignoring Billy and moving rapidly back towards him, its tentacles reaching out to grab him.

Billy held up his hands as if in surrender to the Nurgler, even as it turned away from him.

Maxwell wasn't sure what happened next.

For a second Maxwell saw the Nurgler clearly for the first time - a huge craggy brown thing shaped like a fat bullet, its scaly hide covered in barnacles, with dull milky eyes and a mouth as big as a man filled with dozens - *hundreds* - of jagged green teeth, each tooth as big as a fist.

Then a fireball engulfed the Nurgler. Maxwell was blasted out of the pool into a blue sky. He hit the ground with a bone shaking thud that drove all of the water out of his lungs - and quite a few of the biscuits he had eaten for breakfast out of his stomach into the bargain.

Water fell around him like rain, and to his amazement he saw his denim jacket lying crumpled on the ground where he had thrown in before jumping in the pool.

'I'm back,' he gasped - and his spectacles were *still* on the end of his nose.

Something thumped to the ground beside him. Billy sat up, covered in mud and slimy stuff - bits of the Nurgler.

'See?' said Billy, and he threw up, then gasped, 'I told you it would be fun.'

Chapter Eight: the lost boys

'There's something about Virporta Island, Max. When I got here I found out I could do this.'

Billy clicked his fingers and a jet of blue flame shot from the palm of his hand, and stood there, wavering in the breeze.

'Doesn't ... doesn't it hurt?' said Maxwell in astonishment.

'No, not a bit.'

'Why didn't you tell me about this?'

'What am I supposed to say? "Hello, I'm Billy, I'm new at your school and I tend to burst into flame every now and again?"' Billy sighed. 'I just didn't want you thinking I was a mad weirdo, Max.'

Maxwell looked at the dancing flame and laughed. 'Well, at least you don't talk to ants,' he said.

'Very true!' Billy replied happily. He clicked his fingers and the little blue flame vanished. 'You're the weirdo, not me.'

'You're weirder than me,' said Maxwell.

'I think you'll find you're the weirdest weirdo, mate,' Billy replied.

'You're the king of the weirdoes.'

'You're the queen of the weirdoes.'

The street looked deserted, and in the dying daylight it looked somehow less real than it had seemed that morning. Looking down the street towards the distant potato factory Maxwell wondered how he had not realised immediately that the street had grown. Pugg's Potato Factory was much, much further away. It looked like a model of itself.

'Max?' Billy was looking at the pavement, his usually animated hands twisting together in front of him. 'Max, I ... I was frightened on the ice,' he said quickly.

Maxwell laughed. 'I know! Me too! I was terrified!'

'Yeah, but ... ' Billy sighed, and he looked up at Maxwell. 'I chickened out, Max. I was just, like, frozen, you know? I couldn't do nothing. If you hadn't pushed me over ...'

Was Billy apologising? Maxwell could hardly believe it. 'But you saved us from the Nurgler, Billy!'

'I saved myself,' Billy replied. 'It was going to let you go. I only ... exploded cos I was frightened of what that horrible thing would do to me. You saved us. You got us away from them beasts, and you came after me through the pool. I didn't do nothing!' Billy cried wretchedly.

'We saved each other!' Maxwell said, exasperated. 'I'm not ... I was frightened too, just like you!'

'No mate,' Billy replied. 'Not like me.'

Maxwell grabbed Billy's shoulders and instantly felt Billy's supernatural warmth radiate through him. 'We're a team, Billy,' he said.

Billy looked startled, and then slowly he smiled. He took hold of Maxwell's shoulders, and as Billy's extraordinary heat filled Maxwell he felt all the cold terror of their adventure evaporate.

'A team!' Billy agreed.

'You and me against the world,' said Maxwell.

'Too right, mate. And the world don't stand a chance.'

As soon as Maxwell stepped through his front door he heard his mother cry, 'Maxy!'

Bettie ran from the kitchen, grabbed him, and spun him round. Despite being a small woman his mum was very strong, and she twirled Maxwell round like he was five years old.

When Maxwell finally landed he saw that two other people were standing by their kitchen door - a squat little man with a bald head and a thin moustache and an extremely tall woman with long blond hair that fell all the way to her waist. The man and woman were looking at Maxwell with peculiar expressions on their faces, like they were ready to leap on him and throttle him the second his mum stepped aside.

'Where have you been, Maxy!' his mother cried, shaking him affectionately until his teeth rattled.

'Been . . . ?' said Maxwell, confused. His mother was holding onto him like she was worried he would float away the second she let go, and her eyes were moving rapidly over every inch of Maxwell's body as if she didn't really believe he was standing there. The two odd people, meanwhile, were inching down the hall towards Maxwell looking more and more like they were preparing to spring on him. 'I was just in the woods with Billy--' Maxwell began.

'Where is William?' the long haired woman demanded suddenly. 'What have you done with him?'

'I haven't done anything--'

'Where is Billy, Maxy?' Bettie Jones asked quietly. 'Did he get lost in the woods?' What were they going on about? 'Mr and Mrs Barker have been frantic with worry!'

So his was Billy's mum and dad. They weren't at all what Maxwell had expected. Mr Barker, the intrepid reporter, looked like a bank clerk, or perhaps a funeral director, and Mrs Barker looked more like an Amazonian Warrior than a journalist.

'We were just playing in the woods,' Maxwell said.

'For two days?' Mrs Barker demanded coldly. Two days? It had just been a few hours! What were they talking about?

'People have been searching through the woods all night,' Mr Barker said. 'There are probably still people out searching now, Maxwell. We've been very worried, son, and so has your mum. Where have you been? And where's our Billy?'

'We . . . ' Maxwell thought quickly. 'We went camping.'

'Camping?' exclaimed Mrs Barker, her voice colder than the deepest depths of the frozen river between worlds. 'And it didn't occur to either of you to tell your parents about this little adventure?'

Maxwell paused, and then he said, 'But ... I did tell you, mum.'

Betty Jones frowned. 'You did?' she said slowly.

Maxwell felt sick. 'Yes, I told you yesterday morning, don't you remember?' His mum was running her hand over her forehead, her eyes confused. 'I asked you to tell Billy's mum and dad. Remember?'

'Did you dear?' his mum asked.

'Yes, mum!" Maxwell insisted. "Don't you remember?'

Maxwell felt terrible. This was a horrible, horrible thing to do, he knew - but what choice did he have? How could he possibly tell them what had actually happened?

'Oh ... yes,' his mum said finally. 'Yes, now you come to mention it, I do seem to remember--'

'You knew!' snarled Mrs Barker.

'Now, now, dear.' Mr Barker stepped in front of his wife, and took both of her hands in his. 'It was just a mix up, that's all, and everything's all right now, isn't it?'

'NO!' screamed Mrs Barker. 'Everything is not all right! This stupid boy--'

'I said,' Mr Barker interrupted firmly, 'Everything is all right now, isn't it, Jane?'

Mrs Barker looked furiously from Maxwell to his mum, her jaws working like a leopard denied its dinner. She pulled her hands out of Mr Barker's and marched across the hall, sweeping her husband aside. She pointed a long nailed finger at Maxwell's face. 'In future you will stay away from my son,' she snarled.

'But ... Mrs Barker ...'

'Stay away,' she said slowly. A second later she was gone, the front door slamming behind her.

'Well, well, well,' said Mr Barker shakily. 'Boys will have their adventures, won't they, Mrs Jones?' Bettie Jones did not answer. She was looking up at the ceiling, a perplexed expression on her face. 'Well, Maxwell,' Mr Barker continued with a cough. 'Looks like you got a bit of a soaking. Is it raining out?'

Maxwell looked down at his sopping wet clothes. He was forming a large puddle on the hallway carpet. He looked up at Mr Barker. 'I fell into a stream,' he said.

'Boys and streams, eh? Trying to catch a fish or two, eh?' Mr Barker smiled indulgently - but his eyes narrowed with suspicion. 'Or was it a whale, Maxwell?' he asked. 'Well,' said Mr Barker slowly, 'I'd better be getting back home, stop Jane throttling our Billy, eh?' Seeing Maxwell's startled expression he chuckled, and added, 'Don't worry, lad, Jane's a pussycat, really.'

Maxwell doubted that very much, unless she was a six-foot pussycat with dripping fangs and razor-sharp claws, but he said nothing.

'Well, thanks for the tea, and the ... erm ... potato cake, did you say, Bettie?'

'Chocolate potato surprise,' his mum answered, started out of her daze by her favourite subject. 'Did you like it, Ronnie?'

'It was ... lovely, Bettie,' Mr Barker replied unconvincingly.

'I'll give Jane the recipe,' Maxwell's mum said excitedly. 'It's one of our favourites, isn't it, Maxy? We have it at least twice a week.'

'Well, lucky you, eh?' Mr Barker headed hastily for the door. 'Thanks again! Best be off!'

'Show Mr Barker to the door, Maxwell,' his mum said.

'Yes, mum.' Maxwell walked after Mr Barker and opened the front door for him. Mr Barker smiled, stepped outside ... then he paused, and stepped back inside.

'You're a good lad, aren't you, Maxwell?' he asked.

'I ... I try to be, Mr Barker,' Maxwell replied nervously.

'Good answer.' Mr Barker's round little face stared at Maxwell's with a searching expression. He now no longer looked like a bank clerk, he looked like the toughest journalist in the world, hardboiled by years of lies. 'You be careful, son,' he said at last, 'And make sure my Billy's careful too, right?'

Maxwell nodded. Mr Barker clapped him on the shoulder, an easy grin on his face. He sprang over the doorstep, and strode off down Spudmore Avenue whistling happily.

Maxwell closed the door, and walked back down the hall.

His mum was bent over the kitchen sink, her record breaking fingers peeling their way through a mountain of potatoes. 'Sausage and chips for tea, Maxy,' she said without turning around.

'Lovely, mum,' Maxwell replied. He stood watching her for a second, a little woman concentrating fiercely on a pile of old potatoes. He wanted to tell her that she hadn't forgotten about his camping trip. More than anything else in the world he wanted to tell his mum he had lied, and that he was sorry.

But he could not.

Maxwell turned away and walked upstairs to his room. He lay on his bed for a long time, and he thought about the Nurgler's words:

Who am I?
I am Titus M--

Chapter Nine: the Test

On Monday morning Maxwell woke to the sound of heavy rainfall and his goldfish singing.

Maxwell sat up and peered blearily into the fish bowl on his bedside cabinet. His goldfish, the Handsome Beast, looped under a plastic arch, and sang: 'If I ruled the world, every day would be the first day of spring ...' in a rolling baritone voice.

'Good morning,' said Maxwell.

The Handsome Beast butted its nose against a plastic diver and continued singing.

Maxwell leant over the water. 'You've got a very good voice,' he said.

The fish ignored him and continued looping around the bowl, singing stridently.

Maxwell sighed, took a pinch of fish food, and dropped it into the water. 'It wouldn't hurt you to be polite,' he muttered.

'And it wouldn't hurt you to feed me something decent, you ginger buffoon!' the Handsome Beast replied. It swallowed a lump of fish food, then spat it back out. 'Cheap, tasteless rubbish!' the fish exclaimed, and continued singing.

Maxwell was beginning to suspect that being master of the beasts wasn't all it was cracked up to be.

Mrs Trimm's general store was completely deserted when Maxwell arrived through the jangling front door. He was soaked from the rain, but anxious to see Billy again. Music filled the shop, a waltz, Maxwell realised, and as if to confirm this Mrs Trimm and her husband Hassan waltzed by the open door behind the counter as Maxwell approached. This was not at all unusual. Mr and Mrs Trimm often had a morning waltz, and occasionally a samba, depending on the weather.

'Ah! Maxwell!' Mrs Trimm shouted over the blasting music as Mr Trim dipped her. 'I'm afraid you'll have to do the round your self this morning!'

Maxwell looked aghast at the huge stacks of newspaper that sat on the groaning counter. 'Is Billy all right?' he asked.

But Mrs Trimm and Hassan had waltzed away, and did not answer.

Maxwell picked up a large pile of papers and trudged back out into the rain.

By the time Maxwell finally left the house it was almost nine o'clock, and his arms, shoulders and legs were aching from delivering newspapers to Virporta Island's hundreds of new households.

He was not helped by the fact that his mum had mislaid her umbrella, which was large and brown and, not surprisingly, in the shape of a potato, with "A potato is for life, not just for dinner!" emblazoned on it in pink letter. They finally found the umbrella poked up the chimney, which puzzled Bettie Jones as she was sure she had left it in the bath.

The Handsome Beast, Maxwell discovered, was not the calm gentle creature he had imagined it to be. Between singing light opera the fish constantly complained about the size, shape, and location of its bowl, 'Do you really think I want to see you dribbling in your sleep just inches away?' It complained about its food, the temperature of its water, told Maxwell he dressed shabbily, advised him to dye his hair and informed him he could do with losing some weight, 'You're very doughy around the jaws,' it said in its snooty voice.

The result of all this chaos was that by the time that Maxwell did walk through the front gate of the Watchmen Academy he was in a very bad mood indeed, and he had forgotten two very important things. He should never walk through the Watchmen's front gate, and he should always look over his shoulder.

'Hello, Bumwell,' came a lazy voice from behind him. Maxwell turned, realising his mistake too late - in a flash he was surrounded by Pugg's gang.

Bartholemew Pugg was dressed in a bright yellow poncho, grinning all over his mean face. Pugg's ugly crew were all dressed as Pugg in yellow ponchos, looking like angry blobs of custard.

'I knew we'd catch up with one another eventually,' said Pugg, rubbing his sausage-like fingers together with glee. 'I have *so* been looking forward having a little chat. Nothing to say, Bumwell? Not going to tell us the tale of your little woodland adventure? I hear your mummy forgot you'd gone camping. Now isn't she a silly mummy?'

Maxwell was wet, cold, irritated and, before he knew he was going to say anything, he suddenly found his lips mouthing these words:

'Where did you get that coat, Bartholemew? I'd heard the circus was in town, but do they know you're wearing the Big Top?'

Pugg's mouth fell open. 'Wh ... What did you--' Pugg gasped.

'W-w-w-w,' Maxwell mimicked. 'Where did you get that face, Barty? I've been meaning to ask. Was it Pigs R Us?'

Bartholemew Pugg's face turned a deep shade of crimson. Maxwell had seen Pugg beat up and intimidate dozens of children over the years, but he had never seen Pugg angry. Pugg was one of these odd people who thought that casual brutality was just a little hobby he cultivated, and nothing in particular to get worked up about.

He was worked up now, all right, and it really was a wonderful sight. Maxwell laughed - he just couldn't help himself.

'I ...' snarled Pugg.

'Yes?' Maxwell leaned closer and put a hand to his ear.

'... am ...' he spluttered.

'Ugly?' Maxwell offered. 'Smelly? A fat rat-breathed moron?'

'... going to KILL YOU!' Pugg roared, and he launched himself at Maxwell. Maxwell raised his fists - he was pretty sure he was going to be badly beaten, he was fairly certain he had gone quite mad - but he was absolutely positive he was never going to run away from this fat, repulsive boy ever again, and he was one hundred per cent certain that Bartholemew Pugg was about to receive at least one good punch right in the middle of his stupid face.

Something whizzed past Maxwell's ear, bounced off Pugg's forehead, and then zinged back over Maxwell's shoulder. Pugg stood quite still, a thoughtful, dreamy expression on his face, then suddenly crumpled.

'Sorry!' came a voice. Pugg's gang, who had been looking down at their fallen master with expressions of disbelief on their faces, turned at the sound of the voice.

Billy Barker came striding towards them, a hockey stick over his shoulder. Behind him Daisy, Bella and Jamie stood, all holding hockey sticks, all wearing identical expressions of disbelief.

'Has anyone seen my spud?' Billy said cheerily. 'Bit of a knack to this Potato Hockey lark, in't there? I ain't quite got the hang of it yet.' He stopped in front of Pugg, lying face down in a dirty puddle. 'Oh dear,' he said, he looked up at Maxwell and winked, then looked down at Pugg. 'Did I hit you, mate?'

Pugg bubbled what might have been a threat from his position in the puddle.

'You've killed him!' Tom Chop exclaimed in stunned horror.

'Really? Cor blimey O'Riley - manslaughter! And on my first day at school too!' Billy couched down and took Pugg's arm. 'Up you get - Oh crikey, he's a big un, in he? Give us a hand here, Max.'

Maxwell, lost for words, took Pugg's other arm, and together he and Billy heaved him onto his feet. Even with the two of them it was a strain, but Prickle, Chop and the others seemed to be in shock, and didn't offer help.

'You alright, mate?' Pugg's eyes were vague and dreamy, like Buddha in a yellow poncho. 'Do you want me to get your mum, or something?'

'Mummy?' murmured Pugg in a high, lilting voice. 'Mummy is in Bradford.'

Maxwell and Billy exchanged a look, their eyebrows raised. 'Well that's a shame,' said Billy.

'I was doing something,' Pugg muttered, blinking and shaking his head. 'What was I doing?'

'Well, I believe you were just about to give my mate Max here a good smacking,' said Billy. Maxwell looked at him in alarm. What was he *doing*? 'But that'd be a bit of a shame, Barty. He's quite a nice lad, as it goes.'

'Jones!' hissed Pugg, his eyes clearing. 'You called me a pig!'

'Did you call old Barty a pig, Max?' Billy scolded.

'No, I didn't,' Maxwell replied.

'Yes you did!' Pugg roared, then he winced and grabbed his head in pain.

'Actually,' Maxwell said, 'I asked him if he'd bought his face at Pigs R Us.'

'I'm going to KILL you! OW!' Pugg squeezed his aching head, and Billy laughed. Pugg's eyes widened in fury. 'I'm going to kill BOTH of you!'

'We haven't even been introduced, and already you want to kill me?' Billy said, a wounded expression on his face. 'And, to be perfectly fair, mate, you are a bit on the porky side.'

'Get them!' screamed Pugg. 'Bash them!' But oddly no one moved. Not even the outraged Pugg.

'Well, I suppose we could have a punch up,' Billy sighed in a bored voice. 'But, you see, me and Max's mates over there,' he waved his hand in the vague direction of Daisy, Jamie and Bella, 'We've all got hockey sticks, and a lot of very hard potatoes.' He winked at Pugg. 'Now you don't want me starting my first day at a new school with a blood bath, do you Barty, my old cock sparrow?'

Pugg looked from Billy to Maxwell, and then across at Jamie, Bella and Daisy. Bella was wearing her usual petrified expression, but her feet were planted firmly on the ground. Jamie was twirling a hockey stick in one hand and juggling two potatoes in the other. Daisy look calmly back at Pugg, her hockey stick held in both hands, as if waiting for Ms Hummingbird to blow her whistle.

Pugg fumed and spluttered, caught between murderous wrath and his sly wisdom, which was telling him that this was not the usual inconspicuous bullying he was used to. This was a proper *fight* - it would be loud and dangerous, and he might get hurt, and he would almost certainly get in trouble.

'I'm not fighting you,' Pugg finally barked. 'It's Jones I want.'

'Well, that's a bit of a shame, Barty, cos old Max Jones and Billy Barker are a team,' said Billy. 'So if your fight's with him, your fight's with me, see?'

Pugg glared at Billy, glanced again at the three friends - Jamie was now juggling four potatoes in one hand - and he said: 'That isn't fair. You have hockey sticks. It isn't a fair fight.'

Maxwell gaped at Pugg. 'You and your gang all had hockey stick when you chased me through the Black Woods!' he said angrily.

Pugg gave him a contemptuous look - he obviously thought that wasn't the same thing at all - then stalked past Billy and Maxwell. 'They're not worth it,' he said to his gang. 'Come on, let's go.'

They slouched off, muttering threats under their breaths. 'Bye now!' Jamie said, waving his hockey stick. 'Don't be strangers!'

Pugg bared his teeth at Jamie, who gave him a cheerful wink, and he stalked away, looking like the world's biggest, meanest yellow jelly baby.

'What a ... What a ... What a Pugg!' Billy exclaimed, shaking his head.

'Thanks Billy,' Maxwell said, 'That was a great shot.'

'Yeah, it was,' Billy replied. He turned to Bella, Jamie and Daisy. 'Who did make that shot anyway?'

'It was Daisy,' said Jamie, grinning, and poking Daisy in the ribs with his elbow.

'She's a champion hockey player!' Bella exclaimed.

'Nice shooting there, miss,' Billy said, and he gave Daisy a wink. Daisy turned red to the roots of her hair.

'Thanks, Daisy, you really saved my neck,' Maxwell said. 'Are you okay now? After your accident, I mean?'

'I'm fine,' Daisy muttered, in a most un-Daisy like way. The usually striden girl was looking at the ground, her face deep crimson. 'Are you all right, Maxwell?'

'Wow!' Jamie exclaimed excitedly, jumping between Maxwell and Daisy like a deranged frog. 'I can't believe it, Maxwell! Facing up to Pugg - to Pugg and *all his gang* - fists up! Come on, farty Barty Pigg, have a go!'

'You were so brave!' said Bella, her voice quailing.

'Well, I don't really think ...'

'Billy was very brave too!' Daisy interrupted. Everyone looked at her, and - though Maxwell would have sworn it was impossible - she turned an even deeper shade of red. 'Well, he was,' she murmured.

'What a team, eh?' said Billy. 'Jones, Jugg, Blip, Electra and Barker!'

'The A Team!' exclaimed Jamie, executing a clumsy Kung Fu kick at the air.

They all laughed. It was a wonderful feeling. It was as if Billy coming had filled a last piece in all of them, and they had finally come together.

Maxwell looked round at his happy, laughing friends, and he grinned. We are the A Team, he thought.

'Hey, Jamie, second row,' said Lance the caretaker. 'What's your name, kid? Okay, Billy - you're in row two with Jamie. Row ten, Max. You too, Bella. Row five, Daisy."

Inside, the Hall Tower was filled with chairs and noise. Maxwell and Bella walked to row ten, where they found each chair had a name on it. Maxwell found his seat, and swapped it with a kid named Albert Juble, so he could sit beside Bella.

'Maxwell, look at all these people!' Bella said, looking around in amazement.

Maxwell *was* looking. He had never seen so many people in one place in all his life. There were twenty-six rows of seat, and each of the rows had fifty or more chairs in it. That must mean - Maxwell struggled to work it out - 50 times 26 was . . . erm . . .

'There are over 1300 kids here!' Bella exclaimed. Maxwell stopped calculating. That seemed about right, he thought. To Maxwell, who had only ever seen fifty children at one time in the Hall Tower, the massive space seemed impossibly packed. 1300 seemed like an almost impossible number of children to Maxwell.

The Hall Tower was in absolute chaos, indeed Maxwell and Bella seemed to be the only ones sitting, everyone else was milling around talking and laughing or trying to swap seats to be near friends, and Maxwell heard Dr Silex roaring instructions and threats almost constantly. When everyone finally did begin to settle down Maxwell started noticing some very odd things about the new children.

Almost all of the new children wore spectacles, and those who did not looked . . . Well, a little strange. He saw one boy who was at least seven feet tall who was having extreme difficulty sitting in his chair. He saw a girl who's skin looked distinctly green - not grass green, or even as green as a tennis ball - but definitely green. Several of the children were bald, other had streaks of blue and red in their hair. Pugg and his gang were all sitting together several rows back looking very pleased with themselves until Miss Hummingbird broke them up and sent them to their proper rows. Maxwell watched a boy called Jackson Jakes sat down a couple of seats from Bella. He had a long, horse-like face, his hair a brown mane. He sniffed the piece of paper with his name on it, and sat back with a contented whinny.

There was something else strange about the new pupils, but Maxwell wasn't quite able to grasp exactly what it was until Bella leant over to him and whispered, 'These new kids are so stuck up, aren't they?'

'What do you mean?' Maxwell asked.

'I've said hello to everyone who passed us, and they never even looked at me.' Tears welled in Bella's eyes. 'I can't bear rude people!'

'They're probably just nervous about starting a new school,' Maxwell said reasonably. But looking round he saw that Bella seemed to be right. The new children were talking to other new children, but the kids who lived on Virporta sat alone and ignored amongst the bustle and chatter.

'Well at least Billy isn't like that!' Bella said.

Maxwell could see Billy one row down from the front of the stage, chatting to Jamie. He noticed, however, that though the new children were happy to talk to Billy they pointedly ignored Jamie - and Jamie Blip was a very difficult person to ignore. Maxwell looked along the fourth row and spied Daisy. She was bent over a writing pad - doing homework, Maxwell supposed, even though they had been told they had none. Several girls surrounded Daisy, but as they stood talking they never spoke to Daisy, or even acknowledged that she was sitting right under their noses.

The clear tone of the school bell rang through the air, and everyone in the hall grew silent.

'Good morning ladies and gentlemen and welcome to what for many of you will be your first day at the Watchmen Academy.'

Professor Magister cleared his throat, and his eyes darted around the packed Hall Tower. He was alone on the stage and looked very small and uncomfortable in front of the long, empty teacher's table.

'Of course I am ... erm ... incongruous,' Magister winced at the uncomfortable word, 'in welcoming you to your first day when today is, in fact, anything but.' Several students looked at each other and shrugged. 'This is not your first day at the Watchmen Academy proper, as, of course, there are no formal lessons today. Today you shall be inspected by the school ...' Professor Magister stopped, and then waggled his fingers back and forth, muttering under his breath. 'I'm sorry - what I meant to say was - today you will be *tested* by the school *inspector*, Mr Vim. Yes, that is what I meant.'

There was an excited murmur around the hall, and lots of heads were straining this way and that, evidently trying to catch a glimpse of Mr Vim. But Mr Vim was no where in sight. Maxwell looked up the to the distant ceiling of the tower, half expecting to see Mr Vim hanging in the air, his bat wings flapping as he took the school register, but of course he wasn't there either.

'You will all be tested in the school's gymnasium,' Professor Magister continued. 'The pool and the sport field are also available for those with special requirements.'

Special requirements? What did that mean, Maxwell wondered. He hoped that part of the test would be swimming. If his experiences beneath the ice with the Nurgler had taught him anything they had certainly taught him that he was an excellent swimmer.

'Now,' Magister continued, 'As you have no doubt realised it will take rather a long time to test you all individually. With this in mind we have invited a guest speaker to the Watchmen Academy.' Professor Magister turned to his left and began to clap. The rest of the room began to applaud politely as a large man in a brown suit stood up in the first row. A cacophony of whistles and shouts exploded from behind Maxwell. He turned and saw Pugg and Mickey Prickle applauding and whistling furiously. He turned back to the front just in time to see the large man in the brown suit puff his way to centre stage.

'Oh no,' murmured Maxwell, 'Not *him*.'

'Ladies and gentlemen it gives me great pleasure to introduce the mayor of Virporta Island, Mr George Pugg, who has kindly volunteered to give a short talk.'

George Pugg stood centre stage - he *filled* centre stage - a wide grin on his ruddy face. He waved to the children like a man who had just been elected prime minister.

'A *short* talk,' Maxwell whispered to Bella. 'I *bet*!'

'Do you think he'll talk about potatoes?' Bella asked excitedly.

Maxwell rolled his eyes - what else would George Pugg talk about *but* potatoes?

'... on the shores of that great continent, thousands of miles from civilisation, surrounded by armies of brutal savages, one man stood alone. In his hand he held the beginnings of the modern world. The magical key that would open the door to science, medicine, culture, arts. He held it in his hand, lifted it high against the crashing ocean at the end of one world, and at the beginning of another. Just one man . . . and a potato.'

There were weak applause from the semi-conscious audience - even Bartholemew Pugg seemed to have fallen asleep - and Maxwell stirred out of his daze as George Pugg took several bows, pumped Professor Magister's hand like it was a handle on a slot machine, and walked triumphantly from the stage, waving as he went.

'Who would have thought that a potato could mean so much?' whispered Bella in awe.

George Pugg had spoken for two hours. He had spoken about different varieties of potatoes, and the differing methods various parts of the world used to farm them. He had spoken about the many recipes you could make with potatoes. Maxwell recognised many of these recipes - such as potato jam tarts and potato custard - as his mother's concoctions (though Pugg never mentioned Bettie Jones) and Maxwell had shook with nausea at the memory of their taste. Mayor Pugg had spoken about how the potato had inspired Darwin's theory of evolution, the Wright brothers' first flight, Einstein's theory of relativity and the moon landing.

He had spoken about potatoes a lot, and at length.

Maxwell was having difficulty focusing his eyes, and he seemed to have forgotten how to speak. He sat up and shook himself. He noticed that all but two rows in front of him were empty now. Some people had all the luck. Why couldn't his name be Maxwell Aardvark?

Professor Magister took the stage, looking a lot older than he had at the start of Pugg's speech. 'Well, thank you Mayor Pugg for that . . . instructive talk.' Magister looked ready for his bed. 'Now, the Watchmen Academy's sports and recreation mistress Ms Hummingbird will give a *short*,' he shot Ms Hummingbird a warning looking as she approached the stage, 'a *short* recital of flute music.'

Miss Hummingbird rushed to centre stage, almost knocking Magister into the front row, and started playing a chipped, ancient-looking flute immediately.

'Oh my sweet Lord,' murmured Maxwell as the shrill squealing notes screeched around the Hall Tower.

Bella winced as if hit by a blow. 'She's *terrible!*' she exclaimed, and though Maxwell did not share Bella's dislike of Ms Hummingbird, there was no denying that the sound the flute produced was truly terrible. It was like someone beating a crow to death with an electric violin. And an untuned violin and a crow with a bad throat, at that. 'Still,' Bella said, covering her ears, 'I don't suppose it's easy following George Pugg!'

'No, you're right there,' Maxwell replied, and he slumped back in his seat, wincing at the painful racket.

Twenty long minutes later Maxwell and Bella's row was finally called in to see Mr Vim. Ms Hummingbird was still playing as the long line of Jameses, Joneses and Juggs left the Hall Tower, and Professor Magister, trapped on stage, looked like he was about to burst into tears.

'My brain is melting,' gurgled Bella as Lance led them along a semi-buried corridor towards the sports hall. 'What on earth was that woman trying to play?'

'The Flight of the Bumble Bee,' Maxwell replied. It had taken him a long time to work this out, as Ms Hummingbird had played all the wrong notes in the wrong order and at the wrong speed.

'No bumble bee ever flew like that,' snarled Bella.

They were led around the back of the Watchmen Academy to the squat white sports hall. Inside Lance made them stop inside another corridor which was half-submerged in the ground. He lined them up in alphabetical order.

'Well - good luck,' Maxwell said as he was led forward to stand with half a dozen Joneses.

Bella just nodded. She was shaking with fear.

No one spoke. Perhaps Bella was right about the new people being rude, but now they ignored one another as well as the children who lived on Virporta. Children entered the sports hall one by one. They did not came back out of the door. All that Maxwell could hear was a low electronic buzzing which might have been the lights in the corridor, rather than some strange testing device behind the sports hall doors.

Maxwell tried to remember what Mr Vim had said about the test, but found he could not. His belly kept reminding him that it was almost lunch time, and his brain kept remembering that Mr Vim, qualified school inspector or not, had bat's wings and shot flames out of his eyeballs.

It was all too easy to imagine Mr Vim perched behind the doors roasting the children one by one then eating them soundlessly.

Finally, as Maxwell was beginning to think that he wouldn't mind hearing a few more hours of Ms Hummingbird's flute recital - anything was better than standing here - Lance opened the door, murmured, 'Good luck, Max,' and Maxwell stepped through.

Maxwell hadn't been in the sports hall very often. Ms Hummingbird was a great fan of 'fresh air', even if that fresh air came from a raging tornado and there were two feet of snow on the ground, she rarely held lessons indoors. He had forgotten how truly huge the room was. Gym ropes that even a monkey would think twice about climbing to the top of hung from the ceiling 200 feet above his head. The room was as wide as three football pitches and twice as long.

At the far end of the long hall behind a small table sat Mr Vim. Mr Vim did not move, or make any sign that he had noticed Maxwell entering. If it hadn't been for the distant glint of his metallic sunglasses Maxwell wouldn't have been certain the remote figure was the school inspector.

Maxwell walked nervously towards the distant table. His feet sounded very, very loud on the wooden floor. As he passed the short passage that lead off to the teacher's toilets he was suddenly desperate to wee - and looking that way he could have sworn he saw someone duck back around the wall . . .

Maxwell was puzzled, but immediately forgot that someone might or might not be lurking outside the teacher's lavatory. He was in front of Mr Vim.

Mr Vim did not move. He simply sat and stared at Maxwell, his long gnarled hands crossed on the desk. The desk itself was completely empty - no pens, no paper, nothing at all to indicate that there was a test.

'Mr Jones,' said Mr Vim flatly. Maxwell wasn't sure if he should reply. He hadn't actually seen Mr Vim's lips move. 'You are Maxwell Jones?' asked Mr Vim after a deathly silence, the pale line of his mouth moving only slightly.

'Y-Yes, sir,' Maxwell said. Mr Vim continued to stare at him. He did not move or speak . . . Was this part of the test?

Suddenly Maxwell heard the strange buzzing again, and he saw that Mr Vim desk was not totally empty after all.

A small white box, the size and shape of a shoe box, sat on the desk. There was a small slit in the top of the box, and as Maxwell watched a bell chimed and a piece of paper popped out of the slit.

Mr Vim reached slowly across the desk, tore off the piece of paper which was just a little bigger than a postage stamp, and looked at it. He continued to look at it for what seemed like a very long time, his face motionless. Then he closed his fist around it, and folded his hands in front of him on the table once again.

Thank you,' he said.

Maxwell was confused. 'Is that it?' he asked. 'Is that the test?'

'Yes,' Mr Vim replied. 'Did you want something else? A nice chat, perhaps?' Mr Vim grinned. It was like seeing a dead man smile.

'N-No, sir,' stuttered Maxwell. 'Thank you, sir.'

Mr Vim's grin faded. Maxwell could almost hear his face creak. 'Very well. Please leave through the fire exit.'

Maxwell smiled weakly and began to quickly edge his way from the table, trying not to turn his back on Mr Vim.

'I knew your father, Maxwell,' Mr Vim said suddenly.

Mr Vim was staring straight ahead. Had he spoken, or had Maxwell imagined it?

'I knew your father quite well.' Mr Vim turned to face Maxwell. 'Do you think you take after your father, Maxwell?' he asked.

'I . . . I don't know, sir,' said Maxwell. Mr Vim stared at him. He seemed to be waiting for something. 'He died before I was born.' Maxwell continued. 'I never met him.' And then, for no reason at all, he added: 'He liked superhero comics. I like superhero comics.'

What a stupid thing to say, thought Maxwell, why did I say that?

'I too like superhero comic books,' said Mr Vim, and he returned his attention to the empty hall. 'Thank you, Mr Jones.'

'Thank you,' Maxwell muttered, and he got out of the sports hall as fast as he could without running.

Chapter Ten: Conundrum

A sign on the entrance to the Hall Tower read:

**All pupils have been tested may go home.
Normal lessons commence 9am tomorrow.**

Professor L Z Magister

But either everyone was too keen to discuss the test, or, like Maxwell, they weren't sure whether they had actually been tested. Whichever the case all the pupils with surnames from A to J were crowded around the yard, talking animatedly.

Maxwell walked through chattering groups of children, barely seeing anyone he knew. It was raining, and Maxwell spotted the familiar figure of Tom Chop. He was standing by himself, and was no longer wearing his bright yellow poncho, despite the rain. He looked surly and ready to bite anyone who came too near.

Finally Maxwell spotted Billy standing talking to a boy he didn't recognise. Must be one of the new pupils, Maxwell thought. The boy wasn't even wearing a uniform, but was dressed in a denim jacket just like one Maxwell owned. As he approached he began to think that he *did* know the boy after all. His spikey black hair and handsome, clever face looked very familiar . . .

'Hello Maxwell! That was *we-ird*! Wasn't that weird? That was very weird!'

'Hello Jamie,' said Maxwell. He tried to get another look at the boy, but Jamie bounced up and down in front of him like a deranged puppy.

'That was the strangest test I've ever had,' said Daisy, appearing beside Jamie. 'Did he ask you any questions at all?'

'He told me my dad taught him to play the guitar!' said Jamie, still bouncing madly up and down. 'Isn't that *weird*?'

Daisy shot Jamie a withering look. Maxwell often had the feeling that Daisy didn't like Jamie. 'Did Mr Vim ask you anything, Maxwell?'

'Not really,' said Maxwell after a pause. He wasn't sure he wanted to tell Daisy or Jamie about his dad's superhero comics.

'And what about that machine thing? Weird!' Jamie exclaimed. 'I asked him if I could have a look at the piece of paper that came out of it, but he said "No". Just like that; "No".'

'He told me he was very impressed by my dad's hydroelectric generators.' Daisy frowned, and shook her head.

'I'm off!' Jamie interrupted suddenly. 'Playing hockey later, Maxwell?'

'It's raining,' Maxwell said.

'I'll ring you later!' Jamie yelled as he sped off across the yard.

Daisy tutted in disapproval and turned back to Maxwell. 'Do you think they'll tell us how we did in the test?' she asked anxiously.

'Well . . . Yes, I suppose so,' Maxwell said this to reassure Daisy more than anything else. Daisy was always top of the class at just about everything. But what sort of results Mr Vim would gauge from his questionless, effortless, unexamination . . . Maxwell had no idea.

'I think I'll go and wait for Bella,' Daisy said. 'She's sure to be upset after meeting Mr Vim. She hates people staring at her. I'll see you later, Maxwell.'

Daisy turned to go, and Maxwell took a hesitant step towards her. Now was his chance to ask her about what had happened in Potato Hockey—

'Maxwell Jones?'

Maxwell turned at the sound of his own name, and looked into the eyes of the boy who had been standing talking to Billy. The boy was dressed in jeans and a denim jacket, and his eyes were large and blue and set in a perfectly formed face. He was staring at Maxwell, his expression one of amazement and delight. 'It is . . . you, isn't it?' he asked.

'Do I know you?' Maxwell said.

The boy grinned, and opened his mouth to reply – when a small figure dressed in a yellow poncho and large Wellington boots grabbed the boy's arm.

'Mamble, you fool! What did I tell you!' hissed the small person angrily. The figure in the yellow poncho was very short, barely four feet tall, and the poncho covered every inch of his tiny body . . . except for the hand which was gripping the arm of the boy called Mamble.

'I told you not to call me that!' said the boy, his face furious and at once terrifying – the face of a killer, or a maniac.

'And I told you . . .' the figure turned his head towards Maxwell, but all Maxwell could see under the yellow hood was shadow. 'Come on, we must go now!' he whispered urgently.

'All right, all right,' said the boy. He looked at Maxwell, smiled uncertainly, then walked off with the little figure in yellow.

Maxwell watched them go, frozen to the spot. What was going on? When the man in the yellow poncho had grabbed the boy's arm his hand had been ... What exactly? Not a human hand. It was nobbly and brown and covered in curly hair to its finger tips. Like a monkey's paw.

A hand fell on Maxwell's shoulder, and he let out a screech of terror.

'Bleeding Nora, Max!' exclaimed Billy. 'Didn't give you a fright there, did I mate?'

'No, I scream like that all the time,' Maxwell replied – but Billy did not laugh. 'Are you all right, Billy?'

'Eh? Oh yeah, I'm fine,' Billy smiled weakly.

'What did you think of the test?' Maxwell asked eagerly. Would Billy have a theory about what Mr Vim was planning?

'The test was fine,' Billy said. 'Look, Max, I've got to ... Erm, I've got some stuff to do,' Billy was looking over Maxwell's shoulder. 'Can you meet me at Aunty Magnolia's in about an hour?'

'Sure,' said Maxwell.' 'But who was that you were talking to—'

'I've really got to go now, Max,' Billy interrupted. 'Catch you at the shop, okay?'

Billy was gone before Maxwell could even open his mouth to reply.

Maxwell's mum was in the kitchen when he arrived home. 'Hello, Maxy,' she said brightly. 'I'm having cheese sandwich. Would you like one?'

'Erm ... ' Maxwell looked at the sandwich she was cutting in four. It certainly *looked* like a cheese sandwich. 'Is it a potato cheese sandwich?'

'No, just cheese,' Bettie replied, and then added eagerly, 'I could put some potato in, if you'd like?'

'No - plain cheese is fine,' Maxwell said quickly.

Maxwell's mum took a large slab of cheese from the fridge, placed it on the kitchen bench, and pulled a huge glinting metal meat cleaver from a drawer.

Maxwell watched his mum lift the meat cleaver over her head with an expectant smile on his face. Forget about being a record-breaking potato peeler - this was Bettie Jones's best trick by far.

She brought the glinting metal cleaver down with a *thunk!* . . . and a thin sliver of cheese peeled from the end of the slab. Bettie Jones could cut slices of cheese as thin as paper with that meat cleaver, eccentric or not.

'Would you like some tomato, Maxy?' his mum asked, lifting the wicked-looking meat cleaver again and bringing it down in three blurring swipes. Three curls of cheese landed on the cheese board.

'Yes please!' said Maxwell enthusiastically. He wasn't actually all that keen on tomato, but his mum's trick with a meat cleaver and a tomato was not to be missed. She could throw a tomato into the air, and - *swish-swish-swish!* - it would land on the bread in neat little sections, sliced in mid-air.

'Isn't Archie with you?' his mum asked, raising the meat cleaver.

'Who's Archie?' asked Maxwell.

'*Conundrum!*' his mother cried. The meat cleaver flew backwards out of her hand and shot towards Maxwell. He ducked, and heard it *thunk* into the wall above his head. It hung there, quivering, inches above his scalp.

'Oh dear,' said Bettie Jones.

She walked over to Maxwell and tugged the meat cleaver out of the wall with a grunt. A fair amount of plaster landed on Maxwell's stunned head. Bettie smiled, and returned to the kitchen bench.

'How about some pickle?' she asked.

'Wha- What did you say?' Maxwell stuttered.

'I asked you if you'd like some pickle, dear?' his mum replied.

'Conundrum,' said Maxwell. 'You said "Conundrum".'

'Nonsense, Maxy. Why would I say that?' His mum took a tomato from the fridge. 'I sneezed. That's all.'

She threw the tomato into the air, the meat cleaver flashed, and half a dozen perfect slices of tomato landed in a row beside the cheese.

'Well?' his mum said, turning to him, the meat cleaver, stained with blood-red tomato juice, held in her hand.

Maxwell gulped. 'Well what?'

'Would you like pickle or not?'

'Not,' Maxwell gulped.

Suddenly he didn't feel so hungry.

Billy was waiting by the door of Mrs Trimm's general store. He was hopping impatiently from foot to foot. 'You're late!' he said before Maxwell could even open his mouth. Then, looking Maxwell up and down, he added; 'What on earth are you dressed for, mate?'

Maxwell sighed. His mum had insisted that he put on his wellington boots, two jumpers, gloves, a wooly hat and his huge puffer jacket before she would allow him out. He felt like he was in a sauna, and he looked like a Jelly Baby.

'Never mind all that,' snapped Maxwell impatiently as Billy, who was dressed only in jeans and a sweatshirt, looked him up and down with a wide grin on his face. 'What's going on, Billy?'

'Mr Vim is leaving Virporta Island in an hour,' said Billy, 'and we're following him.'

Billy ushered Maxwell into the shop without another word.

'This way,' Billy said.

Billy lead Maxwell around the counter, crouched down, and swung open a trapdoor.

'We're going into the cellar!' Maxwell exclaimed excitedly.

'Well ... I'm going into the cellar,' said Billy, descending the steps and slowly disappearing into the floor. 'I'm not sure you'll fit through the trapdoor in that coat.'

Maxwell pulled off his gloves, coat and hat as Billy climbed back up the steps. 'What's going on Billy?'

'I'm shutting the trapdoor,' Billy replied. 'There's a light switch on the wall there.'

'Billy!' Maxwell cried in exasperation.

'Just switch it on, I'll explain in a minute,' Billy said.

The trapdoor slammed shut above Maxwell's head, plunging him instantly into total darkness. The darkness reminded him, with a shiver, of the black waters beneath the frozen river, and he fumbled anxiously for the light switch.

The light buzzed and flickered to life - and a thousand glassy eyes glared at Maxwell from white, motionless faces.

'Gruesome, ain't they?' said Billy, climbing down the steps and grabbing a doll from the hundreds that sat on the shelves in front of them. 'This one wets its knickers! Bleugh!' Billy punched the doll in its waxy face, then kicked it onto the air. It flew over the shelf and disappeared.

From where they stood the cellar sloped downward, and the boys could see the full extent of the cellar . . . or, at least, they could see as far as the cellar was lit. In front of them thousands and thousands of shelves swooped down and down and on and on. Maxwell watched tube after tube of neon light flicker to life, lighting even more shelves.

'This place goes on forever!' Maxwell exclaimed.

'You might be right,' Billy answered. 'I've never found the end of it, in any case. Here, take this.' He handed Maxwell a backpack and a piece of paper.

A dozen or more items were listed on the piece of paper - a torch, a compass, a knife (Swiss Army), tin of beans, matches (waterproof)

'What is this for?' Maxwell asked, holding up a backpack which was bright pink with a cat's face on the back.

'All I could find,' said Billy. 'Come on, we ain't got much time.' Billy walked round the corner of the doll shelves. Maxwell looked at the fuzzy pink backpack in disgust, then followed.

Three shelves later Maxwell caught up with Billy as he was pulling pair of walky-talkies out of their packet.

'Here, these'll come in handy,' said Billy, handing Maxwell a walky-talky. 'Batteries? Oh - here we go.' He handed Maxwell a pack of batteries, and dropped a pack into his own, similarly pink and fuzzy, backpack.

'What's going on, Billy?' Maxwell demanded, following Billy as he strode off along the shelves again.

'Provisions for the expedition,' Billy replied patiently. 'Look! Biscuits! These'll be better than tins of beans. Do you want chocolate, plain, or both sorts?'

'What expedition!' Maxwell cried in exasperation as Billy stuffed three packets of chocolate biscuits into his backpack without waiting for a reply.

'I already said! Mr Vim is leaving the island in an hour . . .' He looked at his watch. 'In forty-three minutes Mr Vim is leaving, and we're going to follow him.' Billy walked off again. Maxwell followed, beginning to feel genuinely angry.

'Why are we going to follow Mr Vim?'

'To find out where he's going.'

'Where is he going?'

'Dunno, mate. That's why we're following him.'

'But *why* are we following him?'

'I told you that already! To find out where he's going. Here we are - Swiss Army knives. You can't beat em.' Billy tried unsuccessfully to rip the little red knives from their packaging. 'Blimey, you need a Swiss Army knife to open these Swiss Army knives,' he observed.

Had Maxwell really worried about appearing odd in front of Billy? Billy, who was currently tearing at cardboard package with his teeth like a rabid dog?

'Billy?' Billy was now growling like a rabid dog too as he tried to free the Swiss Army knife. 'Billy!' Maxwell pulled the chewed, battered pack from his teeth.

'What's up, Max?' asked Billy, a puzzled expression on his face.

'What is going on, Billy? How do you know Mr Vim is leaving Virporta?'

'Well ...' Billy sighed. 'That's a little complicated,' he said.

Maxwell didn't know if Billy had gone completely mad, or was trying to drive *him* around the twist. 'Has it got something to do with that boy you were talking to in the yard?' Maxwell asked. Billy nodded, frowning. 'Who was he Billy?'

'That's . . . well, it's complicated,' said Billy. 'It's not who he *was*, it's who he's *going* to be, if you see what I mean?'

Maxwell stared at him blankly. He was now convinced that Billy had gone completely doolally. 'No, Billy,' he said as patiently as he could, 'I don't see what you mean.'

'Come with me,' said Billy, 'and I'll show you.'

Billy led Maxwell across the cellar to the far wall were thick roots twisted from the ceiling to the floor. They must have walked right under Spudmore Avenue to the edge of the Black Woods, Maxwell thought - and this was just the *side wall* of the cellar - how far did it stretch along its *length*? To the sea? *Under* the sea? Dozens of mirrors had been nailed to the roots that grew down the wall, mirrors of all different shapes and sizes. Maxwell looked at himself and Billy reflected back in the flickering fluorescent light.

'I don't get it? Is the boy you were speaking to here?'

'Yeah, he is,' said Billy.

Maxwell looked left and right, but all he could see were more mirrors, more roots, more wall, more shelves. 'Is he hiding?'

'Not exactly,' said Billy, and he reached up and snatched Maxwell's spectacles from his face. 'Look in the mirror.'

Dozens of faces of all different sizes looked back at him from the mirrors. All were wearing the repulsive jumper with a world globe in the shape of potato his mother had knitted for his eleventh birthday. And all of the faces were wearing an open mouthed expression of shock . . . but not one of those faces was the face of Maxwell Jones.

A blue-eyed boy with spiky black hair was looking back at him. The handsome face had something ... something that seemed to *lurk* just under the skin. Something like cruelty. Or evil.

'That's who I was talking to in the playground, Max,' said Billy. 'That boy I was talking to was you.'

'But . . . ?' Maxwell blinked, and the stranger's face blinked back. He stuck out his tongue, and the black haired boy stuck out his. Maxwell felt as if someone had kicked him in the stomach. 'How can that be?' he gasped.

'I dunno,' said Billy. 'He said it was a ... a Corndrum? Some funny word—'

Maxwell remembered the meat cleaver flying out of Bettie's hand and thumping into the wall above his head. 'A ... Conundrum?' Maxwell said.

'Yeah! That's it!' cried Billy, then he frowned. 'How did you know that, Max?'

Maxwell couldn't reply even if he had known what to say. His throat had gone dry, and the stranger's face looking back at him was pale.

'And that's not all,' said Billy. 'Check *this* out!'

Billy reached up and pulled off his own spectacles with a dramatic flourish. His face transformed in front of Maxwell's astonished eyes. Billy's face became longer and changed colour – his skin turning a shimmering silver. Billy's eyes turned from dark brown to purple in a blink, and his messy blond hair grew upwards into spikes as long and thick as ice cream cones, turning from blond to dark blue flecked with zigzags of gold.

'*Ta-da!*' cried Billy, grinning. His teeth glinted gold. 'Now is that cool or *what?*'

Maxwell looked at the two boys looking back at them from the mirrors – one a stranger, the other barely human – and he had to admit it:

'Yes,' Maxwell said, and his unfamiliar face split into a crazy grin. 'That's fairly cool, all right.'

Chapter Eleven: ZØØM

Maxwell and Billy crouched behind a heap of mud, walky-talkies strapped to their belts, backpacks on, binoculars hanging around their necks. They were staring intently at a large steel door marked with a single word:

ZØØM

It had seemed like a very short journey from the basement of Mrs Trimm's General Store to this mountainous stack of wet earth in the grounds of Pugg's Potato Factory, they had so much to talk about and puzzle over.

Maxwell, the Maxwell who Billy had been talking too in the schoolyard, was from the future, Billy explained. The "future Maxwell" had told Billy that Mr Vim was leaving Virporta Island at exactly three o'clock, and it was essential that they followed him.

'How does he know Mr. Vim's leaving at three?' Maxwell asked, as they hurriedly went round Mrs Trimm's basement collecting bits and pieces they needed for their journey.

'Because *he* followed him in the *past*,' Billy grabbed two whistles from a shelf. 'Keep up, will ya?'

'But who told him – me – that Mr Vim would be leaving at three?'

'You did – I mean, he did. In the future – or do I mean in the past? In *our* future, but in *his* past, which is the same as our future. Or maybe I mean his future is the same as our now?' Billy waved his arms to clear his head. 'You know what I mean.'

A conundrum, Maxwell knew, was a very difficult kind of puzzle, and what had happened certainly fitted that description. The other Maxwell, who was really the same Maxwell as him, had travelled into the past somehow, and he had told Billy that Mr Vim was leaving Virporta Island through a door marked ZØØM in the grounds of Pugg's Potato Factory at precisely 3pm, and that Maxwell and Billy must follow Vim. But who had told the future Maxwell that? The Maxwell who had met another Billy before the future Maxwell had followed Mr Vim had told him, of course. And who had told him? *Another* Maxwell from the future had told *another* Billy from the past. Millions, billions of Maxwells and Billys had passed on this information ... Or perhaps, only one Maxwell and Billy had spoken, trapped in the time Conundrum? But where had the information about Mr Vim leaving the island come from? If everyone was passing the information on, where had the information started?

It made Maxwell dizzy to think about it. 'Did he tell you where Mr Vim is going?'

'No,' said Billy. 'You – I mean, *he* – he said he had to arrange with Jamie, Bella and Daisy to meet him at four, so he couldn't hang about.'

'Meet him where at four?' Maxwell asked.

'He didn't say.'

Maxwell found this even more confusing. If the other Maxwell was meeting Jamie, Bella and Daisy at four and they were going to Puggs at three to track Mr Vim as he left Virporta Island that meant they would be wherever they were going for an hour. So why had the future Maxwell told Billy to bring food, compasses, radios, and a dozen other things, for a sixty-minute journey? It didn't make any sense.

'What about the other one?' Maxwell said. 'Who was he?'

'Other one?' Billy frowned. 'What other one? I only talked to you – I mean *him*,' Billy bared his teeth in frustration. 'I only talked to the future Maxwell,' he said. 'You saw someone else?' Billy's face lit up.

'Maybe it was *me*? Me from the future. How cool is that?'

Maxwell pictured the future Maxwell's strange companion, dressed in his yellow poncho.

Maxwell was certain that the short hairy creature with the future Maxwell had not been Billy Barker. So what had happened to Billy?

ZØØM was as big as Pugg's factory itself. It was built into the side of a craggy hill behind a thick line of spruce trees that stretched from the Black Woods like a protective arm surrounding ZØØM. The building was totally invisible even from the front gates of Pugg's Potato Factory. Maxwell was certain that very few people on the island knew it even existed.

Large heaps of muddy earth surrounded ZØØM. Maxwell and Billy hid behind the heap closest to the door and waited.

'Why have we got these binoculars and all this other stuff? Why do we need binoculars? What are we going to do in an hour, in the middle of Virporta, that we'd need binoculars?'

'Will you shaddap about bleeding binoculars!' Billy snapped. Despite Billy's earlier enthusiasm Maxwell could see that he was worried, and Maxwell thought he knew why. What if they followed Mr Vim and found themselves on the frozen river again with the beasts and the Nurgler? They had barely escaped with their lives the first time. 'Anyway,' Billy said, 'the binoculars were your idea, not mine.'

'No they weren't!'

'Yes they were!' Billy paused, and scratched his head. 'Or, at least, they will be your idea.'

'I don't think I like Conundrums,' said Maxwell glumly.

'You and me both, mate,' said Billy. 'Now, *shush*, it's 3 o'clock.'

Maxwell looked at his watch. Just as the second hand reached twelve Maxwell heard a familiar booming voice.

'... oh yes, current production methods are top of the line, tip-tip top.' The voice was followed by the potato-brown shape of George Pugg. At his side, looking as pale and thin as a French fry, was Mr Vim. 'Computerised now, of course, and very advanced. Tesla . . . You'll recall Tesla Electra?'

'Yes,' said Mr Vim in his flat, gravelly voice.

'A good man, Tesla – though not overly gifted in the old grey matter department.' George Pugg chuckled, his belly shaking like an unpleasant brown jelly. 'The initial design was old Archie's, of course, Tesla couldn't design a potato peeler. But he is very gifted mechanically—'

'Archie?' said Mr Vim, stopping suddenly, and turned to Pugg. 'Dr Arcania has been on Virporta Island?'

'Here?' Old Archie? No, no,' Mr Pugg suddenly looked very nervous under Mr Vim's stony glare. 'He designed the Distribution Engine when we built the factory, is what I meant. I haven't seen Archie for years. I'd heard he was dead?'

'I very much doubt Arcania is dead,' said Mr Vim, coldly. 'A clever rat will survive any sinking ship.'

He glared at Pugg for several seconds (the longest seconds of George Pugg's life, judging by the expression on his face) then turned and continued walking.

'Y-Yes . . . The Distribution Engine sorts the tubers by their genetic strands,' Pugg continued. 'They are then relayed to a number of shoots—'

'We are here,' said Mr Vim, stopping in front of the door marked ZØØM.

'Would you like me to show you in?' Pugg stepped importantly towards the door. 'While you're here I could show you our new—'

'No,' said Mr Vim. 'Goodbye, Mr Pugg.'

'Oh ... right ...' Pugg drummed his fingers on his enormous belly, whilst Vim stood in front of the door, motionless. 'Well ... Have a good ... erm ... trip. Will we be seeing you again anytime soon?'

Mr Vim turned his silvery visor to George Pugg's plump red face, and grinned a cold, hard, slow grin. 'I very much doubt we will meet again, Mr Pugg,' he said. He pushed open the door, and it swung closed behind him with a flat *clang*.

George Pugg stood staring at the closed door, rocking slightly backwards and forwards, his fingers drumming on his big gut. 'Good riddance,' he hissed, and waved a chubby fist at the door. He looked around sharply - Maxwell and Billy ducked out of sight just in time – and then scampered away as fast as his fat little legs could carry him.

'Now, that's no way to talk to the mayor, is it?' said Billy, he tutted. 'Teachers today – no respect.'

'You don't know George Pugg,' Maxwell replied.

'No, and I don't want to. Come on.'

The door was thick metal, with the word ZØØM engraved onto it. Beneath this, in very small letters, were the words: level 5 employees only beyond this point – but despite the warning the door seemed to have no lock. It didn't even have a handle.

Billy looked from the door to Maxwell. 'You ready?' he asked nervously.

'No,' Maxwell replied, smiling.

Billy grinned. 'Me neither.'

'Let's go, then,' said Maxwell, and he pushed open the door.

Maxwell wasn't quite sure what he had expected to find inside the large corrugated building – but he had certainly never expected anything like what was hidden behind the door marked ZØØM.

'Cor!' gasped Billy, his mouth hanging open, 'Cor ... *blimey!*' he added.

The inside of the building was huge. In fact it somehow seemed bigger than the outside. In the centre of this massive space an enormous machine hovered. It looked like a robotic octopus. The gleaming octopus machine's body was as big as two double-decker buses, and from the base of its shiny fat body metallic tentacles at least fifty feet long wavered in the air.

'That must be that Distribution Engine what old Pugg was going on about,' said Billy.

Maxwell nodded – that's was it was, all right. The colossal octopus machine was distributing potatoes from its tentacles. But despite its huge size, its eerie slow and silent movements, and the fact that it did not appear to be attached to anything but hung impossibly in mid-air, Maxwell was not looking at the Distribution Engine.

Maxwell was looking at what the engine was distributing its potatoes too.

The floor beneath the Distribution Engine was criss-crossed with dozens of tracks, and on these tracks, weaving busily between each other under the robot octopus' waving tentacles, were dozens of little trains.

The trains were shaped like animals. One load was pulled by what looked like four wild black horses, another by a yellow elephant, another by what looked like a giant purple hamster. Yet Maxwell was sure they were trains – they pulled carriages which were rapidly being filled by the Distribution Engines' tentacles, and red steam belched from the wild horses' nostrils, from the elephant's trunk, from the hamster's ears. Maxwell spotted a pig-shaped engine, which was coloured a vivid green - red steam billowed from its bottom.

Perhaps the most remarkable thing about the trains was that they did not hit each other. They chugged frantically under the Distribution Engine like a madly circling herd of panicking animals, but they never collided, or even came close to colliding.

'Look!' said Billy. Maxwell followed Billy's pointed finger. A yellow camel broke away from the chaos, and switched to another line. The camel chugged to the end of the building, and Maxwell realised that the building only had three walls. The fourth wall was the side of the rocky hill they had seen from the outside, with a large tunnel in its centre. The yellow camel picked up speed, and thundered into the tunnel with a loud whistle. '*That* must be where Mr Vim went,' said Billy.

'That's how they get the potatoes off the island?' said Maxwell in disbelief. It all seemed unnecessarily complicated to Maxwell.

'How'd you think they did it, magic?' said Billy. 'Come on, we've got a train to catch.'

The boys ran along to where they had seen the camel switch tracks. They were now directly under the Distribution Engine, and looking up at the massive body and busy arms of the huge, gleaming machine Maxwell was struck by just how impossible what he was seeing was. To see a man grow bat's wings and shoot flame from his eyes, or to even see yourself transform into a different person in front of your own eyes, was one thing . . . but to see a machine, something as reliable and dull as a machine, hanging in mid-air spitting out potatoes made Maxwell's brain just want to give up and go home for a lie down.

'Here comes one now,' said Billy, 'Get ready.'

Maxwell and Billy watched as the green pig turned onto the track. It steamed slowly past them, and Maxwell read the words – *ZØØM Engineering Inc, proudly serving the 101 Realms since 2025* – scrolled in flowing gold letters on the side of the pig's belly. Then the engine had passed, and Maxwell quickly scrambled up the side of the clattering train. A second later Billy landed in the potatoes beside him, and they found themselves chugging towards the tunnel entrance.

'Typical!' Billy exclaimed in disgust. 'We *would* get the bleeding pig!'

The green pig train let out a high pitched *toot!*, steam rising out of its backside. Clattering and shaking the potato train gained speed and carried the boys into the black tunnel.

Chapter Twelve: Termination Central

'Is it just me, or is it getting quite pleasant in here?'

'If you mean, is it getting absolutely freezing cold in here,' said Maxwell through chattering teeth, 'Then yes, it is.'

They had been on the green pig train for less than five minutes, barely enough time for the light from the Virporta end of the tunnel to fade, and yet it was as cold as if they had travelled miles underground. Where Maxwell's torch light touched the tunnel walls it reflected back off thick sheets of ice, and the train's progress had become unsteady as it skated along, barely able to gain purchase on the frozen track.

'Can you smell bananas?' Billy said suddenly.

'Bananas?' Maxwell sniffed the air, but his nose was almost frozen solid . . . he did smell something. 'I'm not sure,' he said.

'I can smell bananas.' Billy sniffed around like a bloodhound, searching for the scent. Finally he picked up one of the potatoes from the pile he was sitting on and gave it a long hard sniff. 'It's the potatoes!' he exclaimed.

Maxwell picked up a potato and sniffed it. 'This one smells like an apple!' he said, amazed.

'And this one's a melon!' said Billy, holding up a dirt-covered potato. Maxwell picked up a handful of perfectly ordinary looking dirty, nobbly potatoes – one smelled of orange, another of grape, and a third – he sniffed if for a long time until he was sure – had the distinctive aroma of fish and chips. 'It tastes like a melon!' Billy exclaimed.

'Oh! That is disgusting!' said Maxwell, as Billy took a large bite out of a potato. 'They're all covered in dirt!'

'Dirt's good for you,' Billy answered through a mouthful of raw potato. 'Take a bite – they're delicious!'

'I'm not eating raw potatoes,' said Maxwell. 'I hate *cooked* potatoes, never mind raw ones!'

'They're not potatoes. Go on – try a peach, they're lovely and juicey.'

'I am not—' Maxwell began, but he stopped as the train slowed suddenly with a screech of brakes, then thudded to a halt, covering them in billowing red smoke.

'What happened?' said Billy, standing up and dropping a half eaten potato. 'Have we broken down?'

'I don't know,' said Maxwell. 'We can't have come very far.'

The steam slowly cleared, and Maxwell raised his torch to the roof of the tunnel . . . and discovered they we no longer in a tunnel.

His torch beam rose over the train's green head and reflected off a wall of what at first looked to be solid ice. But as Maxwell peered through the steam he saw that the ice coated a red brick wall, and on the wall was a sign, which read:

Termination Central

All exits to Watchmen City and University Connections to all Realms

'I think we've come a tad further than we thought, Max,' said Billy.

They shone their torches around. They were in what appeared to be an underground train station – there was a platform a couple of feet above their heads, and signs pointing in different directions. Maxwell read several of these signs –

Virporta, Newcastle, London, Aberdeen
Prezema, the Bleak Republic, Shamble
Minsk and Moscow

Mab, and the Wooden City

--but most of the signs were unreadable. The entire
platform - the walls, the ceiling, the flinty earth around
the train tracks - was covered in a thick sheet of ice,
and most of the exits to these exotic-sounding places
were blocked by impenetrable walls of ice.

'Nice climate,' said Billy, lowering his torch
and sitting back down, 'But I don't think I'd wanna
spend my holidays here.'

'Me neither,' said Maxwell. 'Look, Mr Vim
went that way,' he shone his torch over fresh
footprints on the frosty platform, 'We'd better follow
him.'

'Right!' said Billy, but his enthusiasm wasn't
very convincing. 'We're on the trail now, Maxy boy.
My old dad'd be proud of us.'

'Right,' Maxwell agreed, but he didn't move. It
occurred to him that it would be a very good idea to
stay on this transdimensional pig train (or whatever it
was) until it decided to return to Virporta. Good old
boring Virporta Island, thought Maxwell wistfully.

With this in mind Maxwell turned to Billy, who
was picking up potatoes, sniffing them, then dropping
the ones he liked the smell of into his backpack. He
had just opened his mouth to ask Billy what he
thought about staying on the train, when Billy said, 'I
wonder who unloads these potatoes?'

Maxwell shot to his feet, and heaved himself
onto the platform as quickly as he could. Whoever, or
whatever, was coming to collect these potatoes
Maxwell was certain he didn't want to meet them.
'Come on, Billy!' he said urgently.

'Hold your water! Daft to leave supplies behind,' said Billy, sniffing a large, very filthy potato. 'Mmm – sausages!' He dropped it into his fluffy pink rucksack.

'Come on! You'll be here for hours! We're supposed to meet the others at four, remember?' said Maxwell anxiously.

Billy shook his head thoughtfully. 'Not necessarily true,' he said. He reached for a potato – and it moved. Maxwell saw the potato sink beneath the pile, but Billy didn't notice, and his fingers closed around another potato. 'You're forgetting the pool under—'

It all happened very fast. One second Billy was kneeling in the train examining a potato, the next second he was gone. The potatoes vanished with a rumble, and Billy vanished with them – he didn't even have time to cry out – and Maxwell found himself looking down at a suddenly empty train.

'Billy!' Maxwell fell onto his knees and leaned over the platform. A trapdoor had opened in the bottom of the train carriage and the potatoes, and Billy, had vanished through it into blackness. 'Billy! Billy can you hear me?'

The trapdoor closed with a ringing *CLANG!* the pig train exhaled a whistling jet of pink steam, and began chugging backwards into the tunnel.

Maxwell jumped back, barely avoiding having his nose clipped off by the pig's metallic ears. He looked around the frozen platform – but if there had ever been a bell or buzzer to alert the station master it had long since been entombed in ice. He sprang forward again as the train passed – and found himself looking down at the frozen tracks.

There was no hole between the tracks, just frozen lumps of dirty shale that looked like they had lain there undisturbed for at least a thousand years.

The pig train gave a final whistle, but when Maxwell looked up to see it leave the tunnel they had come through was no longer there. The tracks ended at a solid wall of black ice.

There was no way back.

'Max?'

Maxwell had kneeling at the edge of the platform for several second staring down at the solid tracks, already bitterly cold and at a loss at what to do next.

'Max? Can you hear me?'

'Billy?' Maxwell spun round, his torch darting across walls of ice. He was alone on the platform. 'Billy? Is that you? Where are you?'

'Max, are you listening?' came Billy's voice. 'Turn on your walky-talky you dim goit!'

Maxwell dragged his walky-talky from his belt. 'Billy!' he cried into the radio. 'Is that you?'

'Who'd you think it was, bleeding Marconi?' Billy replied sarcastically.

Maxwell laughed, relieved to hear his friend's voice again. 'Are you all right, Billy? Where are you?'

'Oh, yeah, I'm just flipping dandy,' answered the crackling voice from the radio. 'I just fell about a mile onto the biggest pile of potatoes you've ever seen. I'm in some sort of cave thing, it's absolutely *huge*. It's got them things on the ceiling – whatcha call those pointy rocks that hang down?'

'Stalactites?' Maxwell suggested.

'That's the fellas,' said Billy. 'Stalacs hanging tight all over the joint. I can't see you, though. Shine your torch down the hole.'

Maxwell looked down at the frozen shale. 'Billy . . . there isn't a hole,' he said.

'What! Oh, that's flipping great!' Billy exclaimed. 'That'd explain why the future you didn't

tell me to bring a rope! Do me a favour, will you –
when you get back to Virporta tell me to get *out* of the
train *before* the potatoes go the journey, okay?'

Maxwell didn't know how to reply. Why
hadn't his future self warned Billy about the train?
'Are you all right?' he said into the walky-talky. 'Can
you see any way out?'

'No, mate. It's as black as Barty Pugg's
underpants down here. I think ...' The radio fell
silent.

'Billy?' Maxwell shook the radio. 'Billy!'

The radio clicked, and then Billy, his voice
barely a whisper, said: 'Someone's coming,' and the
radio went dead.

'Billy? BILLY!'

But Billy did not reply.

Maxwell looked around the platform.

Mr Vim's footprints lead to a dark tunnel
marked **Watchmen City and University**. Perhaps
someone there would know where Billy had gone?

Beyond the platform Maxwell found himself in
a corridor. The only sound was the crunch of ice
crystals under his feet and his own breathing. If it
weren't for the occasional reminder that he was in
some sort of abandoned train station, he could have
been walking through a tunnel carved into solid ice.
He passed other exits, but they were all frozen shut.
Once or twice he thought he glimpsed things deep in
the ice, shapes like people, but he tried not look too
closely.

After what seemed like a very long walk his
torch beam lit up the bottom of a stairway. As he
approached he realised that it wasn't a stairway at all –
it was an escalator, buried under layers of hard frost.

At the bottom of the escalator stood a large
ticket machine, half submerged in ice. The ticket
machine was a peculiar grey colour, not a metallic

colour at all, and a forgotten ticket that was sticking out of it was exactly the same colour. Maxwell reached for the ticket – it snapped off in his hand, and a fine grey dust fell from it. Maxwell stared at the ticket in the palm of his hand. The ticket wasn't frozen.

The ticket and the ticket machine had been fossilised.

'How long has this been here?' Maxwell murmured – but there was no one to answer him. Maxwell checked his radio again, and then continued up the dead escalator, following Mr Vim's footprints.

At the top of the escalator Maxwell found himself facing a thickly packed wall of snow and ice. In the centre of the wall was a hole about the size of a man which, judging by the heaps of snow around it, had been dug very recently. Maxwell felt a chill breeze. He switched off his torch, and stepped through.

The tunnel was filled with pale silver light. All around him the snow groaned, small flurries falling from the roof with every step. As Maxwell walked further into the moaning, crumbling passage the light grew brighter and brighter until at last he stepped out of the tunnel – and gasped.

For several second Maxwell forgot to breathe, he simply looked around, his face expressionless, his mouth hanging open. Then he looked up at the sky and let out a shout of astonishment.

Maxwell's voice did not carry and it did not echo. There was nowhere for his voice to go, and nothing for it to echo off. All around him in every direction stretched a white featureless land. There was not a building, not a tree, not a mountain or a hill. There was just flat, endless snow as far as the eye could see.

And above him Maxwell looked up at a purple cloudless sky dotted with stars that formed shapes that he had never seen before. Above the horizon hung a huge red moon, and above that moon a smaller silver moon, and one, two, three – seven more moons. The smallest of the nine bright blue like a shiny button.

And though Maxwell guessed he could see a hundred miles in every direction, he could not see Mr Vim anywhere.

There was a loud *CRUMP!* sound from behind him. Maxwell spun round. The entrance to the tunnel that led back to Termination Central had collapsed. It was just another heap of featureless snow.

Chapter Thirteen: big green coconut

There was a single pair of footprints in the snow, and then nothing more, just the white, endless, plains.

Maxwell was a brave and quite resourceful boy, but faced with the terrible white *nothing* that seemed to stretch on forever in front of him even the bravest of men could have been forgiven for just sitting down and giving in to the pitiless cold. Mr Vim could be a hundred miles away by now, sipping coco by a heated swimming pool for all Maxwell knew, and Maxwell, who did not have wings, could not follow him.

And even if he could, in which direction should he go?

But the future Maxwell had escaped, Maxwell reminded himself. The future Maxwell had returned to Virporta and had told Billy exactly what he must bring here in order to survive. So Maxwell began digging through the contents of his fluffy pink rucksack, searching for the thing that would save him.

As he pulled knives, biscuits, matches and cans of pop out of the rucksack Maxwell reminded himself that even if he didn't find anything he simply could not give up. Billy has said they were a team, and Maxwell would not leave this alien land without him.

Maxwell stood up straight and looked at the contents of the backpack strewn across the snow. 'Nothing,' he murmured. If he was very careful he could probably survive a couple of days out in the open with the stuff in the backpack, thanks to Miss Hummingbird's extreme wilderness survival lessons, but he could see nothing here that would help him get home.

See nothing ... ? Maxwell looked down at the binoculars hanging around his neck. He could see nothing ... But was there nothing to see?

He lifted the binoculars to his eyes and scanned the horizon.

At first he wasn't sure the binoculars were working, all they showed was white no matter which direction he looked or how much he adjusted the focus. He lifted the binoculars to the sky and the largest of the nine alien moons filled his vision. Well – they worked, anyway. At any other time Maxwell would have been fascinated by the strange craters of the unknown moon, but a nice view wouldn't feed him or stop him freezing to death.

He brought the binoculars back down – and saw something. It was so distant, or perhaps so small, that without the binoculars he would never have spotted it, and even with them he couldn't tell what it was. It was a little spot of green in the endless white. A tree? It was impossible to tell anything – except that it was something that was not white, and for Maxwell, that was enough.

Maxwell dropped the binoculars, shoved his gear back into his rucksack and swung it onto his back, then checked his silent walky-talky was still switched on.

He stepped over Mr Vim's footprints, and walked out into the white wilderness.

Maxwell didn't know how long it took him to get to the green shape, he had long since stopped checking his watch, but long before he stood in front of it he knew exactly what the green shape was.

In front of him was a large green metallic coconut with a ragged hole in its side. It was a thing that he had seen – minus the hole – perhaps a million times in his life; so often, in fact, he had stopped noticing it years ago.

'Professor Magister's office,' he whispered, the words coming out in weak jets of steam. He was looking at the large office where Professor Magister lived, five hundred feet above his students' heads at the crest of the Hall Tower.

Maxwell looked up at the sky, and then down at the green coconut again. The sky still held nine moons and countless unknown stars, and the peak of the Watchmen Academy's tallest building was still in front of him, buried in the snow of an alien world.

'It just *looks* like Magister's office,' he murmured. 'It can't *be* it.'

Of course not. That was just crazy. Had the school hopped on a space ship and gone off on its holidays? It wasn't the same building, no . . . But still Maxwell, who was now so cold he couldn't feel his legs or arms, paused. To see such a familiar thing made this place seem even more alien somehow. Maxwell realised that the shivering he felt wasn't just cold, it was fear too.

He looked down. On the ground in front of him were Mr. Vim's footprints. He had stepped into the hole in the side of the green coconut.

Maxwell looked back, but behind him there was nothing but cold and death.

Maxwell flicked on his torch, and its beam revealed a large empty room, the floor dusted with snow. An open doorway led into darkness.

Maxwell pulled his walky-talky off his belt, and pressed the TALK button. 'Billy?' silence from the radio. 'Billy, can you hear me?' Nothing. Not even the hiss of static.

He clipped the radio back onto his belt. He didn't want to think about what could have happened to Billy, so he walked across the room and through the open door.

Maxwell's feet clanked on something metallic. His torch revealed the top of a rusted staircase which wound downwards into the darkness. He peeked over the edge but the torch beam didn't reach the floor. Maxwell stepped forward. The staircase let out a metallic squeal and swayed like the deck of ship. Maxwell stepped back quickly, his heart lurching. How had Mr Vim, who must weight three times as much as Maxwell, got down this shaky, rusty death trap? He had unfurled those handy wings again, of course, and fluttered gently to the distant floor, with an angelic smile on his face for all Maxwell knew.

'No good, I've got to do it. There's no way back,' Maxwell said to the darkness.

The staircase shuddered and chattered, the squeal of rusting metal echoing off the walls like the screech of bats. He kept reminding himself of the black haired boy he had met in the play yard only that morning. The future Maxwell had no broken bones, all that was missing was his spectacles. As the staircase heaved and howled Maxwell believed he could live without his glasses - yes sir, no problem. In fact he'd take them off right now and drop them over the edge if the tower wanted something to smash at its bottom, that would be no problem at all--

Maxwell's foot came down on empty air, and he grabbed the handrail just in time to stop himself unbalancing. He shone his torch in front of him, his heart pounding. The staircase had broken off, and all that was in front of him was a drop into darkness.

He angled the torch until he saw, a dozen feet below him, the floor of the tower . . . and the glinting, tortured remains of the collapsed staircase.

'Fantastic,' murmured Maxwell. He slowly knelt, then lay on his belly. The staircase *screamed* and shuddered, rivets popping from the wall and pattering to the floor. He shone his torch under the stairs, and saw that the floor was clear directly under him. He could swing under the staircase and drop safely onto the floor. Of course, sure, no problem at all. Just a little swing and a twelve foot drop.

'No sweat,' said Maxwell shakily, 'I can do that.' He turned around and slid his legs over the drop, not giving himself the time to think too much about it. The staircase screeched again, rivets raining onto the floor. 'That's okay, that's fine.' He put the torch in his mouth, and slid backwards until only the top half of his body was on the staircase, his legs dangling stiffly. *I can do this*, he thought, *if I can survive Potato Hockey and double maths with Silex I can survive anything.*

Nevertheless, his belief that he *would* survive because the future Maxwell had of course survived unscratched didn't seem quite so persuasive any more, and it was several minutes before he slid all the way back and was finally dangling by his fingers.

'See!' he gasped. 'I knew it would be—'

The staircase gave a final piercing scream, and tore away from the wall.

Maxwell was suddenly lurched into the centre of the tower, he had a brief glimpse of the staircase unravelling from the wall, twisting and undulating like a snake, and then it shook him free, and Maxwell fell into blackness.

He hit the floor hard. The torch flew out of his mouth and bounced away.

The jumping torch beam flashed upwards and in a second Maxwell saw the whole staircase peel away from the wall and fall like a breaking wave. He scrambled to his feet . . . but the torch light vanished – and suddenly Maxwell didn't know which way to run.

The staircase hit the floor with a massive explosion of sound. Maxwell fell to the floor. He closed his eyes and covered his ears. He felt the ground shudder beneath him. Something buzzed past his ear as fast as a bullet . . . and then there was silence.

Maxwell opened his eyes. The torch lay on the ground a few feet away, its beam lighting on a tortured tangle of broken metal.

'Whoops.' Maxwell picked up the torch and shone it over the contorted remains of the staircase, and then turned to where in his own world the exit to the Hall Tower lay. And sure enough there it was. The doors looked exactly the same as those he passed through on his way to lunch every weekday, if a lot older and a *lot* more in need of a lick of paint. Maxwell couldn't believe his luck; one of the doors was open, and beyond it dim light glowed . . .

'*Hungry* . . .'

Maxwell spun round, the torch beam whipping over the piles of broken metal. The Hall Tower (if that's what it was called on this world) was empty apart from himself and several tons of scrap. He could have sworn . . .

'Hungry, hungry, *HUNGRY!*'

Maxwell took an unsteady step forward, tried to speak, swallowed, then tried again. 'Hello?' he said.

'Hello,' replied a voice that was little more than a whisper.

'Hello? Who's—'

'Hungry hello, hello hungry,' said the voice, and suddenly it was joined by *other* whispering voices, repeating the words like an idiot echo, '*Hungry hello, hello hungry.*'

Maxwell lifted the torch up past the piles of metal, noticing how the beam shook as it moved up bare walls, higher and higher, a hundred feet up to where the wall was no longer smooth, but dotted with large grey shapes.

Moving shapes. Shapes the size of people. Sleeping people curled on the wall like cocoons.

'Hello hungry,' hissed one of the shapes, and as Maxwell's torch beam fell on it, it raised its head and grinned at him.

Maxwell let out a cry of horror. The torch fell from his hand. He heard the smash of glass, and he was plunged into darkness.

'Hello hungry.' Maxwell heard something fall to the floor with a thud. It was followed by another thud, then another, and another. 'Hungry hello.'

Maxwell turned and ran.

He ran towards the dim light that shone through the open door, his mind paralysed with terror, all he could think about was getting away from those grinning *things*.

When the creature hanging on the wall had raised its head it had grinned at him and its mouth had been a glowing hole filled with whirling black shapes like the fast turning blades of a lawnmower. Its grey head had been bald and featureless, with dark holes where its ears should be, and its eyes ...

Maxwell reached the open door and grabbed it, feeling his strength give way as he touched it. Fighting his legs' weakness and the whirling dizziness in his head he turned back to look into the tower.

The grey creatures shambled towards him. They were in no hurry. They chattered and giggled and their terrible heads shook and blurred and twisted and ticked. Their long clawed hands dangled by the sides of their featureless, unclad, stick-thin bodies. Their busy, glowing jaws lit their faces and their eyes ... eyes as black and lifeless as jewels, the eyes of soulless dolls ... or dead men.

'Hungry,' whispered the creatures, whispering it to one another like it was a delicious secret, giggling and chittering. 'Hungry.'

Maxwell grabbed the door in both hands and tried to drag it closed – but the part he was holding simply disintegrated in a cough of sawdust and writhing insects – and he fell back onto the floor.

He lay on the floor, frozen with terror as slowly, unhurriedly, the creatures passed through the door and surrounded him.

They lowered their awful faces to his and grinned.

'*Hungry,*' they hissed.

Chapter Fourteen: the A-Men

The grey men grinned at Maxwell, their whirling, buzzing mouths filled with poisonous black comets, their wet black eyes glinting and Maxwell realised that he had made a terrible mistake. The boy in the school yard had not been him at all. He had not travelled into the past to set himself on this road, because this road ended here. The boy had been the keeper of these monsters, and Maxwell and Billy had been sent here for one purpose – to feed them.

'Face,' hissed one of the creatures. It reached out a hand with fingers as long and thin and sharp as pencils, and stroked Maxwell's temple. Its touch was like ice. 'Mamble,' it said.

The creatures shuddered as one, and a sudden confusion of hissing sounds which may have been words came from them. 'Eat?' said one of the grey men. The creatures chattered and hissed, and drew back, exchanging glances and noises in their secret language.

Maxwell didn't wait for a second chance.

He leapt to his feet and ran head first through the grey men. They flew aside, shrieking with surprise and hitting the floor with a sound like ripe tomatoes, and suddenly Maxwell was free of them. He was running in the wrong direction, back towards the entrance to the Hall Tower, but Maxwell's instinct did not waver, and he barely had a second to consider what he was doing.

Maxwell jumped at the door, his feet hit the ancient wood, and then he ran vertically *up* the door towards the ceiling. He kicked off the roof, spun backwards through the air, and landed neatly on both feet behind the grey men. The creatures blundered into the door, screaming in frustration and fury.

'That's impossible,' said Maxwell, looking down at his feet, which had temporarily forgotten the laws of gravity. When he looked up the creatures were coming towards him again – and this time they were running.

Maxwell spun round, ready to run ... and stopped dead in his tracks.

Ten yards in front of him in the centre of the ice tunnel which ran from the Hall Tower stood Mr Vim. He still wore his shabby electric-blue suit, but now he had added a mangy brown cape that fell from his shoulders to the floor. His metallic glasses were gone – his eyes flaming pits of fire.

Mr Vim let out a terrible roar, and flame shot from his eyes in a horizontal sheet – straight towards Maxwell.

Maxwell threw himself to the ground. He felt the wall of flame sizzle over his head. The creatures buzzing cries became ear piercing shrieks, and Maxwell looked up to see Mr Vim running towards him, flame still spewing from his eyes.

'Your hair is on fire,' said Mr Vim in his flat, inflectionless voice as he ran past Maxwell without even pausing to look at him.

Maxwell stared after Mr Vim dumbly, then grabbed a handful of snow from the floor and put out his rapidly burning hair. He felt like he was operating on autopilot, but when he turned to see where Mr Vim had gone he was jarred back into reality with a sickening jolt.

Mr Vim was advancing steadily on the grey men, burning everything in his path. But the grey men were not running from Mr. Vim, they were struggling forward through the flames even as they burnt, hissing: *'Vim – die – boy – our boy – Mamble-'*

It was too much for Maxwell, and whatever store of bravery he had in him (and he had a lot) ran dry, and he turned and ran. He would realise later that Mr Vim had almost certainly saved his life, but right now all he knew for sure was that he did not want to be here and he did not want to see this.

He ran down the ice tunnel leaving the screams of the grey men and the shout of the awful flames behind him. He ran through a door and found himself in a tower, staircase leading off in all directions. In a second he knew where he was – he had run across the school yard and was now in the main tower which he entered every morning, and he felt a flood of relief – he knew a million places he could hide up any one of these staircases!

Then Maxwell heard the *thud-thud-thud* of bodies hitting the ground and saw all around him the gaping white maws of a hundred grey men.

'Oh ... that is just not fair,' Maxwell said to the chittering, quivering, buzzing army of monsters as they quickly advanced upon him.

Maxwell turned and sprinted across the floor towards the furthest staircase. If this tower was the same as the one in the Watchmen Academy--

Behind him the *thud-thud-thud* of falling bodies continued – how many of these things were there? – and as he reached the staircase and looked up at the thin door at its top Maxwell felt a glimmer of hope – it *was* the same!

Maxwell ran to the top of the stairs, sure that at any moment one of those grey hands was going to grab his ankle, and he squeezed through the open doorway.

Inside a staircase spiralled upwards through a tower that Maxwell recognised very well. He knew that if he held his arms out at his sides he would be able to touch both walls without even stretching.

'Old Squeezy!' he exclaimed in relief, and started up the spiral staircase. In the Watchmen

Academy Old Squeezy was the narrowest of the school's towers, far too cramped for Bartholemew Pugg or Dr Silex to enter, and the ideal place to hide from either of those fat bullies. This tower, though the staircase was rusted and the lamps which lined the walls were either black with dirt or long ago smashed, was exactly the same dimensions, and there was no way even a normal sized adult could climb these stairs. He was safe! The monsters couldn't follow him!

'*Mamble*,' hissed a snake-like voice.

Maxwell looked back with a lurch of fear. The spiral staircase was lit with darting shadows. The grey men were following him up Old Squeezy one by one, their blazing jaws lighting their way, their stick-thin bodies fitting easily in the claustrophobic space.

All hope of escape vanished as the clattering feet and buzzing laughter of the grey men grew closer behind him. Maxwell staggered out of the tower into a glass corridor packed tight inside thick ice and snow. He tried to run but his traitor legs seemed to have turned to rubber under the weight of his terror. He turned back and the grey men were pouring out of Old Squeezy, some lurching after him on their stick-thin legs, some leaping onto the walls and ceilings and crawling towards him with a spider's ease.

He couldn't run, there was no time, the speed the grey men were moving they would fall on him before he got a dozen feet. So Maxwell did they only thing he could do. He pulled out his only weapon – a rather pathetic looking Swiss Army knife – and faced the oncoming monsters.

Maxwell was suddenly plucked from his feet. He was about to thrust the knife upwards – when his eyes met a glinting visor of steel and a thin, emotionless face.

'Are you planning to peel me an apple?' asked Mr Vim. Maxwell shook his head dumbly. 'Well then, kindly put that knife away, boy.'

'Mr Vim!' Maxwell exclaimed. Above him he could see Mr Vim's bat-like wing flapping furiously. 'What are these things? What's going on?'

'They are the Long Men,' replied Mr Vim calmly. 'But I hardly think this is the time or the place for a lengthy discussion about them. Hold on tight.'

They swooped and spun through the air. Maxwell dropped his knife and grabbed Mr Vim's wrists. For a second he was almost face to face with the oncoming grey tide of Long Men, and then they were flying back down the corridor at breakneck speed.

Maxwell hung on for dear life as they shot out of the glass corridor like a cork out of a bottle. They were suddenly spiralling upwards through a tower that whizzed past too fast for Maxwell to recognise. Just as Maxwell was sure their spinning motion was going to make him throw up into the face of any pursuing Long Man they flew into another glass corridor.

But there was no doorway at the end of this corridor - it ended in a solid wall of hard grey ice.

'You've gone the wrong way!' Maxwell yelled, but Mr Vim ignored him, and flew straight at the ice wall. Maxwell craned his neck around. The Long Men were now only a few feet behind them, and surely only seconds from grabbing them and bringing them crashing to the floor. And there were no longer dozens or even hundreds of Long Men chasing them, there were *thousands*. They filled the corridor like a grasping grey tidal wave, growing closer and closer and closer. 'It's a DEAD END!' Maxwell screamed.

'Oh, do shut up,' Mr Vim replied in his calm, gravely voice. 'What a fuss.'

They flew straight at the wall of ice. Maxwell shut his eyes and covered his face with his arms. He heard the buzzing screech of the Long Men and felt the first razor-sharp claw touch the heel of his foot. Maxwell screamed and—

--and opened his eyes to find they were flying up the centre of the Hall Tower. Maxwell turned back and saw the Long Men tumbling out of an apparently solid wall and falling to the floor with outraged screams.

'A magic wall!' Maxwell exclaimed, and Mr Vim tutted in disgust.

'A hologramic projection,' Mr Vim corrected him, curling his lip. 'Magic indeed!' he spat. 'Hold on tight, just another few—'

And suddenly Mr Vim was gone and Maxwell was falling. Black wings whirled above him, and with a terrible screech a Long Man darted out of the darkness and grabbed the straps of Maxwell's rucksack.

'Boy,' hissed the Long Man, its wet black eyes staring into Maxwell's, its burning mouth inches from his own lips. 'Mam—'

Maxwell felt himself jerked upwards, and for a second Mr Vim was looking down at him, his grim face splattered with blood – and then the backpack disintegrated under the combined weight of the boy and the Long Man, and Maxwell was falling again.

He saw Mr Vim's wings spread wide above him, and then with a screech the Long Man grabbed him again. Maxwell felt a flare of pain as the creature's claws raked down his face, his spectacles flew off, and the Long Man fell backwards and down.

'Boy!'

Maxwell did not think – that part of him that he never dreamed existed, that part that was born for falls and fights and chases and knew absolutely no doubt or fear came to life immediately – his arms shot up, and Mr Vim's hands clamped firm as manacles around his wrists.

Maxwell was wrenched downwards. It was as if his weight had inexplicably doubled, and he looked up at Mr Vim, whose stony face was set in agony, his wings beating frantically at the air. 'The Long ... *Man*!' gasped Mr Vim.

Maxwell looked down, and felt a jolt of horror. The Long Man's black eyes looked back up at him, its pencil claws clamped around the walky-talky fixed to Maxwell's belt. Below its dangling feet the floor of the Hall Tower was packed with hungry white jaws. Waiting.

'*Kick it!*' Mr Vim hissed. Maxwell's wrist slid out of his slippery hand, and Mr Vim grabbed Maxwell's right arm with both hands. Maxwell looked down again and drew back his legs to kick the Long Man. He paused, not wanting to kick anywhere near those whirling jaws ... and then with a thin *reep* sound the strap holding walky-talky snapped, and the Long Man fell.

'No!' yelled Maxwell. His hand shot out and he grabbed the walky-talky's aerial.

'Drop it!'

'No!' Maxwell yelled defiantly into Mr Vim's brick-red face. He couldn't lose the walky-talky, it was his only chance of ever finding Billy. 'I need it!'

'Stupid ... boy,' grunted Mr Vim. His wings beat furiously against the air and they rose slowly up the throat of the tower.

Below him the Long Man was grasping the radio tightly in both hands, shaking its body too and fro it chattered and screeched and ranted. Above him Mr Vim's face was drawn in pain as his huge wings battered the air with an enormous sound. Maxwell felt like a bone between two mad dogs. He felt Mr Vim's

hand growing slippery with sweat, felt his own fingers
go numb, his spine surely screeching as loud as the
Long Man's horrible voice. Any second he must fall,
any second the aerial would slip between his numb
fingers; and either he or Billy would be lost forever.

He looked up, sweat and blood pouring into
his eyes, and he saw the Long Men were scaling the
walls all around them, their dead black eyes and
vigorous white jaws following their painfully slow
progress.

'I ... I beg you, boy,' gasped Mr Vim, 'Drop it,
I beg you.'

Maxwell shook his head and closed his eyes.
No. He would never let go.

With a roar of effort Mr Vim wrenched them
into the air. Maxwell snapped his eyes open *hologram*
hologram HOLOGRAM he thought frantically as the
wall hurtled towards them and the Long Men scuttled
urgently forward with frantic screams.

They passed through the wall – Maxwell could
have sworn he heard it *pop!* – and suddenly they were
zooming along a well-lit glass corridor. 'Drop it *now!*'
Mr Vim bellowed, but Maxwell hung grimly on to the
slippery aerial.

The Long Man reached one long clawed hand
towards Maxwell's heart, hissing, '*Mamble!*'

Something flew under Maxwell's legs with a
flumph noise - and suddenly the Long Man was no
longer trying to grab Maxwell, it was screeching and
beating at its chest - where a large metallic spider had
appeared.

'My dog's got no nose,' said the robot spider in
a broad Yorkshire accent. Its eight pincer legs were
sunk deep into the Long Man's bloodless flesh. It
looked up at Maxwell with a round jolly face, and
winked. 'How does he smell? Awful!'

The robot spider chuckled rustily, and then exploded in a blaze of white light. The Long Man simply disintegrated, and Maxwell and Mr Vim were hurled through the air by the force of explosion.

Maxwell hit the ground and skidded along the long corridor. An enormous man jumped over him without even glancing down, a matted grey cape trailing behind him.

'How does he smell - awful!' chuckled the man. 'Those Spankies!'

'Come, boy,' Mr Vim held out his hand, Maxwell took it and Mr Vim pulled him to his feet.

'Who is that?' asked Maxwell. 'What was the spider thing?'

'That was a Spankie. A robotic bomb with a taste for awful jokes.' Mr Vim was pulling Maxwell along the corridor. 'And that man is--'

'Oh, Sid!'

Mr Vim turned towards the sound of the voice, and then back to Maxwell. 'Run,' he said.

Maxwell ran, barely able to keep his feet as Mr Vim, whose skinny legs were just as powerful as his muscular wings, dragged him along. Behind him Maxwell heard the booming, jolly voice of the man in the cape. 'Hello boys!' he yelled happily. Maxwell turned to see what was happening, he stumbled, and the next moment he literally was being dragged along by Mr Vim, whose speed didn't slacken at all.

The man in the cape still has his back to them, but Maxwell could now see that he had a thick matt of curly white hair that cascaded over his ridiculously wide shoulders. The man wasn't tall, he was no taller than Maxwell, but he was twice as broad as he should have been. He looked like a cartoon character that had been squashed by a falling piano.

The Long Men filled the corridor. They roared towards the odd little man in a writhing, screeching flood, as fast and as deadly as an oncoming train. But the white haired man didn't show any fear, he didn't even take a step back from this terrible sight. He was laughing.

'I love a reunion!' he chuckled as he raised what looked like a rusty cannon to his shoulder.

The cannon fired with a pneumatic *flumph* sound, and a bright Spankie flew out of the end. 'I just bought a wooden car,' said the Spankie as it spun towards the Long Men. 'Wooden wheels, wooden body, wooden engine . . . Wooden go!'

The end of the corridor exploded in a blinding flash of white light. Mr Vim's hand was wrenched from Maxwell's as he was hurled from his feet by the blast. A second later Mr Vim was pulling Maxwell to his feet. 'I said *RUN*!' he roared into Maxwell's face. Maxwell didn't need telling twice.

They ran towards the open doorway at the end of the glass corridor, a terrific rumbling crash following them. They reached the tower, and for a second Maxwell looked back and saw the thickset man belting towards him, this time not followed by the Long Men, but by a terrifying avalanche of snow, ice and glass. Maxwell saw that the man had a thick white beard, looked in fact like a demented Santa Claus - then Maxwell's feet were pulled off the ground as Mr Vim unfurled his wings and catapulted them both up the spiral staircase.

The doorway they had run through vanished as snow smashed through and the steel staircase Maxwell had been standing on shattered like it was made from toothpicks. They flew out of the door and fell onto the floor of a glass corridor mere seconds before the snow would have reached up and engulfed them.

Maxwell sat up. The entrance to the tower was choked with snow from doorstep to lintel and

spilled out into the corridor in a hissing triangle. Mr
Vim sat up beside him. 'Are you all right, Mr Vim?'
Maxwell asked.

'I may need stitches,' he replied, unfurling his
batwings and poking a finger into a small rip. 'Your
head is bleeding.'

'The Long Man scratched me,' Maxwell said.
'Mr Vim, your friend--'

'The cut will need to be disinfected,' Mr Vim
interrupted. He clambered to his feet, and put his
hand to his back with a groan. 'You have also lost
your glasses.'

'Mr Vim?' Maxwell pointed anxiously at the
blocked doorway. 'Shouldn't we help your friend?'

Mr Vim waved dismissively at the heap of
snow. 'He'll be fine.' Mr Vim arched his back, and his
spine let out a series of pops. 'I, on the other hand,
am in serious need of a good chiropractor.'

There was a muffled thud behind him.
Maxwell jumped to his feet and spun towards the
noise. A shaggy white head surfaced from the snow,
followed by two arms as thick as a normal man's
thighs, followed finally by a comically broad body.

'What spanking entertainment!' said the man,
turning on his back and pulling his legs free of the
snow. '"Wooden go"! Ha! Ha!'

'I'm so happy you enjoyed yourself,' said Mr
Vim sourly.

The huge man chuckled and shook himself like
a dog. When the snow was shaken off it revealed a
bright red costume and black boots. With his curling
white hair and beard the man could have been Father
Christmas. He reached back into the snow and pulled
something out – but it was no sack filled with
presents, it was the huge rusty canon Maxwell had
seen him fire at the Long Men.

The huge man seemed to notice Maxwell for the first time. He grinned with delight. 'Cyril Jugg's the name.' He held out a hand, Maxwell took it in his and his hand was immediately engulfed in a fist as big as a plucked chicken. 'Also know as Juggernaut,' Cyril Jugg said with a wink. 'And who might you be, young fella?'

Maxwell looked from Juggernaut, who was scratching his backside with a gun a horse would have strained to carry, to Mr Vim, who was fretfully poking at his torn bat wing.

'I'm Maxwell Jones – but *what* are you? Maxwell asked.

Juggernaut laughed uproariously at this rather rude question. He grabbed Mr Vim around his shoulders, and twirled the canon on one finger.

'We are the last of the Good Men,' he said. 'We are,' he paused dramatically, 'The A-Men!'

'You're the who?'

Chapter Fifteen: the Fortress

Juggernaut's face fell. 'You don't know who we are?'

Mr Vim shook Juggernaut's enormous arm off his shoulder. 'Of course he doesn't know who we are. He's from the Big Combination, you fool, the A-Men never even existed in his reality.'

'You've never heard of the A-Men?' Juggernaut looked like he was on the verge of tears.

'No,' Maxwell said, then seeing Juggernaut's crestfallen face, he added quickly: 'Sorry.'

'No need to be sorry, Mr Jones,' said Mr Vim. He took one last poke at his torn wing and then furled them closed with a sigh. 'I would have been more worried if you had know of us.'

'But he is one of us, Sid?' Juggernaut asked.

'Of course. He found his path, didn't he?' Mr Vim looked at Maxwell curiously. 'How exactly did you find your path to Vir, Mr Jones?' he asked.

'Well ... It's a bit complicated,' said Maxwell. 'I was, sort of, told to follow you by, erm ... by myself.'

To Maxwell's surprise Mr Vim nodded. 'A Conundrum,' and Juggernaut added, 'A time rift, of course.'

Maxwell stepped cautiously towards the two men. 'Mr Vim? Mr ... erm ... Jugg?'

'Just call me Juggernaut, wain,' he winked. 'Not even Sid here calls me *Mr* Jugg.'

'Juggernaut – Mr Vim? Where exactly are we?' Maxwell asked.

'Vir,' Mr Vim replied.

'The home of the Good Men,' Juggernaut added.

'Good Men?' Maxwell was puzzled. Nothing he had seen so far – with the possible exception of these two odd men – had struck him as particularly good. 'What where those things chasing me? The Long Men?'

'That is too complicated a story to be told now,' snapped Mr Vim. 'The longer we stay here the more chance there is that more Long Men will find us.'

Juggernaut nodded, chuckling indulgently. 'They're persistent little buggers, right enough,' he said.

'Yes. Quite.' Mr Vim swept his ratty cape over his shoulders. 'We'd best return to the Fortress. Come, Mr Jones.'

'Mr Vim? My friend Billy, he—'

'We can talk once we are safe,' Mr Vim interrupted. 'Right now ... What are you doing, Cyril?' he snapped, turning on Juggernaut.

Juggernaut was fiddling with his canon-gun, deftly pressing a sequence of mildewy buttons on its barrel. 'Uh?' he grunted, looking up at Mr Vim. 'I'm recalling Eric and Ernie, of course,' he said.

'I don't know why you don't just leave those rusty, senile buffoons buried in the snow,' said Mr Vim.

'Oh, I could never do that,' said Juggernaut amicably. He pressed another series of buttons and the gun began to give out a shrill beep. 'Won't take a second.'

'Oh, for goodness ...' Mr Vim turned to Maxwell. 'Come, Mr Jones. Jugg and his pets can catch us up.'

'Pets!' exclaimed Juggernaut, sounding offended. 'I'll have you know that Eric and Ernie have saved me, hair and hide, a hundred times over.'

'And they've almost blown us to the First Place a thousand times over!' Mr Vim replied hotly. 'They are dangerous, unstable—'

'Here they come!'

Mr. Vim wrapped his cloak around him and sighed heavily as Juggernaut stared grinning at the pile of snow blocking the entrance to the tower. As Maxwell watched two black spheres the size of marbles tumbled out of the snow and rolled across the ground into the waiting barrel of the canon.

'Black chips,' Juggernaut said to Maxwell, straightening and patting the huge gun affectionately. 'They store Eric and Ernie's personalities, and rebuild them inside the Big Bopper,' he indicated the canon. 'One of Archie's best inventions.'

'Can we go *now*?' Mr Vim sighed.

'Why of course. Lead the way Good Man Vim,' Juggernaut replied, holding out a hand and bowing.

Mr Vim swept off down the glass corridor. Maxwell began to follow him when a hand roughly the size of a frying pan closed on his shoulder.

'We've met before, haven't we wain?' asked Juggernaut, scrutinizing Maxwell closely. 'What be your name again – Jones, is it?'

Maxwell nodded. 'Maxwell Jones.'

'Maxwell?' Juggernaut scratched his chin thoughtfully, and released Maxwell's shoulder, indicating for him to follow Mr Vim.

They walked out of the corridor and down a flight of spiral stairs. Though Juggernaut barely fit through the door, Maxwell noticed he was actually an inch or two shorter than him. They crossed a large tower - so dark and ruined looking that Maxwell didn't recognise it at all - and up another staircase.

'I like your name, though, wain,' said Juggernaut as they entered another glass tunnel – and this one was familiar to Maxwell, though he couldn't quite think why. 'It's ripe with possibilities, you might say.'

'Possibilities?' asked Maxwell, confused.

'Your Good Man name, boy, your hero name, you ken? Mighty Max? Or Marvellous Max? No, no - too much like an acrobat for my liking.'

'I'm not a ...' he wanted to say superhero, because now he was almost positive that this was precisely what Juggernaut and Mr Vim were. Superheroes, right out of Andy Jones's old comic books - but instead he said, 'I'm not a Good Man, Mr Jugg.'

Juggernaut pointed to the cut the Long Man had made on Maxwell's forehead. 'Faced a thousand monsters and escaped with barely a scratch.' Juggernaut looked at Maxwell thoughtfully. 'You are the first boy - the first apprentice - to find his way to Vir in more than eleven years, Maxwell Jones.'

Juggernaut smiled, and Maxwell returned the smile - it was almost impossible not smile at that broad, happy face. But he could not bring himself to trust that easy smile. Was this Bella's long-lost father? If so, why had Bella been told he was dead? And what was he doing here? In a place where the stars that painted the bleak sky were nothing like the stars that twinkled above earth.

'Mr ... Juggernaut?' Maxwell began slowly. 'There's a girl I know at school, she--'

'We're here,' Juggernaut interrupted, and held open a door for Maxwell.

Maxwell looked at the door through which Mr Vim had just walked. 'This is the girl's toilet!' he exclaimed.

'Toilet?' Juggernaut ushered him through the door. 'This is the Fortress, wain.'

Maxwell walked through the door, expecting to see a line of stalls (and some part of him was horrified they might walk in on a girl, brushing her hair straightening her knickers, or doing whatever girls did in toilets) and discovered Juggernaut was right -

this wasn't the girl's toilets. But it didn't look much like a Fortress either.

'The girls toilets are through this door at the Watchmen Academy?' asked Juggernaut, realisation dawning on his face.

'Yes,' said Maxwell, looking around the room. 'This place looks a lot like my school,' he explained, but Juggernaut was already nodding.

'Of course it does. It is the same place,' said Juggernaut. 'Or rather, the Watchman Academy is the same place as this.'

The small room was packed with rotting cardboard boxes, newspapers and musty cloth bursting out of their sides. Everything was covered in a thick layer of dust, and the light that shone from the ceiling was pallid and lifeless.

'That damned *door* won't let me in!'

Juggernaut pushed past Maxwell, sending him stumbling into a pile of damp old socks without even a glance back at him. 'You've got to be nice to her, that's all,' said Juggernaut, placing his hand on the wall.

'*Nice* to *her*!' exclaimed Mr Vim. '*It* is a damned *machine!*'

'Good afternoon, Linda,' Juggernaut said in an obsequious voice, 'How are you feeling today?' Mr Vim threw up his hands in frustration, and sat down on a stack of old newspapers.

These two are crazy, thought Maxwell, and began to feel distinctly uneasy. Being on the other side of the universe in a building trapped under tons of ice and snow surrounded by cannibal monsters was one thing, but to be trapped, as Jamie Blip would put it, with two people who were obviously as fruity as nut cakes …

'Hello, Cyril,' whispered a breathy voice. 'Where have you been?'

Juggernaut chuckled. 'You know me, dear Linda, running around blowing things up.'

Maxwell looked around, but he couldn't spot where the voice was coming from. It seemed to come from everywhere at once, as if the very air had been given a voice.

'Boys will be boys,' whispered Linda, indulgently. 'I was beginning to think you'd forgotten me?'

'How could I ever forget you, sweet Linda?' said Juggernaut. 'You're on my mind night and day. Like the first dewy flower of spring.'

Mr Vim slapped his forehead in frustration and rage; Maxwell just goggled at the barrel-like shaggy man. Was Juggernaut chatting up a wall?

Linda the wall gave a girly giggle. 'Oh, Cyril, you silver tongued—'

'Will you just open the door you stupid damned machine!' roared Mr Vim.

'Access denied,' brayed a mechanical voice that sounded nothing at all like Linda.

'*Now* look what you've done!' said Juggernaut angrily. He turned to Maxwell. 'I've told him, I've told him a thousand times that the A.I.s are sensitive--'

'Sensitive! They're senile!' Mr Vim aimed a savage kick at the wall.

There was a loud burring rumble. A panel slid open in the wall, and a large machine gun poked out. 'Any attempt to gain forced entry will be met with lethal force,' said the mechanical voice.

'They are *sensitive*,' Juggernaut insisted, one wary eye on the machine gun that was slowly tracking its way between Mr Vim, Juggernaut and Maxwell. 'You talk to her, Maxwell.'

Maxwell looked at Juggernaut, then Mr Vim, then at the gun as its sites snapped towards him.

'Me? Talk?' said Maxwell. 'Talk to who?'

'To Linda, of course,' said Juggernaut.

'The wall?' asked Maxwell.

'The A.I.,' said Mr Vim. 'The machine that operates the door.'

'No, don't talk to the *machine*,' said Juggernaut slowly, as he glared at Mr Vim. 'Talk to *Linda*.'

Mr Vim threw up his hands and sat back down on his stack of newspapers, his head in his hands. 'Just place your hand there and talk,' said Juggernaut. Maxwell walked cautiously towards the wall, the large machine gun tracking his every step.

'Er ... hello? Linda?' Maxwell glanced at Juggernaut, who nodded his big head encouragingly. 'I'm ... erm, Maxwell. Hello.' Silence. The gun did not move. 'Pleased to meet you.'

There was no answer from the wall. If this was a door it was the strangest one Maxwell had ever seen. Apart from the alcove where the machine gun squatted there wasn't a single crack or line on the wall. It just felt like damp cement.

Mr Vim stood up suddenly, the machine gun whipped around towards him. He ignored it. 'Get out of the way, Mr Jones,' he said.

'What are you doing!' said Juggernaut, alarmed.

'I'm going to disable that gun and burn a hole in this damned door before the Long Men find us,' Mr Vim reached up to his visor.

'Maxwell Jones?'

Maxwell looked at the wall in surprise. 'Hello?' he said.

'Maxwell?' came the soft feminine voice of Linda. 'You don't mind if I call you Maxwell, do you?'

'No, of course not, erm ... Linda,' Maxwell replied, feeling slightly ridiculous.

'You're in the wrong place, Maxwell,' said Linda. 'According to my files you belong on Virporta Island, at the Watchmen Academy?'

'Yes, that's right,' said Maxwell.

'It's his first day, Linda,' Juggernaut said suddenly.

'A first day? Oh my, that is a very important occasion,' said the soft voice, and to Maxwell's considerable relief the machine gun withdrew into the wall, and the alcove closed, leaving not a mark to show it had ever been there. 'Are you enjoying your first day at university?'

'Well ...' Maxwell looked at Mr Vim and Juggernaut. Mr Vim was waving his hands up and down; Juggernaut was mouthing some word that might have been "charming". Maxwell turned back to the wall. 'It's a bit cold,' he said.

'You'd better come inside and warm up, then, Maxwell Jones,' said Linda. There was a loud creaking accompanied by a discordant buzzing, and the door slowly rose into the ceiling in front of Maxwell's eyes. 'I do hope you enjoy your first day.'

'Thank you, Linda,' said Maxwell. Mr Vim and Juggernaut dived under the rising wall. 'You're very kind,' he added.

'Thank *you*, Maxwell Jones,' Linda replied, delighted. 'What a polite young man,' she trilled.

Maxwell stepped forward. The wall slid down behind him and closed with a wheezing *clunk* - but Maxwell barely even noticed.

At the room's centre the floor was sunken and a number of plush (if a little threadbare) comfortable-looking sofas sat facing one another. Mr Vim was standing at the far end of the room looking at large silver screen which showed a cross sectional plan of the Watchmen University. The University, Maxwell could see from the plan, was exactly the same layout as the Watchmen Academy. Mr Vim touched a section of the screen that had turned black, it was, Maxwell realised, the tunnel Juggernaut had blown up. 'That's the third section we've lost in as many months,' Mr Vim sighed.

Juggernaut meanwhile had thrown off his ratty cloak and had produced a large sack from somewhere in its folds. He upended the sack into an alcove in the wall, which looked rather like the sort of sink you see in railway station toilets, and dozens of dirty potatoes tumbled out. A bell chimed in the alcove, and a list lit up on the wall above it:

Carrots
Chicken
Curried Goat
Apple
Mince Pie
Grapefruit
Cuthbert

Juggernaut slammed his fist against the display and "Cuthbert" blinked out and was replaced by "Custard". 'Chicken soup or mince pie and carrots, Maxwell? Or would you prefer a curry?'

But Maxwell didn't not reply, *could* not reply. All his words had stuck in his throat as he looked around the remarkable room.

It was difficult to tell just what size and shape the room was. The room appeared to change as Maxwell looked at it, the angles of the wall seemed to move and take different shapes in the corners of his eyes. The ceiling rose and fell and changed colour from black to blue to white to red. At the far end of the room, where Mr Vim stood scowling at his map, was an open doorway. When Maxwell first looked through it had opened into a long corridor that disappeared into its own horizon; the second time he looked through the door it led to a rising staircase; when he looked again the doorway opened onto a large circular room filled with Roman pillars, which ended at an arched courtyard overlooked by a still blue sky.

On the wall to Maxwell's left was the head of a creature that looked like a cross between an elephant and an octopus, with half a dozen tentacle-trunks, a large yellow beak, shiny white eyes and purple skin. The weird animal's head was at the centre of a number of glass shelves, which contained some very odd things. Maxwell recognised a few of these objects – there was a cricket ball, an old-fashioned dial telephone and a ten pound note. There were some object he thought he knew, though he had never seen them in his life – a mobile phone, a video recorder and a silver cappuccino machine. And there were an awful lot of things that could have been anything at all – a silver ball covered in shiny spikes that reminded him unpleasantly of the spiky beast that had jumped on Billy's head at the frozen river; an odd jelly-like shape that floated and pulsed above a black disc; a large metallic eye with a cat-like vertical pupil that blinked unnervingly at him.

'Maxwell Jones,' said Juggernaut. 'Didn't you hear me? What do you want to eat?'

'I'm not hungry,' said Maxwell. 'Juggernaut? Mr Vim? They both turned to him. 'I have to find Billy. My friend, Billy?'

'What precisely happened to Billy, Mr Jones?' asked Mr Vim.

'We were on a train, and the bottom, sort, fell out. Billy fell through, and the ground closed up over him.' Mr Vim and Juggernaut exchanged a frowning glance. 'He said he was in a sort of cavern--'

'Said?' interrupted Mr Vim. 'How did he say this if the earth had swallowed him?'

Maxwell raised the walky-talky. 'He called me on this,' he said.

'So that is why you hung on to that toy,' said Mr Vim.

'We have to find Billy,' Maxwell said urgently. 'He said the cavern was filled with potatoes and it had stalactites on the ceiling--'

'The silo,' said Juggernaut quietly.

'You know where it is? You can take me there, we can ...' but Juggernaut was shaking his head, and would not look up to meet Maxwell's eyes. He turned to Mr Vim. 'You can take me there, Mr Vim. We can find Billy with the walky-talky--'

'Your friend is dead,' said Mr Vim.

Maxwell stared at Mr Vim. Did he just say . . . He couldn't mean *Billy*! Billy couldn't possibly be--

'Dead,' said Juggernaut quietly, 'Or worse than dead.'

Maxwell turned to Juggernaut. Juggernaut lowered his head. 'Billy isn't dead,' said Maxwell. 'He *can't* be dead!'

'The silo is controlled by the Long Men,' said Mr Vim, his voice as flat and emotionless. 'Thousands of them nest there like rats. Even if your friend is alive--'

'Billy!' shouted Maxwell. 'His name is Billy!'

'--even if Billy is still alive,' Mr Vim continued stolidly, 'We would have no hope of rescuing him.'

'But ... but ... Billy has powers! He can--'

'Better that he did not,' said Juggernaut.

'But you don't understand!' said Maxwell, furious. 'He can make flame appear! He can shoot fire out of his hands!'

'The Long Men eat such powers,' said Mr Vim. Juggernaut nodded. 'They suck them from us like vampires.'

'We have lost almost all of our powers, wain,' said Juggernaut sadly.

'And when they have your powers they suck away your life force. They drink away your youth, your memories, your very mind. They take everything you are. And when they are finished, you are like them.'

'I escaped!' said Maxwell angrily.

Mr Vim shook his head. 'If we hadn't come along--'

'I would have escaped without you! They were afraid of me!' Maxwell was furious. Billy *couldn't* be dead. 'They looked at me and they stepped back. They were frightened of me!'

'No, Maxwell, they were not frightened of you.' Mr Vim put a hand on Maxwell's shoulder. 'They recognised you.'

'How could they recognise me! I've never been here before!'

'No,' said Mr Vim. 'But your father has.'

Chapter Sixteen: the history of the future

'Ten years ago Vir wasn't as it is today. It was a lush green land filled with cities and towns and villages and thousands of people. People like us. People with extraordinary abilities. We were called the Good Men. We came from many different Realms - from Earth, from Prezema, Telamore, Mab, a dozen other different worlds. We came here because Vir called to us, and here,' Mr Vim raised his hand and indicated all around him, 'at the Watchmen University we learnt to control our powers, and we were taught to use them for good.'

'I was the librarian,' said Mr Vim. 'Cyril was a professor of philosophy.'

Maxwell looked at them both with frank disbelief. He could just about imagine Mr Vim as a librarian, but Juggernaut - who was currently munching and slurping his way through his sixth bowl of curried goat, his whisker dripping with water and lumps of potato - Juggernaut was a *professor*?

Juggernaut grinned. 'He doesn't look much like a librarian, does he?' he said. Maxwell smiled despite himself and shook his head.

'Yes. That is one drawback with the Good Men,' said Mr Vim. 'After a while we simply don't look like ordinary people any more. So we disguise ourselves.'

'Sid pretended he was blind,' said Juggernaut.

Maxwell frowned, puzzled. 'You pretended you were a blind librarian?'

'Yes. What's wrong with that?' Mr Vim demanded, coldly. He glared at Juggernaut, who was sniggering into his curried goat. 'After all - who would suspect that a blind man working in a library in Fife was, in fact, Optar the all seeing?'

'Who would suspect that a blind man was, in fact, a librarian living in Fife,' said Juggernaut.

'How did you disguise yourself, Juggernaut?' Maxwell asked.

'He drank a lot of beer,' snapped Mr Vim. 'No one suspected for a second that he was anything more than a fat drunken yob. After ten pm he didn't even recognise himself.'

'Oh, they had a lovely student bar at Hull Polytechnic. Lovely beer they had there,' Juggernaut sighed. 'What I wouldn't give for a cold beer now.' He looked down sadly at his bowl of curried goat flavoured potato soup. 'It's a shame old Archie never got round to creating beer flavoured potatoes.'

'Archie?' said Maxwell. 'Who is Archie? I've heard that name before.'

'Where?' said Mr Vim. He leant forward, an urgent look on his face. 'Who mentioned that name to you?'

Maxwell paused before answering. The first time he had actually heard that name was when his mother had almost decapitated Maxwell with a meat cleaver in their kitchen in Spudmore Avenue. His mum had asked 'Is Archie with you?' and when Maxwell had asked who Archie was his mother had shouted, 'Conundrum', and Maxwell had come very close to an unexpected haircut.

'Mr Pugg said that name to you,' Maxwell said innocently. 'Outside that train station place?'

'You were there?' Mr Vim frowned and sat back 'I never saw you.'

'We were hiding behind a big pile of soil,' and he added, just so they wouldn't forget, 'My friend Billy and me.'

'Hmm?' Mr Vim seemed quite put out that he hadn't seen them hiding outside ZØØM. Maxwell didn't add that he had not seen them in the Black

Woods or outside the Black Monastery either. 'Archie is Dr Lambton Arcania. He was our greatest scientist,' said Mr Vim. 'He invented the trans-dimensional trains you rode on, and the Distribution Engine, which sorts the potatoes before they come here. He also created the technique which genetically modifies the potatoes into any flavour you could want.'

'And the Spankies,' said Juggernaut, reaching down and patting the huge cannon-gun which lay at his feet like a sleeping dog. 'And he invented your glasses, of course.'

'My glasses?'

'Your spectacles change your features,' said Mr Vim. 'You look quite different now, Mr Jones.'

'Where is Dr Arcania now?' asked Maxwell.

'Dead,' said Mr Vim.

'How did he--'

'Let me explain,' interrupted Mr Vim. 'Arcania invented many marvellous things. The Distribution Engine, the transdimensional train, your spectacles,' Mr Vim paused, and a slight smile curled at the ends of his thin lips. 'But Arcania considered invention and discovery of paramount importance, and the consequences of his inventions irrelevant. For Arcania the ends always justified the means. He invented things simply because it occurred to him to create them. He did not consider what effect they would have on our world – on all our worlds.'

'But I don't understand what this has to do with me and Billy,' Maxwell said.

Mr Vim held up his hand. 'There was a legend among all the people in the 101 known worlds of a great engine. This engine controls everything in our universe. It controls rainfall, how long stars live, whether a meteor will hit or miss your planet, whether your sausages will be burnt or done to a turn.'

Maxwell was sure all of this was an attempt to distract him from rescuing Billy, but nevertheless he leant forward, and asked: 'What's it called?'

'The Eternal Engine,' said Mr Vim.

'But . . . it's not real, is it? asked Maxwell. Mr Vim frowned. 'You said it was a legend. Doesn't that mean it's not real?'

'You'd be advised to take legends a trifle more seriously from now on, wain,' said Juggernaut ominously. 'You tend to avoid ending up dead that way.'

'But Mr Jones is quite right,' said Mr Vim, a small, tight smile on his face. 'What I should have said was, the Eternal Engine used to be a legend.' Mr Vim paused. 'Until Dr Arcania found it.'

Juggernaut nodded. 'It was old Archie's life's work, finding that divine machine. Not that we knew that, of course.'

'How could you not know?' asked. Maxwell.

'For every machine Arcania built for us, he built ten for himself. Self-evolving super computers, hyper-intelligent androids, time machines, trans-dimensional rockets that could travel from one end of the universe to the other like that,' Mr Vim clicked his fingers. 'And all these things he built with one goal in mind – to find the Eternal Engine.'

Time machines? Rockets that could cross the universe? Those things were impossible . . . weren't they? But in this strange world where men flew with their own wings and bombs cracked jokes was anything impossible?

'Why did Dr Arcania want to find the Eternal Engine?' Maxwell asked.

'Many years ago a young man came to Vir,' said Mr Vim. 'He was an astonishing boy, with remarkable powers, powers beyond anything any of the Good Men had ever encountered before. That boy's name was Titus Mamble.'

The Long Men kept saying that name, Mamble. The Nurgler had said his name was *Titus M*—before he was rudely interrupted by Billy turning into a human fireball. Titus Mamble?

'Titus came here the same way you did, Maxwell,' said Juggernaut. 'A Conundrum brought him to Vir.'

'What is a Conundrum?' asked Maxwell.

'A Conundrum is an event which is constructed out of the heart of space and time,' said Mr Vim. 'It is controlled by the very will of the universe.'

'And this Titus Mamble, he was brought here by a Conundrum?' asked Maxwell.

Mr. Vim nodded. 'You heard us call the world which you come from the Big Combination? Your world - all the known worlds, in fact - are not the same as they once were. The way the universe used to be is a time that we call the First Combination.

'Titus Mamble was born in the First Combination, when your world was a very different place. You study history at school, Mr Jones?'

'Yes, Professor Magister teaches us history,' Maxwell replied.

Both Juggernaut and Mr Vim smiled at the mention of Magister's name. 'I'm sure he teaches you very well,' said Mr Vim. 'Have you studied the second world war, Maxwell? The Nazis? In the First Combination, the reality in which Titus Mamble was born, the Nazi's won the Second World War. 'In Titus's time, the Nazi party, the Third Reich, ruled almost the entire world.'

'Titus grew up in a labour camp,' said Juggernaut quietly. 'His mother and father died there when he was only two years old. When the

Conundrum brought him to Vir he left his sister behind, and she died' Juggernaut sighed heavily. 'Poor Titus.'

'Titus graduated from the Watchmen University with the highest degree marks ever awarded,' said Mr Vim. He pointed to the wall beside the strange sink device that had cooked their meal. The wall, Maxwell saw, was filled with graduation photographs. 'And of course we asked him to join the A-Men.'

Maxwell stood up and walked over to the photographs on the wall. They showed lines of young men and women dressed in academic gowns. Under each photograph was a plaque - "Watchmen University, Graduating Year 2015" - and the names of the people in the pictures. 2015?

'Titus was a great hero,' said Mr Vim. 'He had astonishing powers. He was . . . Titus was a hero to *us*. Compared to Titus we were just like Normals, with no powers at all.'

The Long Men had called Maxwell "Mamble". Bartholemew Pugg had called Maxwell a "Mamble's boy". It all made sense, didn't it? Maxwell felt ill. He felt his whole body shaking uncontrollably as his eyes moved from photo to photo, helpless to stop himself.

'But as great as he was, Titus Mamble was only a boy. A boy who had seen his own mother and father die, and had abandoned his own sister to her death,' Mr Vim continued, though Maxwell barely heard. His eyes moved relentlessly from photo to photo, from face to face. All of the people in the photographs were young; some were human, and some of them obviously not human at all. He even saw a glum-looking chimpanzee dressed in a mortarboard and gown.

At last his eyes rested on one photograph. The plaque beneath it read: "Watchmen University,

Graduating Year 2037". A familiar face smiled back at him from the photograph.

'When Titus discovered that Dr Arcania had found the Eternal Engine . . .' Mr Vim sighed, a sound of terrible exhaustion rather than impatience. 'Juggernaut and I were here, in the Fortress, when it happened. If we hadn't been we would almost certainly have died too.'

'What happened?' said Maxwell.

'Vir froze,' said Juggernaut simply, 'instantly.'

'This entire planet was hurled ten thousand years into the past in the blink of an eye,' said Mr Vim. 'And everyone who was not inside the Watchman was frozen alive – or turned into a fossil where they stood.'

'What happened to Dr Arcania?' asked Maxwell.

'He was killed,' replied Mr Vim. But he didn't sound convinced.

'And Titus Mamble?'

'Obliterated,' said Mr Vim. 'Or so we believed.'

Mr Vim looked at Maxwell. He no doubt expected Maxwell to ask him what he meant by that – but of course Maxwell knew Titus Mamble hadn't been "obliterated" – Titus Mamble still lived, only now he was no Good Man, he wasn't even human any more. He was the Nurgler.

'What about the other people in the university?' asked Maxwell. 'You can't have been the only ones here when Mamble switched on the Eternal Engine?'

'No, we were not,' said Mr Vim. 'All the other survivors are now Long Men.'

'But why haven't you—'

'I think we have answered quite enough questions for one night, Mr Jones,' said Mr Vim curtly. 'I have had a very long, extremely unpleasant day, and if you don't mind I would like to go to bed,' Mr Vim got slowly to his feet.

'Can I ask you one more question, Mr Vim?'

Mr Vim sighed. 'What is it, Mr Jones?'

Maxwell turned back to the wall. In front of him was a photograph of a group of young men and women. This photograph had been taken a dozen or more years in the past, or perhaps thirty years in the future of a past that no longer existed. In the middle of the picture stood a man with a broad smile on his face. It was a face that Maxwell had seen before. He had first seen it in the yard of the Watchmen Academy just that morning, and later in a mirror in the basement of Mrs Trimm's general store.

'Titus Mamble,' said Maxwell, his voice shook, and each word seemed to have a weight his tongue could barely carry. He turned back to the two men. 'Titus Mamble is my father, isn't he?'

Juggernaut's mouth fell open on astonishment. His eyes met Mr Vim's and Juggernaut's mouth snapped closed and he lowered his eyes.

Mr Vim turned back to Maxwell. He was a statue again, his thin face as cold and emotionless as stone.

'Isn't he?' Maxwell insisted.

Mr Vim sighed. 'Yes,' he said, sounding almost relieved.

Chapter Seventeen: Billy

'There I am,' said Juggernaut, tapping one of the photos on the wall with a sausage-thick finger.

Maxwell looked closely at the curly-haired blond boy, whose head was the exact shape of a cube. If it were not for the familiar grin on his face and the fact that his body looked wider than it did tall, Maxwell would never have guessed it was a photograph of Cyril Jugg. The plaque beneath the picture read: "Watchmen University, Graduating Year 1989" which meant that in Maxwell's world the photograph was taken over twenty years ago, but in the topsy-turvy world of Vir Juggernaut had posed with his class almost fifty years ago.

Linda had dimmed the lights in the Fortress to give the illusion of night in this place that the sun never touched. Mr Vim had promised to return with Maxwell to Virporta in the morning, explaining that it would be almost impossible to find the buried entrance to Termination Central by night.

Juggernaut yawned. The big man looked exhausted, but he had been happy to point out some familiar faces from Virporta Island in the graduation photos. Maxwell had spotted a young Professor Magister; Miss Hummingbird (who looked exactly the same, though she had graduated only two years after Juggernaut) and Dr Silex (in her photograph she had looked thin and impossible young, and had been wearing a wicked grin – Maxwell wouldn't have recognised her in a million years).

'Juggernaut?' said Maxwell. 'What my—' Maxwell had almost said "my dad", but stopped himself. 'What Mamble did – it wasn't *that* bad, was it?'

Juggernaut's brow clenched together. 'Not that bad?' he grunted. 'Maxwell – what he did was terrible. *Terrible.*'

'But he changed the world for the better, didn't he?' Maxwell said urgently, desperate to believe what he said. 'Mr Vim said the earth was an awful place. There were labour camps, and children were slaves, and people died all the time.'

'And what about Vir, Maxwell Jones?' said Juggernaut softly. 'Thousands of people died. And what about Mab, or Chof? Those two worlds were destroyed in the Big Combination.' Juggernaut's voice remained soft, and Maxwell realised that Juggernaut was not angry; he was trying to explain something important. '*Billions* of people died on those worlds. Across all the worlds tens of billions of people ceased to exist, as if they had never been born.'

'I didn't think—' Maxwell began to say.

'And on your own world the Big Combination wiped hundreds of thousands of lives from reality. Parents who had lived in the First Combination were dead in the Big Combination, their children never born.' Juggernaut stared at the photograph of Titus Mamble. 'What Titus did was an awful thing, an abomination. An irresponsible, evil act.'

'But he didn't mean to hurt anyone, did he?' Maxwell insisted.

Juggernaut turned on Maxwell, and Maxwell took another step back. Juggernaut's face was as grim as Mr Vim's. 'Everything we do is important, Maxwell,' he said slowly. 'Every moment of our lives we affect history profoundly. We touch the universe and we change it. That is true of every boy and girl alive, but with us . . .' Juggernaut raised his thick stubby hand, and Maxwell shrank back. But Juggernaut smiled, and rested his hand on Maxwell's chest. 'We are the guardians of time and space and of the future. But mostly we are the guardians of people, the protectors and the champions of the innocent and the weak. What is in your heart isn't what makes you, Maxwell Jones, it is our actions that make us what we are.' Juggernaut lowered his hand. 'Titus wasn't evil, but his actions lead to terrible evil. He forgot the power of his hand. Do you understand?'

Maxwell nodded, though really he wasn't sure if he understood at all, and if he did, he was far from sure that Juggernaut was right.

'Good,' said Juggernaut, grinning. 'Time for bed now then, eh?' Juggernaut threw an arm around Maxwell's shoulder and led him through the door at the end of the room.

This part of the Fortress was, according to Mr Vim, an unstable focus-specific wormhole in the space-time continuum. What that meant was that this room existed in all the 101 worlds and shifted constantly between them. It currently looked like an overgrown jungle temple, and Juggernaut guided Maxwell to a moss-green door fixed into the ruined remains of a pyramid.

Juggernaut pulled open the door, and Maxwell looked inside, expecting to see a dark altar lit by flickering candles – but instead found himself looking into a white room with a small bed covered by a grey blanket, a nondescript wooden chair sitting beside the bed. 'It is basic, but the bed is clean,' Juggernaut smiled apologetically, 'Though not particularly comfortable.'

'Juggernaut?' said Maxwell, turning away from the room. 'I know a girl at school called Bella Jugg. You're not . . . ?'

'See you in the morning, Maxwell Jones,' said Juggernaut, guiding Maxwell (almost pushing him, in fact) through the moss coloured door.

'But I'm not—' The door slammed shut in Maxwell's face '... tired,' he finished.

Maxwell sat on the drab bed.

He had never felt less like sleeping in his entire life.

'. . . *Maxwell* . . .'

Maxwell sat up with a start, and looked blearily around. He stared at the blank white walls for several seconds before he remembered where he was. He had been lying on the bed staring up at the ceiling, his head filled with confused thoughts about Titus Mamble, when he must have drifted off to sleep.

'*Maxwell!*' whispered a voice closed by his ear. Maxwell turned blearily towards the voice, and saw the plastic walky-talky lying on the chair. 'Can you hear me?' crackled a voice from the little radio.

Maxwell grabbed the walky-talky. 'Billy?' he said in disbelief.

'Are you alone?' asked Billy. Maxwell frowned at the walky-talky. 'Maxwell? Can you still hear me?'

'I can hear you, Billy,' said Maxwell. Then, after a pause, he added: 'Yes, I'm alone.'

'Good. Look, I can't talk for long. You've got to come and get me. I'm trapped here—'

'Trapped where?' Maxwell asked urgently.

'Listen, Maxwell, just get out of the Fortress quickly, all right?' said Billy's voice on the radio. Maxwell thought he heard a strange noise beneath Billy's voice, like a heartbeat, or perhaps the throbbing sound you heard in your ears underwater. 'Come to the Hall Tower. Radio me when you get there.'

Maxwell looked at the radio. The Hall Tower? Finding his way there wouldn't be a problem, assuming the Watchmen University's layout was the same as the Watchmen Academy's ... but why was Billy there? Had the Long Men trapped him there?

'Billy, there are some . . . some people here who can help us,' he said to the radio. 'I'll bring them. They're called—'

'Don't bring Vim and Jugg!' hissed the voice on the radio urgently. 'Come alone and come *now*, Maxwell!'

'Billy, you don't understand! They're friends. They can help us!'

'No,' said the voice on the radio flatly. 'They are not your friends, Maxwell. They are not what they seem to be.' The noise, a low, dull throb, grew louder and louder behind Billy's voice, sounding now more than ever like an agitated, enormous heart. 'Come quickly, and come alone. Come *now*, Maxwell!'

The radio went dead.

'Billy?' Maxwell pressed the walky-talky speak button again and again. 'Billy?' But there was no answer.

Maxwell pushed open the door and found himself no longer in the jungle ruin, but stepping from beneath an arched entryway. Mist floated across the floor of a large courtyard and curled around bone white pillars, which reached brokenly towards an infinite, black, starless sky.

Maxwell liked Juggernaut, he liked him a lot, and he found he liked Mr Vim too – after all Mr Vim *had* saved his life – but he didn't trust either of them. If they had not lied to him then they most definitely had not told him the whole truth, Maxwell was sure of that.

And, he thought, what was so bad about what Titus Mamble had done? If Mamble hadn't changed history Maxwell was sure that he would have ended up in a labour camp, probably alongside his mum and Daisy, Jamie, Bella, Billy and everyone else on Virporta Island.

Judge people by their actions, not what was in their hearts. Well – okay. Titus Mamble - his dad – his heart had been set on saving his family, and his actions had saved the world from a terrible future.

So Maxwell did not wake Juggernaut or Mr Vim, and he did not leave them a message telling them where he was going and why, and when Linda asked him where he was going he simply replied, 'For a walk.'

'It's really a very bad idea to go walking around the university at night, Maxwell,' said Linda. 'Why don't you have a little sleep and then you can go out with Cyril and ... and *that man* – tomorrow?'

It hadn't occurred to Maxwell that Linda wouldn't open the door, but of course Linda's job was keeping people in, just as much as it was keeping the Long Men out. Then Maxwell remembered what Juggernaut had said to Mr Vim - *Don't talk to the* machine. *Talk to* Linda.

'Linda?' said Maxwell quietly.

'Yes, Maxwell?'

'I really need to go out. You see ... It's a bit embarrassing . . .' Maxwell paused, biting his lip. He could hear the seconds ticking by on his watch, and the ticking seemed to say: *'Billy's in trouble – Billy's hurt – you're already too late.'*

'Embarrassing?' said Linda curiously. Did she – it - even know what that meant?

'I picked you some flowers on Virporta Island,' said Maxwell. He felt a hot flush of guilt – but that was ridiculous. Why should he feel guilty about lying to a machine?

'Flowers!' trilled Linda. 'Flowers for me? Oh, Maxwell, how kind! It's been years since I smelled flowers! But, really, I can't let you—'

'Mr Vim made me leave them behind,' Maxwell interrupted her quickly. 'I didn't see any harm in bringing them ...' Maxwell was surprised, and a little alarmed, by how easily the lies flew from his lips. '... But Mr Vim said robots don't need flowers.'

'*Robots!*' hissed Linda. 'Oh, I'm a *robot*, am I?'

The wall rose instantly.

'Thank you, Linda,' Maxwell said, amazed at how easy it had been. 'I'll be back as soon—'

'I'll be keeping a close eye on you, Maxwell,' Linda interrupted him coldly, and Maxwell could hear a trace of the mechanical heart behind that deceptively human voice. 'I'll light the corridors. Keep away from the red lights and follow the green. Do you understand?'

'Yes, yes, of course,' Maxwell said quickly, stepping into the storage room before Linda could change her mind and close the door again.

'And Maxwell?' Linda purred. 'Say hello to Archie for me.'

Maxwell turned back to the Fortress. 'Archie?' he asked, confused. But he was looking at a dirty wall.

Maxwell walked quickly, pulsing green light accompanying him throughout his journey.

Maxwell saw no sign of the Long Men, and after a while – though he still glanced over his shoulder and moved quickly past every black doorway – he was pretty sure he wasn't going to see them. Open doors led to rooms which Maxwell knew from his own world – Dr Silex's maths class, the common room, Lance's broom closet – but all the rooms were empty and desolate. Snow and ice groaned and he tried not to think of the tons and tons and snow piled above his head.

Maxwell turned a corner, and the light around him turned slowly from green to red. As he stepped into the Hall Tower it was like stepping into a blood-filled artery. Red light lit the tower to its massive ceiling, clinging to the crushed and twisted remains of the metal stairwell like freshly spilled blood.

There were no Long Men in the Hall Tower. The red walls were bare, and all that was on the floor was the stairwell scrap heap and his broken and abandoned torch.

'Maxwell?'

Maxwell pulled his radio from his belt. 'Billy? Is that you?'

Maxwell expected a typical sarcastic reply, but Billy just said: 'Go to the back of the tower.' Maxwell did as he was told. 'And be quiet,' Billy said. 'There are creatures here, monsters, they're called—'

'The Long Men,' Maxwell finished for him. 'I think they've all gone, Billy.'

'No. They're hiding. Be careful, Maxwell,' Billy said.

Maxwell? From the second Billy had met him he had called him 'Max' or 'mate' or 'me old China plate'. Why did Billy keep calling him Maxwell? ... Unless...

'Unless you aren't Billy at all,' Maxwell whispered to the radio.

'There's a door ahead of you,' said the voice on the radio. It was a gargly, stuffed voice, just like the gleeful voice of the Nurgler, now he listened to it properly. 'Go through it quickly.'

Maxwell turned back . . . and saw a thin shadow flicker across the petrified doorway.

The Long Men.

'Maxwell?' said the voice on the radio. 'Maxwell, can you hear me? You have to come quickly. You have to--'

Maxwell threw the radio to the floor. The cheap plastic walky-talky exploded like a bomb.

In the silence that followed a screeching buzz rose all around Maxwell, and from the rubble and debris of the stairwell white lights appeared. Spinning lights full of moving black things.

The Long Men. Hundreds of them. All around him.

Maxwell backed slowly across the Hall Tower, knowing that he had been trapped. There was no door here, no exit, he had been tricked.

So Maxwell was rather surprised that when he finally backed up against the wall, watching the horrible illuminations come on all around him, the wall promptly sprang open, spilling him backwards, and swung efficiently closed behind him.

He was in a long, low area that was filled with pipes that hung from the ceiling and spread across the floor. Maxwell knew where he was, he had been here before - or rather, he had been to this same place on his own world. Lance the caretaker had once taken a science class when Professor Magister had been off on one of his research trips, and (much to Bartholemew Pugg's scorn) had decided to show them some practical engineering.

Maxwell was under the Watchmen's swimming pool. But, Maxwell thought, even the laid back Lance would be upset by the state of the pool room in this world. Those pipes that weren't green with mould were brown with rust, and they all dripped onto the floor, which was ankle deep in grey water.

Then Maxwell realised what the sound he had heard on the walky-talky had been - it was the throbbing sound of the water being pumped into the pool above.

He walked through the room picking his way between dripping, smelly pipes. At the far end he came to a flight of steps covered in black mould.

On the wall beside the steps someone had scratched these words:

MY NAME IS

I AM
MY NAME
I
IMY
MNYM

'Well,' Maxwell murmured, remembering Billy's words as they faced the Nurgler on the frozen river, 'That's not a good sign.'

The Watchmen University's swimming pool was the same size as the Watchmen Academy's, but what had been magnificent in Maxwell's world was mouldering here. The walls and ceiling were black and peeling, reminding Maxwell forcefully of the Black Monastery. The poolside was green and slick with mould, and the water itself was a sticky, polluted black. And it was very polluted, Maxwell saw; newspapers floated in the water beside broken dolls, smashed chairs, lamp stands and chipped cups and plates. It should have been impossible for these things to float - but even larger things floated in the brackish water, impossible or not. Maxwell saw a snooker table, and a street sign, reading: "Melmoth Avenue".

Then Maxwell saw something else floating in the water - something that made his heart jump and his breath escape him in an involuntary shout of horror.

Billy was floating face up just below the surface of the filthy pool, the water scurrying over his open eyes.

Maxwell fell to his knees, and reached out towards Billy. The water shot upwards like a tentacle, wrapped around his wrist, and dragged him forward.

Maxwell felt his knees slide across the mossy poolside and screamed. The water was going to pull him under, that tentacle so much like the Nurgler's was dragging him into its depths. He looked down and he saw a face looking back at him. Not his reflection, but the face of a man, formed entirely from water.

The water around his wrist suddenly disintegrated and fell back into the pool with a *splat!*, and Maxwell fell back.

A filthy black column of water rose from the surface of the pool. It ran and squirmed and twisted and quivered - and suddenly the column wasn't a column at all, it was the shape of a man.

'Hello, Maxwell,' said the man, black water sliding down his cheeks like slugs as he grinned. 'So nice to have you back where you belong.'

Chapter Eighteen: the return of the magnificent two

The man stepped out of the pool, his body shimmering and rippling, and he stood in front of Maxwell. Maxwell could see that he seemed to be wearing a suit and tie, and a long cape just like the ones Juggernaut and Mr Vim wore – except that his, of course, was formed from the pool's dirty water. Every part of him was made of water, even the buttons on his shirt and the curls of his long, shaggy hair.

'Let me help you up, Maxwell,' he said, holding out a dripping black hand.

Maxwell cringed. 'Don't touch me!' he cried. He got quickly to his feet, not taking his eyes off the man for a moment. 'Who – What are you?'

'I thought you knew,' the man replied with a cheery, slimy smile. 'I am Titus Mamble.'

'No you're not!' Maxwell said. 'Titus Mamble is a monster!'

'What an unpleasant thing to say!'

'No, a *real* monster,' every impulse Maxwell possessed was screaming at him to run from this filthy creature, but the sight of Billy floating in the dirty water kept Maxwell's feet rooted to the spot. 'A monster called the Nurgler.'

'Oh! I see what you mean, please excuse me,' said the creature amiably. 'You are quite correct, Maxwell, the Nurgler is Titus Mamble . . . but so am I. I am Titus Mamble's mind, the Nurgler is all that remains of Titus Mamble's body. We were once joined in one great whole.' Maxwell started – those were almost the same words the Nurgler had used. 'There was an accident, an explosion, and I was separated—'

'When you switched on the Eternal Engine,' Maxwell interrupted.

'Oh, you know about that?' asked Mamble. 'Well, I didn't precisely "switch on" the—'

'When you destroyed all those worlds and killed all those people!'

'Killed? I killed?' the water creature looked amazed. 'I have never killed anyone. Destroyed worlds? Which world am I meant to have destroyed?'

'Mab,' said Maxwell, 'and . . . and . . .' he struggled to remember the name Juggernaut had told him. 'Chof!' he remembered suddenly.

'Mab? How could I have destroyed Mab? By your own admission you have been there!' Mamble gave an astonished laugh, and shook his head, black water spraying everywhere. 'Mab is where the Nurgler lives, hidden in the frozen mountains of Shamble. And Chof? Chof was destroyed by the Boshers, everyone knows that!' The creature sighed. 'I'm afraid you have been deceived, Maxwell.'

'You switched on the Eternal Engine! You killed millions – *billions* – of people!' shouted Maxwell. 'You're the liar!'

'I have already told you that I did not switch on the Eternal Engine,' said Mamble patiently. 'It was destroyed by a Spankie. No one switched it on. If you want to blame anyone for what has happened then you should blame Lambton Arcania. Dr Arcania stole the Eternal Engine, and, when I tried to return it to its rightful owner, Dr Arcania sent one of his smart bombs to destroy it.'

Mamble held out his hands and smiled at Maxwell. Maxwell took a step back. Was this true? Any of it? Was anyone telling the truth?

'Billy,' said Maxwell. 'You hurt Billy!'

'I saved Billy,' said Mamble. 'I fought off the Long Men as they were about to kill your friend. I brought him here to heal.'

'In that?' Maxwell exclaimed. 'That water's filthy! It's full of rubbish!'

'It isn't water, Maxwell, and it isn't filthy. Those are my memories you see floating there. These are the things which remind of what I once was,' said Mamble quietly, lowering his rippling head. 'Incidentally,' his head darted up, and Mamble grinned. 'You knew it wasn't Billy on the walky-talky, didn't you, Maxwell? How did you know that?'

'I wasn't sure at first . . .'

'But you worked it out, didn't you?' Mamble winked. 'I've always considered myself an excellent mimic, and I'm intrigued to know how you . . .' Mamble laughed, and waved a watery hand in front of his face '. . . how you saw through me.'

Maxwell smiled despite himself. 'It was just the things you said. You called me "Maxwell", and Billy never calls me that, he always calls me "Max" or "mate". And Billy says sort of funny things like, "cor blimey O'Riley, and "cop a load of this" - stuff like that.'

'I see you're a very observant young man,' said the Mamble. 'Well done you.'

Maxwell smiled uncertainly. He wasn't quite sure what to make of Titus Mamble - if this dirty stack of water in the shape of a man really was Titus Mamble. If this was Titus Mamble then, according to Mr Vim, Maxwell was talking to his own father, so why hadn't this creature mentioned that?

Maxwell heard a distant sound - a shot, or perhaps even a muffled explosion. Mamble glanced towards the steps leading down to the pool room, and then turned back to Maxwell. You should go now,' he said. 'The Long Men fear me, but even that won't keep them back for very long, and they seem intent on capturing you.'

'What about Billy?' asked Maxwell.

'Billy should be fine now,' said Mamble, but when Maxwell stepped towards the pool Mamble darted forward. 'No! Wait! Don't touch the water!'

'Why?' asked Maxwell. 'You said it was safe?'

'It is,' the Mamble said quickly. 'I'll help him out. It will be much easier.' The Mamble walked to the pool and stepped in. The man-shape turned back into a formless column of liquid again, and rejoined the dirty not-water.

There was another heavy sound. Flakes of paint drifted down from the ceiling like black snow.

A shape exploded from the middle of the pool and catapulted through the air followed by a comet tail of water and landed in front of Maxwell.

'All right, me old mate?' said Billy, shaking water off his clothes. 'How's your belly for spots?'

'Billy!' Maxwell cried. He grabbed his friend and shook him. 'Billy! You're alive!'

'I bleeding well won't be much longer if you don't stop shaking me,' Billy replied with a grin as he removed Maxwell's hands from his jacket.

Maxwell noticed that Billy's touch was cold. 'Mamble didn't hurt you?'

'Hurt me? He saved my flipping life, mate,' Billy replied. 'Two more minutes and those Long Men would have been having Billy and chips for tea! We'd better get our skates on, Max. I've seen enough of those Long Men to last me ten lifetimes and no mistake.'

'Me too,' Maxwell agreed - but he paused, and looked again at the pool. The water - or whatever this liquid was - was completely still, and all of the objects in it had sunk, or perhaps vanished. 'Where's Mamble gone?' he said.

'Mamble? Titus Mamble is here?' Maxwell turned to see Juggernaut striding towards them, his large rusty cannon in his hands again, a grim expression on his face. 'Were is he, Maxwell Jones?' he demanded.

'He's in the pool,' said Billy. Juggernaut swung towards him, raising his massive cannon. Billy took a step back.

'Who is this boy?' growled Juggernaut.

'This is my friend, Billy,' said Maxwell.'

'Billy ...' Juggernaut slowly lowered his gun. He glared suspiciously at Billy and Billy smiled weakly back at him. 'Come, boys, we must go,' Juggernaut said suddenly, turning back towards the steps. 'Sid's in trouble,' and he began striding away from the pool.

'What's his problem?' Billy whispered to Maxwell, glaring at Juggernaut's back. 'I'll knock his block off!'

'Juggernaut's okay. He's just--'

'Maxwell Jones! Billy Barker! To me! NOW!' roared Juggernaut. Maxwell and Billy exchanged a frightened look, and ran over to Juggernaut. 'Down the steps, quickly!' the big man barked as they approached him.

Billy started towards the steps, but Maxwell didn't move. 'Juggernaut, what's going on?' he demanded.

'I told you to wait until morning!' Juggernaut spat. He looked furious, looked, in fact, like he wanted to turn his cannon on Maxwell. 'Now do what you're told and get down those stairs, boy, before you cause any more trouble!'

Maxwell looked into Juggernaut's angry eyes, but he did not move, though Billy was now tugging anxiously at his sleeve. 'Juggernaut, I had to help Billy. I never meant—'

'It's what you do that matters, not what you mean to do.' Juggernaut raised the huge gun in both of his hands. 'But now I see that words are not enough for you, and I must show you the consequences of good intentions.'

The cannon jumped in Juggernaut's hands. With a *flumph* a bright Spankie flew into the air.

'I used to be a werewolf!' the little robot spider cried as it spun towards the ceiling. 'But I'm all right NOOOOWWW!'

The Spankie exploded with a massive concussive blast. Blackened masonry fell, followed instantly by a roaring avalanche of ice and snow that crashed into the pool. A second later the ceiling began to collapse in great chunks, snow and ice smashing into the churning black water of Mamble's pool.

Juggernaut grabbed Maxwell and hurled him down the steps after Billy. Maxwell hit the ankle-deep water at the bottom running, and Juggernaut and Billy were running at his side within seconds. All three of them ducked and weaved and jumped through the creaking, shuddering pipes of the pool room, whilst above them the ceiling of the Watchmen University's pool was obliterated by tons of snow and ice with a sound like the end of the world.

Maxwell caught up with Billy, and to his amazement he saw that Billy was actually laughing.

'I bet we don't get invited back to his next pool party,' gasped Billy, unable to control his laughter. Maxwell started laughing too. Behind him he could hear the snow smashing its way down the steps, but he couldn't stop laughing.

They ran towards the door, but before they reached it Juggernaut flew past them. He hit the door head first, square in its centre, and the door flew off its hinges. Maxwell ran through the door after him, and skidded to a stop in front of Mr Vim.

'Hello again, Mr Jones,' Mr. Vim said calmly. 'And Mr Barker. How are you, Billy?'

Neither Maxwell nor Billy replied, they were looking around in amazement at a scene of devastation. The Hall Tower was littered with the burning remains of dozens of Long Men. Mr Vim stood serenely in the middle of this smoking carnage, his hands clasped behind his back.

Juggernaut staggered to his feet rubbing his grey head. 'I'm getting too old for battering down doors with my bonce,' he groaned.

'Aren't we all,' said Mr Vim. 'I think we've outstayed our welcome here, Mr Jones, wouldn't you agree?' Mr Vim unfurled his batwings and held out a hand to Maxwell. 'I'll take you, Mr Jones, Cyril can take Mr Barker. Cyril can't fly, of course, but he's very good--'

Something hit the ground with a heavy thud. Mr Vim spun around as a Long Man uncurled from the floor, grinning fire. There was a second *thud*, followed by another and another. Maxwell looked up and saw that it was raining Long Men. They fell from the ceiling in curled grey balls, bounced, and then sprang to their feet like evil Jack-In-The-Boxes.

Mr Vim grabbed Maxwell's arm. 'GO!' he shouted to Juggernaut, and once again Maxwell was wrenched into the air of the Hall Tower - but Maxwell had barely left the ground before he crashed back down again. He struggled to his feet and saw Mr Vim fighting off three Long Men; one of his bat-like wings had been torn to shreds.

Maxwell launched himself at the closest Long Man. The creature moved with blurring speed, and before he knew what had happened the Long Man was on top of Maxwell, its burning jaws inches from his face.

'*Mamble go*!' it hissed furiously. '*Boy stay!*' Its razor-sharp claws dug into Maxwell's shoulders - and then it vanished. Juggernaut hurled the Long Man over his shoulder with one hand.

'COME ON!' Juggernaut roared, pulling Maxwell to his feet.

'Mr Vim!' yelled Maxwell, but he couldn't even see Mr Vim any more, just a fuming tangle of biting, clawing Long Men where Mr Vim had been standing.

'It's too late for Sid,' said Juggernaut. 'Quickly, boy, grab hold--'

'No!' screamed Maxwell. 'He saved my life! I won't leave him! I won't!'

Juggernaut grabbed Maxwell by the shoulder. Maxwell tried to pull away, but Juggernaut pulled him close to his enormous flat face.

'It's already too late,' said Juggernaut quietly. 'Now put you arms around my neck before it's too late for us too.'

Maxwell looked at Juggernaut, dumbfounded. How could he leave his best friend to die?

'Max,' said Billy, putting his hand on Maxwell's arm, and whispering into Maxwell's ear. 'I'm frightened, mate.'

Maxwell glared at his friend's terrified face. He wanted to yell at Billy that *he* had come to rescue *him*. *Maxwell* had risked his life for Billy, and now Billy wanted to leave Mr Vim to die?

Then Juggernaut leant forward, and whispered into Maxwell's other ear. 'The Conundrum.'

Maxwell looked at Juggernaut's sad face with a start. Was this why Billy didn't return to Virporta? Was Billy about to die because Maxwell stopped them escaping?

Maxwell shrugged off Juggernaut's hand and threw his arms around the old man's massive neck. 'I hate you for this,' he whispered

'Just hold on tight,' he grunted.

Juggernaut ran at the wall, and Maxwell and Billy, clinging around his neck, ran with him. Maxwell heard a final *crump!* of falling masonry and the roar of flood water, and then Juggernaut launched himself at the wall.

Maxwell and Billy screamed in unison as they flew up the tower - then they hit the wall and Juggernaut's sausage-thick fingers sank into the stone up to his knuckles.

Juggernaut began to climb rapidly, his fingers sinking into the stone like it was made of plasticine. Maxwell looked down just as the doorway from the pool room exploded outwards in a tidal wave of black water. The water filled the Hall Tower in a roaring black deluge, swallowing the Long Men and everything else in its path. The waters began to rise quickly towards them . . . *too* quickly - with a start Maxwell realised Juggernaut had stopped climbing.

'Damn,' Juggernaut whispered, and Maxwell looked up.

Long Men crawled rapidly down towards them, their glowing mouths buzzing in triumph.

Chapter Nineteen: Arcania's mountain

Maxwell tore his eyes away from the scuttling Long Men. Below him the black waters were rising higher and higher. He imagined the Long Men circling below their feet like sharks, ready to launch forward as they fell.

Launch?

'We're not going down without a fight, boys,' said Juggernaut. He reached down and unhooked the cannon from his belt. Letters blinked on the complex instrument panel above the trigger. They read: ERNIE.

'Juggernaut!' said Maxwell. 'We have to jump!'

Juggernaut shook his head. 'It's useless, Maxwell.'

'Juggernaut, listen!' If you fire Ernie now, we're all dead. At least my way we have a chance. Please, do as I say – jump!'

'I won't die running from my enemies,' and he turned back to the Long Men.

Maxwell looked at Billy, expecting to see terror in his face . . . But Billy was grinning. He winked at Maxwell. 'Let's take Mr Jugg here for a dip, eh Max?' he whispered, and he raised his legs and began to push himself away from the wall.

Juggernaut, now only holding on by one hand, almost dropped the cannon. 'What are you DOING!' he roared.

'Causing more trouble,' said Maxwell. He placed his feet on the stone wall and pushed with all his strength.

Juggernaut bellowed with rage, but short of throwing the boys off his back to their certain deaths, there was little he could do to stop them. The first of the Long Men reached out a clawed hand towards

Maxwell, its filthy fingers moving closer, closer – then falling away.

'You've killed us!' howled Juggernaut, clawing at the suddenly empty air.

'Fire your gun!' Maxwell yelled, and when Juggernaut raised it towards the Long Men, he shouted: 'Not at them! At the water! FIRE AT THE WATER!'

Juggernaut turned in mid-air, and suddenly they were falling head first, hurtling down the side of the tower towards the churning black waters.

'BANZAI!' roared Juggernaut, and he pulled the trigger.

The end of the cannon ignited like a rocket at take off – and they did take off – they were launched back up the tower by the massive ignition kick of the firing gun. Juggernaut dropped the canon, reached up, and his fingers sank into the stone of the Hall Tower.

Ernie whirled downwards. 'What goes red-black, red-black, red?' the Spankie cackled – but he never delivered the punchline. The black waters engulfed him.

'That's quick thinking, Maxwell Jones,' gasped Juggernaut, looking down. 'It was a quite insane thing to do, but nevertheless, quick thinking.'

'What a ride!' yelled Billy, grinning wildly. 'Let's do it again!'

Maxwell looked down. They were above the Long Men, but not for long. The creatures had already turned and were scurrying up the walls towards them.

'I admire your spirit, Billy Barker, but I don't think we're safe quite--'

Juggernaut's words were drowned out by a huge explosion as the Spankie ignited. Maxwell saw a great plume of fire rise under the black waters. Below them cracks began to race up the tower. A huge slab of wall the Long Men had been climbing up peeled away from the tower and tumbled downwards. Ice and snow roared through the hole it left behind. The tower began to shake itself apart.

Juggernaut began scaling the tower again, but now his movements were slowing as his fingers scrabbled to dig into stone that was cracking and crumbling beneath them.

'Climb over my head!' gasped Juggernaut. Maxwell looked up and saw Billy was already boosting himself onto Juggernaut's shoulders and grabbing the edge of the remains of the metal stairwell.

'It's only a few feet, Juggernaut!' Maxwell yelled over the crash and roar of the collapsing tower. 'You can make it!'

'I can if you get off my bloody back!' Juggernaut shouted back.

Maxwell pulled himself onto Juggernaut's shoulders. Billy grabbed his hand as he reached up, and pulled him onto the metal platform.

'Grab him!' Maxwell yelled.

'We can't--'

'I said GRAB HIM!' Maxwell shouted. Juggernaut was clinging to the wall with his eyes closed. Below the tower was splintering as it whipped from side to side like a snake. 'Take our hands!' Maxwell yelled.

Juggernaut raised his head, and smiled wearily. 'It's too late for me, boys—'

'Like bugger it is!' yelled Billy. 'Remember you are a Good Man and do as your comrade commands!'

Juggernaut's eyes cleared, the exhaustion falling from his face. He grabbed Maxwell's hand, and then Billy's, and swung away from the crumbling wall.

Maxwell felt his arm lock in sudden agony, and he grabbed Juggernaut's hand with both of his own, and saw Billy do the same, his face twisted with pain. The platform screeched and buckled under them.

'Pull!' gasped Billy.

'I ... can't!' Maxwell hissed, 'Too ... heavy!'

'Drop him then!' Billy snapped back.

Maxwell pulled with every last ounce of strength he had. He closed his eyes and ignored the buckling platform and the enormous noise of the falling tower and the pain and he *pulled*.

'Thank you Maxwell Jones and Billy Barker,' gasped Juggernaut, climbing unsteadily to his feet.

'You weigh more than an elephant's toilet!' exclaimed Billy. 'What the bleeding Nora do you eat?'

'Cheeky young boys,' Juggernaut growled, but he winked at Maxwell as he said it. 'Now, lads, I think we should take our leave.'

Without another word Juggernaut grabbed Maxwell and Billy and shoved them under his arms as if they were two pieces of luggage. He ran to the exit. The second he stepped over the threshold the remains of the staircase tore from the wall, and vanished into the thrashing depths of the Hall Tower. Juggernaut ran across the deserted room, jumped through the broken wall, and they landed in a sprawl on the snow packed ground.

Maxwell untangled himself from Juggernaut's thick arm and sat up.

The green coconut crest of the Hall Tower sank slowly into the snow. It sank silently beneath the purple light of Vir's largest moon, puffs of snow squirting into the air, and then drifting away. In just a few seconds it was gone, with no sign that it had ever been there.

They walked through the moons lit night. Juggernaut had taken off his matted cape and given it to Billy and Maxwell to huddle together under, and in his red suit and black boots he looked more than ever like Father Christmas.

Despite the numbing cold, and for the fact that Maxwell expected a Long Man to jump out from behind every heap of snow they passed, it was the most awesome walk of Maxwell's life. Vir's many moons hung in dozens of colours above their heads, indeed it seemed to Maxwell that every time he looked up a new gold or red or green satellite had been added to the sky. The sky itself, with its constellations that no other boy on earth had ever seen, was breathtaking.

'I used to live there,' said Juggernaut, pointing to a bulbous red moon that hung just above the horizon. 'In a city called Pootonville. I taught elementary interspecies philosophy at Pooton University.' He lowered his hand, and sighed. 'Gone now, of course.'

'The Big Combination?' Juggernaut nodded sadly. 'What happened to the people in Pootonville?'

'They were blasted into space,' Juggernaut replied. 'One minute the city was there, the next . . .' Juggernaut clapped his hands together, making Maxwell jump. 'Gone.'

The ground became rocky underfoot, and the endless white snow was now occasionally punctured by black stones. The stone looked fused, as if thrown from the mouth of a volcano. It was obvious they were not returning to Termination Central, and Maxwell couldn't pretend he wasn't happy about that. He would be very happy never to walk through that dead place again.

'He was happy at the end, Maxwell Jones.' Maxwell looked around at Juggernaut, and saw his large eyes looking back at him piercingly. 'I can tell by your face you're thinking about Sid, and I know what I'm telling you is difficult for you to believe, but Sid was glad to go, and he would have been pleased by the manner in which he died.'

Maxwell bit his lip, and shook his head. 'But the Long Men tore him . . .' Juggernaut winced. 'Sorry,' Maxwell said quickly, 'But the way Mr Vim died was *terrible.*'

'Titus Mamble killed all of Sid's friends. He murdered Sid's son, Jake. You're too young to understand this Maxwell, but sometimes it is harder to live than it is to die. And Sid died in battle, as was his destiny. As it is all our destinies.'

Billy made a tutting noise under his breath, and Maxwell suppressed a smile. If Maxwell had let Juggernaut follow *his* destiny he would still have been clinging to the walls of the Hall Tower.

'We're here,' Juggernaut said, 'You boys had best watch your step from now on.'

Ahead of them a gorge opened up in the earth revealing a range of craggy black mountains. The gorge was like a huge black scar on the planet's white skin, the stones shining bleakly beneath Vir's many moons. They were standing right above a huge crater, a long ago erupted volcano, Maxwell supposed.

'Where it all began,' Billy whispered, staring down into the black shadows at the heart of the volcano.

'That's right,' Juggernaut looked at Billy curiously. 'Did Mamble tell you that?'

Billy shrugged, and looked disinterestedly along the mountain gorge. 'Must have,' he said.

Juggernaut's wide brow furrowed. 'What else did Titus—'

'Can we get out of this cold?' Billy interrupted abruptly. 'You might be used to living like a bleeding penguin, but it's killing me. I really don't feel so good.' In fact, Maxwell thought, Billy looked half dead. Billy's face was grey and gaunt, his lips tinged with blue.

'Of course,' Juggernaut said, his suspicious expression changing to one of concern. 'Follow me Maxwell Jones, Billy Barker, we're almost there now.'

'Here, Billy, you take this,' Maxwell pulled the cape from his shoulders and handed it to Billy. Billy took the cape without a word, and pulled it over his head. Maxwell ran and caught up to Juggernaut.

'Is you friend all right?' Juggernaut asked quietly.

Maxwell glanced back at the shambling shapeless figure of Billy. 'I think so. He's just cold.'

'I imagine it's shock that's effecting him the worst,' said Juggernaut. 'He's lucky to have survived at all. Your friend is probably the first person in a decade to face Titus Mamble and come away with his life.'

Maxwell pointed down the side of the gorge at the distant volcano. 'Billy said that was where it all began?' he asked.

'Yes, that is where Titus Mamble switched on the Eternal Engine,' said Juggernaut. He glanced down at the crater, and then quickly looked away, as if he feared to even look at it.

'So the Eternal Engine exploded when Mamble switched it on?'

'No, the Spankie Dr Arcania sent exploded. It destroyed the Engine, Titus Mamble and his followers, and led to the Big Combination. Or, at least, that's what we thought at the time.'

Maxwell looked at the crater, astonished. How big must the explosion have been? 'Mamble had followers?' he asked.

'Yes. Six in all,' Juggernaut replied. 'Jake Silex was his apprentice.'

'Jake *Silex*? Was he any relation to Dr Silex? Dr Flavia Silex?'

'Jake was Flavia's son,' said Juggernaut.

Dr Silex had a son? It was no wonder she disliked him so much. After all, Maxwell was Titus Mamble's son, and Maxwell, unlike Jake Silex, was still very much alive.

Then another thought occurred to him. 'You said Mr Vim's son was called Jake, didn't you?' he asked.

'Yes, Flavia and Sid were married. They separated after Jake's death. It was a very bad business. Heartbreaking.' Juggernaut noticed Maxwell's confused expression. 'Vim isn't Sid's real name, Maxwell. Have you ever heard of anyone called "Vim"?'

'No,' said Maxwell, 'but I've never heard of anyone called Sid Silex either.'

'Hmm, good point,' said Juggernaut with a smile. 'Hurry up there, boy!' he shouted back to Billy. 'We're here,' he said.

Maxwell looked around. The craggy wall of the gorge rose steadily above them, and below them long shadows had begun to stretch across the black mountain range as the first rays of morning sun glowed above the white horizon.

'There's nothing here,' said Maxwell.

Juggernaut chuckled. 'I know. He never fails to amaze me,' and before Maxwell could reply Juggernaut marched smartly up to the rock face . . . and vanished.

'It's easier if you take it at a run the first time,' came Juggernaut's voice from the rock face. 'And hurry up, I'm dying for the toilet!'

Maxwell took a hesitant step towards the rock face, and then turned to Billy. 'It must be another hologram—'

But Billy had gone. Maxwell saw a momentary swish of dirty grey cloth vanishing into the stone, and then he was alone on the mountain track.

Maxwell sighed. 'Hasn't anyone heard of doors in this place?' he murmured, and then he stepped towards the rock – *into* the rock.

Maxwell blinked. He was no longer standing overlooking the gorge, but in a large, well-lit cave. The cave was almost entirely empty . . . almost, but that was one big "almost".

A giant stood in front of him. He was almost thirty feet tall, and dressed in a golden costume with a blood red cape. A dull silver helmet entirely covered his head. In his hands he held a huge, glinting axe

'TRESSPASSER!' roared the golden giant. He pointed a massive finger at Maxwell. *'YOU HAVE TRESSPASSED ON THE FORBIDDEN LAIR OF ARCANIA AND FOR THAT YOU MUST DIE!'*

The giant raised his axe, and with a bellow of rage he swung it down on Maxwell's head.

Chapter Twenty: Archie, Trevor and the Boshers

Maxwell fell back, his arms raised helplessly as the immense axe blade flew downwards, the golden giant bellowing in fury.

Then silence.

The cavern was empty. The giant had vanished.

'Will you stop mucking about and get moving!' said Juggernaut. Juggernaut was standing by a small door at the far wall of the cavern, Billy stood by his side. The top of the door just reached Billy's shoulders.

'What was ... ?' Maxwell began to ask, but he stopped himself. The giant had been another hologram, of course. Maxwell felt quite sure that if he never saw a hologram for the whole of the rest of his life he would be a very happy boy. He hurried over to where Juggernaut and Billy stood. Billy had removed the cape from his head, and wore a humourless smile on his pale face. Maxwell pointed to where the golden giant had stood. 'Is that what Dr Arcania looks like?' he asked.

Juggernaut gave a short laugh. 'In his dreams!' he said. 'Now come on, both of you, through the door.'

Billy ducked through the doorway, and Maxwell followed him at a crouch.

They entered a long steel passage, the roof of which was only four feet from the floor. Maxwell looked back and saw that Juggernaut had just about managed to squeeze himself through the doorway, and was filling every inch of the passage. Juggernaut had evidently sent them through first to save himself the indignity of having Maxwell and Billy pushing his bottom, sweat was already pouring from his red face.

The steel passage seemed to go on for a very long time, or perhaps it was that the cramped walk, the icy cold, the darkness and the unpleasant metallic scent that filled the small space made it seem like a long way. At last they came to spiral staircase, which, apart from being gleamingly clean, looked just like the staircases in the Watchmen.

Unnatural, yellowish light fell down on them from above, the air was filled with a loud buzzing, that strange metallic scent, and the distinctive odour of percolating coffee.

'Up the stairs! Don't dawdle!' gasped Juggernaut, and he popped out of the steel passage like a cork from a bottle.

'Are you all right, Billy?'

Billy was leaning heavily against the staircase. 'Just a bit tired,' he gasped. He looked as pale as a ghost, and shaking with fatigue.

'I don't think Billy can make it up the stairs,' said Maxwell. 'Maybe we should rest for a minute?'

'I'm like a bear stuffed in a shoebox!' Juggernaut roared. 'Get up those stairs! I'll help Billy. Shift boy!'

Maxwell was pushed up the stairs by a large hand that didn't wait for a reply. It was a long and dizzying journey up the stairs. The walls around him were a vertical funnel formed from gleaming, seamless steel. The buzzing noise grew louder, and the coffee smell stronger and at last Maxwell found himself at the top of the stairs.

He was in a cavern. Stalactites hung from the distant ceiling – but in all other aspects the space was nothing like a cavern at all.

The walls and floor were coated in gleaming. On three of the cavern's walls were the most amazing array of machines Maxwell had ever seen. There were benches with dripping, blipping chemistry sets; there were massive computers on the screens of which banks of numbers and symbols tumbled like electronic waterfalls; there were huge machines which Maxwell couldn't even begin to identify, the biggest of which started at the ceiling and swept down like the world's biggest funnel and dripped mysterious black liquid into a small beaker. Set into one wall were glass cases occupied by the most bizarre and deadly-looking animals Maxwell had ever seen: a snake as thick as a telegraph pole, but as short as Maxwell's forearm with a head as big as a man's; a sabre-toothed tiger with two heads lay licking its long-clawed toes; a creature with a man's body, a fish's tail and a squid's head floated serenely in an aquarium filled with blue liquid. In front of this strange menagerie a two-headed parrot with red, blue and yellow feathers sat on a steel perch. The parrot was reading a book of Keats poetry with one head, and a copy of Raymond Chandler's "The Big Sleep" with the other head.

But despite all these wonders it was the fourth wall that Maxwell was unable to stop staring at, because it was not a wall at all, it was—

'Bunch up!' grunted Juggernaut, booting Maxwell up the backside with Billy's feet. Maxwell clambered numbly up the last two steps. Juggernaut laid Billy down gently on the floor, and leant over him. 'Are you all right, Billy Barker?' Juggernaut asked, but if Billy responded Maxwell didn't hear him – he was staring dumbly at the fourth wall.

The wall was glass, and overlooked a vast, steaming jungle that stretched as far as the eye could see in every direction. But it was not the jungle that had so amazed Maxwell. It was what was above the jungle. A small head on the top of a long, graceful neck rose above the jungle canopy, looked around, and then slowly lowered itself back into the undergrowth.

'That's a dinosaur,' Maxwell whispered.

'Hmm?' Juggernaut peered over Maxwell's shoulder into the jungle. 'Yes. Stegosaurus, I think,' he said, dismissively, and then, with real excitement, he said: 'I wonder if Archie's got any new potato flavours?'

'Potatoes!' exclaimed Maxwell. 'That was a *dinosaur!*' Juggernaut shrugged. 'Are we safe here?'

'Safe?' Juggernaut frowned, evidently mystified. 'Oh! I see what you mean!' He chuckled. 'They're not *earth* dinosaurs, Maxwell Jones. They're Killian dinosaurs.'

'And that's good, is it?' Maxwell said.

'Killian dinosaurs are herbivores,' came a voice from behind them. Maxwell turned to see the two-headed parrot's left head looking up from his book of poetry. 'Actually, they're all vegans, and calling them "dinosaur", from the Latin meaning "terrible lizard" is an insult, as well as being inaccurate, as they are neither terrible, nor are they lizards.'

'Maxwell, this is Byron,' said Juggernaut.

'Actually, mate,' said the right head, looking up from its book, 'the name's Brian.' The left head of the parrot eyed the right head with obvious distaste. 'I am Byron,' it said, '*That* is Brian.'

'Pleased to meet you both,' said Maxwell. 'I'm Maxwell Jones.'

'Charmed,' said Byron, with a slight bow. 'How's your belly for spots, Max?' Brian responded with a wink. 'Common,' snapped Byron. 'Snob,' Brian replied.

'Maxwell, give me a hand here,' said Juggernaut. Together Maxwell and Juggernaut helped Billy to his feet and sat him on a chair in front of a complex bank of instruments. Despite Juggernaut's superhuman strength he needed Maxwell's help – Billy felt as heavy as lead, his joints as unwieldy as stone.

'Are you all right, Billy?' Billy's face was pale and drawn, his eyes bloodshot and watery.

'Look at that, Max,' Billy croaked, raising a shaking hand. 'Amazing.'

Above their head a globe spun below the clusters of stalactites. Maxwell followed Billy's fingers as they traced trickles of black rivers across a barren grey planet. A second later the globe changed – and Maxwell was looking up a jungle world, with spots of blue ocean amongst the green.

'The meta globe,' announced Byron grandly, 'A map of all the 101 Realms.'

'What does that mean?' asked Maxwell, looking at the parrot.

'Pictures of all the known worlds, init?' said Brian. 'Pictures!' scoffed Byron. 'What is it then, if it ain't a picture?' growled Brian. 'It is a quad-dimensional multi-engramic hologram, you dolt!' 'Just a fancy name for a picture, if you ask me.' Byron squawked in frustration. How did this bird live with itself, Maxwell wondered.

'Eight o'clock,' said Juggernaut, taking a pocket watch out of a fold in his red suit. 'Shouldn't be long until Archie makes his appearance.' As he spoke the constantly buzzing of the many machine grew suddenly louder and higher in pitch, and odd metallic smell became heavier, almost choking. 'Regular as clockwork is old Archie.'

'Where is he?' asked Maxwell, looking excitedly around the room. After all he had heard he was anxious to meet the famous (or perhaps infamous) Dr Arcania. 'Is he invisible?' he asked.

Byron and Brian cawed and Juggernaut laughed. 'Invisible? Old Archie?'

'He's got no super powers, Max,' said Brian. 'But he is an exceptional individual,' said Byron. Brian nodded in agreement.

Juggernaut snapped closed his watch. 'Here he comes now.'

The buzzing grew louder and louder, and was joined by an electric crackling, fizzing noise. The smell, like an overheated transformer, grew acrid and thick. Then, with a final *KRIKAKOWKOWKAK!* and a puff of smoke, a figure dressed in white from head to foot appeared several inches above the ground, dropped to the floor, and walked quickly past Maxwell without even glancing at him.

'Hello, Archie! How are you—' The figure, dressed in a silvery white costume, pushed Juggernaut roughly aside and made a b-line for the beaker filled with brackish liquid at the base of the enormous funnel Maxwell had noticed earlier. 'Rude swine,' Juggernaut muttered huffily.

The figure in white – who was not an inch over four feet tall – pulled off his silver helmet, revealing a head of lustrous black hair. He picked up the beaker, and drank down the black liquid at a single gulp.

'Ahhh – coffee,' he sighed, and turned to face Juggernaut.

Maxwell's jaw fell open. Dr Lambton Arcania was a chimpanzee. This mysterious and brilliant scientist was a monkey!

'Oh, it's you again, is it?' said Dr Arcania, in an arrogant voice. 'I hope you haven't come all this way for potatoes, because you can't have any. There isn't enough food in all the 101 Realms to feed you, you hairy hog.' Brian cackled with laughter, Byron, with a disgusted tut, returned to his book of poetry. Juggernaut bared his teeth in a dangerous grin, but Dr Arcania seemed not to notice. He leant languorously against the world's biggest coffee maker and sipped from his beaker. 'I hope that maniac Vim hasn't followed you?'

'Sid is—' Juggernaut began.

'And what is that?' Dr Arcania pointed at Billy, whose pale face was lifted to the globe that hung below the ceiling. 'A child? A child in my laboratory? Are you a complete buffoon, Jugg? This a highly dangerous research facility, not a crèche for . . .' Dr Arcania noticed Maxwell for the first time, and his words trailed off.

'Hello, Dr Arcania,' said Maxwell. He stepped forward and held out his hand. He felt slightly foolish doing this – but he was pretty sure you should offer to shake hands with famous scientists. 'I've heard a lot about you. My name is—'

'MAMBLE!' screeched Dr Arcania. The beaker fell from his hand and exploded on the lab floor. 'The Everyman! You brought him here! You've betrayed me!'

'Calm down, Archie! This isn't—'

'The beast is in my home! Traitor! Villain!' Dr Arcania threw himself to his knees in front of Maxwell and clasped his hands together. 'Oh, do not destroy me, great Everyman!' he begged Maxwell, trembling with terror.

'ARCHIE!' roared Juggernaut. Byron and Brian squawked in alarm, and Maxwell jumped. 'This is not the Everyman. This is Maxwell Jones.'

'M-M-M-Maxwell ... J-Jones?' stuttered Dr Arcania, squinting up at Maxwell. 'But he looks—'

'Maxwell is Titus Mamble's son.' Juggernaut helped the trembling chimpanzee to his feet.

'Mamble's son?' gibbered Dr Arcania, looking from Juggernaut to Maxwell. 'But Titus Mamble didn't—'

Juggernaut grasped Dr Arcania's arm in his massive hand, and the little chimpanzee gave a yelp of pain. Juggernaut turned to Maxwell with a smile. 'Why don't you go and take a walk in the Arcanium,

Maxwell? Archie and I have a few matters we need to discuss in private.'

'The what?' asked Maxwell.

'The Arcanium,' Juggernaut pointed at the dense jungle, his other hand still clasped tightly around the wide-eyed monkey's arm. 'The jungle. It's quite safe, isn't it, Archie?'

Dr Arcania looked from Maxwell to stare blankly at Juggernaut's fixed grin. 'Safe? The Arcanium? Safe. Quite safe,' Dr Arcania agreed.

'The pteradons claim they've seen Boshers in the Arcanium,' said Byron, glancing up from his book. 'Pteradons are always seeing things,' said Brian. 'Very true,' Byron replied. 'Most unreliable creatures.'

'Boshers!' exclaimed Dr Arcania, awaking out of his daze and bristling with anger. 'There are no Boshers in my biosphere! The Arcanium is a totally secure environment!'

'It had better be,' growled Juggernaut. He turned to Maxwell and gave him another twinkling smile. 'Why don't you and Billy Barker go and explore, Maxwell?'

'I'll just stay here, if that's all right, Mr Jugg,' said Billy in an exhausted whisper.

'You run along, Maxwell Jones,' said Juggernaut. 'Brian will come with you, won't you, Brian?'

The parrot sighed, and put down its poetry book. 'My name is Byron, you dolt,' said the left hand head. The bird fluttered from its perch, and landed deftly on Maxwell's shoulder. 'I spotted a parakeet in the Arcanium last week, a right looker too, mate,' whispered Brian, and both heads gave Maxwell a sly wink.

'Okay, I'll see you soon, then,' said Maxwell.

Juggernaut waved his hand, a big grin plastered on his face, and he raised Dr Arcania's furry paw and waved it for him.

Billy continued staring up at the meta globe.

Something's not quite right, Maxwell thought as he walked towards the prehistoric jungle with a two-head parrot perched on his shoulder ... but what could that be?

Almost the second Maxwell stepped into the jungle Brian nipped his ear and said, 'We've got a hot date, kid. Catch you later.'

The parrot flew off in a burst of colourful feathers. 'But how will I find you!' Maxwell yelled.

But Byron and Brian had disappeared over the treetops, and Maxwell was alone on the edge of the dense jungle.

Maxwell looked around. Even if the dinosaurs were Killian dinosaurs and not earth dinosaurs a dinosaur was a dinosaur as far as Maxwell was concerned, however vegetarian they claimed to be. And then of course there were the Boshers to worry about. Whatever a Bosher was.

The wet undergrowth grew thick around him. The jungle was almost completely silent. Nothing moved in the trees. If Maxwell had been in the Arcanium before he would have wondered why he could not hear the shouts of allosauruses as they played their own version of potato hockey with sticks and rocks; he would have wondered why he did not hear the constant shrill gossip of the pteradons, or the cackle of the raptors as they played hide and seek among the trees . . .

He did not see the little pink eyes that tracked him from the shadows of the jungle.

The Conundrum had been on Maxwell's mind almost constantly since they had escaped the

Watchmen University. When he had met the other Maxwell, Billy had been missing, and now Billy seemed very ill, and Billy seemed *different*. Perhaps it was the way he walked, or the way he talked now, without his whirling arms punctuating every word, and...

'Jugg,' murmured Maxwell, stopping dead on the jungle track, his eyes widening. 'He called Juggernaut "Jugg"!'

In the Hall Tower as Long Men crawled greedily towards them Billy had turned to Maxwell, and he had said: 'Let's take Mr Jugg for a dip'. But how had Billy know Juggernaut's real name? Unless ...

'Unless Billy isn't Billy at all,' whispered Maxwell. He looked up and found he was looking out of a great glass window. Below him the black gorge spread out under three suns riding low in the pale blue morning sky. But Maxwell did not stop to admire the view. He spun on his heels and began to stride back into the Arcanium. Then he slowed ... and stopped.

He looked around, and frowned. The jungle was completely silent. How could it be silent ...?

Something brushed his ankle.

Maxwell jumped back with a shout of panic. He was on the verge of bolting headlong into the jungle, and almost certainly getting hopelessly lost, when he looked down, and laughed, relieved.

'Hello there,' he said, crouching. 'Are you lost?'

A small white rabbit, barely larger than Maxwell's hand, stood in the path, twitching its tiny pink nose. Maxwell reached out a hand to stroke the rabbit, a delighted smile on his face. 'Are you lost, little bunny?' he asked it again.

'*No!*' grunted the rabbit in a deep, gravely voice. 'But *you* are!' and it launched itself at Maxwell's face, its mouth opening wide to reveal razor-sharp teeth.

Maxwell caught the rabbit in both hands in mid-air, and fell onto his back. The rabbit writhed and snapped its vicious jaws. 'I'll kill you!' it grunted. 'I'll gut you like a pig!'

Maxwell yelled in disgust and fear, and hurled the tiny animal into the jungle. He sat up. What on earth was that . . . that *thing*?

The bunny flew out of the underbrush like a missile, its vicious teeth gnashing, its ears lay back on its skull as it bounded towards Maxwell with terrifying speed.

A terrific noise filled the jungle. A terrible sound that was a cross between a tiger's roar and an elephant's trumpet. Maxwell felt his skull vibrate horribly, and he clapped his hands over his ears. The little rabbit gave a small squeak of alarm, changed direction in mid-air, and bounced back into the jungle.

'Is he gone?' came a tentative voice from above Maxwell's head.

Maxwell looked up. Leaning over him was a head as big as a car, a face with teeth as long and sharp as swords, murderous red eyes glittering in its craggy skull.

The face of a tyrannosaurus rex.

'AHHHHHHH!' Maxwell screamed.

'Yeek!' piped the T-rex, and its head vanished back into the jungle.

Maxwell climbed to his feet. "Yeek" wasn't exactly what you expected to come out of the vicious jaws of history's greatest predator.

The undergrowth burst open, and a grey shape rocketed out and hit Maxwell in the chest, sending him sprawling back onto the floor.

'You want a fight? Is that what you want?' It was another t-rex. This one was no taller than

Maxwell – but its jaws still looked very, very big. 'You after a rumble? Some action?' said the little t-rex. It danced on the spot and raised his stubby arms, forming his little claws into fists. 'Cos if you're looking for some action, I'm your boy, monkey face!'

'I don't think he meant anything by it, dear,' came a timid voice from the jungle. 'The Bosher attacked him, you see, and when I—'

'Fighting Boshers, eh? Tough, eh? Not as tough as me, hairy bum!' snarled the little dinosaur. 'Come on, put em up! I'll have you, no sweat!'

'I'm sorry, I didn't mean to scare anyone,' said Maxwell. 'That rabbit jumped on me, and the next thing I knew a dinosaur was roaring its head off—'

The little dinosaur had stopped weaving and bobbing, and was slowly lowering its fists. 'You speak Killian!' it said in amazement. '*Mum*! Mum – the monkey speaks Killian!'

The big t-rex's terrifying head reappeared from high up in the branches. It stared at Maxwell for a long time, drool dripping from its huge fangs, and then it turned to the little t-rex. 'Don't call him a monkey, Trevor, it's considered very rude,' she said, and then turning to Maxwell she asked in a kindly voice, 'What's your name, dear?'

'M-Maxwell,' said Maxwell, climbing unsteadily to his feet yet again. 'My name is Maxwell Jones, miss.'

'Miss!' the dinosaur giggled girlishly. 'No one's called me "miss" is seven hundred years! What a polite young man! Hello, Maxwell. My name is Trisha, and this is my little boy, Trevor.'

'I'm not little!' Trevor exclaimed in outrage.

'Oh, I know you're not. You're a very big boy, Trevor,' said Trisha. She lowered her head until her huge jaws were close to Maxwell's ear, and whispered: 'You'll have to forgive, Trevor, Maxwell. He's only two hundred and forty years old, and you know how young children can be.'

'Ah ... yes,' said Maxwell. 'I see.'

'We'd better get home now, Trevor,' Trisha said. 'That Bosher will be back with a whole army, if I know those nasty little things.'

'I'm not frightened of Boshers!' growled Trevor. He began dancing around again, throwing punches at the air. 'I'll bash them, smash them, then I'll crunch them!'

'Of course you will, dear,' said Trisha. 'But it's breakfast time. Aren't you hungry?'

'Brek!' exclaimed Trevor. 'Smashing!' and he turned back to the jungle.

'TREVOR!' roared the big t-rex. The little dinosaur stopped dead in its tracks. 'Where are you manners, young man?'

'Sorry mum,' mumbled Trevor. He turned back to Maxwell and held out a stumpy arm. Maxwell took the little t-rex's deadly looking claw in his own hand. 'I'm very pleased to meet you, Maxwell Jones,' said Trevor, and he gave Maxwell's hand a quick shake.

Maxwell grinned. 'Pleased to meet you too, Trevor,' he said. The little dinosaur shuffled his feet, gave Maxwell's hand another quick squeeze, and then bounded off into the jungle.

'He's a lovely boy, really, he just gets a bit overexcited when he hasn't has his breakfast,' said Trisha apologetically. 'Well, it was very nice meeting you, Maxwell. I don't think I've met a human who spoke Killian so fluently--'

'M-*um!*' came Trevor's voice from deep within the jungle. '*I'm starving mum!*'

'Impatient boy,' muttered Trisha, but she looked down fondly through the treetops. She turned back to Maxwell. 'You had better find somewhere safe before the Boshers return. Would you like to come to our house for breakfast? I just made some fresh scones?'

Maxwell couldn't think of anything he would like more than eating scones at a dinosaur's house, but then with a renewed sense of urgency he remembered about Billy. 'No thank you, I really need to get back,' he replied.

'Never mind, perhaps the next time you're in the Arcanium,' Trisha smiled, and despite her gruesome fangs, it was a very pleasant smile. 'And if you do come across any Boshers, just remember that what they really can't *stand* is loud--'

'*M-um!*' came Trevor's whiney voice. '*M-um! M-um! M-um!*'

'Impatient boy,' Trisha tutted and shook her head. 'I'd better be off. Your mum will be wondering where you are too, I expect. Goodbye, Maxwell!' Trisha turned back into the jungle, the earth quivering as she walked away, and Maxwell heard her scolding Trevor for his bad manners as she went.

What would Bettie Jones be doing now? More than anything else Maxwell wanted to get home. Maybe Virporta Island was boring, but one thing he had discovered was that there were worst things in the world - or in the 101 worlds - than being bored. Being ripped to pieces by cute little bunny rabbits, for instance.

Maxwell turned once more back in the direction of Dr Arcania's laboratory ... and then he saw something that made him stop dead.

A man was standing at the huge glass wall at the boundary of the Arcanium. A man who wore a long brown cape over an ugly blue suit; a man with a bald head, a white goatee beard and silver sunglasses.

'Mr Vim!' cried Maxwell. He ran to the window and pressed his hands against it. 'Mr Vim, I thought you were dead!'

Mr Vim pointed to a door set into the glass wall.

Maxwell ran to the door. In its centre was etched the shape of a hand. Maxwell pressed his palm to it.

'Hello, Maxwell,' came a familiar voice. 'How lovely to see you again. Where are my flowers?'

'I haven't had a chance to get them yet, Linda,' said Maxwell quickly, frantic with impatience, 'But I haven't forgotten. I'll bring them later.' Mr Vim was standing calmly outside the door. 'Could you open the door please, Linda?'

'Certainly, Maxwell,' Linda replied. 'And don't you forget those flowers, young man.'

The door hissed open. A blast of icy wind hit Maxwell as Mr Vim stepped into the Arcanium.

'Mr Vim! I thought you were dead! ' exclaimed Maxwell, delighted. 'How did you escape the Long Men?'

Mr Vim placed his hands on Maxwell's shoulders. If anyone had told him yesterday that he would be overjoyed to see this stony faced old librarian again--

'My boy,' said Mr Vim, and his mouth split into a wide grin. '*My* boy!'

Mr Vim's mouth was a roaring white furnace, black particles whirling inside. 'No,' whispered Maxwell, his knees buckling as the Long Man's pencil fingers clamped around his throat, and began to squeeze.

Chapter Twenty-One: prime numbers

'Mamble is gone,' hissed Mr Vim - the creature that was no longer Mr Vim. 'Boy is *ours*!'

Behind Mr Vim Long Men crawled down the glass wall towards the open door. Maxwell tried to pull away, but Mr Vim's grasp was as implacable as stone. Mr Vim's visor tumbled off revealing black, blank eyes - and the jaws moved closer.

Maxwell was freezing, the heat and life being sucked from his body by ... by ... Not by Mr Vim, Maxwell realised, as the blazing white maw moved inexorably towards his face. The cold was not coming from the Long Man Mr Vim's hands at all - it was coming from Maxwell's *own* hands.

'*Eat,*' hissed the Long Man, '*Eat the Mamble child!*'

Maxwell grabbed Mr. Vim's arms in both of his hands, and felt ice pulse through his fingers, ice so cold it burnt, and with a strangled gasp he dragged Mr Vim's hands from his throat.

Mr. Vim's arms snapped off with a loud *CRACK!* and the Long Man fell back, howling in pain. Maxwell looked at the frozen arms held in his frost covered hands in astonishment, and then dropped them hastily.

The Long Men were moving down the glass wall like cockroaches towards the open door as fast as they could as the creature who had been Mr Vim struggled to its knees, screeching in mindless fury, the stubs of its arm jerking at the air.

'The door!' yelled Maxwell. 'Linda – CLOSE THE DOOR!'

'Of course, Maxwell. No need to shout—' Linda's words were lost in a howl of feedback as the Long Men tore the glass door off its hinges and streamed into the Arcanium.

Maxwell turned and ran.

He ran through the thick jungle with no idea whether he was heading back towards the laboratory. He could hear the Long Men behind him, leaping through branches and scrabbling over the forest floor, hissing and giggling.

Maxwell skidded around a bend in the jungle track. He felt slice through the air behind his head – and he ran head first into a nightmare.

Boshers filled the track in front of him. They hopped rapidly towards him, hundreds of them, their fangs gnashing greedily in their cute fluffy faces.

There was no way Maxwell could stop and nowhere left to run, so he did the only thing he could – he jumped.

Maxwell realised too late that all he could possibly succeed in doing was jumping right into the centre of the charging Boshers ... but as he rose he felt a peculiar buzzing sensation in his spine ... and he continued to rise until – somehow, impossibly – his jump had carried him over the gang of Boshers. He continued to rise up and up, his clothes seemingly the only thing about him that had any weight anymore. He popped up above the treetops, and found himself looking into the lab, where the astonished face of Dr Arcania gaped back at him.

He was suddenly falling with sickening speed. In less than a second he hit the track, but with no real impact, and tumbled head over heels over the rough ground.

Maxwell looked back and saw that he had flown – and that was the proper word to describe it, he realised, he had *flown* – right over the heads of the Boshers and landed a hundred metres down the track. The Boshers were attacking the Long Men, flying at them like furry bullets.

Maxwell got unsteadily to his feet, and as he turned to run a powerful hand grabbed his shoulder and stopped him dead in his tracks.

'Boshers!' exclaimed Juggernaut. 'Archie said there weren't any Boshers!' A long Man, covered in biting Boshers, broke from the mêlée and hurled itself at them, snarling. Without a single change in his expression Juggernaut's fist flew out – and the next thing Maxwell knew the Long Man was flying over the treetops. 'And where did all these Long Men come from?' Juggernaut demanded. 'I thought we'd seen the last of them?'

Maxwell gaped at Juggernaut. His perplexed face gave the impression that he had just found mouse droppings in his biscuit tin, rather than a murderous horde of monsters bearing down on him.

'Billy ...' gasped Maxwell, saying the only thing that made any sense any more. 'Juggernaut – Billy isn't Billy!'

'Eh?' exclaimed Juggernaut, looking at Maxwell for the first time.

'Billy—' there was a flutter of feathers and a low *craw!* As Byron Brian landed on Maxwell's shoulder.

'Alright shipmate? Miss me?' asked Brian cheerily. 'Are you quite all right, Mr Jugg? You look a tad perturbed?' enquired Byron.

'A tad perturbed!' Juggernaut grabbed the bird by both of its necks. '*You* were supposed to be looking after the boy!' he roared.

'We did!' gasped Byron. 'Never took me eyes off him!' choked Brian.

Juggernaut shook the parrot in his fist, banging its heads together. 'Then what are they?' he demanded.

'Boshers!' croaked Byron. 'Long Men!' gasped Brian. '*Attacking!*' they both screamed together.

Juggernaut turned, but before he could raise a hand Maxwell had his own hand raised, palms held out to a Long Man as it leapt at him. A beam of white light shot from Maxwell's hand and hit the Long Man. It froze in mid-air, and then fell to the ground and shattered as if it were made of glass.

'Freezing powers!' exclaimed Byron. 'Pow!' Brian added.

Maxwell looked at his hand in amazement. Flakes of snow twirled above the palm. 'How--'

'Come on!' said Juggernaut. He dropped Byron Brian and grabbed Maxwell's hand. 'Those Bosher won't hold them for long!'

They ran through the jungle, Byron Brian flapping and crowing above them.

'Juggernaut!' Maxwell shouted. 'Billy isn't Billy! I think he's Titus Mamble!'

'Nonsense,' said Juggernaut, pushing Maxwell up the narrow staircase that led back to the laboratory and squeezing up after him. 'Mamble can't take a physical form. That is why he is trapped here. Only physical beings can pass from world to world.'

Maxwell wanted to argue, but there wasn't time. Juggernaut pulled him through the door and it slammed closed behind them. 'I seem to spend all my time on this flaming planet running from something,' said Maxwell sourly as they ran across the lab.

'Perhaps you're running towards something,' said Juggernaut.

'I very much doubt it.'

They stopped beside Billy, who had not moved from his chair. 'Where's Archie gone?' Maxwell looked around, Dr Arcania was nowhere to be seen.

Billy was tapping rapidly on a keyboard, his eyes focused on the large globe turning far above his head. 'What?' he looked at Maxwell and Juggernaut as Byron Brian settled on Maxwell's shoulder. 'Oh, he, erm ... whatyamacallit? Disappeared?' Billy pointed at the meta globe. 'He told me to find Virporta on this thingy.'

'You can do that?' asked Maxwell.

Billy grinned. 'There ain't nothing that old Billy Barker can't do, Maxwell.' Billy returned his attention to the globe, and Maxwell followed his intent frown.

World after world flashed by on the globe. Desert worlds, worlds packed with jungle, worlds that seemed to be continuous cities covering every inch of earth. Maxwell felt uneasy again. How was Billy doing that?

'Where's that damned monkey gone!' barked Juggernaut.

'The Well of Realms,' replied Byron mysteriously. 'Third panel on your right, next to the potato dispenser,' said Brian.

Juggernaut marched over to the wall, and slapped his hand on a panel. A door opened with a belch of steam. Inside Dr Arcania was standing by a closed metal door, hopping from foot to foot. He looked around as Juggernaut stepped inside, and let out a gibber of terror.

'I was just ... I was just ...' he stammered.

'I know exactly what you were doing, you hairy little chicken,' growled Juggernaut. He grabbed Dr Arcania by the scruff of the neck and hurled him back into the lab. 'Now, Archie, I suggest you get us some guns. The Long Men will be through that glass wall in about thirty seconds.'

Maxwell turned, and took an involuntary step back.

Long Men covered the glass wall. Hundreds, or perhaps even thousands of them crawled over the glass, throwing writhing shadows across the floor of the lab.

'We have to get out!' cried Dr Arcania. He jumped to his feet and ran bandy legged to the metal room, but Juggernaut, his powerful arms crossed over his chest, barred his way. 'Get out of my way you oaf! I can open the door to the Well of Realms and we can escape!'

'Maxwell can do that,' Juggernaut replied evenly.

Dr Arcania gave Maxwell a disbelieving look – and Maxwell didn't attempt to correct the doctor's obvious assumption. Maxwell had never so much as touched a computer in his life, how could he do anything?

'The Mamble!' spluttered Dr Arcania. 'You want Mamble to—'

'His name,' said Juggernaut, grabbing Dr Arcania by the front of his white suit and lifting him off his feet, 'is *Maxwell*. Now, tell Maxwell Jones the combination that opens that door.'

Dr Arcania, his feet dangling above the floor, looked ready to faint with terror. 'It will take me *seconds*, you buffoon! We can be in Virporta, or anywhere else in the 101 Realms in seconds!'

Juggernaut shook Dr Arcania in his huge fist. The little monkey made a terrified, despairing noise. Maxwell stepped forward, and a hand as hard as stone rested on his chest and stopped him cold.

'We aren't going anywhere, Archie,' said Juggernaut. '*You* are going to grab a weapon and *we* are going to stop those Long Men.'

'Are you insane!' screeched Dr Arcania.

'Very possibly, yes,' Juggernaut grinned, his eyes glinting madly. 'I've spent ten years trapped beneath a glacier only ten seconds away from death for every moment of that decade. So perhaps I am not quite one hundred per cent sane, no. But I have not forgotten the vow I made at the Watchmen

University, "To protect the innocent and serve the weak",' Juggernaut gave Dr Arcania another brutal shake. 'Do these words ring a bell, old friend?'

'I am protecting the innocent! I'm rescuing Mamble and that other brat—'

'MAXWELL!' roared Juggernaut. 'His name is Maxwell! Don't you ever call him by that name again! These boys don't need our protection, they are Good Men, and more than capable of looking after themselves.' Maxwell was extremely doubtful about this, but didn't think it healthy to argue. 'I am talking about the Killians.'

'The *Killians*?' exclaimed Dr Arcania, a perplexed look on his little face. 'The Killians are dinosaurs, you dolt! They're in no danger!'

'Killians are pacifists who spend most of their time gardening and baking scones—'

'*Scones*!?' Dr Arcania looked astonished. Had he really built the Arcanium and never even bothered going in to it, or talking to the Killians?

'I have not spent ten years of my life,' Juggernaut shook Dr Arcania for punctuation, 'Rescuing these creatures from the havoc Titus Mamble inflicted on their planet to just ...'

Juggernaut was silenced by a loud splintering sound, and they all looked around as a huge crack appeared across the centre of the glass wall. Then another crack appeared, and another and another, until, within seconds, the whole wall was a milky system of splintered glass.

'They're coming through,' murmured Juggernaut, and Maxwell could have sworn there was a hint of excitement in his voice. Juggernaut turned to Dr Arcania. 'What is the combination?' he demanded.

'It's prime numbers on a hundred digit number square,' babbled Arcania without taking his eyes from the ruined glass wall.

'Right, get a gun Archie,' Juggernaut dropped Dr Arcania. 'Two guns!'

'Guns!' exclaimed Dr Arcania. 'I have no guns here! Dr Lambton Arcania is a man of science, not violence!'

'Do you have Spankies?'

'Oh, yes, dozens of them.'

'Activate the Spankies,' said Juggernaut. Dr Arcania scampered away. 'Maxwell, you enter the code as quickly as you can manage.' He looked at the ceiling. 'It looks like Billy Barker is almost ready.'

Maxwell looked up at the holographic globe and saw the familiar seas and continents of Earth. As he watched England appeared in a black square.

'Get into the Well of Realms, Maxwell,' said. 'There isn't much time.'

'But I—'

'*Now* Maxwell! I can't do this and baby sit *you!*'

Maxwell turned away, feeling dread and shame at his obvious stupidity. Dr Arcania walked towards him. Around his feet skittered half a dozen Spankies, chuckling and jabbing each other playfully with their deadly looking steel legs.

'Dr Arcania?'

Arcania walked straight past him, and Maxwell realised that the chimpanzee was wearing earmuffs.

What was he supposed to do? He didn't know what he was supposed to do!

Behind him Maxwell heard a loud crash, and then a sound that had become so familiar to him so quickly. The *thud-thud* of falling Long Men.

Maxwell ran to the Well of Realms, with no idea what he had to do to save all their lives.

The square room had only two features – a metal door, which was firmly closed, and beside the door a large keypad, which looked like this:

1	2	3	4	5	6	7	8	9	10
11	12	13	14	15	16	17	18	19	20
21	22	23	24	25	26	27	28	29	30
31	32	33	34	35	36	37	38	39	40

Dr Arcania's exact words had been "Prime numbers on a hundred digit number square". This was obviously the number square, and a prime number was ... is ... What?

Maxwell wracked his brains. 'A prime number is ...' There was a loud explosion behind him. Maxwell jumped. 'A prime number is ...' Dr Silex's puffy, mean face swam into his memory '... is a number you can divide by two?'

That was it. That was almost certainly it. Yes, that was definitely what a prime number was.

Maxwell lifted his hand to the keypad, and carefully pressed the number 2.

The number lit up orange.

'That's it!' hissed Maxwell triumphantly. He pressed 4.

4 lit up.

His finger was poised above the number 6, when the pad suddenly barked: 'INCORRECT CODE' and all of the number went dark.

'Oh that is just . . .' Maxwell closed his teeth on a very rude word that wanted to pop out of his mouth, '. . . *marvellous*,' he finished.

The parrot landed on his shoulder with a loud squawk. 'What a dreadful racket,' said Byron. 'It's like a blinking world war out there,' said Brian.

'Byron - Brian - do either of you know anything about maths?' asked Maxwell hopefully.

The parrot heads looked at one another. 'No,' they replied together. 'I know quite a bit about potato hockey,' said Brian. 'Literature is more my field,' said Byron.

Hockey? *Literature*? What use is literature? 'Do either of you know what a prime number is?' he asked.

The parrot exchanged a glance. 'Prime,' said Byron, 'from the Latin base "primus", meaning "one".' Brian nodded in agreement, 'It must mean the number one,' he said.

Maxwell pressed number 1. The number lit up. It stayed lit up. The door did not open.

Outside Maxwell heard the screams of the Long Men mixed with Dr Arcania's even louder screams, and Juggernaut's booming laughter.

'I pressed two before,' he said, and pressed the number, which lit up as before.

'Perhaps prime numbers are constituents of the number one,' suggested Byron. 'Try number which can be divided by one.'

'That's *all* the numbers, dozy,' said Brian. 'It can't be *all* the numbers, can it?'

'Well, I don't hear you making any constructive suggestions,' Byron replied huffily.

The two heads began to bicker - whoever said that two head were better than one obviously hadn't met this parrot, Maxwell thought - but Maxwell wasn't really listening to their argument, he didn't even hear Dr Arcania's screams of terror, or the Spankies' jokes before they exploded, or the boom of Juggernaut's mad laughter. Maxwell was remembering long dull Friday mornings as Dr Silex wrote calculations as long and deadly as crocodiles on the blackboard while his hockey stick taunted him from his backpack.

'*A prime number*,' he heard Dr Silex's high, bitter voice vibrate through time and space from double maths, '*A prime number, Mr Jones ...*'

'A prime number is a number only divisible by itself and one,' said Maxwell.

'Pardon?' said Byron. 'Yer what?' said Brian.

'That what a prime number is! I remembered!' said Maxwell excitedly. 'It's a number you can only divide by itself and one.'

'Ah - yes,' Byron cleared his throat. 'I was just about to say that.' Brian cackled. 'You were not!' 'I most certainly was!' 'Weren't!' 'Was!' 'Was not!' 'Was-was-was!' 'Not-not-not--'

'Will you two SHUT UP!' shouted Maxwell. The bird fluttered its feathers, and the two heads glared silently at one another.

Maxwell reached for the pad again. 1 and 2 were still lit. He pressed 3 and it lit up. Not 4, thought two time two is four. He pressed 5, then 7, paused, then pressed 9--

'INCORRECT CODE,' barked the keypad, and all the number went dark.

'Three time three is nine,' said Byron snootily.

'I always have problems with nines,' Maxwell said, furious with himself.

'What a noggin,' whispered Brian, Byron sniggered.

Maxwell started again - 1, 2, 3, 5, 7 - not 9 - 11, 13 - he paused at 15 - no, five times three - 17, 19 . . .

Outside the Well of Realms the air was filled with screeches of Long Men and the blasts of exploding Spankies. Both Byron and Brian kept saying helpful things like; 'They're getting closer,' or 'Oh, I say! Old Jugg almost copped it there!'

. . . 53 . . . 57 . . . 61 . . . Maxwell's finger paused above 63.

'Nine times seven,' said Byron. 'Three times twenty-one,' said Brian. 'Or visa versa,' Byron added.

'You're really not helping,' said Maxwell through gritted teeth. This was the worse possible torture anyone could possibly dream up for him. Sweat was pouring down his back, and his hand shook as he moved his finger along the numbers - 64, no - 65, no - 66, no - 67?

The little room shook. Maxwell glanced through the open door, and turned quickly back to the keypad. Even if this was math hell, it was still a lot better than being out there.

Maxwell's finger shook above the number 67. Was that right? Did nine go into 67, or thirteen, or seventeen?

'I can't ... ' Maxwell looked blankly at the numbers; they seemed to tumble and crawl over the keypad like malicious little Long Men. 'I can't do this!' he yelled.

'Course you can,' said Brian.

'I'm not a Good Man, not a hero, I'm not ... Not anything!' Maxwell cried.

'What nonsense,' said Byron. 'But of course ... If you are afraid ... ?'

'I'm doing my best!' said Maxwell angrily.

'He's chicken, that's what I reckon,' said Brian.

'Well ...' breathed Byron loftily. 'He is a *Mamble*, after all. What more can one expect?'

'Bad blood,' Brian nodded sagely.

'I'm not a Mamble!' yelled Maxwell. He grabbed for the bird, but it flew out of his reach. 'I'm Maxwell Jones! You stupid bird!'

Maxwell spun back to the keypad. He hit 67, then, quickly - 73, 79 ... his finger paused over 81 ...

'Nine times nine,' he gasped, and let out a desperate laugh. He pressed 83, 87, 91, 97.

'CORRECT CODE ENTERED,' said the pad, and the steel door opened with barely a hiss.

'I did it,' said Maxwell, hardly able to believe it. 'I did it! God bless you, Dr Silex, you mean old bag!'

Then, with a terrible sinking feel in his stomach watched the door swing silently open.

The door had opened onto a stone wall.

Beneath the stalactites where the meta globe had once hung now there hung a black-framed box. Inside the box the familiar countryside of Virporta Island raced by.

'The door's open,' said Maxwell. 'But—'

'Great,' Billy interrupted without looking around. 'I'm almost ready too – but Arcania didn't tell me how to activate this thing, only how to find the island. I don't know how to open *my* door.'

A huge explosion reverberated through the air, and Maxwell heard a large creaking noise, followed by a terrific crash. They both turned towards the Arcanium, but nothing could be seen except thick wreathes of smoke; licks of flame flickered.

'You better find that monkey fast,' said Billy, 'before the whole bleeding mountain comes down on our heads!'

'Right,' said Maxwell, and he ran into the smoke.

The air was thick and acrid, and after only a few steps Maxwell was almost blind. Things crunched and slid under his feet. There were no more explosions, nor shouts, nor were there the hissing giggles and taunts of the Long Men. There was just an eerie smoky grey silence.

Something grabbed his shoulder. Maxwell spun around raising his hand, feeling ice flashing through his veins.

'What are you doing here?' demanded Juggernaut. 'I told you to go!'

Maxwell lowered his hand. 'I've got the door open, but Dr Arcania didn't tell Billy how to activate the meta globe.'

'ARCHIE!' roared Juggernaut. Dr Arcania hobbled out of the smoke. He was wide eyed and shaking, his white suit streaked with soot. He was holding a Spankie to his chest like it was his favourite teddy bear. 'Tell the boy how to activate the Well of Realms,' Juggernaut said.

'I ...' Dr Arcania looked from Juggernaut to Maxwell, his eyes as big as table tennis balls. 'It ... It's complicated,' he said. 'I'll have to activate it.'

Juggernaut sighed. 'Do it fast, then. Say close to me, Maxwell. The Long Men have withdrawn, but I don't think they're finished fighting yet.'

They marched back through the silent smoke, Maxwell keeping pace with Juggernaut who was walking backwards, his fists raised. Dr Arcania scampered along at his other side, the Spankie still hugged tight to his chest.

Billy was standing beside the keyboard; Byron Brian perched on his shoulder. Above them the box which had replaced the meta globe showed a stretch of beach with a lick of blue ocean at its edge.

'Excellent!' exclaimed Dr Arcania. He shoved the Spankie into Maxwell's hands and ran over to the keyboard. 'Well done, Willy.'

'It's Billy.'

'Just make it quick!' interrupted.

'This is a very complex and delicate sequence,' said Dr Arcania, rubbing his hairy chin and looking thoughtfully at the keyboard. 'It will take me some time to get it right. Why don't you—'

'Get on with it!' barked Juggernaut.

'Very well, very well,' grumbled Arcania. His fingers fluttered above the keys without touching them. 'Now, let me see ...'

Something hissed in the smoke. Juggernaut spun towards the sound, his fists raised.

Dr Arcania grinned slyly. His finger punched down on the ENTER key – and he turned and ran.

'Juggernaut!' cried Maxwell, throwing down the Spankie and grabbing for the monkey – but he was too quick for Maxwell and before Juggernaut could even turn around Dr Arcania had bolted through the hole in the wall of machinery, and escaped into the Well of Realms.

'That damned cheating monkey!' roared Juggernaut. He turned to Billy and Maxwell. 'Go boys – go now, before the door closes!'

Billy ran towards the room, and Maxwell took a step after him – then stopped, his heart hammering in his chest.

'DES!' Juggernaut bellowed into the smoke. The Spankie that Arcania had been holding scuttled to Juggernaut's feet. 'What are you waiting for boy, a warrant from the Vir High Council?'

'I'm staying. I won't leave you alone,' said Maxwell, unable to believe he was really saying what he was saying, but knowing absolutely that it was right. 'I'll help you fight the Long Men.'

Juggernaut grinned, and then with a speed he would not have believed possible, he grabbed Maxwell, and shoved him under his arm as if he were no more than a piece of luggage. 'Des!' he shouted. 'With me.' The Spankie scuttled after them.

'What are you doing!' cried Maxwell, struggling to get free. 'I can help you!'

'No. You can not,' said Juggernaut.

'You can't fight all of these Long Men!'

'I've been fighting them for ten years without your help, Maxwell Jones,' Juggernaut replied impassively. 'And I've faced a lot worse than this and survived, I'll have you know.'

He plonked Maxwell down in the metal room and reached up to close the door.

'I won't go!' yelled Maxwell. 'I'll stay here until you open this door! I won't leave you to die!'

Juggernaut sighed, and lowered his hand. 'I have no intention of dying, Maxwell,' he said.

'But I want to—'

'Shush, boy,' snapped Juggernaut. He placed his hands on Maxwell's shoulders. 'Be quiet and listen.'

Maxwell glared at Juggernaut, ready to answer any argument the big man had ... but Juggernaut did not speak, and Maxwell realised he had not told him to listen to him – he had simply told him to listen.

Bring us the boy!' whispered a voice from the thick rolling smoke. *Bring us Lord Mamble and go free! Bring him to us!'*

'They want you, Maxwell. You are the only reason that they are here. If you go, they will go.'

Maxwell stared at the shapeless smoke in disbelief, and then turned back to Juggernaut's calm, watching eyes. 'Why me?' he whispered.

'Titus Mamble created the Long Men,' said Juggernaut. 'Without him they will die, and now that he has gone, they want you.'

'*Created* them, but how--?'

'He sucked the life from them to keep himself alive,' said Juggernaut, his massive hands tightening painfully on Maxwell's shoulders. 'The Long Men were once Vir's greatest, most noble heroes, Good Men and Women who stood side by side to fight Titus Mamble.' Juggernaut lowered his eyes. 'Mamble ate their souls, and turned them into monsters.' Juggernaut's eyes met his again. 'So you see, Maxwell Jones, you must go.'

'I'm not like Mamble!' said Maxwell fiercely. 'I won't leave you!'

Juggernaut smiled – and for a second Maxwell was sure he was going to take his hand and say, "Yes. You are right, Maxwell Jones" and Maxwell would prove he was not like his father, *he* would stop the Long Men, and then—

Juggernaut picked Maxwell up and hurled him into the room. Maxwell hit the icy floor and skidded into the wall. 'Des,' said Juggernaut, 'Blow this room ten seconds after I close this door.'

'Yes boss,' replied the Spankie, and it scuttled inside.

'Wait!' said Maxwell, struggling to his feet. 'I won't leave, Juggernaut! You can't make me!'

Juggernaut glared at Maxwell, and then grinned. 'Des, this Maxwell Mamble,' he said – and that name, spoken by a friend, hit Maxwell like a blow. 'If he doesn't leave, destroy this room with him in it.'

'Yes boss.' The door slid closed with a thud. 'Mississippi or elephants?' asked the Spankie.

Maxwell looked down at the little metal spider. 'What?'

'Do you prefer Mississippi or elephants, Mamble?' Des enquired.

Maxwell bristled with anger. 'I am not M—'

'Elephants it is, then, Maxwell Mamble,' said Des, and he scuttled into the centre of the room, and began his countdown.

'Ten – elephant – nine – elephant – eight – elephant—'

Maxwell looked frantically around – but there were no hand prints etched in glass or steel here.

'--six – elephant – five – elephant – four – elephant—'

Maxwell turned to the door. Where there had been a rough stone wall before now there was blackness, as flat and featureless as a pool of oil. Maxwell ran towards it.

'--three – elephant – two – elephant – one—'

Maxwell leapt through the door.

Chapter Twenty-Two: return to yesterday

Maxwell fell through blackness that pressed down on him like the waters of the frozen river - but this time there was no Nurgler to give him breath. The dark void stole the scream from his lungs and pressed on his eyes and lips like rude fingers as he was hurled through a vast nothing.

He began to spin and jerk through the void, and now he had glimpses of things; a vast donut constellation of stars; a planet that was a colour Maxwell had never seen before; another planet pulsed and shuddered like a frantic heart; he fell through blades of purple grass as high as mountains. And all the time silence as Maxwell whizzed through the universe like a child's spinning top, and--

--Maxwell was looking up at the moon. Not any moon, *the Moon*. It looked down on him like an old friend from clouds that seemed frozen in the sky.

'I'm home,' Maxwell whispered, and his words broke the frozen night like a spell. Clouds skittered across the moon and rain roared down on him - and he was falling.

Maxwell turned in mid-air. Far, far, *far* below him was Virporta Island. Maxwell was falling towards it with all the grace of a tree trunk.

He hurtled towards the black, boiling sea and knew for certain that when he hit the water he would be knocked out, or break every bone in his body, or maybe just plain old fashioned drown.

Then Maxwell remembered something.

As well as routinely attempting to crack their heads open in Potato hockey and encouraging them to develop gills in her not drowning lessons, Miss Hummingbird also taught her classes extreme survival techniques. This was not as much fun as it sounded, as Miss Hummingbird's lessons were always practical lessons. Maxwell knew how survive an avalanche, a crocodile attack, and accidentally driving your car into a river. Being buried with snow shovels by the rest of the class and then holding your breath before digging your way out had been quite fun, true; but the wild crocodile Miss Hummingbird had brought into the school yard hadn't been her greatest success, and Professor Magister had expressly forbidden Miss Hummingbird from driving her Mini Cooper into the school swimming pool.

And now Maxwell remembered one particular lesson (not a practical lesson, much to Miss Hummingbird's obvious disappointment) which, up until this moment, he had been absolutely certain would never be of any practical use in his life. The lesson had been called How To Fall Out Of A Plane Into A Raging Sea and Survive.

Maxwell straightened his legs, wrapped his arms around his chest, and pushed his chin down into his chest. The black water hurtled towards him and Maxwell forced himself to slow his breathing, filling his lungs as full of air as he could - once, twice, three times - and then he held his breath. He hit the water, his spine buzzing as if it were a cracked whip, and plummeted like a spear into the freezing sea.

Maxwell tried not to panic. As he'd been taught he spread out his arms and legs like a starfish - but all of Maxwell's recent encounters with water had ended badly, and he abandoned Miss Hummingbird's teachings and swam frantically towards what he hoped was the surface.

Maxwell's head broke the water. He let out a whoop of triumph, and was immediately covered by a wave. He struggled back above the wild sea coughing and spluttering, and looked around.

There was the shore! Maxwell let out another shout, and was about to swim to the beach when something caught his eye.

A bird fluttered above the waves a few feet from him. It was Byron Brian, his two beaks pulling frantically at a piece of white cloth. Maxwell quickly swam over to the parrot.

'Maxmell!' both heads cried, their beaks full of the white cloth. 'Melp! Me Moctor!'

'Dr Arcania?' Maxwell grabbed the cloth from the parrot's mouth and pulled. Dr Arcania's still face surfaced, and instantly disappeared again under the fierce waves.

'He's dead!' cried Brian. 'Oh no, oh no, oh no,' sobbed Byron.

Maxwell slipped his hand under Dr Arcania's hairy chin, and began to pull him towards the shore. This was another Hummingbird survival tip - Rescuing A Drowning Man - Maxwell had thought utterly useless. He supposed the same rules applied to a chimpanzee. 'Thank you, Miss Hummingbird,' he muttered as his heels struck sand, and he dragged Dr Arcania ashore.

Maxwell quickly moved the monkey into the recovery position he had learned with a very embarrassed Bella Jugg the summer before. Byron Brian spun around, its heads screeching useless suggestions. Maxwell glanced at the sea - was Billy out there somewhere beneath the waves? He pushed the thought away, bent over Dr Arcania, and began alternately blowing air into his mouth and pumping his small, still chest.

The rain fell in angry blasts, the pale moon blinking down on them through skittering clouds. Maxwell pumped Dr Arcania's heart - one, two, three - listened to his silent chest, then blew air past his cold lips - one, two, three ... but the little chimpanzee did not move.

Byron Brian fluttered to the ground, and lowered his head. The bedraggled parrot began to weep in quiet stereo as Maxwell's hand lay still on Dr Arcania's chest, and he sat back.

'I'm . . .' Maxwell gulped and let out a shaky sigh. 'I'm sorry, but--'

'MOCHACHINO!' screamed Dr Arcania, sitting bolt upright. He looked at Maxwell, his eyes wide, and vomited a great spout of salty water. 'Mamble?' he murmured, confused.

'You're alive! You're alive!' yelled Byron Brian. The parrot landed on Dr Arcania's head and began dancing merrily.

'Get off me you flea infested toilet brush!' bellowed Dr Arcania, trying to beat Byron Brian. But the parrot was to quick for the chimpanzee, and it wasn't about to stop its dance.

Maxwell got to his feet, and squinted out across the rearing black ocean. If Billy was out there ... He turned back to the beach.

Billy was standing only a few yards from where Dr Arcania was currently trying to throttle Byron Brian in the sand. He was staring up at the pale moon, not even blinking at the lashing curtains of rain, and as Maxwell ran up to him he heard Billy whisper: 'One moon, one moon.'

'Billy!' Maxwell exclaimed, grabbing his friend's arm. 'I thought you'd drowned!'

Billy spun around and grabbed Maxwell in an embrace - and Maxwell felt a terrible wave of exhaustion wash over him, as if Billy's touch was draining his strength - then Billy threw his hands up in the air and the feeling evaporated so fast Maxwell wasn't even sure he had felt it.

'We made it!' Billy yelled, dancing on the dark sand. 'Virporta! Earth! We made it back!'

Maxwell reached out to Billy, paused automatically, and then grabbed his arm. To his relief the strange draining sensation did not return. 'Billy--'

'Sand!' yelled Billy. 'Rain! Oh, Maxwell do you know how wonderful it is to see rain after all that snow!' Billy threw back his head and opened his mouth to swallow raindrops, laughing ecstatically.

Maxwell looked up at the pouring rain. Rain was no doubt a wonderful thing, but just now it was chilling him just as efficiently as the frozen planes of Vir.

'Billy!' Maxwell shook him, and Billy looked at him with a bemused grin. 'I thought you were dead! Dr Arcania almost drowned!'

Billy frowned. 'Arcania? I thought he'd run off?'

'Well, he didn't!' Maxwell replied angrily. 'You left him to drown, Billy!'

'He's all right, isn't he?' Billy pointed and chuckled. 'Look at him playing with that parrot. He's full of life!'

Maxwell stared at Billy, dumbstruck. At that moment he knew without a shadow of a doubt that this person in front of him was not Billy Barker. But if this was Titus Mamble standing in front of him, what was he doing here?

And where was Billy?

'Anyway,' said Billy. 'Archie abandoned us, didn't he? Ran off and left us to the Long Men without a backward glance, didn't he?'

'I most certainly did not!' said Dr Arcania. He was holding Byron Brian by its throats, and the parrot's heads both looked ecstatically happy. 'I came here to rescue you! Jugg is more than capable of dealing with those creatures.'

'Rescue us from what?' asked Billy, smiling coldly. 'We're back on Virporta. There's nothing here that can hurt us, is there, Arcania?'

Dr Arcania bristled - literally - Maxwell saw the hairs on his head rise half an inch. 'If you believe you are safe because you are home,' he said grimly, 'you are more foolish than you look, little boy. We are at the centre of a temporal omniscient retro-helix, or Conundrum if you prefer, and whether on Earth or Vir, our problems have only just begun.'

Billy opened his mouth to argue, but Maxwell held up his hand.

'Look, we can talk about this later,' he said. 'Right now we have to get somewhere dry and warm before this rain drowns us all.'

'Well put, Mamble,' said Dr Arcania. He released Byron Brian, who fluttered onto his shoulder, and looked at the doctor with adoration. 'We shall go to your home,' he looked around. 'Which way is it? Do you have coffee beans and a grinder? I do so detest instant coffee.'

It took them longer to get from the Long Beach to Front Street than Maxwell ever would have imagined. Grey daylight had begun to light the sand by the time they spotted the chimneys of the terraced houses. Virporta Island was still growing it seemed - but why?

'You are thinking of it in completely the wrong way,' said Dr Arcania impatiently as they marched wearily over the sand dunes. 'Of course Virporta is growing. It is meant to grow to accommodate its population's needs.'

'But ... islands don't grow,' said Maxwell.

'Quite right, Mamble, islands do not grow. But Virporta is not an island.'

'Will you stop calling me that!' snapped Maxwell. 'My name is Maxwell Jones, not Mamble!'

Billy grinned, 'You tell him,' he said, and chuckled.

Maxwell ignored him. He had a lot of questions to ask Billy, but right here and now, out of sight of help, could be a very bad place to ask them. 'So if Virporta isn't an island what is it?'

'It is very complicated,' said Dr Arcania airily. 'I hardly think--'

'Explain it to me, then Archie,' he interrupted tersely. Maxwell was beginning to fell that even if Dr Arcania hadn't tried to abandon them he still wouldn't have liked the doctor. He might look like a cute monkey, but he was the least cute creature Maxwell had ever met. 'Tell me what you mean, if you know so much.'

Dr Arcania sighed heavily. 'Virporta is a crossroads,' he explained slowly. 'It is the meeting point of all possible realities on this planet, and all possible combinations of reality. Do you understand so far?' Dr Arcania let out a bark of laughter. 'What am I saying? Of course you don't understand! Let me put it simply for you. Virporta is not an island because it is not a fixed mass of land connected to this planet - it moves around this world as it chooses. It is not an island because - though every planet can be said to be a living organism - Virporta is literally alive. Virporta is a thinking, growing, self-aware creature. It does not exist on any maps of this world, because it does not exist in any one place in this world. Not even this planet's primitive satellites can locate it. Virporta is not part of planet earth - it is a doorway to a billion realities and countless worlds which exists within this reality and on this world.' Dr Arcania gave Maxwell a patronising pat on the head. 'Understand now, do you Mamble?'

Maxwell ground his teeth. 'I think so, yes,' he replied.

Dr Arcania hooted with laughter. 'Of course you do,' he said sarcastically.

They reached the top of a sand dune, and Maxwell felt a great weight lift from his heart. Here was Front Street, to the west the clean unbroken towers of the Watchmen Academy, and just a few minutes north Spudmore Avenue and Bettie Jones with her potatoes, her useless inventions and her simple heart. This street which had seemed so drab and mundane just a few hours before now seemed magical and fantastic after the cold horror of the dead world Vir, and in a few minutes . . .

Maxwell looked down at his watch, then around him at the soggy spring morning.

'Wait!' shouted Maxwell as Dr Arcania and Billy began to stride down the sand dune towards Front Street. 'Come back up! We've got to hide!'

'Hide!' Dr Arcania snorted derisively. 'Dr Lambton Arcania does not hide!'

'What are you on about, Max?' asked Billy without slowly his stride. 'We're back home. What have we got to hide from in Virporta?'

'I know *where* we are,' said Maxwell urgently, 'But do either of you know *when* we are?'

Billy frowned, but Dr Arcania's eyes widened in shock. 'The retro helix!' he cried, and he scrambled back up the dune.

'What are you two on about?' said Billy, exasperated. 'I am freezing cold, I haven't eaten all bleeding day and I want to go home!'

'My watch says it's seven o'clock in the evening,' said Maxwell, 'But it's morning, Billy. It's the morning of the Test!'

Understanding dawned on Billy's face. He ran back up the sand dune.

'It should have occurred to me immediately!' Dr Arcania cursed. They all sat on the dune out of sight of the houses. 'We are at the edge of the counter-helix. The Murdnunoc.'

'The Murd ...' Billy frowned. 'What does that mean?'

'We've gone back to yesterday,' said Maxwell. 'To the day that you met the Maxwell from the future.'

'Indeed,' said Dr Arcania. 'And we must follow precisely the sequence of events which led to the Conundrum within this time frame. What happened during the Conundrum, Mamble?'

'It Maxwell, *Archie*,' said Maxwell through gritted teeth.

'*Maxwell*, then,' said Dr Arcania. 'If you wouldn't mind, *Maxwell*, could you please describe in detail the events of the Conundrum, *Maxwell*.'

Between them Maxwell and Billy explained what had happened to them the day before. While they were talking Byron Brian landed on Dr Arcania's shoulder and listened in silence.

'So you do not approach the boy here until 2pm,' said Dr Arcania when they had finished. 'Unless the orbital cycle of this world has changed since last I visited I would imagine that our timing is overtly prescient.'

Maxwell and Billy looked at him blankly.

'He means we're too early,' said Brian, Byron nodded in agreement.

'Precisely,' said Dr Arcania. 'And even the slightest alteration in timing would cause a chaotic change in the inversion helix of the probable Conundrum.'

Maxwell looked at Byron Brian. The parrot's heads looked at one another, then they both turned back to Maxwell and Billy and it shrugged its shoulders.

Dr Arcania covered his eyes and shook his head in frustration. 'It means reality would change catastrophically,' said Dr Arcania. 'It means that all that has happened since Billy met you Mam ... Maxwell, would cease to exist. Indeed, this reality would be utterly destroyed.'

Chapter Twenty-Three: the eternal engine

Maxwell thought that by now he would have been
used to long, miserable journeys - but whilst his was
by no means the longest, it was by far the most
miserable hour Maxwell ever spent in his life.

Now that Dr Arcania had realised that they
were part of the Conundrum he insisted that they stay
out of sight of any islanders. They walked along the
beach hidden from Front Street and the Watchmen
Academy hidden by sand dunes as stinging rain
whipped at their exposed faces as icy sea winds lashed
at them. They finally entered the Black Woods almost
two miles from the grounds of the school. At least
they would be out of the wind and the rain here,
Maxwell thought, but his optimism was short lived.
The woods were muddy and dank, and if anything it
was even colder under the trees. And it wasn't just
discomfort and cold they had to worry about -
Virporta had gained several new inhabitants, and none
of them looked particularly friendly. Maxwell
glimpsed what looked like a giant blue hedgehog with
a body as big as a man's and a wrinkled and vicious
face beneath a crown of quills. He watched as it
jumped from branch to branch high above them,
letting out a blood-curdling yammering noise. He saw
a snake wrapped around a tree trunk; the snake was as
long and thick as a telegraph pole, with a head shaped
like a barbed arrow.

They walked on, not talking, growing wider
and wider apart as they trudged through the dripping,
rustling woods.

Byron Brian landed on Maxwell's shoulder and
shook himself. 'How are you my boy?' asked Byron.

'Cold,' Maxwell answered shortly.

'We've got something to ask you,' whispered
Brian.

Maxwell looked around, and noticed for the first time that Byron's eyes were blue, and Brian's were green. Despite his discomfort and growing exhaustion he couldn't help but smile to think that he was talking to such a remarkable creature as if he were just a casual friend, when only a few hours ago a talking ant had filled him with wonder. 'What's your question?' he asked the parrot.

Byron looked around conspiratorially, 'Your friend Willie--' 'Billy,' Brian corrected him, 'Billy,' Byron continued in a whisper, 'Is he . . . is he quite the ticket, do you think?'

'Quite the ticket?' Maxwell repeated, mystified.

'Is he acting funny?' asked Brian.

'He ...' Maxwell thought. Was Billy acting funny? He had thought so when they had landed on the beach, and again in the Arcanium, but Billy seemed more like his old self again now. Perhaps his friend had been in shock, as Juggernaut thought? And Juggernaut had also said that Mamble couldn't leave Vir. He had assured Maxwell that Titus Mamble could not take physical form. 'I'm not sure I know what you mean,' Maxwell said.

Byron Brian sighed unhappily and ruffled its feathers. 'It is just . . .' Byron began, 'He doesn't smell quite right,' Brian finished.

'Smell?' Maxwell wiped rain from his face, and was surprised again to find his spectacles gone. 'I thought parrots didn't have a sense of smell?'

'Perhaps they do not, I am not an anthropologist' said Byron huffily, 'And I ain't a parrot neither,' added Brian icily. He turned to Byron and whispered in his ear. Byron nodded, then said: 'He has a scent about him, a most distinctive odor, which we have only detected once before.'

'Where was that?' asked Maxwell.

'At Arcania Mountain,' said Byron. 'Just after Mamble was destroyed by the Eternal Engine,' said Brian.

Maxwell felt his heart freeze in his chest. Ahead of him Dr Arcania was writing in a note pad, oblivious to his surroundings, and ahead of the doctor Billy was striding purposefully through the woods, looking alertly around.

But where was Billy leading them?

'Do you have a dog?' asked Byron suddenly. 'Or a cat?' asked Brian.

'No. Why?'

'Have you got any sort of pet, Max?' insisted Brian. 'It is vitally important,' said Byron.

'Well ... I've got a gold fish?'

'A fish!' exclaimed Byron excitedly. 'Of course!' Brian leant close to Maxwell's ear and whispered, 'You must take us to the fish, Max!'

Maxwell looked at the parrot, bemused, but its eyes were filled with urgent worry, and both heads were nodding rapidly. 'Okay, then,' he said, 'I'll try my best.'

Maxwell caught up with Dr Arcania. 'Billy!' he shouted. 'We've got to go to my house!'

Billy stopped and turned back. 'Your house? What for?'

'Your teddy bear, perhaps?' snorted Dr Arcania. 'Don't be ludicrous, Mamble. What if someone sees us? What if *you* see us? We can not risk upsetting the Conundrum, you idiot boy.' Dr Arcania started walking again.

'It's okay, Maxwell, I know somewhere we can stop up ahead,' said Billy, and he began striding forward again.

And how would you know that? Thought Maxwell, you've lived on this island less than a week ...

and Billy was calling him "Maxwell" again - not "Max" or "mate" or "me old China plate".

But I bet you do know somewhere nice and quiet up ahead - the perfect place to cut our throats in peace.

'I need my glasses!' said Maxwell desperately.

'Squint,' said Dr Arcania without slowing his pace, his eyes fixed on his notebook. 'You've managed perfectly adequately without them up until now.' Billy chuckled, a distinctly watery and unpleasant chuckle.

'I don't need them to *see*,' said Maxwell. 'I need them so people can't see *me*.'

Dr Arcania stopped in his tracks, and looked at Maxwell. 'Your spectacles make you look different?'

'Yes,' said Maxwell. 'And when Billy met the future me I put them on so he knew I was who I said I was.'

'Good Lord!' cried Dr Arcania, slapping his forehead. 'This is vital! If you had forgotten . . . !' he threw his hands up. 'Catastrophe! Chaos!'

'The end of reality,' said Byron from Maxwell's shoulder. 'Well done, Max,' Brian whispered in his ear.

'The end of reality!' Dr Arcania agreed with emphasis. 'Billy, you utter moron, how could you forget such a vital fact!'

Billy was staring at Maxwell, his face impassive, 'I don't know,' he said slowly. 'Silly me.'

'Idiot!' cried Dr Arcania. 'Quickly - to Mamble's house!'

Maxwell turned back and led them towards Spudmore Avenue. Dr Arcania followed, muttering to himself and furiously crossing out calculations on his note pad.

Billy stood watching them, the small unpleasant smile still fixed on his face, his eyes as cold and emotionless as a Long Man's.

After a while he followed them.

Maxwell pushed open the back door to number thirteen Spudmore Avenue and stepped into the small kitchen. He stood looking around with a feeling of such intense happiness he could barely stand it. Just a few short hours ago he had been sure he would never stand in this place again, never see his mum's potatoes of the world tea towel again, never--

'Coffee!' cried Dr Arcania. He pushed Maxwell rudely aside and galloped over to the coffee machine. He opened the lid and sniffed inside. 'Nutty Cuban! Wondrous!' he cried in rapture, and switched on the machine.

Byron Brian landed on the kitchen table. 'Can I have one of these, Max?' Brian asked, pointing a claw at a packet of digestive biscuits. 'I am absolutely famished, my dear boy.'

'Of course,' said Maxwell. He heard the kitchen door slam closed, and turned to see Billy leaning back against it. That small smile had reappeared on Billy's lips, a smile that did not reach his calculating eyes.

Billy stepped forward, and held out his hand to Maxwell. 'I have something--' he began.

The front door slammed open. They all froze and turned towards the sound.

Bettie Jones bustled into the kitchen, an umbrella held in her hand, her hair plastered to her head from the rain.

'Oh! Maxy!' she said in surprise. 'I thought you'd left for school?'

Everyone looked from Bettie to Maxwell.

'I ... I forgot my glasses,' Maxwell said.

'Oh, Maxy, you'd forget your head if it wasn't stuck on,' she said with a beaming smile. 'Hello there,

Archie,' she said, noticing Dr Arcania beside the coffee machine.

'Ah ... Ha - Hello Bathsheba,' Dr Arcania stammered. Bathsheba? Maxwell didn't know his mum was called Bathsheba! Dr Arcania's lips tried the shape of several words, and finally he settled on: 'How are you today?'

'Dripping wet, Archie, absolutely sopping.' She shook her hair over Dr Arcania, laughing, and the monkey grinned in alarm. She turned to Maxwell. 'You haven't seen my umbrella, have you Maxy?'

Maxwell's mouth worked, but no words came out.

'It's in your hand, Mrs Jones,' said Billy.

Maxwell's mum lifted her hand and looked at the umbrella she held there in surprise. 'So it is! Thank you ...' Bettie stopped. She looked at Billy closely, a frown furrowing her usually unlined brow. Then she stepped back, shook her head, and smiled again. 'Thank you Billy,' she finished. She turned back to the door, and noticed Byron Brian sitting on the kitchen table, half a digestive biscuit sticking out of each of his beaks. 'What a pretty parrot!' she said cheerily, and she walked out of the house and slammed the front door closed behind her.

Everyone was looking at Maxwell. He shrugged. 'That's just mum,' he said.

Dr Arcania returned his attention to the coffee pot as it began to bubble and hiss. Brian swallowed his biscuit. 'You'd better go and get your specs before anyone else turns up, Max,' he said. 'Go with him, Billy, and get yourself some dry clothes,' Byron added through a mouthful of digestive, with a quick sideways glance at Maxwell.

'You can get me some clothes while you're there, Mamble,' said Dr Arcania without looking up from the dripping coffee pot. 'Nothing yellow. I can't bear yellow.'

'Okay,' said Maxwell. He turned to Billy, and in an even voice he asked: 'Coming?'

Billy raised a hand and grinned coldly. 'Lead on,' he said.

They walked out of the kitchen. Byron was still crunching his biscuit, and Brian plucked another one from the packet. Neither of them looked up at Maxwell as he passed.

He ran quickly up the stairs and Billy followed him at a leisurely pace. The second Maxwell walked through the bedroom door he looked over at the handsome Beast. Loud snores rose from the fish bowl. The Handsome Beast was asleep.

'You must feed him too much,' came a voice from behind Maxwell. 'Only an overweight fish would snore like that.'

Billy walked into the bedroom, and looked around slowly, a large smile on his face. 'I forgot you could hear him too,' said Maxwell.

'Yes. We are both Master of the Beasts, aren't we, Maxwell?' said Billy - but the voice was not Billy's, and the way he moved, slow and calm and flowing like water, was not the way Billy Barker moved. It was Titus Mamble's voice, and every movement was that of a creature which had spent a decade little more than water. 'There are some advantages to being master of all beasts, but on the down side animals can make a terrible racket.'

Titus Mamble walked past Maxwell and stood in front of his bookshelf. He took a comic from a shelf and opened it, smiling.

Maxwell walked backwards until his back was to the fish bowl. He reached behind him and started flicking the water with his fingers.

'It's pointless trying to run, you know,' said Mamble without looking up from the comic book. 'There really is no possibility of escape.'

'I'm not running,' said Maxwell. He flicked the water harder. The Handsome Beast gave a grunt - then continued snoring.

'And if you were thinking of using any of your powers, you shouldn't bother. You won't hurt me, and you'll almost certainly kill Billy Barker.'

Maxwell felt a glimmer of hope. 'Billy is ... Billy isn't dead?' he said.

Mamble grinned viciously. 'I've already told you I'm not a murderer, Maxwell,' he said. 'Billy is fine, or I should say when I leave this body Billy will recover almost immediately.' He walked over to where Maxwell stood, and Maxwell shrank back. Mamble grinned even wider, and held up the comic book. 'I am so pleased to see we share similar interests,' he said. 'That will make things so much easier for both of us.'

'What things?' asked Maxwell.

'Don't worry, Maxwell, there will be no pain,' said Mamble, his voice soothing. He grabbed Maxwell's arm with eerie speed. 'But if you resist I will kill your friend. I can kill him as easily as switching off a light. Do you understand, Maxwell Jones?' Maxwell nodded dumbly. 'Good boy,' said the creature silkily.

Mamble threw back his head. A spout of black water rose from his open mouth. It formed into a spinning black column, and then slowly transformed into a grinning human face. Titus Mamble's gurgling voice whispered: 'Basilica Astrosus. The three reunited.'

The water face moved slowly towards Maxwell. He felt Billy's grip loosen on his arms as the creature Mamble slowly left his friend's body - but Maxwell didn't pull away. He knew that if he showed any resistance the creature would kill Billy immediately.

Something flew over Maxwell's head in a burst of colour and landed behind him with a splash. Maxwell heard Brian curse, then Byron hissed, 'Wake up you stupid fish!'

Dr Arcania stepped through the bedroom door and stopped, frozen in terror, a coffee cup held inches from his slack mouth. The black water touched Maxwell's brow, and Maxwell stared into the wide, hungry eyes of Titus Mamble

'The circle closes, Basilica Astrosus,' gurgled Titus Mamble. 'Make me whole again.' His lips closed on Maxwell's.

'W-What? What!' came a grumpy voice from behind Maxwell. 'What are you doing, you feathered freak! Get your claws off me!'

'Wake up you brainless guppy!' yelled Brian.

'How dare you! I'll have you know ...' the Handsome Beast's self-important voice trailed off. 'Mamble!' he gasped.

Maxwell felt a wave of exhaustion flow through his body. His knees loosened, and only Billy's weak grip kept him standing. He felt the thick black liquid push open his numb lips. He felt its rancid burning touch on his tongue, and suddenly he was falling - no, he was *flying* backwards into--

'--the face of creation,' he whispered. In front of him was a small glass cube, roughly the size of a house brick. The cube was filled with swirling primary colours, and in the centre of all these colours swam a tiny silver fish.

'The Eternal Engine,' came a voice from behind him. He turned and saw a boy of about fifteen with a round face, spiky black hair and large green eyes like the eyes of a cat. 'That's what it is, isn't it Titus?'

Titus! This was Titus Mamble's memory! This was the day Titus Mamble discovered where Dr Arcania had hidden the Eternal Engine, and the boy with the green cats eyes was Jake Silex - now only moments from his destruction . . . And Maxwell's own birth.

Maxwell turned back to the Eternal Engine, reached out his hand, and--

--He ran down a dark corridor. Bleak stones flew by, the walls and ceiling and floor dripping and oozing and *moving*. The stones were alive.

'Basilica Astrosus,' came a voice from behind him. 'We should not go any further, Titus Mamble.'

Maxwell turned towards the voice.

Juggernaut stood in the passageway. But this was a young Juggernaut; his black beard had a single vertical streak of grey bisecting his chin.

'We must go on, Juggernaut,' said Maxwell - but it was Titus Mamble's voice that came from his mouth. 'You can see for yourself that this is no legend! And if the black palace is real, then perhaps the Astrosus--'

'I tell you we must go back, apprentice,' said Juggernaut grimly, 'or risk our very souls.'

Mamble laughed. 'Souls! More myth and superstition!'

'We are going back,' said Juggernaut, and he stepped forward, his huge hands raised to grab Mamble.

Maxwell/Mamble skipped back, laughing, and Juggernaut's hands closed on empty air. 'You'll have to be quicker than that, Cyril!' he said. Then he turned and ran, Juggernaut stomping and bellowing after him.

He ran and ran. The corridor rose and fell, undulating like a snake. As he left behind Juggernaut's thundering feet and colourful curses, the feeling that

these dripping flagstones were somehow alive grew
and grew until it was a certainty.

He slowed to a walk and, cresting a slippery
black corridor, looked down into an older passage that
looked on the verge of collapse. At the end of the
passage was an open doorway, and through the
doorway a beam of light shone from the room
beyond. Only *light* wasn't really the right word - it was
a beam of *black*.

'The Astrosus,' whispered Titus Mamble, and
he started down the ruined passage to the doorway
that gaped and twitched like a hungry mouth.

Maxwell/Mamble's foot pressed down on the
slimy cobbles and he/they felt it vibrate and then
shatter. The passage shimmered - and then began to
break apart. A terrible sound filled his/their heads, a
scream that tore apart the nightmare memory like an
opera singer shattering a glass.

Maxwell fell to his knees. He realised in an
instant that he *was* Maxwell. He was back in his own
bedroom, and Billy was staggering backwards holding
his head as the black waters of Titus Mamble's
consciousness pushed their way back into his mouth.
But these things barely registered with Maxwell. Every
thought was blasted apart by the terrible sound. His
brain seemed to swell inside his tight skull; the organs
of his body vibrated sickeningly; his skin seemed to
want to tear from his flesh to escape the monstrous
sound.

Billy staggered back, fell, and then crawled
across the room past Dr Arcania, who stood with his
coffee cup still held inches from his slack lips. He
seemed totally unaffected by the abominable sound.

Tears filled Maxwell's vision. He heard a small *crack*
inside his head and blood gushed from his nose. 'Stop
... it ...' he croaked. 'Stop it ... please!'

Billy screamed, and lunged to his feet. In two bounding steps he was across the room. Without pausing he hurled himself through the bedroom window.

The terrible sound stopped instantly. Maxwell collapsed onto the bedroom carpet.

Darkness crowded into his vision. He heard the slap of his curtains as wind and rain blew through the broken window pane, and distantly he heard the sound of running feet.

Then blackness engulfed him, and he knew nothing else.

Chapter Twenty-Four: Murdnunoc

From somewhere far away Maxwell could hear the sound of singing. A deep, velvety voice slowly sang a song he had never heard before. It was a song about red skies and orange fields.

Maxwell opened his eyes, and found he was looking at a sky filled with a dozen moons and a billion unfamiliar stars.

'Oh no,' he murmured.

'Don't like that one, Max?' asked a familiar voice. 'How about midnight on Mab?' The sky above Maxwell turned a gorgeous deep blue without moon, stars or clouds.

Maxwell sat up. He was in a bed. Dr Arcania sat at the bottom of the bed in a fat white leather chair. He was fast asleep, the Handsome Beast's fish bowl wedged between the monkey's knees, his hairy fingers clasped tightly around the glass.

'How you doing?'

Maxwell gaped at young man who sat beside his bed, smiling a languid, almost disinterested smile. 'Lance?' Maxwell spluttered. 'What are you doing here?'

'I live here,' the caretaker replied.

'But where--'

The question was answered before Maxwell had time to finish it, by a purring female voice, 'How are you, Maxwell?'

'Linda?' Maxwell looked around the room. The walls and ceiling showed a landscape of swaying golden corn under an unfamiliar deep blue sky - and looking around Maxwell realised he had been in a room the size and shape of this one before. 'I'm in the Fortress, aren't I? He said, turning back to Lance.

'You're in a Fortress,' Lance replied. 'But not the one you were in yesterday. This is the Fortress in the Watchmen Academy, not the Watchmen University.'

'I'm still in Virporta?' Lance nodded. 'Is Billy-'

Linda's interrupted: 'Twenty-three minutes to the Murdnunoc, Maxwell.'

Maxwell looked up at the ceiling blankly. 'To the what?'

'The Murdnunoc. What your future self did when you experienced the Conundrum in the past,' Lance replied. 'You must now go back and complete the Conundrum.'

Maxwell laughed. 'Absolutely not!' he exclaimed. 'I'm not going to complete the Conundrum, or the Murdnunoc, or whatever you want to call it. I'm not doing anything. I'm not moving from this bed!'

Lance looked at him, perplexed. Then he rose quickly to his feet, leant across the bed and shook Dr Arcania. 'Dad! Wake up!' he said.

Dad? Thought Maxwell.

Dr Arcania awoke with a chatter of alarm, and wrapped himself around the fish bowl, the water slopping around furiously. 'Do you *mind!* exclaimed the Handsome Beast, and then he began singing his odd song again, beginning a new verse about long-legged purple crocodiles making pottery.

'Dad – Max says he isn't going to complete the Conundrum.'

'What? Of course he is. What nonsense!' He turned to Maxwell. 'Get up and get dressed, Mamble. Time is of the essence. You must—'

'I'm not getting dressed and I'm not getting up,' said Maxwell firmly. 'I'm not going anywhere.' He glared at Dr Arcania. 'And *don't* call me Mamble again, *Archie.*'

'But ... but!' Dr Arcania threw up his hands, then quickly grabbed the fish bowl again as more water slopped onto the floor. 'But the consequences of not completing the Murdnunoc would be catastrophic!'

'More catastrophic than what's already happened?' Maxwell looked from Dr Arcania to Lance. 'Billy has been taken over by Titus Mamble. Mr Vim is ...' The image of Mr Vim's face transformed into the cold, insane features of a Long Man rose in Maxwell's mind, and he pushed the terrible picture away. 'Mr Vim is dead,' he continued. 'Juggernaut is probably dead too. I'm not doing it,' said Maxwell, glaring at Dr Arcania. 'If I stay here Billy will be all right, and Mr Vim and Juggernaut will be alive. I'm not going to send Billy to Vir! Never!'

'It's a temporal omniscient retro-helix you moron!' roared Dr Arcania. He sprang to his feet, even more water slopping over the lip of the Handsome Beast's bowl.

'That doesn't mean anything!' Maxwell replied. 'I think you just make those words up. Murdnunoc's just Conundrum backwards. Why don't you admit it? You just made that up, didn't you?'

'Made ...!' Dr Arcania's lips twisted into a furious grimace. 'Made it up! Made it up, you impudent little pea brain! I am Dr Lambton Arcania! I am the continuum's foremost authority on cosmology, astrophysics, genetics, omniology and ... and ... And everything!' The little chimpanzee was now jumping up and down, he was so angry, and the Handsome Beast was swearing and cursing loudly as he was slopped about in his bowl – though of course only Maxwell could hear him. 'Made it up! I created the Uniscope! The Trans-Dimensional Matter Escalator! *I* discovered the Eternal Engine! And I do not make things up!'

'Calm down, dad,' said Lance in a soothing voice, putting a hand on Dr Arcania's arm.

Dr Arcania shrugged his hand away, jumped up onto the bed and thrust his face into Maxwell's. 'You will complete the Conundrum,' he snarled. 'You will close the temporal omniscient retro-helix, and you will deal with the consequences of the Murdnunoc, you . . . you *Mamble!*'

Dr Arcania leapt off the bed in a spray of water and stormed out of the room, the Handsome Beast screaming abuse as his bowl was slammed into the door.

Lance watched him leave, and then slowly sat.

Maxwell glared at him. 'I'm not doing it, Lance!'

'Okay,' Lance replied evenly. 'That's cool.'

Maxwell looked at Lance questioningly – but Lance just smiled calmly back at him, as composed as he always was.

Maxwell climbed out of bed. He was fully dressed apart from his trainers, which he retrieved from under the bed and pulled on.

'Where are you going, Max?' Lance asked.

'Nowhere!' Maxwell snapped. He sat down on the bed, his back to Lance. 'I'm just going to sit here, and when the Conundrum's over I'm going to go and see Billy.'

'You won't find him,' Lance said.

Maxwell turned to face him. 'What do you mean?'

'Billy won't be there,' Lance said, smiling sadly. 'Just because you don't complete the Conundrum it doesn't mean everything will go back to the way it was.'

'But if I don't tell Billy to follow Mr Vim—'

'Billy will follow Mr Vim to Vir just the same. That's Billy's fate, Max.'

Maxwell bristled. 'There's no such thing as fate!' he snapped.

'Sure there is,' said Lance gently. 'Billy's fate is set. He will go through Termination Central, the Long Men will catch him, and Titus Mamble will possess his body. It has happened, Max, and it will happen again, no matter what you do.'

'But if I don't tell him about Mr Vim—'

'If you don't tell him Billy will find out some other way, and he probably won't tell you that he is following Mr Vim,' said Lance. 'The Conundrum affects you, not Billy. Billy will never even know there was a Conundrum. When Billy comes back he'll be Titus Mamble, and you won't be able to stop him. You won't even know you have to stop him.'

'But I *do* know!' said Maxwell in exasperation.

'You know you have to stop him now,' said Lance, 'because the Conundrum happened in your past, but if the Murdnunoc isn't completed there is no Conundrum. You'll forget everything that happened in Vir, because it never will have happened.'

Maxwell thought hard. Would that be such a terrible thing? The wonder of being on a different world, looking up at a different sky with its different stars and its many moons had quickly been eclipsed by the terror of the Long Men and the horror of Titus Mamble.

'What will happen to Billy if I don't complete the Murdnunoc?' Maxwell asked.

'He'll die,' said Lance flatly. 'He'll become like the Long Men. In a very short time everyone on Virporta Island will be Long Men unless you stop Titus Mamble, and you can't stop him if you don't complete the Murdnunoc.'

Maxwell nodded. It seemed that after all he didn't have a choice. But this wasn't a third rate thug like Bartholemew Pugg, he was facing Titus Mamble, a creature who had destroyed billions of people with his extraordinary supernatural abilities and his cunning.

What could Maxwell do? Talk to animals, run up walls and freeze things. It wasn't much of a competition, was it?

'I see you mean to do it,' said Lance. He got to his feet. 'In that case you'd better get a move on, Max. You've only got ten minutes—'

'Eleven minutes fourteen seconds,' interrupted Linda's velvety tones.

'Whatever,' said Lance. 'You'd better get in gear, and I'd better get back to the Hall Tower before I'm missed.'

Maxwell looked up at Lance, and asked the question that had been bothering him since Juggernaut had forced him back into his own world. 'Why is it me, Lance?' he asked. 'Why do I have to stop Mamble?'

Lance shrugged, and smiled.

'Because no one else can,' he replied.

The main room of the Fortress was almost exactly the same as the one where Maxwell had sat eating potato soup with Juggernaut and Mr. Vim on Vir. Graduation pictures lined one wall, shelves filled with weird artifacts and the mounted head of a very peculiar beast on the other wall. The main difference was that the room was clean and well maintained on Virporta. And of course the Vir Fortress hadn't had an anxious monkey in a space suit carrying a goldfish bowl.

'Come on, come on!' snapped Dr Arcania. 'What have you been doing in there? There are only eight minutes to the Murdnunoc, Mamble!'

'It's Maxwell, you hairy nit!' squawked a familiar voice. Maxwell looked up and saw Byron Brian was perched on the head of the elephant-octopus thing. 'His name is Maxwell Jones, Dr Arcania,' Byron said soothingly.

'Frippery! Irrelevance! Semantics! Get down to the yard immediately, *Maxwell*,' Dr Arcania emphasized Maxwell's name with a sour look at the two-headed parrot. 'And try to remember every last detail of the Conundrum. It is essential that you do not deviate from the temporal matrix in even the smallest detail. Do you understand me, you idiot boy?'

'Oh yes,' said Maxwell. 'I understand you perfectly, Dr Arcania. Have you got a coat for Dr Arcania, Lance?'

'Coat?' said Lance. 'I don't have any that would fit him, Max.'

'You'd better find one that will, then,' said Maxwell.

Lance shrugged, and walked out of the room. Dr Arcania watched him go, then turned back to Maxwell, a look of panic rising on his face. 'Coat? Why would I need a coat?'

'Because you're coming with me, Dr Arcania,' Maxwell answered.

'Me?' squeaked the monkey.

'Can I come too, Max?' asked Brian. 'And me!' added Byron excitedly.

'Sorry Brian, sorry Byron, but you weren't part of the Conundrum,' said Maxwell. He turned back to the quivering chimpanzee with a smile. 'But Dr Arcania was.'

Dr Arcania shrank back and pulled the fish bowl closer to his chest. 'Me? I can't come! It's far too dangerous! What if I'm seen?'

'You have to come if Max saw you before,' said Brian, fluttering onto Maxwell's shoulder. 'It is inevitable,' said Byron.

'I'm sorry, Dr Arcania,' said Maxwell, 'But you have to come. I saw you before, so you have to be there now, don't you?'

'I won't come!' The little chimpanzee was close to tears, and whatever satisfaction Maxwell had thought he would get from making Dr Arcania come with him quickly disappeared. What must it be like for a person as extraordinary as Dr Arcania to discover that fate had decided exactly what he must do and when he must do it, and no extraordinary machine or brilliant idea could change it.

'Very well!' barked Dr Arcania. He was shaking with fear – but he looked Maxwell in the eye and he was no longer holding the Handsome Beast's bowl quite so tightly. 'I will come with you, Maxwell.'

Maxwell smiled. 'Thank you, Dr Arcania,' he said.

Dr Arcania waved airily. 'All circumstances must be duplicated precisely or, naturally, temporal wave anomalies will cause multiple modular crises.'

'Erm ... right,' said Maxwell. 'We'd better get going, then.'

Maxwell walked quickly to the door, already trying to remember exactly what had happened the day before.

'Maxwell?' Maxwell stopped and turned back to Dr Arcania, who was smiling hopefully. 'Could I possibly bring the Handsome Beast with me?'

'I don't think so, Dr Arcania,' said Maxwell.

'Oh.' Dr Arcania slowly put the fish bowl down on a table with a sigh. 'The Conundrum must be replicated precisely. I understand.'

Maxwell didn't reply. He didn't know if bringing along a goldfish bowl would cause temporal thingies and modular whatsits – but he was absolutely certain he couldn't stand another second of the Handsome Beast's singing.

'Bless you, Dr Arcania,' said Byron, fluttering back onto the mounted head. 'You're a champ, doc,' said Brian. Dr Arcania puffed out his chest importantly, and waved the praise away.

'Come along, Maxwell, there's hero work to be done,' said Dr Arcania.

'Thank goodness for that,' said the Handsome Beast. 'That monkey stank to high Heaven! And you, ginger, bring me back some food!'

Maxwell ignored the fish, and side-by-side he and Dr Arcania stepped out of the Fortress, and into a very certain future.

Maxwell looked out across the rain swept towers to the sports hall. Mr Vim would be sitting in that building right now. He would be behind his almost empty desk right this second, grim and silent as a child with a surname beginning G, H or I quivered in front of him. It was tempting to think about that – to think that it would take him only two minutes to cross the fields, enter through the back door of the sports hall and come face to face with Sid Vim. But it was a terrible thought too, because Maxwell knew that this was something he could not do. He could not save Mr Vim from his inevitable and horrible future.

Something occurred to him then, and he turned to Dr Arcania, who was now virtually unrecognizable beneath the floor-length yellow poncho Lance had "borrowed" from Tom Chop's coat peg. 'Dr Arcania? Mr Vim made us take a test—'

'Vim!' cried Dr Arcania in sudden alarm. 'Vim is here?'

'It's all right, he's nowhere near,' Maxwell said soothingly. 'Mr Vim had this sort of machine? A sort of white box about the size of a shoe box, and a piece of paper came out of the top of it?'

'A genome developmental articulator,' said Dr Arcania. 'Undoubtedly one of my greatest inventions.'

Maxwell had noticed that all of Dr Arcania's inventions had long-winded titles that didn't seem to mean anything. 'What does it do?' Maxwell asked.

'It predicts the genetic development of an individual,' replied Dr Arcania. He added, in a weary patronizing voice, 'It tells you what powers a person has, or will develop.'

Maxwell nodded. So that explained what Mr Vim had been testing them for; to find out if they had any supernatural powers. But that explained what Mr Vim had been doing, not why he had been doing it.

A terrible thought struck Maxwell, but he pushed the idea away before it had a chance to form properly in his head. Mr Vim was his friend, Mr Vim had saved his life, Mr Vim wouldn't—

'What is that noise?' hissed Dr Arcania. An awful discordant howl rose up from a tower. Dr Arcania spun around to Maxwell, a look of terror on his face. 'Long Men!' he cried, and he turned to run.

Maxwell grabbed the hood of his poncho before Dr Arcania had the chance to scarper. 'It isn't Long Men,' Maxwell said. 'It's a flute recital.'

Dr Arcania looked at Maxwell with frank disbelief. '*That*,' he said, pointing down the spiral staircase to the screeching that rose from the Hall Tower, 'is the sound of music? Are you joking?'

Maxwell remembered sitting through Miss Hummingbird's torturous murdering of "Flight of the Bumble Bee" with a wince. 'Come on, we're running out of time.'

Minutes later Maxwell and Dr Arcania stood by an open door looking out at the rain swept schoolyard.

'You've remembered everything?' Dr Arcania asked anxiously.

Maxwell nodded, though in truth he did not feel at all confident. Billy had told him very little of

what the future Maxwell had said to him. And what
would happen if he got it wrong? It was all very well
talking about fate, but Maxwell knew what Dr Arcania
was talking about was Fate – with a big "F" – a future
that could very well alter the lives of everyone in the
101 Realms. And what if one subtle change – one
wrong word or gesture from Maxwell – altered that
Fate in some terrible way?

'Wait here,' Maxwell said. 'I won't be long,'
and he forced his feet to move.

Maxwell stepped through the open door and
into the yard, and was just about to start looking for
Billy, when Arcania grabbed his arm.

'Wait Mamble, you fool!' Dr Arcania hissed.
'Your spectacles!'

Maxwell grabbed the thick-rimmed black
spectacles out of Dr Arcania's hairy hand and shoved
them into his pocket with one hand, while shoving
Arcania back into the shadows with the other. 'Stay
out of sight!' he whispered angrily. If one person in
the schoolyard glimpsed the chimpanzee there would
be uproar.

Maxwell stepped into the schoolyard. He was
acutely aware of the fact that all of the children around
him were dressed in the Watchmen's drab gray
uniform, whilst he was conspicuously dressed in jeans
and a denim jacket.

Maxwell found himself wondering again why
on earth Mr Vim was here. If Dr Arcania had known
what the purpose of the Test was he would certainly
have told Maxwell - Dr Arcania delighted in displaying
his superior knowledge and intellect, after all. So why
was there a test? If all the children here were like him
then their powers were only just beginning to reveal
themselves - and what use would such unreliable
powers be against a creature like Titus Mamble, who

had drank dry the lives and souls of thousands of much more powerful adults?

And now other memories were tugging at those suspicions. How had Mr Vim known where to find him when the Long Men had first cornered him in the Hall Tower of Vir? And why hadn't Mr Vim mentioned his trip to Virporta Island to Juggernaut? How had Mr Vim know the way to Mab? And when he had arrived there how was it he hadn't been able to find the Nurgler, when he and Billy had found the creature after taking a single step into the frozen forest?

And, must worryingly of all, why had the Black Monastery only appeared after Mr Vim had set out to find it?

Maxwell was consumed by these terrible suspicions, so much so in fact that he walked right into someone.

'Oi!' came a familiar voice. 'Sorry I wasn't watching where you were going, mate!'

Maxwell looked up and almost whooped in delight. 'Billy!'

'That's the handle, me old duck salad,' Billy replied.

'I never thought I'd see you again!' Maxwell exclaimed. He felt like hugging the gawky boy. 'It's wonderful to see you!'

Billy gave Maxwell a nervous smile. 'Yeah, well, it's wonderful to be seen,' he said, edging away, 'But you'll have to excuse me, I've got some other fans waiting.'

Of course! *Billy didn't recognise him!* 'It's me, Billy, it's Maxwell,' he said, reaching into his jacket pocket.

'Course it is,' said Billy, edging further away still. 'How could I ever forget you?'

'It's a little complicated ... '

'Course. Very complicated, yeah.'

'And I don't have much time ... '

'Me neither, mate. So - must be trotting off, yeah? Lovely to meet you and all that.' Billy turned to walk away.

Maxwell grabbed his arm and turned him back to face him, and the same time he flicked open his spectacles and put them on.

'It's me, Billy,' he said.

Billy's face drooped in astonishment. 'M-Max?' he stuttered. 'How did you . . .?'

'I don't have time to explain,' Maxwell said. He pulled off his spectacles and shoved them back into his pocket. Billy's face went through several amazed expressions as Maxwell transformed again in front of him. 'I've got a lot to tell you ... ' But Maxwell stopped dead as he looked over Billy's shoulder and saw a quite amazing sight.

He was looking at himself, or rather the him from yesterday. Maxwell Jones was walking across the yard towards them.

'Is it something to do with Mr Vim?' Billy asked suddenly.

Maxwell snapped his head back to Billy - did he suspect ... ? But of course at this time they had thought of Mr Vim as a monster - Billy hadn't yet been to Vir. He glanced back at the other Maxwell and saw Jamie Blip bouncing up and down in front of his past self excitedly, stopping him coming any closer.

'Come on,' he said to Billy. 'There are too many familiar faces here.'

Maxwell had been on the verge of taking Billy back to the Watchmen where Dr Arcania was still hiding, but then he remembered that Billy had said he had seen no one with the future Maxwell, and Billy wasn't likely to have forgotten meeting a talking chimp. So he led

Billy out of the school gates, and they stood out of sight behind the large stone pillars at the entrance.

Billy started talking immediately: 'What's happened to you? Did Mr Vim do that to you? Did you find out what Mr Vim is?'

Maxwell held up his hand, stopping Billy's flood of questions. He paused before he spoke, because what Maxwell wanted to do more than anything else was to tell Billy *exactly* what had happened and beg him *not* to follow Mr Vim.

But he remembered Lance's warning about what could happen if he tried to change the Conundrum, and the seeing the other had confirmed that what was happening to him now was exactly as he remembered it happening to him in the past.

'I don't have much time, Billy,' he said carefully. 'I have to see Jamie, Bella and Daisy before they go home ...'

'What for?' Billy asked, barely able to contain his excitement.

'I've got meet them back here at four,' and before Billy could open his mouth he added quickly; 'Don't ask me why, because I can't tell you.' And that was true – Maxwell couldn't tell Billy why he had to meet them, because he didn't know himself. 'Billy ...' he began, and Billy nodded excitedly. Maxwell thought hard – how could he explain what was happening without explaining too much? Finally he simply said, 'I'm from the future.'

Billy's face, with had been tense with excitement, changed into an expression of disbelief. 'You're from the bleedin what?' he exclaimed. 'On yer bike!'

'When we followed Mr Vim to—' Maxwell had almost said "to Mab" before he remembered that he had not known the name of the Nurgler's home until Mr Vim had told him it in the Vir Fortress, '—to the frozen forest, it was two days later when we came back, remember?'

'Hardly likely to forget am I?' Billy replied bitterly. 'My mum bleedin grounded me for a week!'

'Well, this time I went to another world, and I've come back a day in the past.' Billy looked unconvinced, so Maxwell took him by the shoulders, and turned him towards the schoolyard. 'Look over there,' he said.

'What exactly am I looking ... ?' Billy's voice trailed off as he followed Maxwell's pointed finger. Daisy had emerged from the sports hall now, and beside her, talking animatedly, was the other Maxwell Jones. 'Blimey,' croaked Billy. 'You're from the future!' He turned back to Maxwell. 'How did it happen?'

'It's called a Conundrum,' Maxwell said. 'I don't really understand it myself.'

'So you really know what happens in the future?' Billy asked. Maxwell nodded. 'Excellent! Come on, then, spill the beans!'

Maxwell looked at his friend's expectant face and felt a deep pain in his chest. If Lance was right and Maxwell was not effected by fate he now had the choice of telling Billy the truth and saving him – or of telling Billy nothing and betraying him.

But if Lance *was* right then soon all of Maxwell's memories of Vir would fade, and he would not even know that Titus Mamble would return hidden behind Billy's face. And Billy, his Billy from his own time, was still alive, and there was still perhaps a chance to save him ...

'I've only got one chance to help you, Billy, and I don't have much time,' Maxwell said, and Billy nodded attentively. Maxwell paused, and then quickly said: 'You have to follow Mr Vim. He's leaving the island at 3 o'clock today, and you and Maxwell have to follow him.'

'The past Max, you mean? The Max from my present?' Maxwell just nodded. He was afraid to say any more, and he did not want to get into confusing conversations about the past, present and future. 'Why do we have to follow Mr Vim? Is it something to do with the Nurgler?'

'We have to follow him because we followed him in my past,' Maxwell said. It seemed like a feeble explanation, but Billy nodded firmly.

'How do we find him, then?' Billy asked.

Maxwell told Billy the directions to the door marked ZØØM, and then gave him a list of the things he would need for his journey. Billy wrote these down on the piece of paper Maxwell remembered seeing in Mrs Trimm's cellar.

'And binoculars, don't forget binoculars,' Maxwell said, remembering his own binoculars had saved him from being lost on the freezing planes of Vir. 'That's very important.'

'Bin-oc-ul-ars,' Billy wrote it down. 'Blimey, where we going? Up the blinking Amazon?' He shoved the piece of paper in his pocket. 'Well, I'd better get a wiggle on if I've got to get all this stuff by three,' he said. He grinned at Maxwell. 'See you soon, future Maxwell.'

Billy turned to leave, and suddenly the horrible consequences of what Maxwell was doing hit him. He could not send Billy to his doom with a backpack filled with chocolate biscuits and beans.

'Billy! Wait!' Billy turned back to him, an impatient expression on his face – he was obviously anxious to begin his adventure. Maxwell glanced back at the Watchmen, and thought he saw a glimpse of Dr Arcania's yellow poncho in the dark doorway.

'You forget to give me the ray gun or the secret password of something?' Billy said, grinning.

Maxwell looked at his friend, opened his mouth to speak, stopped, and then said: 'I've stolen Tom Chop's coat.'

Billy shrugged. 'So what? Who's Tom Chop?'

Maxwell pointed Chop out. He was standing alone in the yard, looking sullen and very wet. 'He's one of Pugg's gang. Can you see him?'

'Course I can see him, he's difficult to miss. Did someone bash him on the head or something?'

'No, he always looks like that,' Maxwell replied. Billy snorted laughter. 'Go and talk to him. Ask him where his raincoat is,' Billy looked at him questioningly. 'It's important,' Maxwell said.

To Maxwell's relief Billy simply said, 'Sure,' turned on his heels and marched through the school gates and towards Tom Chop without another word.

Maxwell walked quickly through the school gates and back into the yard. He walked towards where the door to the school stood ajar, and then stopped to allow a group of chattering children past. Immediately he was out of sight behind the crowd of children he spun on his heels and ran towards where a small red haired boy stood with his back to him.

Maxwell stopped and reached out a hand – but then stopped again. Would something happen to him if he touched the other Maxwell? He didn't know, but it seemed like a bad idea to test it out.

'Maxwell Jones?' he said, and the red haired boy turned to face him. 'It is ...' Maxwell paused. What could he say? '... It is you, isn't it?'

The red haired boy's brow crinkled in a frown and he took a step back. 'Do I know you?' he asked.

Maxwell grinned, he couldn't help himself. The other Maxwell was him, he knew that for sure, and yet he didn't look exactly how he remembered, or perhaps imagined, himself to look. He was shorter than he'd thought for one thing, and his face looked ... Well, different, somehow. It was like seeing yourself on film, or hearing your voice on tape, not strange or alien exactly, just somehow different from what you expected.

Maxwell opened his mouth, not exactly sure what he was going to say next, and someone grabbed his arm.

'Mamble, you fool, what did I tell you?' snarled Dr Arcania.

'I told you not to call me that!' Maxwell snapped. He turned back to the red haired boy, but Dr Arcania, unrecognizable in the yellow poncho, jerked his arm again.

'And I told you ...' Dr Arcania's voice trailed. Maxwell followed his gaze, and saw that the other Maxwell was staring at Dr Arcania's hand in shock.

Maxwell felt a terrible dread rise in his chest. Everything that was happening, everything he and Dr Arcania had said to one another, was exactly the same as he remembered it.

'Come on, we must go now!' Dr Arcania said urgently, and it was like the little chimpanzee was an actor, repeating lines Maxwell had already heard.

With a feeling of despair Maxwell said, 'All right, all right.' It was as if his voice were unconnected to him. He looked at the Maxwell he had once been, and smiled sadly. He allowed Dr Arcania to lead him away.

'What did you think you were doing?' Dr Arcania said angrily when they were both out of earshot.

Maxwell shook his head. 'It doesn't matter, Archie. It was exactly the same as I remembered it,' he said. 'Everything, every word, was just like I remembered it!'

'Well thank goodness for that!' Dr Arcania exclaimed.

'But isn't there anything I can do about it?' Maxwell asked desperately. 'Isn't there anything I can change? Lance said I was outside of fate—'

'Fate!' Dr Arcania exclaimed. 'There is no fate, Mamble, except that which idiotic human beings imagine. Your backwards, superstitious race has done more than any other to suffocate rational thought, Mamble, and what's more—'

'But what about the Eternal Engine?' Maxwell said. 'You found that, didn't you? Doesn't that prove—'

'The Eternal Engine was nothing more than a machine, albeit a highly sophisticated one. The existence of the Engine proves nothing,' Dr Arcania snorted derisively. 'Even the creation of the Engine is surrounded by ridiculous human myth! Do you know that Vim, *Vim*, of all people, believed that God created the Eternal Engine so mankind could combat the forces of the Basilica Astrosus! What ... What flimflam!' They were now back inside the Watchmen, and Dr Arcania's voice was becoming increasingly strident and loud . . . but despite that Maxwell barely heard what he said next. 'Gods and monsters in the twenty-first century, for pity's sake! I despair, absolutely despair of your whole undeveloped, backwards, superstitious—'

'What did you say?' Maxwell interrupted. 'The Basilica . . . what?'

Dr Arcania sighed and rolled his eyes. 'I am not a philosoper, Mamble, I am a scientist.'

'But what is it?'

Dr Arcania covered his face with his hands. He sighed through his fingers, then lowered his hands, and said, his voice full of impatience and irritation:

'The Basilica Astrosus is a legendary temple of evil built by Satan to tempt the good and give them unlimited magical powers. They would in turn trade their souls for these powers.'

'Mamble – Titus Mamble – he said "Basilica Astrosus" when he tried to . . . Whatever he tried to do in my room,' said Maxwell.

'Another clucking superstitious idiot,' said Dr Arcania sourly.

'But ...' Maxwell remembered clearly the dream, or memory, or whatever it had been. Titus Mamble had been standing in a black and dripping corridor with Juggernaut. 'What does it look like? The Basilica Astrosus?' he asked.

'It doesn't look like anything, it doesn't exist!' Dr Arcania snapped irritably. 'It's a legend, Mamble!'

'What does the legend say it looks like, then?' Maxwell persisted.

For a moment it didn't look like Dr Arcania was going to reply – he looked extremely angry – and Maxwell realized something. Dr Arcania was only angry because he was afraid. The little chimpanzee, so far from home, was terrified.

Finally Dr Arcania said slowly, apparently resigned to Maxwell's stupid and irrelevant questions: 'The legend says it is a large black castle, or church, which stands at the borders of the physical world. Its stones are living, and at its centre is the Astrosus, a black jewel that pulses beams of black energy. "Basilica" is from the Latin meaning "fortress" or "temple" and Astrosus literally means "of evil stars". The temple of evil stars. Now,' Dr Arcania slapped his hands on his thighs and stood. 'You've had your bedtime story, can we go, Mamble?'

Arcania turned and walked away, but Maxwell didn't follow him. He was remembering the memory he had experienced when Titus Mamble had touched him – of the black and breathing stone corridor and of the pulses of black light at its end.

And he was remembering something else too, and this thing was not someone else's memory. He remembered looking out across a field of bloody poppies at a huge, crumbling black ruin that vanished into the air at the borders of another world.

'The Black Monastery,' Maxwell whispered.

Chapter Twenty-Five: Mr Vim splits

'Mr Zubrolenko,' said Mr Vim with a voice as deep and cracked as an earthquake fault line. 'I have always admired your father's fencing skills.'

The small dark boy in front of Mr Vim's desk looked at the grim statue in front of him in surprise. 'T-Thank you, sir,' he stammered.

'What's he saying! What's he saying!' hissed Dr Arcania.

Maxwell turned to him, annoyed. 'Why don't you come over here where you can hear him?' he whispered.

'I can hear him quite adequately, thank you Mamble,' Dr Arcania replied, his furry head poking out of a hole in the wall. 'I just don't happen to speak Russian!'

Maxwell was about to reply that he didn't speak Russian either – then realized that of course he must do. He had spoken to the Killian dinosaurs, and despite their appearance they were not beasts, so presumably he could understand every language.

Maxwell peaked around the wall again. Young Mr Zubrolenko was swaying uncomfortably from foot to foot while Mr Vim stared at him, as immobile as stone.

They were in the sports hall, in a small corridor that led to the teachers' toilets. Maxwell had forced Dr Arcania to come with him – literally forced him, freezing Tom Chop's poncho into a solid block of ice with his newly discovered power, and threatening to do the same to the terrified chimpanzee.

Dr Arcania had led Maxwell through a maze of small tunnels which, up until the moment Dr Arcania opened a small door in the wall inside Old Squeezy, Maxwell had had no idea existed. The tunnels were metallic, square, ice cold to the touch with a roof just high enough for Dr Arcania to walk upright comfortably. Maxwell had been forced to stoop throughout the journey. The passages were exactly the same design as the one at the entrance to Dr Arcania's laboratory that Juggernaut had squeezed so painfully into.

Dr Arcania had refused to leave the tunnels, apparently more frightened of Mr Vim's wrath than by Maxwell's threats. He was now sitting in the wall of the hallway leading to the teachers' toilets.

They had watched Mr Vim test student after student. The only variation in the Test was the comment the school inspector made about the students' parents - it seemed that Mr Vim knew everyone who lived or had lived on Virporta Island.

'What are we doing here?' Dr Arcania asked irritably for perhaps the twentieth time. 'This is an utter waste of my valuable time.'

Maxwell didn't answer, couldn't answer, because he didn't really know why they were here. But he kept remembering Billy's theory of "conspicuous disconnections", and that on Vir all his suspicions about Mr Vim had been forgotten in the scramble to survive. Now these suspicions nagged at him again, steadily revealing some awful, unthinkable truth about Sidney Vim.

Instead of answering Dr Arcania's question Maxwell ask him one. 'Archie? When we were in the Fortress, why did Lance call you dad?'

'Will you kindly refrain from calling me "Archie", Mamble!' Dr Arcania said sniffily. 'I find that name deeply insulting.'

'Okay, sorry.' Maxwell didn't point out that it was nowhere near as insulting as Dr Arcania calling him "Mamble". 'But ... Lance isn't your son, is he? He can't be!'

Dr Arcania shrugged. 'In a sense he is my son. I built Lancelot, you see.'

'Built him? You mean ... Lance is a *robot*!'

'Certainly not! As if Dr Lambton Arcania would build a mere *robot*,' he scoffed. 'Lancelot is a cyborg. An artificial intelligence with a titanium endoskeletal frame, an artificial neural network, and an organic exoskeleton.'

Maxwell was shocked. 'He must be really strong, then?' he said.

'Of course. He is programmed to protect the Watchmen Academy. Naturally he is strong. What use would he be if he were merely human?' In answer to Maxwell's confused expression he said slowly, so as even the dim-witted boy could understand him: 'What use would he have been when the Goregoths attacked the school if had merely human strength? What possible use would he be on the many occasions the Long Men have broken through Termination Central into this world?' Dr Arcania raised his hairy chin proudly. 'He was the strength of ten Juggernauts. He is, the perfect caretaker.'

Maxwell saw a glimmer of hope for the first time. A creature ten times stronger than Juggernaut! Perhaps with Lance's help it was possible to defeat Titus Mamble . . .

But a voice interrupted this thought. He peaked around the wall and saw that a small, round man in a brown suit was standing in front of Mr Vim.

'All done and dusted, are we?' asked George Pugg cheerily. 'Well, if you're all set I'll take you—'

'You will have to excuse me for a moment,' said Mr Vim, rising slowly to his feet.

'Oh,' said Mayor Pugg, blinking up at the towering figure. 'Isn't the Test finished, then? Magister told me you would have to leave at three?'

'The Test is finished,' said Mr Vim. 'You will have to excuse me while I go to the toilet.'

'Of course, of course!' said Pugg, chuckling. He took a nervous step back as Mr Vim walked around the table. 'Long, long day, eh? I have murderous trouble with my bladder myself. Must be my age, eh?'

'Thank you for sharing that with me,' said Mr Vim, and without another word he walked across the gym floor – straight towards Maxwell.

'Mr Vim's coming!' hissed Maxwell. He spun around. 'We'll have to hide . . .' his voice trailed off as he looked down the empty corridor. 'You hairy bugger!' he cursed.

Maxwell ran quickly to the Staff Toilets. He eased open the door, and silently slipped inside.

Maxwell slipped into the nearest toilet cubicle, closed the door behind him and crouched on top of the toilet seat.

A few second passed, and then Maxwell heard the entrance door creak slowly open then swing closed again. Mr Vim's feet clicked across the tiled floor. Maxwell heard the furthest of the three toilet cubicle doors open and close again.

Maxwell relaxed, and began to feel more than a little foolish crouching on a toilet seat like a garden gnome while the school inspector went to the loo. His suspicions about Mr Vim suddenly seemed ridiculous! After all, how—

Mr Vim's toilet cubicle door creaked open and Maxwell's heart stopped in his chest. He heard the door swish closed, Mr Vim's feet clicked across the tiles, and the door of the toilet cubicle next to Maxwell creaked open.

Maxwell looked around frantically. What a stupid place to hide - he was trapped! He could slip under the wall into the next cubicle, but Mr Vim would surely see him, and any second the door would open ...

Maxwell reached forward to bolt the door as Mr Vim's feet began to move stealthily towards him – then his fingers stopped as he looked up at the coat hook that was fixed to the back of the door.

He reached up and grabbed it with both hands. A second later the door swung open, Maxwell clinging to the back of it.

He heard Mr Vim breathing on the other side of the door, bear millimeters away. Mr Vim paused . . . and then with a grunt of satisfaction turned away – leaving the door wide open.

Maxwell clung on, the coat hook cutting into his hands as his full weight bore down on the little curl of metal. But he did not dare move an inch.

Through the crack of the open door he watched Mr Vim step up to a line of sinks. He stared at himself in one of the dirty mirrors, then reached forward and touched his reflection.

Maxwell hung on, sweat running into his eyes in stinging streams. He felt totally stupid. Here he was hanging on to the back of a toilet door while Mr Vim admired himself in the mirror ...

Maxwell almost fell to the floor with shock.

Mr Vim touched the mirror then drew back his hand – and the fingers of his reflection followed him. Mr Vim's reflection reached out of the mirror, and Mr Vim took its hand.

Mr. Vim's reflection stepped over the basin and onto the tiled floor. Two Mr Vim's stood straightening their cheap suits in front of the sinks, their twin reflections looking back at them from the mirrors.

They did not speak, but merely nodded curtly to one another, and then one turned, walked to the toilet cubicle beside Maxwell's, stepped inside and closed the door.

The other Mr Vim straightened his lapels, brushed his goatee flat, and turned to the exit.

At that moment the door burst open and George Pugg hurried in. 'Hope you don't mind,' he said. 'Caught short, won't be a moment.'

His fat legs carried him quickly towards the open door behind which Maxwell hung, and even a dunderhead like Mayor George Pugg couldn't fail to spot him!

Mr Vim seized Pugg by the shoulder with one of his long bony hands. 'We must leave now,' he said.

Sweat coursing down the mayor's red face. 'But I'll only be—'

'We must leave now,' Mr Vim repeated. He released Pugg from his grip and walked out of the toilets without a backwards glance.

George Pugg took another step towards the toilet cubicle, then a ripple of fear passed over his usually jolly, vapid face.

He spun round and hurried out of the door after Mr Vim.

Maxwell let out a sigh of relief.

'Who is there?' hissed Mr Vim.

Maxwell froze in terror. The cubicle door creaked open, and Mr. Vim moved in front of the door where Maxwell hung.

'Who is there!' he demanded, and Maxwell opened his mouth to speak – and heard a small squeak of alarm. But it didn't come from Maxwell – it came from above his head.

It was a squeak that Maxwell recognised immediately – and Mr Vim recognised it too.

'ARCANIA!' Mr Vim roared, and he thundered into the centre of the room. Above his head came another whimper of fear, and a metallic thud-thud as Dr Arcania scrambled through the ventilation pipes hung from the ceiling.

Mr Vim let out a bellow of rage. His suit bulged as his shoulders rippled and grew.

He was unfurling his bat wings to fly up to the ceiling and rip Dr Arcania from his secret tunnel, and he would see Maxwell!

The bathroom door opened with a creak. Mr Vim's head snapped around, his teeth bared.

'Hey there, Mr Vim,' said Lance mildly. He wheeled a mop and bucket into the room in front of him. 'I thought I saw you leave with Mayor Pugg?'

'I ... ' Mr Vim glanced back up at the ceiling, his face working with frustration. 'I forgot something,' he said.

'Oh yeah?' Lance leaned against his mop. 'Maybe I can help you find it?'

No, no, no! thought Maxwell frantically. His fingers felt like they were made of dumb wood and stabs of pain dug into his shoulders in agonizing jabs – he couldn't hold to the coat hook for another second, not another second!

Mr Vim smiled coldly at Lance. 'I found it, thank you,' he replied, and he walked out of the toilet.

'Catch you later, Mr V,' Lance said to Mr Vim's back. The door slammed closed and immediately Maxwell fell to the floor in a boneless heap.

Lance raised an eyebrow. 'Hey, Max. How's it hanging?'

When they got back to the Fortress Maxwell discovered that the Handsome Beast's bowl had gone, and there was no sign of Dr Arcania.

Maxwell collapsed into one of the overstuffed armchairs, rubbing his numb fingers and aching shoulders.

'Why did he take my fish?'

'It's a Cerberus Fish,' the caretaker replied. 'Your fish could spot Titus Mamble from ten miles away.' Lance sat, and then went on awkwardly, without looking at Maxwell, 'Dad is ... He probably went to get something to help you, you know? One of his machines, or something?'

They both new that Dr Arcania was doing nothing of the sort. The devious little chimpanzee had stolen the Handsome Beast and run away.

'Dad's a brilliant man, you know,' said Lance quietly. 'He's probably the most brilliant man who ever lived, but he ... He's not a brave person, you know?'

Maxwell looked at Lance, but Lance did not return his gaze. But who was Maxwell to judge Lance's father? After all, his own father had been responsible for thousands, millions, perhaps billions of deaths, and worse. If only Titus Mamble had been a fish-stealing coward!

'He saved my life on Vir,' Maxwell said.

'Really?'

'Yes. He opened a doorway back to this world so we could escape the Long Men.' Lance nodded, a disappointed smile creased his lips, and Maxwell quickly added, 'And he fought off the Long Men.'

Lance's eyes widened in surprise. 'Dad did?' he asked incredulously.

'Yes. Your dad and Juggernaut fought the Long Men off, hundreds of them, while we escaped.' This was not of course strictly true. The little monkey had not been knuckles bared shoulder to shoulder with Juggernaut, and of course Dr Arcania had not politely waited for the boys to escape with him.

'What else did he do?' Lance asked, leaning forward intently.

'He ... er ...' That was the problems with lying to people, Maxwell realized, you always need a hundred more lies ready in your back pocket to convince people your first lie was the truth. 'He ... He saw that Billy had been taken over by Titus Mamble,' said Maxwell.

'Saved you twice, then?' said Lance, grinning and shaking his head in admiration. 'Twice!'

'No he did not!' came a voice, making them both jump. 'It was I who spotted Mamble, not Dr Arcania!'

Byron Brian was looking at them from the top of the mounted head. 'Yeah, but the doc told us he was suspicious first of all, Byron, *remember?*' said Brian. 'I most certainly do not recall – *OW!* Byron exclaimed as Brian pecked him on the head. 'Yes,' he said, grudgingly, 'Now I do recall that the doctor did tell us about Billy's possession by the Mamble.' He clicked his beak angrily at Brian, who looked mildly back at him.

'I thought you'd left too,' said Maxwell, as the parrot fluttered from the wall and landed on the coffee table in front of them.

'The doc told us to stay with you,' said Brian, and he gave Byron another quick peck. '*OW!* Yes! Yes, all right!' Byron sighed dramatically. 'He said he was returning to the Hill to find ways to fight the Mamble.'

'Is that why he took the fish?' asked Lance, delighted. The parrot's two heads nodded as one.

Maxwell was quite certain that the parrot was lying. 'What's the Hill?'

'Arcania Hill on the west coast of the island,' said Brian. 'It is where the doctor's lab is hidden in this realm,' added Byron.

Maxwell had never heard of Arcania Hill, but he did know of a hill that overlooked the sea to the west of Virporta, indeed he had often stopped to rest there on his explorations of the island. He had been sitting on top of one of Dr Arcania's fabulous laboratories, and had never known.

'Arcania Hill's where he built me,' said Lance, nodding. 'But I thought he'd abandoned that place years ago?'

'No, we often come here in the summer,' said Byron, and Brian nodded in agreement.

Maxwell was puzzled. 'Why would he abandon his lab?' he asked. 'Was it attacked by Long Men, or Goregoths?'

'Dr Arcania was banished from both Earth and Vir,' said Byron. 'He was exiled to Killian – but that of course was before the Boshers invaded that world.' And Brian added. 'Those thickos on Vir couldn't find the doc in million years, even if the doc built a lab right under their noses!'

Maxwell was still confused. 'But why was Dr Arcania banished?' he asked.

Byron Brian and Lance looked at him as if he were a complete idiot. 'Because he caused the Big Combination, of course,' said Lance, as if everyone in the world should know this.

'But ... I thought Dr Arcania destroyed the Eternal Engine to stop Titus Mamble?'

'He did,' said Lance. 'He had Spankies guarding the Engine. It was the destruction of the Eternal Engine that caused the Big Combination.'

'The Vir High Council said he should never have tried to find the Eternal Engine,' said Byron. 'Mr Vim wanted him executed,' said Brian, 'But most of the High Council thought that was because the explosion had killed Jake Silex. And of course he didn't *mean* to kill anyone. He didn't mean to kill Jake, or Titus. He'd just been protecting the Engine. So they exiled him.'

So Titus Mamble wasn't responsible at all. The Big Combination and the catastrophe that followed it had been nothing more than an *accident*.

'So what are you going to do now, Max?' Lance asked.

Maxwell did not reply for a moment. He was thinking of Titus Mamble, hunted and formless on Vir, and of the Nurgler, lost and hounded on Mab. Then he thought of the Long Men, and what Juggernaut had said about Mamble eating their souls. He thought about the Nurgler, and how it had intended, somehow, to take over Billy's body and in the process wipe Billy's memories clean, and live in his body like a murderer in his victim's house.

And he came to a decision.

'I'm going to stop Titus Mamble,' Maxwell said, 'and I'm going to save Billy.' He looked hopefully at Lance. 'Will you help me?'

The parrot's head nodded in unison immediately. 'Certainly,' said Byron. 'Kick ass!' Brian added.

But Lance was shaking his head. 'I can't, Max,' he said. 'I have to stay here and protect the school.'

'But if Mamble regains his powers he'll destroy the Watchmen! You won't be able to stop him!' said Maxwell.

'I'm sorry, Max,' Lance said, and he walked out of the room.

They needed Lance's supernatural strength against Titus Mamble but before he could run out of the room after the caretaker, Brian said, 'Leave him alone, Max. He can't help us.'

'We can't do this alone!'

'He can not help us,' said Byron. 'After Dr Arcania was exiled the Vir High Council destroyed all of his inventions. They questioned Lance and decided he should not be destroyed, but they reprogrammed him so he could never leave the grounds of the Watchmen Academy.' Brian nodded. 'If he as much as steps outside the gates of the school Lance would shut down,' he said. 'Lance would die.'

Maxwell sat back down. So that was that. Maxwell and a parrot against the greatest monster in the history of the universe.

Chapter Twenty-Six: target practice

'We'd better hide, Maxwell, better Brian and I not meet your friends until you have had the opportunity to explain.' Maxwell nodded, and Brian added. 'We'll meet you in the woods.'

The parrot flew from Maxwell's shoulder, over the walls of the Watchmen Academy and disappeared into the torrential rain. As Maxwell walked out of the gate he slipped on his spectacles.

'Hello, Maxwell, been taking extra lessons?' asked Jamie, grinning and bouncing up and down on his elastic legs.

Bella was staring at Maxwell's filthy, torn clothes. Daisy frowned at Maxwell. 'Where's Billy?' she asked at once, obviously disappointed that Maxwell was alone.

Maxwell looked at his three oldest friends, wondering just what exactly he should tell them.

Then he noticed something very odd. All three of them were carrying their hockey sticks; indeed Jamie was carrying Maxwell's broken hockey stick, bound up with white tape. Billy must have told them to bring the sticks; Maxwell hadn't mentioned them at all. But why?

They were all staring at him impatiently, and Maxwell said, 'Come on.'

Maxwell crossed the road to Spudmore Avenue, and the others followed, though Maxwell was not exactly sure where he was leading them.

Maxwell stopped at the edge of the Black Woods, and turned to his friends.

'What is going on, Maxwell?' Daisy demanded. 'Where is Billy?'

Maxwell replied immediately; 'Billy has been kidnapped by Titus Mamble.'

Their reactions amazed Maxwell: Bella threw her hands up to her mouth as if to stop a scream; Daisy's eyes widened in horror and she whispered, 'No! No! That just isn't possible!'. Only Jamie acted the way Maxwell had expected them all too. He looked at Maxwell, obviously mystified, and said, 'Who's Titus Mamble?'

But before Maxwell could answer Daisy shouted, 'Titus Mamble is dead!'

'No,' Maxwell replied, 'I've been to Vir and I've seen him.'

'You've been to Vir?' Bella gasped. 'Did you ... Have you seen my--'

'You have *not* been to Vir!' Daisy interrupted her angrily. 'No one has been to Vir for ten years! All the doors to Vir are closed! My dad told me so! You're a liar, Maxwell Jones!'

Maxwell was dumbstruck. How did Daisy and Bella know so much about Vir, when he himself hadn't even heard of the place until he had found himself gazing up at its alien moons?

'Perhaps I'm being a little thick-headed,' said Jamie, looking from Daisy to Bella, and then turning to Maxwell, 'But what exactly is "Vir"? And who on earth is Titus Mamble?'

'Titus Mamble is my father,' said Maxwell. Daisy threw her hockey stick angrily to the ground, and Bella let out a wail. Maxwell turned to Jamie. 'And what and where Vir is, is a long story, but I think I'm going to have to tell you all of it if you're going to believe me,' he said. He turned to Daisy and Bella. 'And I need you all to believe me, because if you don't believe me, and you won't help me, then I think Billy is going to die.'

He looked at Jamie, Daisy and Bella and they all looked back at him, curious, angry and terrified.

'It all began last Friday, the day we played hockey against Pugg,' he began.

Maxwell told them the story of his adventures, and though it was a long story, and he was almost certain that time was running out very quickly, he tried his best to tell them the whole story.

He told them about the growing island (and, of course, they had had noticed this, except for Jamie. 'The streets have grown?' he said in disbelief. 'I thought it took me a long time to get to school this morning!'); he told them about following Mr Vim, about the dinosaur, the Black Monastery, the talking seagull and squirrel, Mr Vim's transformation into a bat winged monster; about the swim to Mab, the frozen river, the Nurgler and the Beasts.

He was aware all of the time that he was telling this story that Billy was lost somewhere in the Black Woods, and that Daisy was growing increasingly impatient and angry, but he forced himself to go on, and he told them about Vir.

Maxwell told them about the frozen desolation of Termination Central and how Billy had been lost. He told them about his long hike to the Watchmen University under that alien sky, about the Long Men, Mr Vim, Juggernaut and Linda.

Maxwell paused, expecting Bella to question him about Juggernaut, but Bella did not speak, so he went on.

Maxwell told the rest of his tale very carefully. He did not mention the Long Men's attack on Dr Arcania's lab, and he kept his fear that Juggernaut was dead to himself.

Finally he had finished his story, and he sat in silence, waiting his friends' next words anxiously.

'What absolute rubbish!' cried Daisy, startling everyone. She got angrily to her feet. 'How dare you lie to us like that! Is this some kind of joke? Where is Billy? Hiding in the trees somewhere, I'll bet!'

Maxwell closed his eyes for a second. This was exactly the reaction he had feared, and of course he should have expected just such a reaction from logical, sensible Daisy Electra.

'Billy is not here,' Maxwell said, opening his eyes and looking pleadingly up at Daisy. 'He has been captured by Titus Mamble—'

'Rubbish! Titus Mamble is dead!' Daisy shouted. 'He was blown to pieces! To atoms! There's no possible way he could be alive!'

'He was never dead, Daisy,' said Maxwell patiently. 'He is in the Basilica Astrosus—'

'A fairy tale!' Daisy laughed angrily. 'Really, Maxwell, just listen to yourself!'

'How do you know all of this stuff, Daisy?' Maxwell asked. 'How do you know about Titus Mamble, and about Vir and Mab?'

'We all know, Maxwell,' said Daisy. 'Every child on Virporta Island knows about the Eternal Engine and the Big Combination. Everyone but you.'

'I didn't know about it!' Jamie exclaimed. 'How come I didn't know about it?'

'Work it out for yourself,' Daisy replied, and she turned and walked away from them.

They all watched her disappear down the alley that led back to Spudmore Avenue.

'What did she mean by that?' Jamie asked Bella. 'Work what out?'

Bella didn't seem to hear his question. 'The Watchmen University has been destroyed?' she asked, Maxwell nodded. 'But ... But my mum said we were beating the Long Men! She said in a few years we would all be going back there!'

'I don't think so, Bella,' Maxwell said as gently as he could.

'But Mr Vim can't be evil,' Bella insisted. 'He's Jangle Mumbles! He's my dad's best friend! How could Jangle Mumble have betrayed my dad?'

Maxwell was saved from trying to answer Bella by something bursting from the leaves above and landed on Maxwell's shoulder with a shrill cry. Bella let out a shocked scream, and Jamie's eyes widened in amazement.

'Are you lot thick or what?' demanded Brian, glaring at the two astonished children. Byron reached up with his beak and pulled Maxwell's spectacles from his face. 'If you don't believe this fine young man's words, then perhaps you will believe the evidence of your own eyes.'

Bella's eyes opened so wide they threatened to roll down her cheeks, and Jamie clapped his hands in delight and began bouncing up and down. 'Magical glasses!' he said. 'That's absolutely fantastic! Where can I get a pair?'

Maxwell stood up. He took his spectacles from Byron's beak with a 'Thank you' and slipped them back on, to a gasp from Bella and a cackle of obvious delight from Jamie.

'They're not magical spectacles,' said Maxwell, 'And my story isn't made up. I can't make you come with me, I'm not even sure I want to you to come with me, but the Conundrum made me meet you here, and that must have happened for a reason. Are you going to help me or not?'

Before they could answer a long, high scream ripped across the quiet glade. Bella scrambled to her feet, 'Daisy!' she exclaimed.

Maxwell was instantly running back to the alley, Byron Brian taking flight from his shoulder.

'Well, well, well,' said Bartholemew Pugg, a cheerless grin on his podgy face. 'If it isn't your boyfriend come to rescue you. Hello there, Bumwell, where's your lanky pal?'

Pugg's knees were planted on Daisy's arms as she struggled on the ground beneath him. Her hockey stick was held in Pugg's hands. 'Help me you idiot!' she shouted at Maxwell, her eyes brimming with tears of shame.

Maxwell took a step towards Pugg – and Tom Chop and Mickey Prickle appeared at the end of the alley and moved rapidly forward, triumphant grins on their ugly faces.

'Yes, why don't you help her?' asked Pugg mildly. 'Look, here come your little friends the weasel and the hippo to give you a hand.'

Maxwell looked around as Jamie and Bella appeared beside him. He turned back to Pugg. 'Let her go,' he said flatly.

'And what are you going to do about it if I don't?' Pugg asked with a contemptuous grin.

Maxwell didn't answer. He simply raised his hand to Pugg, palm open, and raised his eyebrows questioningly.

Pugg frowned. 'And what exactly is *that* supposed to—' the next sound out of his mouth was a howl of pain and surprise as a hailstone the size of a ping-pong ball rocketed from the palm of Maxwell's hand and hit Pugg square in the centre of his eyebrows sending him sprawling backwards.

Daisy scrambled free. 'Maxwell, how did you—' she began, but Pugg jumped back to his feet and roared: 'GET HIM! GET HIM, YOU MORONS!'

Maxwell didn't hesitate. He pushed Daisy to one side and ran full pelt towards the three bullies – and was that a look of fear on Pugg's face? It certainly was.

Maxwell spun around, rising in the air as he turned. He raised both hands to Daisy, Bella and Jamie, who were staring at him in amazement as he rose above their heads.

'Think fast!' he shouted, and hailstones began to pour from his hands towards his three friends in whistling volleys.

Those long, torturous years of Potato Hockey paid off, and Daisy, Jamie and Bella sliced their hockey sticks through the air unerringly, hitting back every ball of ice that came within their range.

Pugg, Chop and Prickle suddenly found themselves overcome by a storm of rock-hard hailstones. They ran from the alley howling and blundering into one another in panic.

Maxwell lowered his hands and floated gently back to the ground, a wide grin on his face.

'That looked like fun!' said Brian, cackling enthusiastically as he fluttered down onto Maxwell's shoulder. 'Are we ready to go now?' Byron asked wearily.

Maxwell turned to his friends, 'I am,' he replied.

Chapter Twenty-seven: the gargoyle

Maxwell pushed through a clump of thorn bushes and stepped out onto a small patch of grass that overhung a rocky streambed.

It had taken him almost three hours to get here through the Black Woods. He looked up at the red glow of the rapidly setting sun above the prehistoric trees and he knew that Virporta Island had grown again.

There was a loud curse from behind him. Bella delicately picked her way out of the thorn bushes, her arms and legs bleeding in several places. A second later Jamie appeared, miraculously unscratched. He was followed by Daisy, who was hacking furiously at the bushes with her hockey stick.

'I'm bleeding like a stuck pig!' exclaimed Bella, fingering her various wounds gingerly.

'Funny you should say that ... ' Jamie began.

'Shut up, Jamie!' said Daisy. She stood beside Maxwell and looked over the edge at the wicked-looking rocks below. 'And exactly *how* are we supposed to get across there?' she demanded.

'Don't worry,' Maxwell replied, taking a step towards the edge. 'It's easy, you just--'

'Easy as pie!' shouted Brian as the parrot burst from the trees behind them, flew over the ravine and landed on the far bank. 'All you need to do is grow wings!' added Byron, and the parrot's heads cackled at one another.

'Exactly,' said Maxwell, and he jumped lightly from the bank.

'MAXWELL DON'T ... !' Bella's cry ended in a gasp of astonishment as Maxwell landed delicately on the far bank. Byron Brian goggled at him, its beaks hanging open.

Maxwell gave the parrot a wink, turned back to his friends and called across the gap, 'Just step off, it's easy!'

Bella and Daisy looked at the drop uneasily, but Jamie, who had never cracked a bone, sprained a muscle or even had a bloody nose in all his life, immediately leapt from the edge with a cackle of glee.

And now it was Maxwell's turn to be amazed.

Jamie jumped, and for a second he seemed certain to hurtle down to the streambed - and then, for only a fraction of a second, barely enough time for Maxwell's eyes to perceive it, Jamie stopped in mid-air. He was suddenly scooped up as if by an invisible hand, and he landed gently beside Maxwell.

'Remarkable, quite remarkable,' said Byron as he watched first Bella then finally Daisy fly over the stream. 'Dr Arcania will be most fascinated by this phenomenon.'

They clambered up through the bushes on the far bank, and Maxwell, in the lead, was halfway down the hill that led to the poppy field before he noticed the others weren't following.

He turned back and saw that Jamie, Bella and Daisy were staring across the land in front of them, and Byron Brian, perched on Bella's shoulder, looked as dumbstruck as the three friends.

'Satan's black palace!' whispered Daisy, her voice cracking with fear. 'I didn't think ... I never imagined it was real.'

Maxwell turned back to the sea. The black Monastery stood on its bleak hill, the red sun dipping slowly beneath the ocean behind it. But the red rays of the sun did not touch its stones, and the darkening blue sky did not illuminate its black shape.

It was as if the building was cut from black card, or had imposed its shape over reality itself. It no longer looked like a crumbling, abandoned old building, but like a living creature steeped in black and terrible evil.

Maxwell lowered his eyes and continued down the hill. After a minute his friends followed him.

At the crest of the graveyard they stopped, and found themselves looking down into a round, dirty-brown pond.

'I thought you said it was just a puddle?' Daisy said this as if she were accusing Maxwell of something.

'It was!' Maxwell said defensively. 'It's grown!'

Daisy snorted, and scrambled lightly down into the moat. The others followed.

'What's *her* problem?' muttered Jamie in Maxwell's ear. 'We just walked ten miles across a mile wide island, everything's grown!'

'She doesn't believe your story,' said Bella quietly. Maxwell gave her a questioning look, but Bella lowered her eyes and said nothing more.

'How come I didn't know about all this 101 Realms and superpowers and all this other stuff when everyone else did?' asked Jamie crossly for perhaps the dozenth time.

'I don't know, but I'd keep away from the edge of that pool if *you* believe my story,' said Maxwell. 'I never saw the Nurgler die, remember?'

Jamie jumped away from the edge, and Bella backed from the brown swirling waters fearfully.

Byron Brian, who had now found a permanent perch on Bella's broad shoulders squawked, and Byron said, 'I don't think you need worry about going too near to the Void pool, Maxwell.'

At the far bank of the moat Daisy was looking down at a wide muddy track that led from the pool. Around the track lines were drawn through the mud, as if a huge tree had been dragged from the water, its branches cutting divots in the sticky earth.

Or tentacles, though Maxwell, and not the trunk of a tree, but the trunk of a monstrous body.

The Nurgler.

Daisy pointed at the Nurgler's trail. 'It looks like something was pulled from the water,' she said, 'There are footprints here.'

'Mr Vim,' he whispered. 'Byron? Brian?' The bird's two heads turned to him. 'I need you to do something.'

'Certainly,' said Byron. 'No sweat, Max,' Brian replied.

Maxwell looked at the prints again, and then up at the Black Monastery. The ghastly building seemed more solid now, more alive, and Maxwell had the horrible feeling that the building was waiting for them. But what else was waiting? Mr Vim? The Nurgler? Titus Mamble? An army of Long Men?

For the first time since he had plunged into the Void pool Maxwell felt as he had for most of his life – hopeless, helpless, small and unimportant. He had spent most of his life walking away – or more often than not running away - from trouble. Could he really face this?

'Fly back to the Black Woods,' he said to the parrot. 'See if you can find any one . . . any *thing* there than can help us,' and before the bird could protest he turned to the others. 'And you should go back to the village and see if you can get help there.'

A look of relief flooded Bella's face, but it vanished as quickly as it had appeared when Daisy answered, 'Don't be an idiot, Maxwell.'

'Are you mad?' said Jamie. 'You think I'm really going to miss out on this? Do you have any idea how truly *boring* my life is?'

'I should never have brought you here. This isn't your fight.' Maxwell saw Daisy's stubborn expression and was suddenly furious. 'Don't you understand? Don't you get it? Titus Mamble is waiting in there for us! If you go into that castle, or whatever that foul place is, he won't just hurt you – he'll *kill* you! Or worse, the next time you walk out here you could be a Long Man!'

'I know!' said Jamie, rubbing his hands together with glee. 'Exciting, isn't it?'

'Exciting ... ?' Maxwell goggled at Jamie in amazement. 'Bella? Go home Bella. I mean it! It's not safe.'

'Don't be an idiot, Maxwell,' Daisy repeated. 'It will take at least five hours to get to the village and back, and by that time it will be too late for you and for Billy. We either go together, or none of us go at all,' she said firmly. 'I'm not leaving Billy, and that's that!'

Maxwell and Daisy glared at each other. He should have felt grateful, he knew that, but Maxwell only felt anger. Titus Mamble was his father, it was up to him to stop him ... And at the back of his mind a small voice that he hardly dared listen to thought – he won't hurt *me*.

'Anyway,' said Jamie. 'Why should you have all the fun?'

Maxwell looked around at Jamie who was grinning widely. 'You're sure?' he asked. Jamie nodded his head, beaming; Daisy nodded firmly, and finally Bella, her face pale and shocked and her voice barely a whisper, said, 'Yes.'

'As if we would leave a skinny little prat like you to battle the Mamble!' exclaimed Brian. 'My suggestion,' said Byron, 'is that we approach the north tower—'

'You're not going anywhere,' Daisy interrupted. 'Maxwell's right, we can't go back for help, but you can fly to the village in minutes. Off you go, and be quick about it!'

Daisy turned and began clambering up the muddy bank in the Nurgler's wake. Jamie followed her. Maxwell turned to the parrot, still perched on Bella's shoulder.

'I can help you, Maxwell,' Byron pleaded. 'We'll be more help to you than those daft kids,' Brian added, and both the parrot's heads nodded in agreement.

'You can help me best by bringing more people,' he looked at Bella's pale face. 'We can't stop Mamble, but there may be people – Good Men - in Virporta who can.'

Both of the heads nodded. 'Be careful,' said Brian. 'And remember what Mamble is, and who you are,' added Byron, but before Maxwell could ask him to explain this remark the parrot took flight and disappeared over the top of the moat.

Bella watched him go, then sighed and turned to Maxwell. 'I like having a parrot,' she said.

'Your dad liked him too,' said Maxwell, and he smiled. 'That is, when he wasn't trying to throttle him.'

Bella looked at him hopefully. 'Do you think my dad will come to help us?' she asked.

'Maybe,' he said, and then seeing the expression on Bella's face he said, 'Probably.'

Bella smiled, and then she turned and climbed to where Jamie and Bella stood at the top of the moat.

Daisy, Jamie and Bella had stopped at the end of the Nurgler's trail, and as Maxwell climbed up beside them he instantly saw why.

The ground in front of the Black Monastery was moving. It took a few seconds for Maxwell's eyes to adjust to this bizarre sight, and then with a shudder of revulsion he realized what it was he was looking at. Worms. Millions, perhaps even billions of worms carpeted the ground, writhing and twisting wetly.

'Oh, that's horrible, *horrible!*' gasped Bella.

'Perhaps you shouldn't have sent your parrot away, Maxwell,' said Daisy. She didn't look as horrified as Bella, but she did look slightly queasy. 'He would have had plenty to eat here.'

'Oh, for goodness sake, they're only worms!' said Jamie. 'Who cares if we squash a few stupid—'

The instant he stepped forward the worms rose up into a pillar six feet high – and they rocketed towards Jamie like a breaking wave.

Maxwell jumped forward his hand held in front of him, ready to freeze the racing column ... but the second Maxwell stepped in front of Jamie the worm-wave collapsed, and he heard the worms – though *heard* was perhaps not the correct word; he read the worms' language in the writhing movements of their tiny bodies – saying: *The Mamble! The boy! The Mamble!*

A path opened in front of Maxwell's feet revealing scorched black flagstones.

Maxwell walked forward and the others followed him, staying as close as they could. When Maxwell looked back he saw the worms closing back over the path behind Daisy's heels at the end of their nervous conga line.

'How did you do that, Maxwell?' Bella asked, her voice shaking, as they stepped onto a wall of black cobblestones that lay against the face of the Black Monastery.

'I didn't do anything,' Maxwell replied truthfully. 'I think they knew I was coming. I think they were waiting to let me in.'

'Waiting ... ?' murmured Daisy incredulously, and she looked back. The worms had formed their unbroken carpet again, stretching from the raised stones on which the friends stood to the edge of the moat.

The walls of the Black Monastery rose to a dizzying height, almost seeming to touch the stars which had begun appear in the rapidly darkening sky. At the crest of the wall Maxwell spotted a gargoyle deeply shrouded in shadow. Its leathery wings were arched above its featureless head, its dark face seeming to stare down at him.

'Where do we go now?' Jamie asked.

'That way,' said Daisy, pointing to a large oval opening in the wall.

They all looked at the opening. It looked worryingly like an open mouth.

'Come on,' he said, and they began to walk along the raised cobble track, all very conscious of their feet on the slippery, uneven stones.

Maxwell reached the hole in the castle wall. Beyond the opening was utter blackness. Not an inch could be seen off any passage or room beyond the entrance.

'We should have brought some torches,' said Jamie. 'And perhaps a flame thrower.'

Maxwell turned to Jamie; he had been about to tell him about the gear he and Billy had taken to Vir in the fluffy pink backpacks, when he noticed Bella was staring upwards. 'Bella?'

Jamie and Daisy turned to look at her. 'Hey! Jugg!' cried Jamie impatiently. 'What are you looking at? Come on!' But Bella did not move, she just continued to stare upwards.

Daisy dug Jamie in his ribs. 'She's terrified, you moron!' she whispered fiercely. Daisy reached out to touch Bella's arm. 'It's all right--'

Bella suddenly screamed: 'HE'S HERE! HE'S HERE, MR VIM! QUICKLY! COME QUICKLY!'

'No!' shouted Maxwell. He stepped forward to grab Bella, and heard Jamie and Bella cry out. Maxwell followed their staring eyes up the walls of the castle.

Above them the gargoyle's wings unfurled and it launched itself from the Black Monastery. They all watched in terror as it glided over the moat - and then turned and swooped down towards them.

'Inside!' yelled Maxwell. 'Get inside now!'

But Daisy and Jamie were staring at the swooping creature, frozen with terror as it flew ever closer. Maxwell pushed them aside and raised his hands to the gargoyle, felt the ice coursing through his veins, and aimed at the monster.

A blast of red flame shot from the gargoyle's eyes and hit Maxwell. He was hurled from his feet and slammed against the wall.

He slid to the cobbled ground, blackness crowding into his vision. In the last second before he lost consciousness he heard the thump of the gargoyle's feet hitting the ground, and a searing bolt of red light split the black clouds that were rolling over him. Then his friends started to scream - and Maxwell was sucked into utter darkness and knew no more.

Chapter Twenty Eight: Mamble's boys

Maxwell drifted slowly out of deep darkness to the sound of many small, eager voices:

'Stay-stay-hold-eat-kill-no-no-stay-stay . . ."

He slowly opened his eyes. He was on a stone floor and was surrounded by darkness. He sat up with difficulty, he was aching all over his body.

His eyes slowly adjusted to the gloom until he could see that he was kneeling on black flagstones . . . and all around him the whispering dry voice continued.

'Who's there?' he said, but the voices did not answer, they just continued to talk, to argue with one another in low, urgent voices.

'Stay-stay-hold-hungry-stay-stay . . .'

Maxwell got to his feet, and as soon as he did beetles, thousands of them, raced out of the gloom and surrounded him in a rustling black circle.

'Get back,' he said, but the beetles did not move. 'Back!'

'They will not listen to your commands.' Out of the darkness, like a shimmering ghost, came Titus Mamble. He drifted over the beetles. Where the tails of his cape covered the beetles they struggled desperately, drowning inside the dirty liquid that was his body. He stopped inside the ring of beetles, the filthy water of his face forming into a smile. 'Hello Maxwell, nice to see you again.' He chuckled wetly. 'Though, of course, as time is reckoned in this realm we haven't met for the first time yet. By my calculations you're lying on a bed in the Fortress around about now, aren't you?'

'Where are my friends?' Maxwell demanded.

'They are quite safe, I assure you,' said Mamble. 'Safe for now, anyway.'

'Where's Billy? Have you ...' Maxwell paused, an image appearing in his mind – a Long Man – and Mamble seemed to read his thought, because before Maxwell could continue he said:

'He isn't a Long Man, Maxwell. Would I do that to a friend?' Mamble held his watery hand to his chest, as though Maxwell had struck a blow to his heart. 'Billy is quite safe. Though a little ... A little tired, you might say.'

'Where is he? I want to see him!'

Mamble sighed, and raised his hands. Light slowly filtered into the space around them, revealing a large, featureless stone chamber. Beetles covered every inch of the floor, heaped in black masses by the only exit to the chamber. 'Show them,' Mamble commanded, and the heaps of beetles suddenly scattered and revealed what was beneath. With sick horror Maxwell saw Billy, Jamie, Bella and Daisy. 'Return,' commanded Titus Mamble, and in a second all four of his friends were covered by beetles again, not an inch of their bodies could be seen under the squirming masses of bugs.

'My power is weakening, Maxwell,' said Mamble with a deep, watery sigh. 'Without the life force of others this form will lose cohesion. If that happens I will not be able to command the beetles, and they will devour your friends.'

'Really?' said Maxwell. He raised his hands as fast as a gunslinger and ice blasted from his palms.

The blast glanced off Mamble and deflected onto the floor, freezing a circle of beetles solid. Mamble looked at the beetles, his eyebrow rose, and he sighed wearily.

'I said my powers were weakening, not gone, Maxwell,' he said. 'Attempt anything like that again and I will let the beetles eat one of your friends. Perhaps Bella? No, Bella is too big, they wouldn't be able to eat another thing!' Mamble chuckled. 'Daisy, then? Or Billy?'

Maxwell lowered his hands. Titus Mamble smiled, and slipped an arm around Maxwell's shoulder.

'Time is short, Maxwell, and you would be best advised to stop wasting it if you want your friends to live.' He led Maxwell across the chamber, the beetles moving with them, forming a clear circle of black stone wherever Maxwell and Mamble stepped. 'You have elemental powers, Maxwell. That is quite impressive! I was your age when I discovered I could talk to animals and fire ice and snow from my hands, just as you can. I remember I was in Haggerston, a little place just outside Edinburgh—'

'I thought you said time was short?' Maxwell interrupted.

Mamble's face darkened. 'Don't you ever interrupt me!' he hissed, and his cold arm tightened around Maxwell's shoulders. It was like being clamped in an enormous vice. Maxwell gasped in pain. Mamble smiled, and his grip relaxed. 'We still have time, and this is a story you need to hear.

'When I was eleven my sister Rebecca and I were sent to a detention camp in a place called Haggerston. From there detainees were assigned to different parts of the country – Aberdeen, Glasgow, Edinburgh – to work as labourers, digging ditches, clearing rubble and so on.'

'Rubble from what?' Maxwell asked, and then flinched, expecting Mamble's unyielding arms to crush him once more.

'Good question,' said the creature, smiling. 'This was during the First Combination, which I believe you now know a little about?' Maxwell nodded. 'German forces had controlled Europe and Asia for more than fifty years, and during all that time the war with America had continued. But the Nazis were of at a great advantage, they developed the atom bomb before the USA. But the Americans continued the war for many years with conventional weapons and had bombed most of the major cities in Europe. By the time Rebecca and I were sent to Scotland the war had been over for almost a decade, and America by that time of course was almost entirely uninhabitable. Nuclear fallout,' Mamble added in answer to Maxwell's confused expression.

Maxwell listened while Titus Mamble described his and his sister's long journey from Lithuania to Scotland, and how they had laboured in Edinburgh, clearing the rubble from a lifetime of war.

Maxwell imagined it. Cities filled with children dressed in gray uniforms, red stars upon their chest to mark them as the children of political criminals, clearing stone and metal and glass with their bare hands. Many, many children died, Mamble told him, crushed or lost beneath the shifting, deadly wreckage of the demolished cities.

And oddly it almost seemed to Maxwell that he was not actually *imagining* these scenes – it was as if he was *remembering them*. In his mind he saw the smoking, shifting ruins of Edinburgh, heard the constant sounds of heavy machinery and the bellow of never ending demolition, and felt the furious cold bite at his fingers and toes ... But how was that possible? These scenes were from another world, these sounds from a history that did not exist, and the clear vision that Maxwell had of Titus Mamble's twin sister Rebecca – Maxwell's aunty – as a dirty, grinning girl with vivid black hair were from a time over thirty years before he was born.

He could not possibly remember these things. And yet somehow he did.

They had stopped in the centre of the room, and as the beetles cleared a space at their feet Maxwell

saw that they were standing in the middle three
concentric circles etched in the stone.

'Ice,' said Mamble, 'That is how I escaped. I
was at the edge of the city, near the river, and when I
looked around I could see no guards – so I ran. I
don't know what made me do it. And as I approached
the river I raised my hands, and I created a path of ice
for myself across to the far bank.'

'You left Rebecca behind?' Maxwell said.

'I intended to go back for her,' said Mamble.
'Even after Vim found me and took me to Vir I always
knew I would go back and rescue Rebecca. But the
Vir High Council wouldn't allow it.'

'Why not?' asked Maxwell.

'Why not indeed? Because Good Men must
not interfere in other cultures' development. Good
Men must not use their powers to help friends or
loved ones when others are in peril. That was the law
if the "heroes" of Vir,' Mamble laughed bitterly. 'Fight
for goodness and light, but do not feel love. Battle
evil, but do not feel hatred or anger. They could have
swept into my world and wiped the armies of the
Nazis from its face . . . But they would not. They were
the Good Men, guardians of 101 Realms, not one
world, and they would not change the course of one
world's history, no matter what monstrous future grew
from that history.'

'And Rebecca died?' Maxwell asked.

'Yes,' said Mamble, but then he smiled. 'But
when I touched the Eternal Engine she lived again.
Rebecca is alive now, Maxwell. I saved her in the end,
you see?'

'But ...' Maxwell looked at Mamble's smiling
face and shook his head. 'But *billions* died because of
you!'

'The Good Men of Vir died,' said Mamble
quietly. 'And there is no tragedy in that. Remember

that these *Good Men* stood by while millions were slaughter and tortured and enslaved by evil men, and they did nothing.'

'But the Big Combination was an accident,' said Maxwell. 'The Eternal Engine exploded, didn't it?'

'It exploded after I began the Big Combination,' said Mamble. '*I* changed the history of this world. *I* froze Vir and smashed the Good Men's reign on 101 worlds. And if Arcania had not destroyed the Eternal Engine, believe me, I would have done much, much more.'

Maxwell stared at Mamble, and the creature looked back serenely, a calm smile on his monstrous face.

'You can't believe that,' Maxwell said at last. 'You can't believe that it was right that all of those people died so your sister could live.'

'I know it was right,' Titus Mamble replied. 'My sister deserved life, they did not. The High Council would not judge the actions of the Good Men, but I would, and I did, and I judged them to be wrong.'

'*You're wrong,*' said Maxwell. 'What you did was terrible, and nothing you can say can change that. I don't care what happened to you,' he said, growing angrier at Mamble's calm expression with each word he spoke, 'and I don't care that you're my father! It was wrong, and it was evil!'

'Your father?' said Mamble. He laughed. 'I'm not your father,' he said.

At that moment a great commotion rose from the passage leading to the chamber. Maxwell turned and saw the beetles quickly scurry away, clearing a broad path from the exit. Then, with an ear-splitting roar, a massive creature thundered into the chamber, rearing and shaking its deformed head, its tentacles thrashing on the stone floor in fury and pain. The monster's filmy gray eyes turned to Mamble, and with a bellow that shook the stones beneath their feet, it rocketed towards them, its misshapen teeth, as long and sharp as sabers, gnashing.

Maxwell took a step back, but Mamble's liquid yet powerful hand grasped his shoulder and held him still.

The thing pistoned towards them, its mouth roaring open, and then, only half a dozen feet from where Maxwell stood, it reared to strike. There was a sudden burst of red light and it fell lifelessly to the floor. Maxwell felt the stones shudder beneath his feet.

'The Nurgler,' Maxwell whispered.

'Indeed!' said Mamble cheerfully. He stepped forward and laid his hand gently on the Nurgler's barnacle-encrusted snout. It shuddered and whimpered with fear. 'So nice to see old friends together again, don't you think, Professor Silex?'

Maxwell gasped and looked up from the beast. He half expected to see his grim maths teacher waddle into the hall, but of course the figure he saw was not Flavia Silex, but a tall, gaunt man as thin as a whip. The beetles closed their path behind him as he stood beside Titus Mamble.

'A pleasure,' said Mr Vim, his thin lips barely moving, his face as impassive as rock.

'You said Mamble was my father,' Maxwell whispered – and he did not feel fear or hatred looking at Vim's expressionless face – he felt hope.

But Mamble was laughing, and even Mr Vim's cold lips curled into a hint of a smile.

'Of course he told you that, Maxwell, and that fool Juggernaut backed him up,' laughed Mamble, thumping Mr Vim heartily on the back. 'The Professor could not possibly have told you the truth.'

They both laughed, and Maxwell stared at them. 'The truth?' he said, and they both looked at him. Maxwell licked his lips. The sounds in the room suddenly seemed too loud – the scuttling of the beetles, the whimpering Nurgler, the distant whine of the wind in the tunnels and passages of the Black Monastery. 'What truth?' he asked.

Mamble smiled. 'When the Eternal Engine exploded I was torn apart. But not destroyed. My mind, my memories, they became a vapor which eventually became this form,' he held out his watery arms, 'And my powers, also a vapor, fell through the 101 Realms into Mab, where they became the Nurgler.'

Titus Mamble leant towards Maxwell, and whispered, 'But I was not torn in two, Maxwell. I was torn in three. My life force became another being. A baby, born out of the devastation that followed the destruction of the Eternal Engine.'

He leaned closer, until his watery lips bushed Maxwell's ear, and his voice was barely even a whisper:

'You are not Maxwell Jones,' hissed Titus Mamble. 'You are me.'

Chapter Twenty-Nine: the Astrosus

'You're lying,' Maxwell said, his voice a breathless croak.

Mamble shook his head, a fine spray of water flying into Maxwell's face. 'I do not lie,' the creature replied.

'You told me you'd never killed anyone but you killed billions of people!' Maxwell said, anger growing in his voice, just as aching fear grew in his bones. 'You're a liar!'

'Ah,' said Mamble, smiling, 'there you are mistaken, Maxwell. I said I never murdered anyone, and I never have. The Good Men who died, died as an act of war. A war against the evil misrule of the Vir High Council.' He stood up straight, and stalked towards the Nurgler. The creature whimpered again, and a tear ran from its squinting eyes as Mamble laid his hand on its head. 'And now that war must continue. The Eternal Engine must be reassembled and all of the accidents of chance put right by my hand,' he held out his other hand to Maxwell, 'By our hands, Maxwell.'

'You're lying!' Maxwell cried. 'I'm not you! I'm me! My dad was Andy Jones, not you!'

'Andronocus is my middle name,' said Mamble. 'Many people called me Andy.'

'What about my mum!' said Maxwell desperately. 'How can I be you? My mum is Bettie Jones!'

'Your mum?' Mamble laughed. 'I barely knew her! She had just graduated from the Watchmen when the Engine was destroyed. I think I had spoken to her once in my life to ask her where Arcania kept his chocolate biscuits!'

'Bettie was with Arcania when the Engine exploded,' said Mr Vim. 'She was his apprentice. She pulled you out of the ruins and took you to Virporta. She is not your mother, Mr Jones. But she did protect you when many wanted you dead.'

'You see, Maxwell?' said Mamble, 'These people, these Good Men, would have killed you - they would have killed a *newborn baby* - out of fear and ignorance. And you want ally yourself with them?'

'I am not you!' shouted Maxwell. 'I'm me! I'm Maxwell Jones!'

'That,' said Mamble. 'Is an illusion. There is no Maxwell Jones, just as there is no Nurgler.' The Nurgler let out a sob of fear at the mention of its name. 'You have no mother, no father, no past and no future. You are an illusion, a device by which I protected myself from destruction. You were born from me, your life is my life, and your future is mine to take back.'

Could it possibly be true that he was this monster? Could it be that everything he was, everything he remembered and he hoped for was a dream? No. No, I'm more than that, he thought. I wouldn't have run and let my sister die. I wouldn't have unleashed the power of the Eternal Engine. I wouldn't have lived in a filthy pool feeding off people like a vampire.

'I'm more than that,' Maxwell said. 'I'm more than a part of you!'

Mamble looked at him thoughtfully. 'Perhaps you are,' he said at last. He raised his hand and behind the Nurgler a trail opened in the beetles. 'Go then, Maxwell Jones. Both of you - go.'

The Nurgler's eyes sprang open. It looked desperately from Mamble to Mr Vim, and then with a roared it reared up, turned and fled.

'What are you *doing!*' bellowed Mr Vim. 'It will escape!'

Mr Vim started forward after the Nurgler, but Mamble laid a hand on his chest. 'I told the boy I have never murdered anyone, and I told him the truth. If they do not want to join with me again, then I will not force them.'

'You fool!' spat Mr Vim.

Maxwell looked at the creature in disbelief, but Titus Mamble stepped aside and smiled. 'Go, Maxwell,' he said, 'with my blessing and my hopes for your future.'

Maxwell took a hesitant step forward. 'I can just leave?' Mamble nodded. 'And my friends can leave with me?'

'Of course.' Titus Mamble waved his hand once more, and the beetles receded, revealing Billy, Daisy, Jamie and Bella.

Maxwell turned back to Titus Mamble, and said slowly, 'But ... But what happens after we leave?'

'I will continue,' Mamble said. 'To keep myself alive I will have consume everyone on this island. Then I will go beyond these shores out into this world and consume everything that lives, until this entire planet is populated with Long Men. I will continue, Maxwell Jones, make no mistake about that.' The creature grinned. 'But don't worry, Maxwell, I won't touch you, or your friends. You will be allowed to live as long as you wish, unmolested and free in my new world.'

Mr Vim laughed harshly. 'If you hurry,' he said, his cracked voice filled with glee, 'you may still catch the Nurgler.'

'Your choice, Maxwell Jones.' Mamble held his hands like scales, weighing Maxwell's life against the doom of an entire world. 'Your choice.'

Maxwell ran along the black corridor, and though he

felt despair tug at his feet and the foul air of the Black Monastery choked him, he could not stop.

Around him the stones seemed to quiver as he passed, and he knew that if he could stop and scrape back the centuries-old dirt the stones beneath would be flesh-pink and soft to the touch. Because now he understood that the Black Monastery was not a monastery, or a castle, a church or a mansion – it was a living creature, and it had him in its belly.

But Maxwell did not stop; he could not stop, though his lungs felt stuffed with cotton wool. He ran through the undulating corridor and out through the gaping door and into the night.

The carpet of worms was gone, but Maxwell barely noticed, if they had been there he wouldn't even have slowed his run. He ran out under the moon and down the side of the moat, at the bottom of which a huge shape was slipping towards the water.

'Nurgler!' Maxwell cried. The beast moved faster at the sound of his voice, its tentacles thumping on the mud. 'Stop! It's me! It's Maxwell!'

The Nurgler stopped, and turned back. Maxwell fell to his knees in the mud in front of the monster's glistening jaws.

'You have escaped!' gurgled the Nurgler in delight. 'Good! Good! We can escape to Mab together! There are many places to hide! A million places! We can—'

'We have to go back,' gasped Maxwell.

'Back?' the Nurgler's fearsome brow creased, making his appearance even more terrifying. 'Don't be foolish, Maxwell, we can not defeat the Titus Mamble! We must escape!'

The Nurgler began to slide towards the pool again. Maxwell struggled to his feet and grabbed one of the beast's tentacles.

'We have to go back!' he shouted. 'If we don't Mamble will turn everyone into Long Men! Don't you see - we don't have any choice but to go back!'

'You go back if you wish, little Maxwell. I have a choice, and I would rather spend eternity hounded and tormented by the Beasts of Mab than face what awaits me in the Basilica Astrosus!'

'But everyone will die!' said Maxwell. 'He'll kill everyone!'

'They will be Long Men. No one will die. Indeed, they will live forever!'

'But that's worse than death!' Maxwell cried in desperation as he felt the powerful tentacle gently but firmly drag free of his fingers.

'No, Maxwell. What we face if we surrender to Mamble is worse than death,' it said, its voice quavering. 'The Long Men remember who they were, though that memory is unbearable torture, and if they are killed they are set free. But the creature does not mean to kill us and set free our spirits, or trap us in wisps of bodies that torture and revolt us for all eternity. He means to obliterate us absolutely. He means to suck the life from us and make our spirits evaporate so that not a single memory of our lives exists in either spirit or body. We will not be dead, Maxwell, we will be as if we never existed.'

Maxwell shivered, and turned his eyes back to the Monastery. Could he face that? Then he thought of his friends, and of his batty old mother, and Mrs Trimm and even the horrible Bartholemew Pugg and the mean walnut eyes of Dr Silex ... And he remembered the empty, hungry eyes of the Long Men.

'If my friends become Long Men it will be like I never existed anyway,' Maxwell said, turning back to the Nurgler. 'I won't let that happen. I can't let him do that to my mum. And don't tell me she isn't my mum, Nurgler, because she is. *She is!* It won't be like I never existed because while my mum is alive I'll be alive. Even if I'm only alive as a memory.'

Maxwell stood facing the Nurgler, and neither of them moved, or lowered their eyes.

The Nurgler sighed, and raised its monstrous face to the sky.

'Mab is so distant, barely even a twinkle in this sky,' it said. 'But the Beasts of Mab will remember me.' It grinned at Maxwell, a terrifying grin, filled with hundreds of wicked, glittering teeth. 'I will live in their nightmares for centuries.' It winked one grey, filmy eye. 'What more could a monster like me dream of?'

The Nurgler's tentacle wrapped itself gently around Maxwell's waist, and squeezed him affectionately. Maxwell buried his face in the creature's thick hide, and tried not to weep as he heard its massive pounding heart.

'Come then!' said the Nurgler. 'If we are to be part of Mamble, let him eat us quickly . . . and maybe we will give him indigestion!'

The monster chuckled, and they walked together to the Black Monastery.

At the door Maxwell paused, and looked back.

Above the Black Woods a full moon had risen, its light painting the boughs of the trees silver. The sky above was dotted with countless familiar stars, and around those stars, Maxwell knew, on countless worlds people beyond reckoning looked up at the sky and hoped.

Maxwell turned away and walked into darkness.

In the grim chamber at the centre of the Black Monastery the beetles parted before Maxwell and the Nurgler. Titus Mamble still stood with his arms held out like scales. At his side Mr Vim smiled coldly.

'You have brought me back my monster,' said Mamble, lowering his arms. 'What a grand reunion this is, Maxwell. You should have rode in on its back.'

'There's only one monster here,' said Maxwell.

'Perhaps two,' growled the Nurgler, glaring at Vim.

Titus Mamble laughed. 'Two mortal enemies brought together in brotherhood, how delightful,' he said. 'But soon all three of us will be closer than brothers, my dear Maxwell and Nurgler. Now – step into the circle please.'

They moved forward, and Maxwell saw that beneath the undulating folds of Mamble's cape the concentric circles, like a target patterned in stone, had reappeared. Maxwell and the Nurgler stood on the outermost circle under Mr Vim's instruction, and Mamble stood opposite them.

'I found this place many years ago,' he said. 'Or do I mean many years from now? Time travel can be so confusing. Whatever – it was here that I first discovered the secret of the Eternal Engine, and here that I was shown my destiny.'

Mamble bent forward and touched the innermost circle, then stood up straight, and solemnly bowed his head. For several seconds nothing happened, and then, with a deep-throated rumble, the outer circle they were standing on began to rise into the air. In front of them the inner circle also rose in a column to the height of Maxwell's chest. In a few moments the three were standing on the lip of a column rising twenty feet from the stone floor, the inner circle like a table in front of them. Then, with an eye-watering screech, a third column rose in the centre of the table-like column, and at its crest, turning in the air, floated a black jewel as big as a football.

'The Astrosus.' Maxwell looked around. Mr Vim was flying beside them, his great bat wings beating, his face slack with wonder and fear.

'The Astrosus,' Mamble agreed. 'Now place your hands upon the column in front of you.' Titus Mamble chuckled. 'And if you can't give a hand a tentacle or two will do just fine, we're not biased.' Maxwell reached for the column, and he felt something – Titus Mamble's will, his own desire, or the Astrosus's dark power, Maxwell didn't know which – drag his hands forward. 'But do not touch the stone!' hissed Mamble, a note of alarm in his voice. 'To touch it is certain death!'

For a second Maxwell's fingers stretched towards the Astrosus – it was almost as if his hands were made of metal and the stone a powerful magnet – and then with an effort he rested his hands on the circular ridge beneath the Astrosus. The moment his palms touched the top of the column they stuck to it like glue.

Mr Vim rose above them, and at a nod from Mamble he pulled a knife from his pocket and cut a slit in the palm of his hand, then closed it into a fist. Blood dripped onto the black jewel.

A beam of black . . . light, Maxwell supposed – he could think of no other word to describe the beam – rose vertically from the Astrosus, and then slowly began to move downwards, turning like the beam of a light house as it descended towards them.

The Nurgler let out a whimper of fear. 'Don't worry,' Maxwell whispered, but the creature was overcome with terror, and continued to shiver and whimper, and Mamble laughed.

'Now all of my designs have come to this,' said Titus Mamble. 'Eleven long years of agony and despair will end today.' He glared at the Nurgler and

Maxwell and grinned, his polluted black teeth glinting wetly. 'And all your hopes have ended.'

The black beam struck Titus Mamble's face. His face became a grinning skeleton's skull. The beam turned slowly around the circle, and Maxwell saw out of the corner of his eye Mr Vim let out a cry of alarm and swoop down to the floor to avoid the black light. The beam turned slowly towards Maxwell. He squirmed and ducked his head – but it was no use, his hands were stuck fast. The beam enveloped him.

The room was suddenly filled with men dressed in armour and chain mail staring up at the Astrosus column. Maxwell recognised them as knights – but he also knew immediately that they were not humans. They were Good Men, many with silver hair, black and red eyes and green and purple skins. The knights raised their swords with a roar of some lost language, then rose up into the air, and flew from the room in a glittering tide of death and destruction.

Maxwell fell forward onto the column as the beam released him – and below the ringing laughter of Titus Mamble and the blood-curdling screams of the terrified Nurgler, Maxwell heard another sound.

A popping noise. Like popcorn cooking.

Maxwell looked up as the black light of the Astrosus hit the Nurgler. The creature let out a terrific scream – and began to *change*. Its thick hide bubbled, its shape shifted, its gnashing, screeching jaws shrank, and its wildly thrashing tentacles vanished.

And suddenly the Nurgler was laughing. When finally the black light released him, it was no longer the Nurgler standing there – it was Titus Mamble, now flesh and blood.

'It's good to be back in the flesh,' said Mamble. He spat something from his mouth. 'Though I do have the most peculiar taste in my mouth. Goodness knows what the dear departed

Nurgler has been eating for the last eleven years!' He leant towards Maxwell. 'Time to say goodbye, my dear little body thief,' he whispered.

The black light turned slowly, past the place where the watery Titus Mamble had stood, moving inexorably towards Maxwell.

'All that you are and were will be forgotten,' whispered Mamble. 'All that you loved will be destroyed and lain waste. In all the universe only I will know your name, Maxwell Jones, and if I live a hundred trillion years I will never speak it again. You will be wiped from history absolutely.'

'You promised to let my friends go!' cried Maxwell desperately as the beam edged closer and closer.

Titus Mamble grinned. 'I lied,' he said.

Maxwell struggled, but it was no use. He had been tricked, trapped, and now there was nothing he could do. The black light of the Astrosus moved closer, now only inches from him ...

... and it stuttered and stopped dead.

'What a remarkably inefficient piece of engineering,' came a familiar voice. 'Early Phoenician, isn't it, Titus? They never were much shakes with mechanics.'

Dr Arcania stood beside Maxwell, carefully examining the black jewel. In the palm of his upheld hand a white ball of light spun, drawing the black beam of the Astrosus into its heart.

'Arcania!' screeched Mamble, twisting frantically as Dr Arcania began to pull the black light back round towards him.

'How are you Maxwell?' asked Dr Arcania. 'Sorry about all that business with the fish--'

'Look out!' cried Maxwell - but he was too late.

Mr Vim swept down on the little chimpanzee with a bellow of fury, his fingers drawn into claws, his teeth bared in a triumphant snarl - and passed right through Dr Arcania. He crashed into the column with bone-shaking impact, and thudded to the floor.

'You're a hologram!' hissed Mamble.

'Slightly more advanced than a mere "hologram". I think you'll find that technology has moved on a little since your time, Titus,' he turned to Maxwell and chuckled. 'As if I, Dr Lambton Arcania, the greatest mind in history, would invent a mere "hologram". This is a Photonogram.' He saw Maxwell's confused expression and raised his eyes and sighed. 'You can look "Photon" up as soon as I get you out of here, Maxwell.' Dr Arcania pushed the ball of light towards the black jewel. 'This is rather harder going than I'd calculated,' he grunted, 'And I do so detest physical labour. Be prepared to run as soon as I deactivate the Astrosus, Maxwell.'

'If you run I will make good on my threat!' shouted Mamble. 'I will destroy this island! I will kill everyone you love!'

Dr Arcania laughed. 'What utter fantasy. If he does not draw your life force from you, Maxwell, Titus will be a Long Man in a matter of minutes, and you can defeat him easily.'

Maxwell looked at Titus Mamble, and to his amazement, he saw that it was true! Mamble's face was losing its healthy pink colour and his fingers were elongating into tapered claws. The water Mamble was now joined with the Nurgler's body - and it was quickly sucking the life from the new form the Astrosus had created.

Mr Vim rose into the air again. His nose was bleeding heavily, and one of his wings looked broken. 'What shall I do?' he implored Mamble. 'I can't touch him! What can I do!'

Titus Mamble's eyes darted from Vim to Dr Arcania, his face working in terror, his skin quickly turning the colour of ash.

'You're finished,' said Maxwell, and Mamble tried to launch himself at Maxwell - but his hands were still fixed to the column, and he howled with impotent rage.

'Almost!' grunted Dr Arcania, pushing against the black light with all his might. 'Just another inch ...'

'The stone!' screeched Mamble suddenly. 'Burn the stone, Vim!'

Mr Vim snatched off his visor and red rays shot from his eyes. The rays hit the Astrosus and a ball of red light exploded from it, engulfing the whole column. Maxwell turned his face away with a cry.

He did not open his eyes again for a second, the red blooming afterimage of the explosion imprinted on the darkness behind his eyelids ... and he heard Mamble's laughter, now unmistakably like the hissing rattle of a Long Man.

Maxwell opened his eyes.

Dr Arcania was gone. The beam of black light was moving steadily towards Maxwell again.

'Finished?' hissed Mamble, white light spilling from his mouth, his eyes turning from blue to black. 'Finished? I have only just begun.'

Maxwell slumped back. If his hands hadn't been welded to the column he would have fallen to the floor. He was lost. Dr Arcania's hologram had been destroyed, and now he had no hope, no chance ...

Maxwell heard the sound again. A sound like cooking popcorn.

He followed the sound and saw that it was coming from the heaps of beetles by the door. Only now the beetles were fleeing from one of those heaps in a tide, and even as they ran the bugs were exploding and bursting into flame. The fleeing beetles revealed a face. The eyes opened, and one winked.

Billy held up a hand, burning beetles falling from his arm, and bent his thumb, then his index finger towards his palm - 5, 4 ...

Maxwell turned back to Mamble. The creature was hissing impatiently at the black beam as it moved slowly towards Maxwell. Titus Mamble's once fine blue eyes were now as black as coals, his mouth a blazing slit of white, his hair falling onto his shoulders in limp drifts. In a matter of minutes he would be completely transformed into a Long Man. Above them Mr Vim hung in the air, his face as expressionless as ever.

'How did you do it?' Maxwell asked, hoping to draw Vim's attention from the popping noise and the scurrying of the panicked beetles. 'How did you find the Nurgler and me?'

Mr Vim allowed a slight smile. 'I did not find you,' he said. 'You found me. In the Watchmen University. You told me about the Black Monastery, and the Nurgler, and after you fled the lab I used Arcania's matter transfer devise to send me back in time to Virporta.'

Maxwell goggled in amazement, Billy temporarily forgotten. 'It was the Conundrum?'

'It was a Conundrum. Not the Conundrum you experienced,' Mr Vim replied. 'The Conundrum showed me the Everyman would rise again, and through my Test I would find you, and you would lead me to the Nurgler, and the completion of my destiny.' He grinned, his teeth as white as sun-bleached bone. 'Well done, Mr Jones, you have fulfilled your own destiny admirably. You have closed the circle that began when Arcania destroyed the Eternal Engine. And now, Mr Jones--'

'And now we can have a barbeque, followed by pop and jelly,' interrupted a voice. 'Anyone bring any burgers?'

Mr Vim began to turn and a torrent of flame engulfed him and hurled him, burning, across the chamber. Mr Vim hit the wall and fell smoking and unconscious to the floor.

A burning figure was suspended in the air in front of the Astrosus column. Its entire form was consumed by flame, from its burning toes and fingers to its red licks of hair. Eyes, bright, glistening silver eyes, shone from its burning face.

'Alright, Max?' said Billy. He floated closer and turned his fierce silver eyes on Mamble, who cowered away, squinting his black eyes and hissing like a kettle. 'A Long Man?' Billy exclaimed, confused. 'Where the bleeding hell's that bum paper Titus Mamble got too?'

'That is—' Maxwell began – and then the beam of black light, which had been turning unhurriedly towards him all the time, hit him square in the face and all words stopped.

Maxwell screamed into the blackness, but no sound came from his straining throat, and then, like air leaking from a balloon, everything he knew and felt and remembered was sucked from his mind.

Frantic with terror Maxwell looked up at ... at ... at the boy ... the boy was on fire for some reason ... his name ...

'Maxwell!' yelled the burning boy. 'Maxwell! What's wrong!'

Maxwell? He thought. Who's Maxwell?

He looked into the black heart of the Astrosus and saw nothing. A blank nothing that was not even darkness. He looked up again and saw that the burning boy was flying closer, trying to smash the black jewel with balls of white fire thrown from his hands – but the flames simply evaporated into harmless smoke a foot or more from the Astrosus.

'MAXWELL!' screamed the burning boy, but now his cries were growing tinny and distant like the volume turned down on a radio, and his flames were fading before the nameless boys dimming eyes.

'Traitor!' hissed a voice. He turned towards it and saw a man was standing where before there had stood a wasted grey creature of some sort. The man tore his hand from the top of the column, leaving the skin of his palm behind. He raised his bloody hand to the burning boy who raised his own hand – a second too late.

A blue sphere encircled the burning boy – and suddenly he wasn't burning any longer. He transformed in an instant into a blond haired boy wearing silver spectacles. He fell to his hands and knees in the blue sphere, gasping.

'There can be no fire without air, traitor,' said the young man, his bleeding hand held high. 'There can be no life without air, either, Mr Barker,' he laughed. 'And now my destiny begins again, life and power fill me, and you shall all die with my name on your lips – Titus Mamble, the Everyman!'

The man turned, grinning triumphantly, and black light filled the boy with no name and no memory, and his mind filled with nothing and he felt himself crumbling into the heart of the jewel, into oblivion.

The boy in the bubble rose painfully to his knees. 'Maxwell,' he whispered with his last gasp of air. 'Oh, bleeding Nora Max, he can't ... can't win ...' He crumpled to the bottom of the bubble.

The boy with no memory looked up at the unmoving figure and heard the triumphant laughter of the man. He opened his mouth, and whispered, 'Billy ... ?'

Everything came back to Maxwell in a dizzying rush. For a second the black beam of the Astrosus guttered and blinked. Mamble's head whipped around, his laughter dying and his face contorting with shock and fear.

The light of the Astrosus steadied, and the memories began to tumble from Maxwell's head again. Titus Mamble grinned, and turned back to his victim.

He looked down at his hands, then squinted his eyes closed. 'I am Maxwell Jones,' he whispered. He leaned back, and began to pull at his left hand with all his strength. 'I am Maxwell ... Maxwell ...' He felt the skin on the palm of his hand begin to tear, excruciating pain setting every nerve in his body on fire – but he did not stop. He gritted his teeth until his jaws ached, tears rolled down his face –he pulled harder. 'I am ... I ...' He wrenched his hand free of the column with the horrible wet ripping sound of his own skin, his blood splattering the Astrosus.

'I AM MAXWELL JONES!' he screamed.

Mamble spun towards him with a shout of rage and alarm, blue electricity arcing across his fingers as he reached for Maxwell's throat. Maxwell grabbed his wrist and plunged Mamble's hand into the Astrosus.

'NO!' screeched Mamble. The blue bubble vanished and Billy crashed to the floor. 'NO!' he screamed as his hand and then his arm were sucked into the Astrosus. Titus Mamble let out a terrible warbling scream – cut off suddenly as the Astrosus sucked him whole into its heart.

The black light beam blinked out. The Astrosus sank slowly back into the central column. Maxwell's hand suddenly came free. He fell back without the strength to cry out and hit the floor.

Maxwell watched, gasping for breath, as the Astrosus column sank into the floor. He discovered he was barely able to move, even breathing was exhausting him. Billy lay unconscious or dead on the other side of the descending column. Maxwell tried to call out his name, but all that came from his throat was a reedy whisper.

Maxwell closed his eyes and felt himself slowly sinking into unconsciousness even as the Astrosus sank back into the floor with a shiver that ran through the Black Monastery.

The last thing he felt was a thousand tiny feet covering his body, and he realised that the beetles had him, and he was finished. They would eat him and Billy and Bella and Daisy and Jamie, and probably Mr Vim too, and none of them would ever wake.

Then, just before the darkness took him completely, he heard a small, strident voice, a voice that was barely even a whisper.

'*Attack!*' cried the voice. '*Drive them back, lads! Onwards! Liberate the feet! 987326 – drop that leaf, laddie!*'

The ants! realised Maxwell, and then he knew nothing but blackness.

Chapter Thirty: the handsome beast's secret

Maxwell felt something leathery and hard beneath him. He opened his eyes. Needles of pain jabbed into his eyeballs and settled at the front of his brain. He saw that he was on the back of some creature that in his confusion he thought at first was a bald horse.

He quickly realised it wasn't a horse at all. It was a small tyrannosaurus rex who smelled unmistakably of fruit scones.

'Trevor?' he murmured.

'Oh, you're awake *now*,' said Trevor sarcastically. 'I hope you *enjoyed* your little snooze!'

Maxwell was hardly able to lift his head, and his vision seemed dim and hazy, but nevertheless he could clearly see that Trevor was carrying him on his back through the Black Woods, and Trevor was setting a breakneck pace.

'Are the others all right?' Maxwell asked, his voice was just a shaky whisper.

'Do you see a stethoscope around my neck? Do I look like a doctor to you?' Without his mother around to correct him Trevor's manners weren't at their best. 'I'm not a horse or a pony either, but I've still ended up with you on my back,' he added sulkily.

'I can walk,' Maxwell said, not sure if this was actually true at all, but he did not relish the thought of upsetting a moody adolescent dinosaur.

'You monkeys move like a fat diplodocus even when you're fit!' Trevor exclaimed. 'And there's no way I'm letting those smelly birds beat *me!*'

Smelly birds? What on earth did that mean? Maxwell looked up and immediately found his answer. Above the trees a great flock of seagulls soared, and beneath them, carried by dozens of beating wings, hung Billy, Bella, Daisy and Jamie.

Trevor leapt over a fallen tree, and Maxwell gripped the t-rex's neck as well as he could, which was not very well at all. His muscles felt rubbery and wasted, and he barely had the strength to cling on.

'That stupid parrot said there was going to be a big fight!' said Trevor bitterly. 'Big fight! Huh! I get to that castle thingy expecting a serious rumble and all that's there is a bunch of stupid kids fast asleep and crawly ants all over the place!' Trevor shivered. 'I *hate* insects, me!'

'What happened to Mr Vim?' Maxwell asked urgently.

But Trevor did not hear him, or more likely decided to ignore the question. He cried, 'Nearly there!' and surged forward with dizzying speed. He left the Black Woods like a tiger leaping from his den and flew across the Watchmen Academy's sports field. They crossed the field in barely ten seconds – a feat that not even Miss Hummingbird could have hoped to match – belted past the sports hall and skidded to a halt in the schoolyard.

Trevor gave a terrific roar of triumph. 'Beat you, you stinky birds!' Maxwell spilled from his back and landed gasping on the hard ground.

Trevor didn't even notice. 'I am the cham-pion! I am the cham-pion!' the little dinosaur chanted, and suddenly Maxwell was surrounded by noise and movement. An enormous flock of birds – though *flock* was not really a big enough word, it seemed like every bird in the world had suddenly descended on the yard – landed, and while Trevor goaded them and snapped his jaws, they spilled their cargo onto the wet yard. Billy, Daisy, Jamie and Bella lay unmoving beside Maxwell.

The seagulls perched on the Watchmen's railings, eyeing Trevor disdainfully as he jumped up and down in front of them, blowing raspberries and waggling his tail at them.

Maxwell tried to get to his feet, but found he barely had the strength to push himself onto his knees. 'Bella?' he gasped. 'Are you hurt?'

Bella was weeping and shaking, and for a moment Maxwell was sure she wasn't going to speak – then, so suddenly that Maxwell felt his heart quiver in his chest like a startled moth, she bawled, 'I'm sorry! I'M SORRY! I didn't know Mr Vim was bad! I didn't KNOW!'

'It's all right, Bella,' Maxwell tried to say, but Bella continued bawling.

'He told me he was trying to help my dad, and that you ... You had tried to kill my dad! He said you were turning into the Mamble! He said you were evil! He told me to call for him when we got to the Basilica Astrosus, and then ... and then ...' Bella stammered something Maxwell could not hear, her eyes fixed on the ground beneath her arm. 'I'm so sorry, Maxwell! He was evil, not you! Oh, Maxwell, how can you ever forgive me?'

Maxwell laid his hand on Bella's head – and he noticed with a chill that his hand didn't look right. His fingers were bony and knotted around the joints, and the back of his hand was covered in brown blemishes like big freckles. He turned his hand over, and saw that there was not a single scar on the palm – yet he remembered, with an uneasy feeling in his stomach, tearing the skin from this hand ...

'Bella,' he whispered, laying his hand on her meaty shoulder. 'Vim fooled us all. There's nothing I have to forgive you for.'

Bella's wails turned to snuffles, and she raised her head, her cheeks glistening with tears ... and the grateful smile that had begun to form on her face was replaced with an expression of horror.

'BELLA!' came a frantic shout, and a second later Bella was whipped away. Maxwell looked up and saw Bella's mother, Jaqui, lifting the muscular girl right off her feet, despite the fact that Bella must have outweighed her by at least a hundred pounds.

Looking around Maxwell realised that the yard was quickly filling with people from the village. There were shouts as they saw the children (and some shouts of alarm as the excited Trevor bounced up to them snarling), but as they saw Maxwell their voices died into silence as they all stood staring at him.

'Help me!' gasped Maxwell, and though his voice was just a reedy, quavering whisper it carried to all the people's ears in the sudden, shocked silence – but no one came forward to help Maxwell.

'What's the matter?' demanded Trevor. 'I got your monkey boy back, didn't I? Why don't you help him you stupid old gits?'

'Please?' gasped Maxwell. He began to crawl forward, but as he inched towards them the crowd fell back, terror and revulsion on their faces. Exhausted, Maxwell collapsed face down onto the dirty ground.

'Excuse me!' came a voice. 'Coming through! Clear a space, thank you! Oh, hello Mr Shinbat, how are your sprouts doing?'

'Mum?' Bettie Jones pushed her way through the shocked crowd. She was dressed in her potato slippers, and she wore her favourite pink nightie with "Call me a Tatty – Please!' written on the front, her hair in curlers.

When she saw Maxwell she stopped dead – and if that same look of horror and revulsion crossed Bettie's face it was gone in an instant. She ran over to Maxwell and knelt down beside him.

'Mum?' he whispered. 'Mum, what is it? What's wrong with me?'

'It's all right, Maxy,' Bettie Jones replied, her voice not quite steady. She scooped him up into her arms and lifted him as if he weighed no more than a baby. 'It's all right, my darling.'

She carried him back through the crowd. Maxwell closed his eyes and turned his face against his mother's shoulder, no longer able to bear the staring eyes of the villagers.

Bettie Jones carried Maxwell out of the gates of the Watchmen Academy and down Spudmore Avenue to their little house. Behind her the villagers followed at a distance, led by Bella's mum, Tesla Electra, Monica Blip and Ronnie Barker (walking side by side with his terrifying wife) all carrying their children.

They crowded into the Jones's small garden, but at the door Jane Barker turned on them.

'That is as far as you go!' she exclaimed, and slammed the front door in their faces.

The villagers gathered in the garden, dressed in slippers, pyjamas and nightgowns, muttering to one another darkly while Trevor ran round and around the little house, shouting abuse at the seagulls that landed on the roof and covered it like a blanket of snow.

And they all waited.

Bettie Jones laid Maxwell on his bed. She quickly stripped off his dirty, torn clothes, pulled on his pyjamas and pulled the bed covers up to his chin. Normally Maxwell would have been absolutely horrified at the idea of his mum dressing him for bed, but he was so weak and exhausted that he could barely lift his arms to help her, and all he felt was grateful that she was here.

'Mum?' he said when Bettie had tucked him in and was fussing around his room tidying up the mess left after that morning's clash with Titus Mamble. 'What's wrong with me?'

Bettie stopped buzzing around and looked at Maxwell. Her mouth opened and closed. 'You're very tired, Maxy dear, that's all,' she said at last. 'I'm going to fetch Professor Magister, I'm sure he'll know what to do.'

'Mum?'

'Yes, Maxy?'

Maxwell opened his mouth to speak ... and stopped.

What had he been about to say? Perhaps that he knew that Bettie Jones was not really his mother, but that it didn't make any difference. Perhaps he was going to tell her that he was not Titus Mamble, and if he lived to be a man he would be Maxwell Jones, because Bettie Jones had been kind to him and had loved him and had taught him that the word was full of kindness and love, not evil and terror. Perhaps he simply meant to tell her that he loved her more than anything else in the world.

There were a million things his tired lips wanted to tell her, but there was only one thing that really mattered to him.

'I lied to you when I said Billy and me had gone camping,' he said. 'You didn't forget, mum. I'm sorry I lied.'

Bettie Jones smiled. She leant over the bed and kissed Maxwell's forehead.

'I knew that all along you silly boy, and I knew you'd have a good reason to lie to me. You did, didn't you?' Maxwell nodded, and his mum smiled. 'Of course I forgive you. Now,' she stood up, 'get some sleep. When you wake up in the morning everything will be right as rain!'

Maxwell smiled. 'As perfect as potatoes,' he said, using one of Bettie's favourite phrases.

His mum beamed, and walked quickly to the door. She turned to look at him, and then stepped out onto the landing, gently pulling the door closed behind her.

But she did not turn away quickly enough for Maxwell to miss the single tear glistening on her cheek before the door closed.

Maxwell closed his eyes, and the darkness took him away.

A shrill whistling noise drilled down into the darkness, bringing Maxwell coughing and gasping back into consciousness in his little room.

He sat up - his heart fluttering like a trapped bird even at this small exertion - but he could see nothing to explain the strange whistling.

Maxwell climbed laboriously out of bed and limped across his bedroom to his shelves of comic books, the floor reverberating with many voices from the lounge below. The whistling sound seemed to be coming from here - but ...

A dark, ghastly face leered at him from the darkness. He stumbled back with a weak cry and almost fell - if he had fallen he would almost certainly have broken every brittle bone in his body.

The dark face was still glaring at him, but the eyes, he saw, were not filled with madness, but with confusion and fear. The face did not move until Maxwell stepped cautiously forward.

'My mirror,' Maxwell realised.

An old man looked back at him from the mirror. But old was not an adequate word for the face he saw - it was an ancient face; a ghastly skull hung with sagging grey flesh and a few wisps of downy hair.

So this is what Titus Mamble had done to him. This was why the villagers had looked so horrified.

The Astrosus had sucked almost every second of life from him, leaving behind this bag of bones.

Maxwell sank to the floor and wept. He cried in fear and anger at the unfairness of it all. Titus Mamble had defeated him, finally and absolutely, and had left him with enough life so that he would know that he had been beaten.

Maxwell wept into his old knotted hands - and he did not notice that the whistling sound grew louder and was accompanied by an electric crackling noise, nor did he see the shelves of comic books swing open like a door letting through a brilliant shaft of light, and he did not hear the tread of a pair of very large boots.

'What have we here?' asked a loud, booming, kindly voice. A pair of muscular arms lifted Maxwell off the floor. 'Good Man Jones out of bed at this hour? That is most irregular.'

'Juggernaut?' gasped Maxwell, seeing the broad white-bearded face through his tears.

'Sorry I'm a little late,' said Juggernaut, laying Maxwell back on his bed. 'It was a long dig into Termination Central, and it took quite a few trips to get the Killians through.'

Juggernaut sat on Maxwell's beanbag, instantly flattening it, and laid a large sack down beside him. It seemed he had been collecting potatoes again.

'I thought you were dead!' said Maxwell.

'Dead? Me! Far from it. Just busy,' Juggernaut replied. 'Which reminds me, I have something which belongs to you.' He struggled back onto his feet and took something from the inside of his cape and placed it on Maxwell's bedside table. 'He seems none the worse for his adventure,' Juggernaut said, bending over and looking into the Handsome Beast's goldfish bowl, which he had retrieved from his cape. Indeed, the little goldfish seemed to be asleep.

'Thank you,' said Maxwell, and he began to cry again.

'Why all these tears?' asked Juggernaut gruffly. He looked momentarily embarrassed – Maxwell guessed that after all he had seen Juggernaut never shed tears of his own – but then sat on the bed (the springs *boinging!* as if in agony under his massive weight) and took Maxwell's frail hand in his meaty fist.

'I'm ... I'm dying,' said Maxwell, and saying these words made the tears run even faster down his face. 'Titus Mamble beat me, Juggernaut. After all that we did, after everything we risked, he still beat me.'

Juggernaut considered this. 'Do you regret what you did, Maxwell Jones?' he asked after a long pause. Maxwell shook his head immediately. He did not regret his adventures for one moment, even if they had to end in this room today. It was better that he should die today than live and see Mamble destroy everything and everyone he loved. 'Then he didn't beat you, did he?' Juggernaut placed a hand on Maxwell's head. 'And as for dying!' Juggernaut laughed. It was such an unexpected thing for him to do that Maxwell's tears stopped immediately, and he gaped at the big man as his laughter rocked the small bed. 'Who said you were dying?' he asked.

'But ... I'm old ...' Maxwell said, confused.

'Nonsense. Why, you're only an eleven year-old boy! Old indeed! I'm sixty-two, and *I'm* not old!'

'But ...' Maxwell felt sudden anger, his weak heart fluttering ever harder. 'Look at me Juggernaut! The Astrosus suck the life out of me!'

Juggernaut smiled. 'Don't worry, Maxwell, the end of your story is a long way off yet.'

Juggernaut stood, the bedsprings groaning with relief. 'Now I must be off, for I fear my story is not yet finished, and I have much more work to do.'

He leant over the bed and tapped the goldfish bowl, then turned to Maxwell and smiled. 'I'll see you soon, Maxwell Jones.'

Maxwell watched Juggernaut walk across the room with growing disbelief and resentment. Was Juggernaut just going to leave him here like this? Did he really intend to abandon him to his death?

'Where are you going?' Maxwell demanded, anger rising in his voice. Juggernaut turned back to him, surprised.

'I am going to deal with the good doctor,' he replied. He kicked the sack, which Maxwell had assumed contained potatoes, and it gave a moan and shuddered.

'Dr Arcania is in that *sack*?' Maxwell exclaimed in horror. 'Let him out! You'll hurt him!'

'Hurt him? I'll do a deal more than that, boy,' growled Juggernaut, and he kicked the sack again, this time hard enough to make its occupant yelp in pain. 'This ... This *creature* abandoned us to our fate on Vir, and all our present disasters began solely with *him*! Hurt him? I'll pluck every hair from his worthless hide!' He kicked the bag. 'I'll strap him to a plank and carry him through this village displaying his cowardice and deceit for all to see!' He leant forward and whispered to the bag, 'I'll take you home, Arcania, to Siluria, I'm sure your father would be delighted to get his hands on your worthless, miserable hide!'

'Ha!' came Dr Arcania's voice from the bag. 'You couldn't find Siluria if I gave you directions, you fat moron!' he said defiantly (if a little muffled).

Juggernaut's brows contracted in fury. 'Then I'll be carrying you in this sack for a very, very long time, won't I, you little wretch!'

Dr Arcania moaned with fear, and Juggernaut nodded, satisfied. He threw the sack over his shoulder and turned to walk out of the door.

'Let him go,' said Maxwell.

'Never,' Juggernaut replied, and he took a single step towards the door.

The next moment Juggernaut was hanging upside down in mid-air, the sack abandoned and temporarily forgotten on the floor beneath him.

'What are you doing boy!' he sputtered furiously. 'Put me down!'

And Maxwell, who wasn't aware that he had done anything, saw that his hand was held out towards Juggernaut. Somehow *he* was holding Juggernaut above the bedroom carpet. 'He saved my life, Juggernaut. Or at least, he tried too.'

'Nonsense!' Juggernaut roared, kicking his stubby legs at the air in his fury. 'He is a coward and a traitor! He would trade your life for a cup of coffee! Now – *PUT ME DOWN!*'

'No,' Maxwell replied calmly. He raised his other hand, and without even being aware what he was doing he opened his hand wide. The sack flew apart. Dr Arcania scampered to Maxwell's side, shaking with terror.

'Put me *DOWN!*' Juggernaut demanded, and Maxwell slowly lowered his right hand. Juggernaut drifted gently to the floor. He stood up quickly and straightened his cape with as much dignity as he could muster. 'I see your mind is fixed on sparing this loathsome creature?'

'Yes,' Maxwell replied. 'He saved me,' and he added – though it was not strictly true, 'Dr Arcania risked his life to stop Mamble. If it wasn't for him we wouldn't have escaped.'

Juggernaut glared at Dr Arcania with utter contempt, and then he looked at Maxwell and his expression seemed to soften a little – but only a degree.

'You may live to regret this foolish act of mercy,' he said. 'But I respect your loyalty, Maxwell Jones ... Even if it is misplaced. And I will be keeping a very close watch on you, Arcania.'

With that he swept from the room and slammed the door closed behind him. The soft murmur of voices in the lounge below stopped as Juggernaut thundered down the stairs, and then several voices cried out in surprise and delight, and Maxwell heard Bella's voice, clear and joyful above the rest, cry, 'Daddy!'

'Cretin,' murmured Dr Arcania. He was still shuddering with shock. 'Neanderthal! He broke into my lab and threw me into a *sack!* Me! Lambton Arcania! I wouldn't mind, but I'd just put on a fresh jug of coffee!'

'Archie?' said Maxwell, staring at his wizen hands. 'How did I *do* that?'

'You have Mamble's powers, of course,' said Dr Arcania dismissively, as if this was of no interest to him at all. He shook his hairy little fist at the closed door. 'A sack! A stinking potato sack! Just you wait, Cyril Jugg, you'll get yours! Put *me* in a potato sack, will you? I? Dr Lambton Arcania, PhD, the greatest mind—'

'What do you mean I have Mamble's powers?' Maxwell interrupted.

'You were bound with Mamble when the Astrosus was merging you and he into one being. You got his power, and he got your life force – not that it will do him much good where he is. Pay attention, you idiot boy!' Dr Arcania was fuming, either as a result of being thrown into a sack or from missing his morning coffee. 'The effects are temporary. *However* the effect on my dignity of being bundled into a rotten potato sack—'

'You mean I'm going to be all right?' A flood of relief ran through Maxwell's aching body. He would be young again, this nightmare was only temporary! Everything would go back to normal!

Dr Arcania stopped dead. He opened his mouth to speak – but before he could another voice said, 'No, of course you're not going to be all right. Only the Eternal Engine can restore your life force.'

Maxwell looked round and saw the Handsome Beast was looking back at him, a bored expression on its face ... and then Maxwell realised something very strange – Dr Arcania had turned at the sound of the fish's voice too.

'Did ... ' Dr Arcania gulped. 'Did that goldfish just speak?' he asked in disbelief.

'You can understand him?'

'Of course he understands me,' said the Handsome Beast. 'I'm speaking the Common Tongue – English, as you call it – though "Common" is more apt a description. Such an ugly and common language!'

'Remarkable!' gasped Dr Arcania, and he leant closer to the bowl, his eyes glittering with excitement. 'Astonishing! A genetic freak, no doubt, but this still deserves some serious research!'

'*FREAK!?*' howled the Handsome Beast, outraged. 'A talking monkey dares call me a *freak!* Come closer and I'll bite your nose off, you furry fool!' The fish thrashed around the water, evidently building up speed to jump out of the bowl and do just that. Dr Arcania sat back hastily.

'You said only the Eternal Engine can help me?' Maxwell sat up painfully. 'But the Eternal Engine was destroyed by Dr Arcania's bomb, wasn't it?'

'The vanity of you idiotic creatures!' exclaimed the fish. 'As if *he* could destroy the Eternal Engine!'

Maxwell and Dr Arcania exchanged an excited glance. 'Well if it wasn't destroyed, where is it?' asked Arcania.

'It is here,' said the Handsome Beast, and both Maxwell and Dr Arcania looked excitedly around the room. 'Not *there*, you underdeveloped simian morons, *here*! I am the Eternal Engine!'

There was a moment's silence while the Handsome Beast swam regally around its small goldfish bowl.

'You?' exclaimed Arcania. '*You* are the *Eternal Engine?*'

'You're a goldfish!' said Maxwell, thinking that

the vain creature had finally gone quite mad.

'And you are a rude ginger haired yob with poor taste in clothes,' snapped the Handsome Beast. 'However ... You do feed me – though not very well – and you do change my water – though not often enough by my standards ... So, I suppose I *should* help you ...' The fish sighed wearily. 'It is such a burden being me.'

'But—' Maxwell began to say – but in the next instant he let out a cry of alarm. The Handsome Beast launched himself from his bowl, flew through the air and shot into Maxwell's open mouth. A second later the goldfish had wriggled across his tongue and down his throat.

'Ahhh!' cried Maxwell grabbing his throat, and then his belly as he felt the fish wriggled down inside him.

'You swallowed the fish! You swallowed the fish!' screeched Dr Arcania hysterically. He leapt back, fell over Maxwell's beanbag, and landed on the floor in the remains of the potato sack.

'Ahhh!' Maxwell replied, and he jumped out of bed in panic.

The commotion brought a thunder of feet up the stairs. Maxwell's door burst open and Bettie Jones, Juggernaut, Billy and his mum and dad, Bella and her mum, Daisy and Tesla Electra, Jamie and Monica Blip, Professor Magister, and (most bizarrely of all, to Maxwell's reeling mind) Dr Flavia Silex all staggered into the room.

They all stopped dead, staring at Maxwell in amazement.

'Maxwell you - my goodness gracious - cor blimey O'Riley - oh, Maxwell - Mr Jones, what on earth--'

Maxwell looked from them to Dr Arcania. The chimpanzee was sprawled across the beanbag looking up at Maxwell with horror, or perhaps awe, his hairy little face bathed in golden light.

The light shimmered across the walls of Maxwell's little bedroom, making it look like a brightly lit aquarium. *Where is that coming from?* But Maxwell had only to raise his hands to know the answer - the light was coming from *him!* It moved across his hands in gentle billowing clouds of gold, and as he watched in amazement his long arthritis-swollen fingers changed.

Maxwell turned quickly and shuffled to the mirror. The people packed into his bedroom door stepped back as he passed them, their eyes wide with that same mix of horror and awe he had seen in Arcania's eyes. Maxwell felt his steps grow stronger, felt his brittle bones harden, and when he looked in the mirror he saw that it was *his* face that looked the most shocked, *his* eyes that were wide with horrified awe.

His head and shoulders were ringed with fierce clouds of golden light. The light moved over his features, and wherever it touched him it changed him. In a moment his bald head was covered with wispy grey hair that turned black as if each strand of hair were being filled with black ink. The deep, ugly lines around his eyes and mouth thinned, and then vanished. The sunken skull of his ancient face was replaced with healthy pink flesh. In less than a minute he was looking at his own face again. No longer the face of an old man; it was the face of eleven year-old Maxwell Jones.

What if it doesn't stop? He thought with a thrill of panic. *What if I become ten, then nine, then eight - what if I become a baby ... and then I become* him?

But even as he was thinking this Maxwell saw the golden glow flicker and then snuff out, and in the light from his bedside lamp Maxwell found himself looking at his own ordinary face again.

For the first time since standing in front of the wall of mirrors beneath Mrs Trimm's general store Maxwell Jones was truly happy to see that face.

He turned back to the room, to the faces of his friends and family (and a few people who he was not that keen on, if he was honest), who all looked back at him with that expression of horrified awe undiminished.

And, of course, of all of them, or all the warriors, scientists and professors, it was Billy Barker who spoke first:

'What the bleeding Nora on a flipping unicycle heck just happened there!' he exclaimed.

'I think--' Maxwell began, but in the next moment something thick and slimy rose up his throat, stopping his words.

The Handsome Beast shot from his mouth, and Maxwell caught the fish in his open hand.

Professor Magister stepped forward and peered down at the small goldfish in Maxwell's palm. 'What is that, Maxwell?' he asked.

'It's the Eternal Engine,' Maxwell replied, and he couldn't stop himself grinning at the gasps of amazement that followed these words. 'It wasn't destroyed at all, it changed--'

'Into a FISH!' bellowed the Handsome Beast, and they all cried out in shock, Bella fainted and crumpled to the floor, unnoticed. 'A water-breathing FISH, you rusty-headed TIT-MOUSE!' gasped the Handsome Beast. 'Put me back in my BOWL!'

Maxwell ran across the room and dropped the Handsome Beast back into its bowl. The goldfish dived beneath its stone arch, and skulked there, muttering darkly.

'How ... er ... How surprising,' said Professor Magister, looking into the bowl.

'Professor Magister?' the old man looked up at Maxwell, his eyebrows raised. Maxwell paused, he looked round at Dr Arcania, who was still sprawled across the beanbag with a stunned expression on his hairy face. 'Professor? What will happen to Dr Arcania now?'

'He'll be sent back into exile, of course!' barked Dr Silex, Juggernaut nodded in agreement, and added, 'And that's more than he deserves!'

Professor Magister held up his hands, a hopeless gesture that seemed to say there was nothing he could do about it. 'I'm afraid that is true, Maxwell. I understanding that Lambton helped you in some way—'

'He saved my life,' said Maxwell, looking around at the shocked chimp, who seemed to be totally unaware that they were talking about him.

'Be that as it may the fact remains that his meddling unleashed the power of the Eternal Engine!' said Dr Silex hotly.

'But he didn't!' said Maxwell.

'That's right!' said Billy stoutly. 'Old Archie had nothing to do with it!'

'I don't know what ridiculous fantasies Arcania has been spinning, but I can tell you right now—' Professor Magister held up a hand again, this time silencing Juggernaut.

'Boys?' invited Professor Magister, raising a nervously ticking eyebrow. So Maxwell told him what Titus Mamble had said in the Black Monastery, when Mamble's words had seemed to him not to be words at all, but forgotten memories from Maxwell's own mind. 'So,' said Professor Magister, when Maxwell had finished. 'Lambton did not switch on the Eternal Engine at all, is that what you are saying?'

'He probably did at some time, I don't think he'd be able to resist seeing how the Eternal Engine worked,' said Maxwell. 'And he probably shouldn't even have done that if it's as dangerous as you say it is. But Dr Arcania didn't cause the Big Combination, and his bomb didn't cause it. It was Titus Mamble and ...' He almost added "and Jake Silex", but remembering that Dr Silex was standing not ten feet from him, he simply said. 'Dr Arcania wasn't there. He didn't do anything, Professor!'

Professor Magister was silent for a few seconds, thoughtfully rubbing his hand over his bald head. 'Well,' he said at last, 'That puts a whole new, erm, complexion on the situation, does it not?' He turned to where Dr Arcania lay. 'However, you did hide the Eternal Engine from us Lambton, a device of potentially immense ...' Professor Magister's words trailed off. He shook his head and sighed. ' Ah. I see.' he murmured sadly.

Maxwell turned, and saw that the beanbag where Dr Arcania had been lying was empty. He turned back to his bedside table, and that too was empty apart from the useless potato clock and his spectacles – the goldfish bowl with the Handsome Beast inside had gone.

'That thieving hair bag!' Billy exclaimed.

'Hmm,' said Professor Magister, a look of deep disappointment on his face. 'Quite.'

Chapter Thirty-One: the watch men

They all trailed down the stairs, leaving Juggernaut attempting to revive Bella. No one spoke, and when they were all finally packed into the small lounge Maxwell's mother said, 'I'll just get Bella some Spud O'Cola – that'll bring her round in no time!'

Or kill her outright, thought Maxwell.

'Can I have some Spud O'Cola too Mrs Jones?' asked Billy. 'I love Spud O'Cola, me!'

Bettie treated Billy to a brilliant smile, and they both disappeared into the kitchen.

Maxwell opened the curtains and looked out into the front garden. Hundreds of people were gathered outside, spilling into Spudmore Avenue in their pyjamas and nightdresses. They were all talking quietly to one another, and kept glancing expectantly – or perhaps fearfully – at the house.

'I dare say they are worried about you,' came a voice from over Maxwell's shoulder. He looked up and was surprised (and not a little unnerved) to see Dr Silex peering out of the window, her small walnut eyes narrowed.

'Worried about me?'

'Of course, boy,' Dr Silex answered crisply. 'A lot of people have been worried about you. Now come away from the window before someone sees you.'

Maxwell frowned at Dr Silex, confused ... and then in a flash he realised what she meant. He wasn't wearing his spectacles, and if anyone should see him at the window they wouldn't see ginger haired Maxwell Jones – they would see the black hair and cruel-handsome face of young Titus Mamble. He quickly closed the curtains and stepped back.

'It's going to be like this for the rest of my life, isn't it?' Maxwell said, and the words felt like ash in his mouth. 'Every time they look at me they'll see Titus Mamble, not me at all.'

Dr Silex pursed her small lips. 'In my experience, Mr Jones, most people are ignorant and wilfully mean spirited when it comes to young people.' She glared at Maxwell, and then nodded, as if confirming this to her self. Then she turned her head – Maxwell followed her gaze to Jamie, who was jabbering animatedly at Professor Magister. Magister was holding his head, no doubt preparing for a headache. 'But ...' Dr Silex sighed, and astonished Maxwell with a beaming smile. The smile transformed her face, and for a moment she was that pretty young girl in the graduation photograph again, 'A Good Man – a good hearted young man – may be able to change the minds of even the ignorant and the wilful.' She scowled again. 'Thought I doubt it,' she added, back to her old self in the blink of an eye.

Maxwell smiled. 'Thank you, Dr Silex,' she waved the compliment away with mock contempt – but Maxwell could tell that she was secretly pleased with him. Perhaps, at last, he had understood one of her complex puzzles. 'Excuse me for a moment,' he said.

He walked across the room and tapped Jamie and Daisy on their shoulders, and beckoning for them to follow him to the kitchen. In the kitchen Billy was busily guzzling foul brown Spud O'Cola as if it were the best thing he'd ever tasted. Maxwell took a second glass from Bettie Jones's hand. 'I'll take that up for Bella, mum,' he said.

'Oh! Thank you ... Maxwell?' The befuddled expression Bettie Jones normally wore was nowhere to be seen on her pretty face. 'What are you up to?' she asked.

'A little adventure,' said Maxwell, and in answer to Bettie's alarmed expression he added quickly, 'Nothing dangerous, mum. Honest.'

'Are you sure, Maxwell Jones?' she asked.

'Yes, mum,' he answered innocently. It might be a *little* dangerous, he thought. *Might be* – but probably not. Probably. 'Why don't you make something for everyone to eat?' he said suddenly, struck by inspiration. 'They must all be starving.'

This distracted his mum marvellously. She clapped her hands together with glee. 'What a good idea!' she exclaimed, and she spun back to the oven, almost knocking Billy flying, and making him cough up quite a bit of his smelly potato drink. Bettie didn't even notice. 'Fish and chips for everyone! I'm sure I've got some potatoes here somewhere . . .'

'Come on,' said Maxwell.

'Where the bleeding hell we going now?' coughed Billy, wiping Spud O'Cola from his chin.

'You can count me out of any more adventures today,' said Daisy. 'If I never see another beetle for the rest of my life I'll die happy!'

Maxwell laughed. 'No beetles, no castles, and no evil monsters, either,' he said. 'Now come on, won't you?'

Bella was sitting on Maxwell's bed, Juggernaut beside her, both of her hands swallowed in his massive paws. It was a miracle the bed didn't go straight through the floor with the Juggs's combined weight on it.

Maxwell placed the glass of Spud O'Cola on the bedside cabinet. 'I wouldn't drink that if I were you,' he said as Bella reached for it, and she snatched her hand away as if the glass were hot.

He stood back and looked at them all - Billy, Daisy, Jamie, Bella and Juggernaut. Standing shoulder to shoulder they barely fit in his small bedroom. His eye caught a glint of reflected light beside the glass of Spud O'Cola - Maxwell's spectacles sat, still looking ugly and uncomfortable and cheap, but now they also looked very, very important. These spectacles were a little thing that could change the whole of the rest of his life.

'What is it, Maxwell Jones?' asked Juggernaut, his brow furrowed.

Maxwell closed his eyes for a moment. It was not that he was unsure how to continue; it was that he did not really want to say what he was about to say. Nevertheless, he opened his eyes, looked at their faces one by one, and said, 'Titus Mamble is alive.'

Their response was immediate and loud - they all started arguing with him at once. Bella looked on the verge of fainting again.

Maxwell held up his hand, and waited until they were silent.

'You know that I'm right, even if we don't want to believe it. Everyone thought he was dead before, and look what happened - he almost killed us all.' There were no arguments this time, and though Maxwell had said this, he still felt a chill of fear - because saying a thing and knowing that thing to be the truth was not the same thing at all. Not at all. 'He'll come back, won't he?' he asked Juggernaut.

Juggernaut nodded. 'Yes,' he answered simply.

Maxwell returned Juggernaut's nod. 'If we know that, if we remember that, I think we have a chance of being ready for him next time,' said Maxwell. 'I think the people outside want to believe he's gone. I think they're waiting for me to go out there and tell them that I killed Titus Mamble, and he's never coming back. But I can't do that.'

'So what is it you suggest we do?' Daisy asked impatiently. 'Put on capes and masks and go flying around the 101 worlds searching for Titus Mamble?

In case you haven't noticed, Maxwell, we're kids! We were almost killed today! What do you think we can do about it even if you're right? What would you do if Titus Mamble walked through your bedroom door right now?'

'There's nothing I could do,' said Maxwell honestly, 'But I think Juggernaut would do plenty.'

Juggernaut nodded grimly. 'Oh yes,' he growled. 'Oh yes indeed.'

'We're not Good Men, we're too young for that,' said Maxwell, 'But we can be Watch Men. We can watch out for ... for ...'

'Conspicuous disconnections?' Billy suggested.

'Yes. Exactly. We can watch out for things that seem wrong, or strange, and Juggernaut will help us if we find anything, won't you, Juggernaut?'

'Naturally,' Juggernaut replied. He put his beefy arm around Bella's shoulder. 'I was looking for an excuse not to return to Vir, and I think that is a very good one, Maxwell Jones.' Bella threw her arms around his neck and hugged him.

'So that's what we'll be,' said Maxwell. 'We'll be Watch Men, right?' They all nodded, but Billy, sipping his Spud O'Cola thoughtfully, held up his hand.

'I hate to, like, burst your bubble, Max, me old mate,' he said, 'But this whole blinking island seems wrong and strange to me. So how exactly will we know if there is anything weird going on? It's weird here all the time!'

'Well,' said Maxwell. 'Let's go and take a look.'

He walked over to the bedroom window, and the others followed. The glass had been smashed out when Titus Mamble jumped through it to escape the Handsome Beast's song. His mum had replaced the window pane with a piece of cardboard. Maxwell pulled the cardboard out of the window frame. The villagers still filled the small front garden and much of the street beyond. Despite the fact that it must have been approaching dawn no one looking ready to go home.

Maxwell turned around, sat on the windowsill, waved at his baffled-looking friends, and then fell backwards.

They all shouted in alarm and raced forward . . . but too late - Maxwell was hurtling downwards towards the gathered villagers, his arms outheld, a big grin on his face.

'Don't show off, boy,' muttered Juggernaut under his breath, and Billy looked round sharply. If he shows off it will frighten them,' Juggernaut said.

'What do you mean?' asked Billy, but Juggernaut just pointed out of the window. Billy turned back, and there stood Maxwell, that big grin still on his face. Billy stuck his head out of the window and saw that Maxwell's feet were planted firmly on absolutely nothing - he was floating twenty feet above the heads of the crowd, not one of who had noticed him.

'Come out,' said Maxwell, 'It's perfectly safe.' For a moment no one moved, they simply stared, dumbfounded, at the boy who was floating impossibly in front of their eyes. Then Jamie, who Daisy had always maintained had not half the brains he needed to keep his mischievous body in one piece, simply leapt through the window head first, as if he were diving into a pool of water rather than thin air. A second later he was hanging in the air beside Maxwell, bobbing up and down and whooping with delight.

One by one the friends stepped through the window (Bella came last of all, and extremely gingerly) until they were all floating in the air above the garden, and Juggernaut stood alone at the window.

'Don't you want to come too, Juggernaut?' asked Maxwell.

'No,' Juggernaut replied immediately. 'I don't approve of flying. It isn't natural, and ...' Juggernaut twitched, and then he stiffened his jaw and glared at Maxwell, there was a glint of danger in those eyes – *don't you dare laugh, boy* – those eyes clearly warned Maxwell. 'I'm afraid of heights,' he said, his voice a gruff whisper. Maxwell and Billy looked at one another and raised their eyebrows, and both had to look away quickly to stop themselves from laughing. They were both remembering how Juggernaut had clung to the collapsing wall of the Hall Tower in Vir. He had claimed he was exhausted and unable to climb any further, but just perhaps the fearless warrior had taken a peek between his dangling toes and had been frozen with simple fright.

Below them the villagers – who couldn't very well miss them now that Jamie was whooping like it was Christmas morning and spinning head over heels through the air – were shouting questions up at them. Maxwell ignored them, and turned back to the grim faced Juggernaut.

'Juggernaut?' The big man's eyes narrowed, no doubt he was expecting a joke at his expense about his vertigo. 'Would you get my spectacles?' Maxwell asked. 'They're on my bedside cabinet.' Juggernaut nodded his head, satisfied that Maxwell wasn't about to risk a joke, and dutifully fetched the spectacles and held them out to him. Maxwell looked down at them, thinking fast and hard, but he knew he had made his decision, so he looked into Juggernaut's eyes and said, 'Smash them for me, would you?'

Juggernaut looked astonished. 'Are you sure, Maxwell Jones? The way you look ... What I mean to say is, you look a lot like—'

'Like Titus Mamble,' said Maxwell. 'But everyone already knows what I look like under those spectacles, don't they?'

'If you're sure?' Maxwell nodded, and Juggernaut clenched his hand into a fist. When he opened it again all that remained of the spectacles were a few chunks of black plastic and glittering shards of glass.

'Enjoy yourself, and look after my daughter, boy,' Juggernaut said. 'And don't forget that the powers you have are on loan, they are not yours. You'd do well to remember that it's a long fall back to Virporta Island, Maxwell Jones.'

'Thanks, Juggernaut, I won't forget.' Maxwell turned to the others and grinned. 'Here we go, then!'

'Hang on a minutes,' said Billy, 'Where exactly are we bleeding well going, cos I for one—' but the next second his words were shut off with a scream of delight as all five of them rocketed into the night sky and disappeared from view.

Juggernaut smiled and clapped his hands together, scattering the remains of Maxwell's amazing spectacles all over the bedroom carpet. 'Kids!' he grunted.

He turned from the window and walked back down stairs to the smell of frying potatoes.

They soared into the sky, up and up and up, hurtling through a freezing bank of cloud and then out of the top where they stopped, bobbing above a vast vista of perfect white, the moon a massive silver disk in the star strewn sky.

It was nice to be in the right world with the right moon and stars above him, Maxwell thought. No – it was better than nice, it was *right*. No matter how many other worlds he would see, no matter how many other skies he would stand beneath, Maxwell knew that this would always be the right place for him, for all of them.

There was a commotion from below and they all looked down as a massive flock of seagulls burst from the cloud at their feet and took to the air around them, crying harshly (but, of course, only Maxwell knew that this was the seagull version of hip-hip-hooray!).

'You could have flaming waited for us!' came a familiar voice at Maxwell's ear. He turned towards it and was delighted to find himself looking at a two-headed parrot fluttering its wings at his side. 'Most impolite!' said one of the heads in a plumy accent.

'Sorry Brian, sorry Byron,' said Maxwell.

'It's all right, I *suppose*,' said Brian sniffily. 'As long as you didn't *forget* about us,' added Byron sulkily.

Maxwell reached up and ruffled the feathers on the parrot's heads, laughing. Both heads rolled their eyes at one another comically. 'Ten flaming seconds off the ground and he thinks he's Superman,' said Brian. 'Typical human,' Byron agreed.

'It is wonderful, though, isn't it?' said Maxwell. 'I know you must be used to flying but it ... it is just ... just so fantastic!'

'It is wonderful and fantastic - and if you have half an ounce of imagination you never get used to it,' replied Byron. 'But it ain't a good idea to spend too long up here,' said Brian.

'Why not?'

'B-Because,' said Daisy, floating over to join them, 'You'll f-freeze to d-d-d-d—'

'Oh!' exclaimed Maxwell, and looking round he noticed for the first time that Daisy, Jamie and even Bella (who had a lot more padding than the rest of them put together) were shaking with cold, their teeth chattering like maracas. Billy, of course, was not affected by the cold, and was swooping blythely above the clouds, whilst ice was forming on the ends of the others' noses. 'Sorry! I didn't realise!' and that was true – oddly, Maxwell didn't feel cold in the slightest.

'That is not what we mean,' said Byron. 'What we mean is it ain't a good idea to stay out of sight of the island too long,' said Brian patiently, 'Cos when you go looking for it again, you might not find it.' Byron nodded. 'Virporta does tend to wander off, remember?'

'Oh!' cried Maxwell – and in a second they were plummeting down through the cloud. Rain lashed Maxwell, and he heard the others screaming – with panic this time, not excitement – because they were not flying down through the cloud, they were falling down.

'MAXWELL!' screamed Billy. 'KEEP US UP! KEEP US UP!'

But Maxwell barely heard him, he too was in the grip of panic, and he spun in mid-air and dived head first through the cloud, leaving the others screaming behind him.

What would he do if he got through this cloud and all that was below them was the dark ocean? Fly to the mainland? What mainland? How far was it? Which way was it? What if his powers failed before they got there?

The cloud thinned and then evaporated, and Maxwell came to a halt.

The clouds burst open above him and Billy, Daisy, Jamie and Bella hurtled out of it in a shower of rain, whirling their arms and legs and screaming in terror. Maxwell raised a hand and they all came to a gentle stop. They drifted down towards him, gasping and shaking with shock (except for Jamie, who was gasping not out of fear, but because he had been laughing so hard) and came to a stop, floating together side by side.

'That ... That was *BRILLIANT!*' exclaimed Jamie, between hysterical giggles.

'Brilliant? Are you mad?' gasped a wide-eyed Bella. 'I thought we were all going to die!'

'You'd be all right, Bella, you'd bounce!' Jamie replied, laughing even harder.

'Shut up, Jamie!' they all shouted.

'You maniac, Maxwell!' yelled Daisy. 'What did you think you were doing!'

'Sorry,' said Maxwell, 'I, sort of, panicked a bit.'

'A bleeding bit!' exclaimed Billy. 'A bleeding *bit*, he says!'

Byron Brian fluttered out of the cloud and landed on Bella's broad shoulder in a spray of rain. 'Takes a bit of getting used too this flying lark, don't it?' asked Brian. 'Yes, but what a wonderful view!' said Byron.

'Yes,' said Maxwell, 'It is wonderful, isn't it?'

Below them Virporta Island floated in the dark sea. To the west was the hump of land which Maxwell now knew was called Arcania Hill; to the north the wide planes where the Black Monastery had stood (though Maxwell was sure it stood there no longer, though they were far too high to see for sure one way or the other); to the east were the craggy hills beneath which the weird animals trains ran from ZØØM to places Maxwell could not imagine; to the south the Long Beach where Maxwell, Dr Arcania, Billy (and, unknown to them, Titus Mamble) had re-entered this world. The Black Woods covered the island from all these points. And how big was Virporta Island now? Twenty miles across? Fifty miles? A hundred?

And there, in the centre of the island, barely visible, was a small cluster of lights. Home.

'I think I've had enough adventures for one day,' said Maxwell. 'Let's go home.'

They all agreed immediately – even Jamie – and with a slight flick of Maxwell's hand they all began to descend slowly towards the small cluster of lights.

'Maxwell?' Maxwell looked up and saw Billy floating beside him, his corkscrew blond hair blowing all over the place. He moved closer, and whispered in Maxwell's ear, 'You're okay, aren't you, mate? I mean. After all that stuff that happened you still feel, like, all right, don't you?' Billy looked at him anxiously.

'I feel ...' Maxwell grinned at Billy, and Billy grinned back. 'I feel super,' he said.

And smiling and laughing the six friends (or seven, if you counted Byron Brian as two people, which both Byron and Brian most definitely did) descended gently to Spudmore Avenue, and walked up the garden path of number 13, following the delicious aroma of fish and chips.

The end

Super Maxwell
and the Burning Boys

Tony Kerr

The explosion boomed across the sands and jungle and streets and mountains of Virporta Island. Windows shattered up and down Spudmore Avenue, and vibrated and cracked on Front Street. The ancient trees of the Black Woods shuddered. Seagulls (and other birds, which did not strictly speaking belong on the planet earth) took to the skies, crying out in terror. An old and well-respected pteradon named Norman fell out of the sky and lay stunned on the hockey pitch of the Watchmen Academy.

'What the bleeding Nora O'Riley on a unicycle was THAT!' exclaimed Billy Barker, stumbling off his skateboard.

Maxwell Jones stepped off his own skateboard and dumbly pointed at the rooftops, too amazed to speak.

A huge mushroom cloud of soil and grass and leaves had risen into the air, momentarily obscuring the ugly shape of Pugg's Potato Factory. A figure rose above the cloud, like a cork fired from a bottle of Champagne. The figure was dressed entirely in red. He flew over Spudmore Avenue, hit (and totally demolished) the chimney of Balthazar Kane's house, and came to a bouncing halt in front of the two stunned boys.

'Good morning Maxwell Jones, good morning Billy Barker,' the huge man in red. He sprang to his feet and carelessly beat out the flames that were licking at his white beard. 'Just finished your paper round?'

'Juggernaut?' said Maxwell. The huge man was dressed in a red boiler suit and wore red Wellington boots and a jaunty red cap on his oversized head. He was covered from top to toe in soil, but seemed none the worse for his explosive journey over the rooftops. 'What happened to you?'

Cyril Jugg, or Juggernaut as he much preferred to be called, grinned sheepishly. 'Just a slight miscalculation, wains, nothing to get excited about!'

'What were you doing?' asked Maxwell suspiciously. 'You weren't messing around with Spankies, were you?'

'Spankies! What do you take me for? I'm retired, Maxwell Jones. I haven't touched a Spankie in weeks!' He said these words quite sincerely, indeed Juggernaut seemed offended by the suggestion . . . But Maxwell and Billy didn't believe a word of it.

Up until a month before Juggernaut had spent almost all of his spare time running around blowing things up. Juggernaut was a Good Man, a name that Maxwell and Billy had come to understand actually meant superhero. Juggernaut had spent the last ten years on Vir, a planet that was the original home of the Good Men. There Juggernaut had fought the Long Men, former Good Men who had been turned into vampiric monsters. Juggernaut main weapon in his battles had been Spankies; spider-like robot bombs who, when they weren't assisting Juggernaut demolishing everything in his sight, rather fancied themselves as amateur comedians.

Maxwell and Billy had reunited Juggernaut with his wife Jaqui and his daughter Bella, and Juggernaut had declared himself retired from the hero business, and had settled down to the quiet life on Virporta Island.

Maxwell and Billy exchanged a knowing look. They both knew that Juggernaut had spent most of his "retirement" hunting monsters in the woods and secretly designing highly destructive weapons in his garden shed.

'Are you sure?' asked Billy, giving Juggernaut a knowing wink,

'Of course I'm sure! What are you suggesting?'
Juggernaut exclaimed huffily. Another fire had started
in his hair, and he quickly beat it out. 'I have a mole
problem, that's all. It's nothing to get excited about.'

'Moles?'

'Yes, moles.'

'Garden moles?'

'No, space moles! Yes, obviously garden
moles, you idiot wain!'

Billy raised an eyebrow. 'And what were you
using to solve this problem with garden pests?
Bleeding dynamite?'

'Dynamite! Of course not!' exclaimed
Juggernaut. 'Where would I get dynamite? Is used
nitro glycerine.'

'Nitro . . .?' Maxwell goggled at him. 'Where
did you get nitro glycerine on Virporta Island!' Mrs
Trimm, who was Billy's auntie and ran the island's
general store, often boasted that she sold absolutely
everything anyone could possibly want or need.
Maxwell wondered if that included high explosives.

'I made it myself . . . Or at least I was making it
myself until my little accident,' Juggernaut's eyes
glittered madly, and he went on excitedly, 'It really
quite simple. You see, you take some garden weed
killer and some sugar--'

'JUGG!' they all looked round at the angry
shout. Balthazar Kane, father of Tamara Kane (one of
the most unpleasant girls Maxwell had ever had the
misfortune to meet) and editor of the island's
newspaper, the Virporta Herald, was advancing on
Juggernaut, a house brick held in both hands. Mr.
Kane, who usually wore a natty white suit and Panama
hat and had the shiny flawless complexion of a doll,
was covered from head to foot in black soot. 'My
CHIMNEY!' he bellowed. 'Look what you did to my
CHIMNEY, you MANIAC!' He held up the bricks,

either as evidence, or in preparation to beat Juggernaut over his sturdy head.

'Me?' Juggernaut's face took on an expression of wounded astonishment. 'I think you must be mistaken Balth--'

His words were interrupted by the loud whistling sound of a large object descending through the atmosphere. A large shed landed in the middle of the road with a splintering *CRASH!* Above the shed door were painted the words: "Cyril's Shed - KEEP OUT!!!" in large red letters. As they all stared at the shed in astonishment the door creaked open, revealing a sheet of paper tacked to the inside depicting a troup of moles being blown into the air under a cheering stick-figure drawing of Juggernaut. Beside the drawing was a formulae for making nitro glycerine.

'Ah,' said Juggernaut. The shed collapsed with a pitiful groan. 'Yes . . . ' a half brick fell from Juggernaut's hair and landed on Balthazar Kane's foot.

'I think we'd better get out of here sharpish, mate,' whispered Billy. Maxwell nodded in agreement.

They both climbed onto their skateboards and continued down Spudmore Avenue as Mr Kane was joined by Juggernaut's wife, Jaqui. Mrs Jugg was holding a burnt and blackened bedsheet, and both her and Mr. Kane were advancing on Juggernaut with murder in their eyes.

'See what I mean?' said Billy, when they had turned into Front Street and were out of sight of an ever-increasing mob of villagers who were all advancing murderously towards Juggernaut. 'This place is just too flippin weird, Max.'

* * *